MW01168938

Matriarchs

by
Kevin B. Niblet

[handwritten signature: Kevin B. Niblet]

[handwritten note: Hope you enjoy]

authorHOUSE™

1663 LIBERTY DRIVE, SUITE 200
BLOOMINGTON, INDIANA 47403
(800) 839-8640
WWW.AUTHORHOUSE.COM

First published by AuthorHouse 07/13/05

ISBN: 1-4208-4607-8 (sc)

Printed in the United States of America
Bloomington, Indiana

This book is printed on acid-free paper.

THANK YOU BLACK WOMAN

Black Woman, decade after decade you have toiled in America without being honored or given the dignified recognition that you so richly deserve for your secular work and the many tireless hours spent being a homemaker, mother, friend and an all around superwoman.

Black Woman, standing on the merits of your immeasurable inner and outer strengths; you alone have reared innumerable children. Instilling in them black folkways, and high moral standards, thus safeguarding black culture for your posterity.

Black Woman, you are the backbone of our black community and without you not even a remnant of it would remain. You with your spirit and will beyond that which is normal have pulled our community from its deepest darkest historical depths to its modern day majestic moments.

Black Woman, through your steadfast determination, dedication, sacrifice and love; you alone by example have proven that any obstacle can be overcome.

Black Woman, you are the mother of all humanity and deserve to be acknowledged as such.

This book is dedicated to Black Women everywhere and is meant to say 'Thank You.' As a black man I humbly thank you, and honor all women of color as queens for eternity.

Kevin B. Niblet

ACKNOWLEDGMENTS

I would like to extend a special thank you to Ms. Sophie Lucas, Leroy Price III, Michael Kostas and Barbara Stephens. That thank you is extended to Kathy Price for cover photos and to Tom Sawyer and Susan Douglas Sawyer for the use of their wedding facility, The Southern Plantation "Heaven On Earth" Missouri City, Texas.

CHAPTER I

"Not on this day, not on Pappa's day," Minnie thought. "Out of all the days of the year, why would there have to be trouble today? And such terrible trouble at that. Lord have mercy on my soul, how could I have caused a scandal like this on my pappa's birthday?" The majority of Minnie's extended family had made wonderful plans for the day. Family and friends would gather together and surprise Minnie's father, William Heard, for his birthday. The family always had huge celebrations, both on his birthday and for Christmas. There would be lots of food, drinks, and a treasure trove of memories. The white folk would be standing out on their porches gawking at the large crowd of birthday revelers gathering at the huge house William and his brothers had built. Even though an inordinate number of her immediate family lived in such close quarters, they never allowed familiarity or petulance to breed contempt for one another. All the folk Minnie loved and knew to be kin planned to be here tonight. The fact that this horrible sequence of events had happened today caused her to cry until her lovely hazel eyes were red and swollen. At the vibrant age of nineteen, Minnie herself was probably the most beautiful young lady in north Georgia. She had a voluptuous body, long black hair that streamed down her back, and a beautiful, fair complexion.

The events of this morning had changed Minnie's entire life course. All because Will Jennings had to be such a low down dirty dog, as Minnie's mother, Jane Heard so aptly labeled him. At least that's what Jane called him when out of hearing range of any white folk. Will Jennings happened to be one of the richest, most powerful white men in the state of Georgia. He was a very animus man who had an eye for enticing black females, a sexual deviant who spent most of his time having illicit sexual thoughts about alluring black females. Yet he had total disdain for the black male. Will Jennings used the

1

black family for producing money off the sweat of their brow. Mr. Jennings also hid many deep dark personal and family secrets from his prominent cabal of southern gentlemen that he called friends. One of his most closely guarded secrets was his verbal and physical abuse of both his son Will Jr. and Heather, his devoted wife. Heather and everyone else called Will Jr. by his nickname " Beau."

As for the Heard family members who built this spacious house that had such beautiful carpentry and craftsmanship, not one of them, neither man nor woman, even shared partial ownership of the home. Each in some capacity or another worked for and lived on Will Jennings's property as either blacksmiths or sharecroppers in this, the year of our Lord 1911.

That morning, Minnie's uncles, Frank and Buddy Lee, had convinced her father and their oldest brother William to slip off into town so that they could privately celebrate his birthday. His brothers would start him out with a haircut, a hot lather shave, a hot scented bubble bath, and some new coveralls. After all, Jane had been hinting that he could use some new britches and a shirt. Surprisingly, William agreed to go. More than anything else, the man was a sun up to sun down workaholic. Meanwhile, while the men were off in town, back at the house, William's other seven brothers and two sisters-in-law were cooking, cleaning, and doing whatever it took helping Jane with preparing the house, and back yard garden area for this grand event. The pungent aroma of smoke rose from charcoals on the open pit built in the ground behind the house. The pit was filled to capacity with too many chickens to count. Then there were delectable slabs of ribs, numerous rabbits, and other wild game to be roasted. The Heard family was planning on having a good time this evening.

Minnie was down at the barn, which had always been one of her favorite places to go and do what she loved most, shoeing horses. It was in this barn that she convinced her father to let her work with him as a blacksmith. She had only been begging for three years before he finally caved in and agreed. "Pappa' s loyal 'sistant" Jane always called her. William was Will Jennings's blacksmith and the best in north Georgia. Minnie was almost as good after five short years. William also made and sold the best corn whiskey in the area. He was a very successful bootlegger. The poker had no sooner turned red when Minnie heard the barn door creaking open. Will Jennings entered as cautiously as a serpent, much more so than usual. He was always so very bold, always boasting loudly about being the biggest land owner in north

Georgia. "Where's your pappy, gal?" he said in his usual strong Southern patois.

"Pappa done gone to town," Minnie answered swiftly and strongly, yet, remembering to be respectful. She never looked him directly in his eyes.

"For what, to pick up my supplies?" he retorted.

"Mr. Will, we may only be your blacksmiths and sharecroppers, but we goes to town for more than your supplies."

At that, he slapped her full across the face, sending blue lights flashing through her head. Before she could gather her faculties, he was ripping at her blouse, tearing it open, exposing her voluptuous breasts. She tried to strike out with both hands but she was temporarily blinded by the force of his blow. Suddenly, she was on the ground and he was on top of her. Minnie could smell the corn whiskey on Will Jennings's breath. With her skirt torn and open, Will Jennings was pulling her panties to the side trying to force his penis inside her. But he had underestimated her strength and resolve. Suddenly, Minnie flipped him over and leaped to her feet. Grabbing the poker, she held it out, pointing it in the direction of his head, hoping that the threat of it would stave off his vicious attack. After rolling over and regaining his footing, Will Jennings was now running towards her in a drunken stagger. At that very moment, he lost his balance. Before Minnie could pull the poker back, Will Jennings was falling face down to the barn's dirt floor with the poker embedded through his throat. Letting out a low groan and a few gurgles, Will Jennings was dead.

Stepping back gasping, Minnie shrieked, " Lord have mercy" Lord have mercy, Jesus" Mr. Will", Mr. Will" " she called out frantically. But there was no reply or movement from the man who most surely had always had a more than passing interest in the young beautiful Negro girl who now stood over his corpse.

She couldn't let anybody find out what had just happened." Gotta tell Pappa first." Minnie pulled Will Jennings's limp body to the end stall, where she and her father kept their blacksmith tools, and hid him real good. "Only Pappa and I ever go in there anyway," she thought aloud. Wild thoughts raced through her head now as she left the barn running toward the house. "White folk gonna lynch us all. Maybe they gonna beat me to death. Ma" Ma" Ma"" she yelled, as she approached the front porch.

3

Startled by the shrieking cries coming from Minnie, Jane leaped up and met her on the porch. "Good Lawd, child, what done happened ta you?"

"It was that dirty dog, Mr. Will, Ma, he tried to ravish me down at the barn and I done killed him... What's gonna happen to me, Ma? Ma I'll die fighting before I let these white folks lynch me or my family."

"Shhh child, shhh," Jane comforted her, stroking her long black hair. "Gwoin be all right, you's gwoin be all right, Mama sees to that. That peckawood got just what he had a comin. Callin' his self, gone take my child. Now where's dat dirty dog's body at, child? We can' t let nobody find him till we tells Pappa and he figures out what ta do."

"I hid Mr Will in me and Pappa's stall."

"Child, why didn't ya jes run?"

"Before I knowed anything, Ma, he was on me. He was hittin' me and grabbin' and tearin' my clothes. The next thing I knew, he was on top of me, but I flipped him off me like Uncle Johnny taught me. I grabbed the poker to scare him off a little, but that fool fell into it and it went into his throat and he fell and just lay there, he just... ohh... Ma." Minnie finally gave way to the tears and overwhelming emotion she felt.

"It's gone be all right," Jane said as she once again attempted to comfort her child. "How in the world I'm gwoin tell William dis?" Jane mumbled to herself. She then began to prepare for his arrival and entrance. She pulled out his bottle of good corn liquor from the trunk and took a big gulp. Afterward, she poured a cup for him. This prepared drink always signaled trouble. William was in a celebrating mode, not in his normal state of mind. So today a poured drink was only part of the birthday festivities. William and his brothers were already feeling pretty good. They had been sipping from his personal stash of good corn whiskey he kept hid in the wagon.

As William Heard and his brothers approached the house, Jane instructed Minnie to go into her room and stay there until she could explain everything to William and get him calmed down. She wanted to spare Minnie the terrible pain of explaining it all over again to her father, although she was sure William would want to hear it from Minnie himself. As he entered the house, William was all smiles showing off his clean- shaven face, fine new britches, and new shirt his brothers had given him. He noticed immediately that Jane was disturbed about something. He thought she was mad about him spending all day in town. Jane assured him it was not that and began to break the terrible news to him.

When she had finished, William went directly to Minnie and gave her a loving and secure hug. William assured his only daughter that everything would be all right. But this was said only as a fatherly duty to give comfort and assurance to his daughter. William and Minnie both knew that it would not be all right ever again. Then William walked Minnie out into the backyard garden area that Minnie and Jane had planted when she was a little girl. The garden was another place of peace and serenity to Minnie. After a brief word of comfort and another strong hug, they returned inside. William called everyone together in the living room and began to get everyone's opinion on the course of action to take. This is how he and his brothers had survived the brutal battles of the Civil War, by always strategically planning every move together. William had always made the final decisions on crucial matters, just as he would now. Buddy Lee had grabbed William's ear early and suggested that they not panic and just bury the old dirty son of a bitch late at night and go on as if nothing had happened. After a few of the other brothers had spoken, it was agreed that no matter what the repercussions, this night's incident would hence forth never be spoken of again to a living soul outside of the Heard family.

Young Johnny spoke with wisdom beyond his years when he suggested that Minnie, Jane, Frank, and Buddy Lee leave town and head south that night, as soon as possible. Upon hearing this, William finally spoke up, saying slowly and strongly, "Not Buddy and Frank, I'll need them with me. I'm gone send you, Johnny, with Jane and Minnie, not south but north to Chattanooga. I hears colored folk do well in business up yonder. All the rest of us will come later. You can cover tracks better than any man we knows of. We'll give y'all all the money we been saving so you won't have to struggle none and make a quiet settlin' in. Frank, you hitch up the buckboard right now."

"Leaving tonight might look 'spicious to everybody," Frank rebutted." We s'pose to be having a party the way we do every year near-bout this time."

William thought about it and quickly agreed with Frank, saying, "Yes, it would look 'spicious. This is how it's gone be tonight. Now y'all know we ain't got no business looking long- faced to these white folks this evenin', and we won't be. We s'pose to be having a party here tonight and that's what we gone be having. We all know that Mr. Will done spent the night away from the house plenty of times in the past. So we gone pray that nobody comes around here asking us about him. Let's just go on like everything is fine."

"Mama, how much money we done saved?" William asked Jane.

She replied, "Almost 12,000 dollars and 8,000 in gold."

"Johnny, you see to it that this money is safe, you hear me?" William said sternly.

Johnny replied, "You know I will." William also had another 4.000 dollars saving and that too would be sent with those who were being forced to take this heart- wrenching exodus.

William picked up his personal batch of corn liquor and swallowed real deep and yelled out, "What the hell gonna come of us? Don't know, but let's give a good show for ourselves tonight." Right then, five horses pulled up in the yard and everyone got real silent. Turns out it was just William's Uncle Ricky Lee, his wife Lillie, and their sons and daughters Buster, Ricky Jr., Babe, and Tara. As they entered the front door, everybody managed to look happy and not let the cat out of the bag.

Other family members and friends started to arrive shortly after the initial guests. Soon it was as if nothing had ever happened. The music was being played and everyone was singing and dancing, jukin' like never before. All the folk kept asking for Minnie. They knew she adored her father and wouldn't miss this for the world. Minnie decided she had better join the others and her father like never before. As soon as she entered the living room, William grabbed her and started dancing away with her. Softly he sang to her, "Everything, everything, everything gone be all right this evening." Yet, an eerie feeling came over Minnie. A feeling that this would be her last evening with her father. She kept wondering why they all were not leaving together. To Minnie it didn't seem right that only she, Jane, and Johnny would leave. Why leave the rest behind, she wondered in silence as she danced with her father. Minnie finally forced herself not to think of what was going to become of her father and uncles.

The night seemed to last forever. At one point, Minnie thought that Will Jennings would come bursting through the door, laugh, and say this afternoon was all a figment of her imagination and tomorrow would never have to happen as planned. But now the friends were beginning to say their good- byes and express to William and Jane how much they had enjoyed themselves. As the last guests left, Jane started to clean up the massive mess left behind. Most of the other family members were either sleep or well on their way. Minnie went out on the back porch to clean the back toilet, and heard deep moaning noises through the door. It sounded like a girl Minnie knew named Pearl Jones. Pearl was about twenty-two; she was Buddy Lee's first love. "Pearl is that you?" Minnie asked from the back door.

Pearl answered as best she could. "Uummm huh, it's me. I'm just a little constipated, girl, uhhhh... I'll be all right though."

Buddy Lee must be in there with that hussy, Minnie thought as she returned to the front of the house to wrap up the cleaning there. Buddy Lee had a notorious reputation with the young ladies. It was widely rumored that he was hung like a mule and knew how to move the crowd in bed. Minnie had heard some of her girl friends' infamous gossip about how he had ruptured a girl from Dalton, Georgia. Minnie never let the rumors or gossip bother her. He was just Uncle Buddy Lee to her.

Finally the house was cleaned and the sun had begun to creep over the horizon. Frank had the buckboard ready. William called Minnie to him and hugged her like never before. She felt moisture on her shoulders and thought, Not Pappa, he couldn't cry. Jane came over and joined the embrace. The three of them told each other how much they loved one another. William turned to Jane and repeated what he had told her last night while they were alone: That she had been his first and only love, and nothing but his end could keep him from coming to her. He then asked her to let him speak to Minnie alone for a few minutes. William told Minnie that the next house he stepped foot in he wanted his family to own. He wanted her to think about owning property and starting a family business. William had no doubt that Minnie would bring his instructions to fruition. "Do your best, baby girl, and we'll see y'all in Chattanooga in a couple of months." Forcing himself to smile, William added, "You know once we get up yonder, whatever you get started we gone work it till it make us some money. I don't ever want my family working for nobody but ourselves, baby girl. I promise you I won't ever let another white man be over my family again. We made Mr. Will rich; hell, we can make ourselves rich."

This was William's way of showing Minnie that she had to mature mentally for this awesome task ahead of her. His commission to look for and purchase a home and think of a business to start gave Minnie something positive to look forward to. William hugged Minnie again and held her head up and told her to always hold her head up high. He jokingly told her it was too big to let hang down anyway. "You better watch out for them slick city boys. You gone be the new girl in town, dumb country gal, right off the farm to them young boys. I betta not catch one of 'em at my house when I get up yonder. Now you listen to me real good, baby girl. This is all part of the Master's plan. As a family, we have always been willing to go wherever he leads us. The Good Lord led us from the ocean side of Georgia to the north side of this state safely after we were emancipated. God led us to this day and he will lead us through it. We never know if his plan will keep us near each other or take us long and far apart. But one thing I can tell you for sure is no distance can take away the love we have for each other, or the faith we have that God can keep us safe and out of harm's way. Put God and family first and you will be fine. Teach your young'uns to be like yourself not fearing any man, only God. You ain't got a thing to feel bad about. It's a brand new day for the Heard family. You remember that charity starts at home and ends abroad. Baby girl, spread your blessings to the needy and the needy will always look out for you when your day of need comes. You can't save everybody, but you help those that you can and don't be nobody's fool. Now I want you to go take the lead until I can get back with you." William then slipped Minnie a tightly wrapped bundle covered with brown paper. He told her this was for all the years she had worked with him down at that ole musty barn, and to do the things he was asking her to do.

"Now," William said as he took a big, deep breath, "let's get along before they start waking up around here and come ah asking about Mr. Will. Johnny, y'all be careful." William and Johnny embraced and whispered something to one another. As the buckboard pulled off, Minnie and Jane kept looking back, waving until their loved ones were no longer in sight. In a low voice, Minnie said a prayer hoping to see her father soon.

As they traveled along, Johnny kept pulling to the side of the road into the bush. He would travel back by foot for some distance to cover the tracks. It seemed like a short while to Minnie, although it had been nine hours and they were now in Tennessee. And what seemed like a few more minutes put them in the midst of the growing city of Chattanooga. That evening, they stayed at the hotel, the first hotel stay of Minnie's life. The room was beautifully decorated, real fancy and all. The drapery was the color of cinnamon and apricot. The most impressive place here to Minnie was the dining area. She loved the lighting and how soft the tables appeared, being lit by candle. Small portions were the only negative she could find here. Johnny had a room next to Minnie and Jane's. There were a few young men in the lobby who spoke and seemed real nice.

Whenever Minnie was alone, her every thought always turned to her father, wondering what was he doing at the time. Boy, she wished he were here with her. A lot of memories came flooding through Minnie's head that night as she lay in bed — the good times back home with her cousins Babe and Tara, whom she had always stitched quilts with. She had always been fondest of Babe and missed her terribly, not that she didn't like Tara. It was just a special bond that she and Babe shared. They were seven days apart in age and had the exact same birth mark on their chests. Babe said the marks resembled the continent of Africa and that God meant for them to go there together one day. The two would spend hours as young girls letting their imaginations run wild about how fascinating Africa must to be. Creating stories about being together on walking safaris across the Serengeti of Tanzania to Lake Victoria then north across the Mara River, all the time watching different grazing animals like zebra, wildebeest, and impala up close.

The forest of Africa is where Minnie often said she wanted to explore observing the habits of carnivores like leopard, serval, and genet from a distance. Minnie thought about the time her father thought she had intercourse because her menstrual cycle had started for the first time and she had been playing with all the boys around. But Jane convinced him she was just coming into womanhood.. Finally, she thought about the most traumatic thing her father ever did to her, the day he gave her the only beating he ever had to administer to her rear end. Minnie was instructed to wash and cook a mess of collard greens. There was only one problem : Babe had come to visit. She and some other girls were waiting outside to go uptown that day. Therefore, Minnie just rinsed the greens off a couple of times, chopped up some onions, washed off three big ham hocks, added them to some water, threw the greens in the pot, dashed a little salt in them, and hauled her self off to town. She had no way of knowing that the greens had turned out gritty because she had not washed them properly. Minnie returned home to the worst behind whipping of her life. After that day, she began to wash her greens leaf by leaf for the rest of her life. As Minnie drifted off to sleep, she was resolved that she had to become a stronger person for herself and her mother.

CHAPTER II

The next morning, Minnie rose to find Jane and Johnny already dressed. She immediately suggested to her mother that they go out and start looking for a house. Jane told her that she and Johnny were thinking the same thing but she did not want to rush into anything. The three of them went out looking together. After lunch, they split up. Jane went back to the room to rest a little. She had gotten tired from all the walking they had done. That's when Minnie found the best house of all. The owner was an old colored lady named Mae Lewis, whose husband had recently passed on. She was selling her home because her only surviving child was living up North and wanted her to come live with her in Detroit, Michigan. Minnie used 1,500 of the 4,000 dollars her father had given her before they departed. It would take two weeks for the sale to be final; afterward, Minnie could take possession of the property. Little did she know, Johnny had just purchased a house two doors down for them to live in. That sale would take a month to finalize.

As Minnie was telling her mother and uncle about her purchase, they turned and looked at each other, puzzled. "Where did you get money to buy a house?" Jane asked. "And secondly, who do ya think ya is deciding on where we gone live?"

Minnie answered carefully because she knew Jane would not tolerate any disrespect. "First of all, the money is mine, Pappa said so. It's for all the years I done worked with him, and I was not trying to make a decision for the three of us. Ma, Pappa made me promise him that I would buy a house with this money."

Johnny interrupted, "This is even better because I can have the house that Jane and I purchased and the two of you can live in Minnie's house. Minnie done gotten herself a house, who'd of thought you would own a house?"

"Me," Minnie answered boldly. "Forget you, Uncle Johnny," she said as they started to cut the fool.

After two weeks, the small room had begun to close in on them. Soon afterward, they received their paper work and settled into their new homes. They were now ready for some of Jane's good cooking. Jane cooked a roast, some snap beans, macaroni and cheese, and cornbread. They ate home cooking for the first time in these strange new surroundings. "That was a fine meal Jane," Johnny said as he began to clear the table.

"We need a church to attend Sunday, and I need some work," Minnie said.

"So do I," Johnny added.

Jane just hung her head and said, "I ain't never worked for money."

Johnny turned to Jane, took her hands in his, "That ain't true, Jane, there ain't been a day gone by that me and my brothers didn't eat a meal fit for kings and we never slept on a cold bed, 'cause you quilted the best covers. Those things made the way easy for us to make money. So you done worked a heap for money. You can ask any of us Heard men, all you've done is worked. You and all the black women like you deserve to be treated like queens for all the work you do to make us men feel like real men, and we've appreciated that very much. You like a mother to us all."

Jane's eyes began to fill with water, but she managed to tell Johnny to get on home and let her be.

Sunday morning, Minnie and Jane went to the church Mae Lewis had told her about after she sold Minnie the house, the Gospel Temple. Rev. Thomas Foster was the pastor, and a young, handsome creature he was, Minnie thought. The neighborhood was abuzz about the new folk that nobody knew. Emma Mae Johnson, the gossip queen of the colored community, wanted to know where they came from, if they were of good stock, and who was that fine boy Johnny. She always found a receptive ear in Mrs. Rhae Hollings, Deacon Louis Hollings's wife. Deacon Hollings worked in the coal mines during the week and at the church most all weekends. Therefore, Rhae had plenty of time for the fine art of gossip. Rhae and Emma Mae had aptly tagged the Timmons family as the "Dirt

Dobbers," whose children were always dirty and wore ragged clothes. Tim and Louise Roberts were a young, recently married couple, and were still considered kids by the rumor mongers. Old Man Worthy and his son Tom stayed mostly to themselves, so they remained subjects of non- interest most of the time, except to scandalize Tom for a lack of female dates. Naturally, some said he was sweet.

Emma Mae had seven children of her own, and not all had the same daddy. She was hardly the one to be speculating as to who had come from good stock. Mrs. Cole, the "number lady" as she was called, had two sons and two daughters, Walter, Michael, Renee, and Brenda, all little snobs because Mrs. Cole had more money than she or they knew what to do with. Minnie met all or most of them that first Sunday at the church service. Rev. Foster preached a stirring sermon this morning. "That Rev. Foster can really move the spirit," Jane announced as they walked home, "and that choir can sang up a storm."

The church members had been real friendly after the service by coming up and introducing themselves and their children to Minnie and Jane. While Jane was talking, Minnie's thoughts turned to her father. "Ma, we've got to write Pappa and let him know how we doing and find out how he's been and what's going on with Mr. Will."

"Child, your Uncle Johnny done gone ta north Georgia this morning ta wire Lillie 'bout what's been going on since we left."

Minnie had inquired about some work after the church service. She got a good tip from Emma Mae Johnson about some house cleaning jobs that had come about since Mae Lewis had left for Detroit. All her customers were looking for someone to clean their homes. Emma had latched on to Minnie as soon as she met her, and she was proving to be a good friend. At times, Emma could even be a great confidant because she listened intently to whomever was speaking to her. She loved small details because these improved the juiciness of her gossip. Emma made it a point to be there for Minnie anytime she could from day one of meeting her. Minnie did her best to overlook this flaw in Emma that irked her to no end. Even if she happened to be in another town at the time that a supposed incident occurred, she had to add her bit on the situation.

With all the new changes and adjustments going on, Minnie's thoughts turned to the long, hard hours sweating sun up to sun down in that barn with her father. Minnie's father's physical image haunted her. William Heard instilled the thought pattern in his daughter that hard work, punctuality, and responsibility went hand- in- hand. Her father had set up the barn logistically for labor to be performed with the efficiency of an automated assembly line. The work techniques he employed pushed away from any negativity and always toward a positive conclusion to every day's labor. He never arrived late at the barn and neither did Minnie, and most nights, she was still working after he went to the house. Meanwhile, Jane had Sunday dinner smelling up the house. She was baking a hen, made some dressing and gravy, candy yams, collard greens with pig tails and ham hocks and hot water cornbread.

When they sat down and blessed the food, Johnny knocked softly at the door. As he came into the kitchen, Minnie could see that he had been crying. "Sit down, y'all." Jane sat down; Minnie was already sitting. Johnny grabbed Jane's hand and began to tell them the horrible news. "All my brothers is dead, all my brothers is gone."

"No" no" no" no" " Jane cried out. "Ahh Lawd, not my William" Not my William."

"Oh, Ma, it's all my fault. I did it, I got my Pappa and my uncles kilt." The three of them sobbed uncontrollably.

Then Jane stood up and said, "It's just us now, y'all all I got now and we won't let each other down; y'all hear me? I mean it, we won't let each other down. Johnny, what they say happened?"

"You don't want to know," he said.

"We gots to know, boy, now tell us."

Johnny began speaking. "After they found Will Jennings's body in the stall that morning, they figured my brother killed him, and the white folk wasn't gone give him no trial, just a lynching. And y'all know William and the rest of my brothers wasn't gone go for that. They were all sharp shooters and they fought the whites and killed seventy-two white men, so when the white folks seen they couldn't out shoot them, they set the house on fire with them in it. Five of my brothers got to the outside before they killed them, and the others burned alive."

"And Pappa, did he burn alive?"

"Nah, baby girl," Johnny said, "he was found outside in the garden. He drug himself out there and that was probably where he felt at peace before he expired."

"My pappa's gone." Minnie could not get over the feeling that she had caused all this calamity to come upon her family, and now what would she and her mama do without Pappa and her uncles? They had never considered how life would be without them. Now all of a sudden they were gone. Jane, Johnny, and Minnie made a vow not to talk about this with any person outside their family circle. A lot of crying and secret blame clouded thoughts and ruined dinner; the night was terrible for all three to sleep through. Only time was going to make this tragedy more bearable and easier to understand. They needed to ground themselves in their faith, is what Jane suggested. "Let's turn to the Lawd, children," was the last thing she said to them that night.

For weeks, Minnie, Jane, and Johnny were not themselves. They had suffered this terrible loss and were not able to bury their family members or even know if it was carried out properly. Johnny kept in touch with Aunt Lillie from that time on through friends of his in North Georgia. He found out that his relatives had taken care to bury his brothers properly. Meanwhile, Rev. Foster had noticed the change in the happy-go-lucky young lady he had first met a month ago, and asked if he might be of some help to her. Minnie at first declined the offer, but Jane invited him over to dinner despite Minnie's objections. Jane had been invited to join a quilt club with about seven other elderly ladies in the congregation of which she accepted. It seemed almost medicinal for her to have their company. They were with her all the time, either stitching rags or just talking. Jane needed this association now more than at any time in her life.

Jane also instituted what would become a family tradition from now on. She, Minnie, and Johnny would meet on Saturday evenings to plan for themselves thoughts and ideas that may have crossed their minds. They also discussed problems they were having either with each other or any other person or thing. The dinner with Rev. Foster was set up for the next Sunday after the church service. Jane had stitched Minnie a new dress and gave it to her at the family meeting so Uncle Johnny could tease her. And sure enough, tease her he did until she was threatening to flip him on his rear end. Minnie and Mamma cleaned chittlins and cooked greens, field peas, macaroni and cheese, ham, hen, and dressing and gravy, corn bread and baked pies and cakes. Uncle Johnny couldn't stay out of the kitchen. He kept coming in, tasting everything he could sneak into without Jane tapping his hand with a spoon to keep him out of the pots.

Rev. Foster whooped so good preaching that morning until Minnie got happy and started shouting and praising the Lord for the first time in her life. She had never shown her emotions in public before. When some ladies came over to calm her, she felt a little embarrassed, but Jane told her it was good to feel the joy of the spirit. As Rev. Foster made the offering for new ones to join the church, Jane and Minnie were surprised to see Johnny walking to the altar. Minnie immediately got up and went down and joined him. They were joining the church together, and it felt so good as they knelt and offered their lives to the Lord together. Tears streamed down Johnny's face as he kept saying, "Amen, amen, thank you, Jesus." It brought joy to Minnie's heart to see tears of joy rather than tears of sadness and pain falling from her uncle's eyes. Rev. Foster acknowledged then commended them both for making the choice to serve God. On the way home, Jane was beside herself beaming with joy. She was so proud of them. As the conversation shifted from the church ceremonies, Minnie informed them that she had accepted some day work cleaning several homes in the area starting next week.

Rev. Foster was expected to arrive for dinner at three o'clock that afternoon. So Jane went through the house making sure everything was just so. Johnny teasingly said to Jane, "You know full well preachers always late, so take your time and stop acting like the Lord himself is coming."

Jane replied, "Boy, you jugging now, shut up dat kind of talk, 'cause the Reverend is the Lord's mouthpiece." Wouldn't you know, as fate would have it, punctually and promptly at three o'clock sharp, Rev. Foster and Deacon Hollings pulled around front in the special buggy the church had given to him last year on his third anniversary.

As they entered the house, Johnny greeted them, "Rev. Foster, you the first preacher I know who set a time to arrive at a place and shows up on time." Rev. Foster was laughing at Johnny's brutally honest greeting, and at the same time trying to ask if it was all right for Deacon Hollings to join them for dinner.

Jane then greeted the young minister and Deacon Hollings. "Of course it's ok for the Deacon to have dinner. He your deacon ain't he, and you the Good Lord's mouthpiece, so I'm honored to have y'all here."

After some small talk and Jane had finished setting the table, she announced that it was time to eat. Rev. Foster said blessings and commented on how good the food smelled. The Reverend asked, " Who did all this cooking?" He really wanted to know if Minnie could cook.

"Ma and I did, Rev. Foster," Minnie replied shyly. "Uncle Johnny ain't did nothing but tote bags of food in from the store and taste all he could while the food was cooking." Everyone burst into laughter and that set the mood for a fun afternoon.

The food was scrumptious, Rev. Foster said, and Deacon Hollings chimed right in, "Lord... Lord...Lord, y'all should get awards for these chittlins, for all of this tasty food."

"Y'all should sell this food, it's too good to give away," the Reverend said. "I ain't jokin'," he said and they burst into laughter again.

"Sell it to who?" Minnie asked. "W e don't know nobody but the church folks."

Deacon Hollings said, thoroughly satisfied, "I know one thing, we done ate at nearly every church member's house in Chattanooga and ain't nobody done cooked like this. Y'all should think about selling plates after the service next Sunday."

"We can't do that, we don't even know how much a plate of food should cost," Minnie said.

"The white folk restaurant charging two dollars a plate uptown. You can easily get two dollars too for your good food." Deacon Hollings replied. Both men had eaten their food up so fast, they hadn't realized that Jane was already piling on seconds.

Minnie spoke up. "I'll try it."

"Try what, child?" Jane asked.

"I'll try selling the dinners next week after church is over, and if it don't work out, the subject is forgotten. So will you help me, Ma?"

"We is in dis together, baby, you know dat, child. Now we didn't invite Rev. Foster over ta dinner ta talk about selling food around town."

"Now, now, Mrs. Heard, nobody thinks this conversation is a bother, it's just that meals like this I would love to have from now on. Believe me, Mrs. Heard, this delicious food will sell," Rev. Foster admitted.

Jane put on some coffee while Johnny, Rev. Foster, and Deacon Hollings shared small talk about planting spring gardens. Deacon Hollings said he always planted twice a year and got just as much in the winter as he did in the spring and summer months. Everyone was stuffed and had to wait awhile before dessert and coffee. Johnny was now interested in this way of planting that Deacon Hollings had mentioned. So he asked him if he had time to help him get started on planting a garden. All the time, Johnny had a plan. He knew that he could be of great assistance to Jane and Minnie if he could cut the cost of vegetable purchases for the dinners they would be selling, so what better way could he help than to use the skills he had gained share cropping.

After dessert, Rev. Foster announced that he hated to eat and run but he didn't have any more free time due to the demands of preaching work. He said to the group of them that Twenty-third Street would never be the same if the plan worked out. At that moment, Minnie thought aloud, "I've never even thought about the name of this street, except that it was on the deed that we signed."

Deacon Hollings snapped a reply, "Girl, this ain't the country town people think it is, you best be paying attention to every street and person you walk down and pass."

"Amen, we hears ya, Deacon," Jane chimed.

Later that evening, Minnie decided to spread her wings a little and take a short walk. She walked toward the corner where First Baptist Church was sitting on Fourth Avenue. When she turned at the next corner, a large crowd was gathered. As she got closer, she heard the most beautiful voice she had ever heard in her entire life. There at East Main Street and Fourth Avenue, a beautiful young colored girl was belting out blues song after blues song, and the crowd kept handing her coins. Minnie thought this was an insult to just give her coins for such an angelic voice. Who is she? Minnie wondered. She tried to get closer but the people wouldn't budge from their positions. Minnie looked around to see if she recognized any of the faces around, but she didn't. She had never heard this kind of music before or been around a crowd of strangers drinking alcohol and whistling and wailing at someone while they sang. They were dancing so close to each other, they almost kissed with every movement. She was excited and liked most of what she was seeing. As she looked behind her, she saw Tom

Worthy and Emma Mae Johnson approaching. Tom was smiling and doing a little dance that made him look silly and gruesomely girlish.

"Hello Miss Lady, what are we doing here this evening?" Tom asked with all his feminine wiles at high peak.

"I was out taking a walk and heard this gal singing and hear I am. I ain't never heard nobody sang that good before or that kind of soulful singing. Who is she?" Minnie whispered to Tom.

"Child, that's Miss Bessie Smith, she's just like me, 'a hot thang' on Friday and Saturday in this town. At least to the folk around here that know how to juke. It sounds like Bessie's in rare form tonight, and so am I, honey." As Tom was about to go off on a tangent about the weekend night life of Chattanooga, the singing stopped. The crowd started yelling for more, but Miss Smith said that she was too tired to continue, and the highly charged revelers would have to wait until tomorrow.

Minnie, Emma, and Tom waited for the crowd to die down before they approached Miss Smith and complimented her on how lovely she sang. Minnie openly admitted that it was her first time hearing that kind of music performed live. "The Blues," Emma said, "everybody done heard the blues or had 'em before."

"Of course I done heard the blues before, Emma. I guess I can relate to some of them thangs she sang about but I ain't never seen nobody sang about 'em as hard as she just did. Miss Smith had those folks dancing hard, right out there in the streets."

"Girl, where you come from? Straight off the farm?"

"I'm from Georgia and you know it, stop trying to show your rump, Miss Emma."

"Girl, you know I'm not showing off on you. What you doin' here in Chattanooga not knowing who Bessie Smith is?"

"We just moved here and you know it," Minnie told her.

"You must of been shut up in the house since you got to town, not to have heard Bessie Smith sing before now."

"You real sharp tonight ain't you, Emma?" Minnie laughed.

Tom chimed in at that point, "She up in your personal business at this point, Minnie. It ain't none of Emma's concern what you been doing since you got to town honey."

"Now I know you ain't callin' me nosey, are you, Tom?"

"Oh, no ma'am, not me, not Miss gossiping know everybody's business in town except her own Emma. Not the mouth almighty."

"You both can call me Emma, not mouth almighty or whatever else you decide on calling me. And that goes for you, Tom, and you Miss Minnie. Now where y'all say we walking to tonight?"

"I didn't say, but I live on East Twenty- third Street."

"Well I live on Third Street and Twenty- third is not on the way. We can split at South Willow."

The three of them walked along chatting all the way. Minnie wanted to know how Miss Smith got started singing the blues. The informed Emma proceeded to let her know that Bessie told her she started off singing in church. But when she could, she would go off and sing the blues. Emma acted as if she knew everything about everyone in Chattanooga. She always did, even while she was growing up. Emma said that Bessie had even told her singing the blues always made her feel happy and good even when she had the blues. "What do you mean when you have the blues?" Minnie asked naively.

"You know, when you feelin' down or sad about something or nothing is going right in your life," Emma explained.

Minnie immediately thought about her father and uncles, "Yeah I done had the blues a lot lately."

"What, you got man troubles?" Emma asked.

"Heck no; what man? I'm not old enough to be thinking about having me a man. I'm only nineteen."

Emma replied, "I'm only twenty and holding, child. I been twenty for five years now and if you ask me how old I am in twenty- five more years, I'm gone still be twenty." Minnie knew then that Emma was a habitual joker.

The two of them continued walking past the corner of Central down to South Willow past the Warner Park Zoo. Minnie had never visited a city zoo, so this entire evening was turning into a group of first- time experiences for her. The zoo facilities were closed for the day, but Minnie knew she was going to have to come back here as soon as possible. Tom and the young ladies decided to call it a night after reaching the corner at South Willow.

Neither Tom or Emma could resist a little more light conversation about the eligible young bucks in town before the three of them split up for the night.

Minnie walked home raring to tell her uncle about the wonderful experience she had enjoyed this fine Tennessee night. She approached his house on a mental high she had not felt since before all the drama and trouble had begun a few months ago. When Johnny answered the door, he encountered a ball of energy and excitement that he had not seen from his niece in a long time. Johnny was smiling through the whole story as she told about the lovely young girl named Bessie and her angelic voice. The happy and sad songs she sang. The two of them decided that they would go and see her sing together Saturday night.

The next morning, Minnie woke up to find Jane sewing some new curtains for the living room and kitchen. Jane told Minnie to clean the house while she finished sewing the curtains. Minnie was still excited from the night before and told Jane she would get to it later. Before she could explain, Jane was up on her feet, and material and sewing tools were on the floor. She grabbed Minnie by the collar and in her coldest tone "You do what I say when I say do it."

When she turned the girl loose, Minnie said, " Mama, I'm sorry, but I'm grown now and I didn't mean no disrespect but I'll clean up later."

Jane calmly turned and walked toward the front closet. Not in a billion billion years would Minnie have conceived what Jane was going to the closet to retrieve. Minnie walked on toward the kitchen to start cleaning. As she turned toward her mother to apologize, she saw that she was holding Johnny's shotgun. Jane said, "I'm still your mama and I don't allow no sassin'. I brought ya in dis world and I'll take ya away from here." She aimed the gun at Minnie, and Minnie turned and ran toward the back door. As she opened the door and started across the yard, she heard Jane yell, "Get back here, hussy." As she jumped up on the fence, she heard the blast from the shotgun. That was the last thing she remembered before waking up to the sound of her mother's voice saying, "I'm sorry, child, I lost my head."

She stirred around in the little bed and felt the sharp pain in her left leg. "Where am I, Ma?"

"You in the hospital, child."

"What happened?"

"You sassed off ta me and I was gone kill ya but ya jumped at the last minute and the bullet caught you in the leg."

"I didn't mean to sass you, Ma, I was just so happy..."

Jane cut her off. "I know, Johnny done told me. I'm sorry, baby, I didn't mean ta shoot ya, I jes miss your pappa so much and I was sitting there thinking 'bout him and how happy we was and I guess I kinda blamed ya for him not being here. So when I saw you so happy..." Jane broke down crying, unable to finish her sentence.

From that day on, Minnie wondered if her mother hated her for what had happened to their family. "Ma, I'm so sorry, can you ever forgive me for getting my pappa took away from us?"

"I shouldn't be blaming ya any how. William could have left with us if'n he wanted to. You and Johnny is all I got left. I'm jes lonely for my man, I reckon."

CHAPTER III

Two days later, the doctor released Minnie from the hospital because Jane told him he was nothing but a quack and a thief and she didn't trust doctors any how. Minnie never sassed her mother again and when she had her own children, she decided they would never talk back to her. The experience only forged a more galvanized bond between Jane and Minnie. Minnie, after that, always shared any experience she had, first with her mother then with Johnny.

It was two months later before Minnie and Johnny got to hear the blues again. They discovered Cameron Hill, where the rich folk lived and no color mattered as long as you had the cash. Johnny had bought a used Ford, so all the young girls wanted to get to know him. It was early, so Minnie, Johnny, and Emma went for a ride through Cameron Hills and surprisingly to them, not one person made a racist or nasty remark to any of them. Emma said she would own one of these fancy houses one day. "Me too," Johnny added, "and it won't be too long either." They rode across the Market Street bridge because Minnie wanted to take a fast ride across. The three of them had a ball that night. It all ended too soon, Minnie thought as they dropped Emma off at home and headed around the corner to Twenty- third Street.

The next Sunday, Rev. Foster asked Minnie to go on a picnic with him to Booker T. Washington Park. Minnie accepted right away. She went home and fixed a picnic basket. The Reverend came over at three that afternoon. They took two blankets and headed for the park. It was a nice warm day, partly cloudy but optimal weather. "Perfect day for a picnic, ain't it, Reverend?" Minnie asked with a coy grin hanging on the corner of her pert young lips as they drove along.

"Yes ma'am, it is and you're the perfect lady to be with on a fine day like this, both just beautiful."

"You're just saying that to make me feel good. You don't really mean it," Minnie replied.

"No lawd, umm umm, I means every word of it." Minnie turned her head because she was blushing. "What's wrong? I say something wrong?"

"No, I was just wondering why a man like you ain't married already."

"I'm still too young."

"So why you want to be out with me?"

"Well, I figured you gonna be needing to have some fun, plus I want to get to know you better, 'cause I liked you from the first moment I saw you."

"But you're a preacher, a man of God's work. You can't be liking nobody you ain't wanting to marry."

"Who made that law, girl, cause God sho' didn't. Besides, I'm starting to like you more and more as the minutes go by."

"You 'bout crazy for a preacher," Minnie laughed as they arrived at the park. Rev. Foster said he had the perfect place to spread the blanket. It was under a big oak tree where he always came to write his weekly sermons.

They got settled in under the tree and had a nice big sandwich and two glasses of sun tea. "Minnie, why don't you start calling me Thomas if you don't mind? Rev. Foster sounds so official."

"If you want me to I will, but only when we ain't 'round nobody else."

"Can I lay on your lap, Minnie?"

"Heck no"" Minnie exclaimed. "What you think I am?"

"No, no, not all of me, just my big head," he laughed.

Minnie started laughing too. "Oh, I thought you was talking 'bout getting on top of me. I don't think so, Mister."

"I wouldn't try nothing like that with you....yet."

"Humph, you better not; I guess it'll be all right to put that old fat head on my lap."

"Y'all selling dinners next week?" Thomas asked. Before she could answer, he went on to say that he had set up accounts for her to get all the food she needed from the grocery store at a discount rate.

"Thank you, Thomas, that was sweet of you to do that. In that case, I guess we'll be open for business."

Minnie didn't pay any attention to the fact that she had started rubbing Thomas's hair while they chatted. "Soft, ain't it?" he smiled, looking up at her as he complimented himself.

"You're conceited too, ain't you?"

"Not me. I just know it is."

"Yeah, Thomas, you got some soft and pretty hair."

"It's not as soft and pretty as you though, Minnie. You smile so beautiful, all I ever want to see you do is smile."

"You know all the right stuff to say to gals, don't you, Mr. Foster?"

"Ok, I'll stop talking so much."

"You better not, Mr. Smooth."

Just then he raised his head slightly and kissed her on the lips and she returned the kiss. Suddenly she stopped and drew her head back. "That's enough of that, I'm ready to go home. I've enjoyed you enough for one day."

"Ok, Minnie, but only if you'll agree to go to the zoo with me next Saturday."

"You know I will," Minnie answered. They gathered the blankets, and in doing so, they bumped into each other, and another kissing session started. This time Thomas stopped and asked Minnie to excuse him because he couldn't help himself.

As they started home, Minnie started thinking about what she had forced herself not to think about the last two months, and how her mama had nursed and waited on her hand and foot, changing her bandages morning and night. When Thomas asked her what she was day dreaming about, she just smiled and said, " My mama."

"You and your mother are real close ain't y'all?"

"Ummm hum, I love my mama, if she ever need anything, I'll be there for her."

"That sure is good to hear, Minnie."

"What about your folks, Thomas?" she inquired.

"Well, my daddy and my mama was born into slavery. My granddaddy was considered the preacher on Langston Plantation where my folk come from. I guess that's where I got it from."

"I should have known it was in your blood"" Minnie exclaimed. "You preach like you was born to preach."

"That's what my mama always say too. My daddy dead too, just like yours. The white folks hung him."

"I'm so sorry to hear that, Thomas; one thing we all need is our pappas."

"I do all right with my mama and so do you, Minnie. You is right, we do need our pappas, but if we lose them to death, life for us goes on, no matter how hard it is to face."

The next week, all the folks from the church came to buy dinners. Most of them had told other folk that they knew about the dinners, so the turn out was overwhelming. Jane was so happy, she forgot about all the complaining she had been doing the night before to Minnie and Johnny about the preparation and cooking of so much food. Rev. Foster came by right after the service as he had promised Minnie, to help with the serving of dinners. Johnny was serving too, until the food started running out. Then he decided it was time to put him a plate up for later on that night.

Minnie had spent 102 dollars at the store, an unheard-of sum of money for a colored woman to spend on food. They made 260- plus dollars in profits that Sunday. That was even more unheard of, and not one person went away complaining, neither about the portions nor the quality. The food was delicious. more than 180 dinners sold on the strength of Rev. Foster's compliments to the chefs passed on from the pulpit and some timely gossip by a deacon's wife.

The many sacrifices Minnie observed her father make gave her the discipline she needed to manage her finances and save most every penny she earned. Most Saturday afternoons were filled with pleasurable outings with Thomas and hard evenings in the kitchen preparing and cooking for the dinners sold on Sundays and the family meetings. Minnie had picked up all Mrs. Mae Lewis's cleaning accounts. Her customer s were very pleased with her work ethics. Though her days and weeks were full with activities, she still missed her pappa dearly.

Minnie and Thomas's relationship was growing more and more with the kissing and petting, and Minnie liked it more and more. Finally they got around to discussing making love. Thomas convinced her that as long as two people were in love, they did not have to be married. Minnie asked

Jane if all the folks she knew who had young'uns were married. Jane said no, "But that don't make it right."

"Do it make it wrong if they love each other and wants to stay together?" she asked.

"No, child. What's on your mind, Minnie? I hope you ain't thankin 'bout doin' nothin' foolish."

"No, Mama, ain't no foolishness on my mind." Deep down inside, Minnie knew she wanted to make love to Thomas Foster. She felt herself pining for him whenever they were apart. Even when she was at work, her thoughts would automatically shift from sweeping the house she was in to her sweeping the house that Thomas had bought for them in her imaginary thoughts. She knew they would be happy if only he wanted to marry.

That Friday after the family meeting, Minnie and Johnny followed through on their plans to go see Bessie sing on Ninth Street. When the singing was over and the two of them waited for the crowd to leave, Minnie felt someone was staring at her from behind. When she turned, she thought she saw Thomas. Naw, it couldn't be, she thought to herself. What would a preacher be doing out here? She turned back around, convincing herself it could not possibly be the man she had fallen in love with. But the voice whispering in her ear was none other than Thomas. "I love you, Minnie, and I want to spend the rest of my life showing you how much."

"What you saying, Thomas, you wanting to marry me?"

"You know I do, but we should wait and see if we gone like making love together."

"Thomas Carter, what kind of foolishness you trying to trick me into?" Minnie snickered.

"You know I ain't fooling, Minnie." He planted a big kiss on her lips.

"I love you too, Thomas," she said as they were getting ready to part ways.

"Then be with me, Minnie. Can't be nothing worse than getting married first then finding out you don't want each other."

"Yes, Thomas, I'll try it. So where and when?"

"I got a place, and what better time than now, Minnie. We won't regret it," he promised.

"I ain't never been with no man, Thomas. I'm so scared, I don't know what to do."

"I'll make it all right, sweet baby, don't be scared."

Minnie told Johnny that she was leaving with Thomas, going for a walk. As they walked off holding hands, Thomas could feel Minnie shaking, and again he tried to reassure her that he would be gentle and not hurt her. "I know you won't hurt me, Thomas, but I had always told my ma and myself that I would be married before I did something like this."

"And you will be married to the man that you do this with, real soon. Now don't it feel good when we kissing and petting each other, girl? Now you know you want to do this as much as I do, don't you?"

"Yeah Thomas but...."

"But nothin," he said and pulled her into his arms and kissed her like never before. As the heat built up in his loins, he slowly walked her backwards down the walkway to the door and opened it, continuing the heated kiss into the bedroom. Minnie was panting and Thomas was touching her in places he had never touched before, all the while taking off her clothes and his at the same time. When he had finally undressed her, he stood back and took a long look at the voluptuous young lady in front of him. "Lawd... lawd... lawd'" he exclaimed. " Wheeew... woman, you so fine, it don't make no sense."

Thomas laid her on the bed and began sucking her breasts very gently. He slowly slid his tongue down her stomach, flick ing it around her navel.

Minnie was at this point somewhat beside herself in ecstasy. Thomas continued teasing Minnie, moving down to her pelvic area. Then he attempted to penetrate. She was wet but still he couldn't. Suddenly he cried out in pain and jumped up. He ran out of the room and Minnie followed him into the bathroom. He was bleeding from his penis.

"What happened, Thomas?" she asked.

"I ain't been circumcised, but it's gone be all right."

"Oh Thomas, I'm so sorry, it's my fault ain't it?"

"No, it's not your fault, we'll try again soon."

"Let me see."

"No way, it's just a little tear at the bottom of this thang."

"I still want to see, it's gone be part mine anyways," she said with a sly smile on her face.

"Woman, get yo'self back in that bedroom", he smiled as he gave a stern mock order.

Minnie returned to the bedroom and started to dress. She was happier than she had been in a long, long time. Thomas returned to the room fully dressed, making sure that they could try again soon. "Maybe so, but then maybe I won't be able to."

"But if you is able, we try, right baby?"

"Yes sir, Mr. Foster, we will try." They made the trek back to Twenty-third Street, kissed and said good night. Jane was standing at the front door. She simply cleared her throat, letting them know that she was present.

"Get in here, gal, and you to Mr. Preacher Boy." Minnie was both ashamed and scared as she passed her mother. Thomas did not know what to expect as he approached the front porch. "What your 'tentions for my child, boy?"

"Well, Mrs. Jane, I loves Minnie and I wants to marry her soon, but we too young right now."

"Son, I'm gone tell you dis one time and only one time : Don't try to make no fool of my baby or ya gone be sorry."

"Yes ma'am, Mrs. Jane," he replied.

"Something else, boy —ya better keep your hands off her til you's married." He gave her a sly smile and said, "Now, I'm a minister, Mrs. Jane. I wouldn't do nothing like that." Minnie was at the front door and heard the entire exchange between the two of them. When Jane reentered the house, she told Minnie to go to bed and think about what she was getting into. But all that night, the only thing Minnie could think about was how good it had felt when Thomas was about to enter her and she wanted him to finish the job.

The following day, Johnny and Thomas came to Minnie with a plan to post menus at some of the local businesses. This turned out to be a good idea. Regular orders came in from some of the local merchants located on 9th St. —B. H. Franklin undertaker, James Knox barber shop, and the sales staff at Evatt Furniture store ordered on a weekly basis. Also, there was an order that came in weekly for ten plates to be delivered to a pool hall in the name of Frank Whatley. Little did any of them know that Rev. Foster had cut a deal with the grocery store to give him ten percent of the gross that was spent on the grossly inflated prices that Minnie was paying. After all the cooking was done, Jane again admonished Minnie to be careful with Thomas. She gave a stern maternal admonition that warned Minnie about the spiritual and physical struggle that was going on inside of Thomas. Jane warned Minnie that while he was wonderful preacher and a fine servant of God, he was still an imperfect human and a man with physical needs and desires.

Even after all these verbal warnings from Jane, the next Friday, Minnie and Thomas had been together all day and ended up at Thomas's house, and again their fleshly desires took over. Minnie was the aggressor. She started stripping Thomas and telling him she had to have him, and how much their last intimate encounter had dominated her every thought the past few days. Thomas went into the bathroom and returned with a jar of petroleum jelly and applied some to his member and to Minnie's private area. This application of lubricant worked to perfection and they spent two and a half hours making wild, passionate love. When they had finished, the blood on the sheets this time indicated that Minnie was no longer a virgin.

Trying to catch his breath, Thomas was all smiles. "Right or wrong, Thomas, it was better than good. Hmmm...I see you been doing this for a while, hadn't you?"

"Naw, woman, what you talking 'bout?"

"Oh, you know what you doing," she laughed.

"Well, I got to clean myself up, Minnie. I got a meeting to attend this evening and I ain't no specialist at this, I just love being with you."

"Yeah, tell me anything, Thomas, I ain't no dumb country gal like you thinking."

At that, Thomas stopped in his tracks and said, "I don't think you no dumb country gal, Minnie, why would you say something like that?"

"Then don't start to," she shot back.

"Minnie" I'm your man and you're my woman."

The meeting Rev. Foster went to that night involved Minnie and the dinners. After dropping her off, he met with Mr. J.D. Lang, the grocery store owner to discuss a gradual price hike of Minnie's purchases and the amount of kickback he would receive. The prices had already been inflated beyond wholesale by five percent. The meeting concluded with an additional five percent to go to the Rev. Thomas Foster.

Meanwhile, the torrid intimacy between Minnie and Rev. Foster continued for the next two months. It was June now and the dinners were selling like hot cakes all over Chattanooga. Jane had noticed that Minnie was sleeping later in the mornings and napping in the evenings. She suspected that something was wrong. She woke Minnie up early one morning, and sure enough, she awoke with morning sickness. "Child, you done got yo'self knocked up, ain't you."

"No, Mama, I ain't knocked up."

But Jane knew she was pregnant. "I knowed it a week ago. You go get that dog and bring him here to me... Preacha my foot... a self- righteous, low... go...go get him."

"Yes Mama, I'm going right now."

As Minnie entered the church, she could hear voices coming from the pastor's office. She recognized Thomas's and Deacon Hollings's voice; the third voice sounded familiar too. She heard Thomas saying, "Minnie say she ain't no dumb country gal, but she ain't suspecting that we marking up her prices by ten percent. Ain't that right, Mr. Lang?" That was the third voice that sounded familiar to Minnie.

"Yes, she's making us plenty of money, Rev. Foster, so you be sure to keep her happy, son, ya hear?" Mr. Lang said in reply.

"Oh you can bet your last dollar that I keep her happy these days, in more ways than one, you can believe that." The three men broke into uncontrollable laughter.

Just then, Deacon Hollings spotted Minnie out of the corner of his eye and before he could warn the other two, a loud slap rang out, then another one. Thomas was covering himself now as the onslaught was stopped by Deacon Hollings grabbing Minnie from behind. "I would cut yo neck right now if I could," Minnie said to Thomas.

"Oh, I'm so sorry, Minnie, we was just cuttin' the fool. Men talk is all, I didn't mean no harm."

"Get your hands off me, man," Minnie said to Deacon Hollings. He immediately let her go and she walked right up to Thomas, who began to cower away from her. "Keep making your money off us, you jack leg supposed-to- be preacher. Because it won't be long now before you'll be stealing from your own child too. Fool, I know that in this world, you're either a wolf in sheep's clothing or a sheep amongst wolves. I thought you were a good man, but you ain't turned out to be nothing but a phony, low down, dirty dog.

You got to answer to the Lord one day just like I do for what we done created together, fool. But I don't want to see your ass ever again in this life." Tears were streaming down her face and she never raised her voice. " I was loving you with all my heart, you stupid bastard. Now your name tastes like shit in my mouth." Minnie turned and slowly walked out. Thomas tried to follow her but she stopped cold in her tracks, and told him to never say another word to her as long as he lived.

As she left the church walking home, Minnie was keenly aware of everything around her — the men in the alley shooting craps, the folk who just stood on the corners every day that she never paid any attention to now stood out. The whistle that warned the crap shooters that the police were coming sounded so loud to her today, although she had heard it many times in the past. Minnie was so mad, she felt as if she could kill someone with her bare hands for a mere mean stare. The tears were still streaming down her face as she opened the front screen door to the house. She calmly told Jane everything that had just taken place at the church. By the time Minnie had finished, there was a knock at the door; Deacon Hollings was on the porch. As Jane opened the door, she told Deacon Hollings to leave and don't come back.

"I'm leavin', Mrs. Jane, just wanted to make sure y'all was all right."

"We gone be all right, and tell that chuckle headed, buck dancing preacha not to come here no more or his folks gone be eating chicken over his ass, and not to ever say nothing else to me or my child."

After a few weeks, Jane noticed that her daughter's melancholy mood began to subside. Minnie was no longer crying over her broken heart trauma. Almost every conversation about her pregnancy went along a one- way line. Like a self- appointed coach, Minnie would spend time every day in front of her bedroom mirror saying, "I'm gone have my young'un and I'm gone raise my young'un and I ain't askin' for a crust of bread from that no- good man."

There was a cold look in Minnie's eyes that Jane had not seen before, and had only seen in one other pair before, William Heard's.

One morning, after Minnie had finished cleaning for her customers, she went and registered for the evening classes at the Alton Park Colored College. She had thought about going many times in the past, but her evenings had been filled by her hunger for Thomas. Although she convinced herself that she hated his guts, she still found herself pining for him. Minnie registered at the right time ; the classes she wanted to take were starting in two weeks. She agreed to pay the five dollar registration fee and pick up the three books she would need. The business book was a lot thicker than the accounting and math books, but Minnie didn't care; she was determined not to be thought of as a dumb country gal or to be stolen from again. That night, she read about as much as she could, trying to get a jump on the accounting class. When she awoke the next morning, it was still on her chest. All day at work, she couldn't wait to get home to read more.

CHAPTER IV

The family agreed to keep selling the dinners and allow the stealing to continue until the garden they had helped Uncle Johnny plant could be harvested to help cut the cost of the grocery bill. After the first harvest went so well, Johnny could see that this small plot wouldn't suffice, and that he could make a huge profit selling his crops to the stores in town himself. So he purchased several acres of land outside of town. Johnny secretly started growing greens, cabbages, cucumbers, green beans, field peas, tomatoes, onions, corn, sweet potatoes, and okra. Johnny also started raising chickens, hogs, cows, and some horses. Along with his own sharecropping skills, he employed some of the methods that he and Deacon Hollings discussed.

Emma was offered a job by Minnie to help with the cooking of the dinners, and she gladly accepted the work. She needed the extra cash any way, so Emma fit right in with Jane and Minnie in the kitchen. The next few months seemed to take a heavy toll on Minnie; the cleaning, the schooling, and the cooking, none of which she minded doing. Minnie was starting to show, and this was either going to be a big baby or she was gaining a lot of water weight. She loved cooking, so that was always pleasing to her. The school work was getting easier, plus there was a fine man named Frank Whatley who was always trying to help Minnie with her school work. Minnie would always decline any help, although they would still engage in some casual conversation.

One Thursday evening, he asked to walk her home and she accepted. They talked about all sorts of things, including the baby on the way. He then asked her if she had ever heard his name before. Then it came to her about the ten dinners every week in that name, Frank Whatley. Suddenly, the talk turned serious when Frank mentioned that a baby needs a father. Frank told Minnie about some of his former school mates who had children before marriage. He spoke of how some guys abandoned the young ladies after they got them pregnant. Minnie took offense at the statement, and said that she didn't need a man to raise her baby. "Okay now, Minnie, I'm sure you don't. I was just sayin' that it don't matter who knocked you up. Anybody can do that, but everybody can't be a father, and sooner or later, a baby might need a father.

"Well mines won't; anyway, you ain't got no young'uns, do you?"

"Naw, big mama, I ain't got none yet, but I want a house full. "They both agreed that they wanted lots of children and a big loving home to raise them in. They shared a common goal: to raise their children not to be afraid of any man and face life's challenges like racism in the manner in which they were dealing with them. The two of them agreed that they were never going to allow racism to hinder them in how they approached every day life or business matters. Frank told Minnie that he wasn't going to wait for racial hatred to die; he was going to help bury it. Both laughed when Minnie said that she never wanted to take a back seat to anyone.

As they approached Jabbo's Pool Room, someone ran out and passed them in a hurry. Frank quickly pulled Minnie to the side. As they came up on the door, they looked inside and a man lay on the sawdust- covered floor, bleeding. He had been stabbed by the person who rushed past them. Stupid fools, Minnie thought to herself, hurtin' and killin' one another up for no good reason. "Hmmm, you knew somethin' was wrong, Frank? You be in them kinda places."

"Sometimes, I ain't gone lie to you, but I knows that scamp Lee Oscar that ran outta there, and if Lee's a running, somebody else done probably fared pretty bad. "

"How do you know Lee Oscar?"

"I've known him since we was boys, we use to do a little running around together on the weekends sometimes."

"What kinda runnin' you talkin' 'bout."

"Business running, that's all, justa lil business."

"You some kinda gangsta or somethin? Cause if you is, I don't want to be seen with you."

"No, no, no I'm going to school to learn about the minerals and precious substances like gold, silver, copper, the ecological balances and such. I want to help preserve this region of this country; it belonged to my ancestors. I don't want it to end up as polluted and eroded as some portions of Europe have been. I'm just a country boy trapped in the city. I love hunting and fishing like everybody else."

"Why you want to know how to preserve this region, you can't run it?"

"Cause I know one day it won't be the way it is now as far as who runs things and who getting ran. So now I want to figure out how to stop this land from getting stripped away before it ain't nothing left for our young'uns."

"Why you stop that kind of talk, man, I'm already knocked up for another man."

"Yeah, for a fool who don't want to be responsible for an innocent child who don't know or care who planted it. That ain't the kind of man I want to be."

"Was you ever in a relationship where you had another man's child to raise, Mister Frank?"

"Naw, but I know some boys I went to school with that did."

"So now you want to learn to be a step- daddy, ha?"

"I reckon so, and why you going to school? To be smarter than everybody else or what, big mama?"

"Nope," Minnie replied, "so that nobody can think they can ever take advantage of me again. Plus I need to learn the proper way to run a business so I can open up my restaurant."

"Well, well, well, and who is this that done took advantage of you?"

"Nobody ain't took nothin' from me and they never will," Minnie snapped.

"Come on now, big mama, I want you to be able to talk to me about anything."

For some strange reason, Minnie felt that she could talk to Frank about anything. She confided in Frank her hatred for Thomas and Mr. Lang for cheating her, and the helplessness that she felt. There was no way for her to strike back at them and she wanted to. "Anyway, this is my house, Frank. Thanks for walking with me. I sure didn't mean to trouble you with my troubles. I'm not looking for a pity party.

See you in school tomorrow."

"Well, thank you for letting me walk you home. I've enjoyed listening to you talk. We might just be able to get back at them slicksters of yours yet. Will it be all right to come by and sit with you sometime?"

"Why you want to come by and sit with me when I'm already knocked up?"

" Ain't worried 'bout that belly none, it might bring me luck in the Alabama or Vegas woman."

"What's the Alabama and the Vegas woman?" Minnie asked.

"Just business," Frank answered. They both laughed and said good night.

The next afternoon after work, Minnie decided to visit with Emma. It had been a while since she had discussed her secret ardent admirer with a living soul. Minnie had noticed that on their walks, he always strolled through some shady area of town, teaching her about pick pockets, thugs, and other games r un on the streets. She decided she would go to Emma to see if she knew anything about him. The two of them could never talk like this in the kitchen with Jane right there all the time.

"What a surprise, what else besides being pregnant as a fish going on in your life?"

"I'm just trying to survive like everybody else, Emma. Trying to hang in there with college learning."

"What's that you learning?"

"Business and accounting," Minnie replied. "There's this young man I met at the school named Frank. He's always sayin' everything is business."

"You ain't talking 'bout that fine thang, Frank Whatley, is you, Minnie? All the young girls is interested in that young buck. Ever'body knows him. He runs the Georgia, Alabama, Las Vegas street numbers, and on Sunday, you can get your bootleg whiskey."

"I knew that Negro was a gangsta," Minnie said, smiling.

"He ain't no gangsta, Minnie, he just ain't to be fooled wit'. I don't think nobody is stupid enough to mess with him, he got Mr. Moore backing him up. Now that's the gangsta. Frank, though, is a nice person. Minnie, you should hear how folks go on 'round here 'bout how he treats his niece Savannah. She's his only sister, Anna's daughter. Anna got married and moved away to Pittsburgh, Pennsylvania. It wasn't no scandal or nothing like that ; she left town with her new preacher husband." Minnie couldn't get a word in. "What I heard," Emma continued, "is that Frank's mother, Mrs. Frankie, wanted Savannah raised down here so she would know her roots and where she came from. Savannah goes up to visit her every summer and she knows who her mother is and she loves her to death for leaving her down here. Folks say that man acts like she his child, he spoiling that little girl to death. So you know he gone be good to his own young'uns."

"That's good to know, Emma, but I got to get my mind on something else besides Frank."

"By the way, Minnie, what you want, a boy or girl?"

"You know what? I ain't even thought about it. But I reckon a boy so he can stick by his mama."

"Well good luck wit school, and I hope I'm around when the baby come along, and good luck wit Frank too."

"Child, I ain't got a chance with Frank or nobody else, being knocked up like this. See you later, Emma." With that, they gave each other a big hug and Minnie started her short walk home.

On Minnie's walk home, she had a flurry of thoughts. What's it gone take to keep the dinners selling? Can I finish school and raise a young'un too? What's gone come of my cleaning customers? I'm gone have to give 'em up soon. I wish Babe was here. Minnie wondered how would she stand a chance of gettin' Frank interested in her, with her being knocked up for Thomas. Minnie decided to let her weary mind rest and enjoy the lovely day. But little did she know that Frank had been doing his inquiring too.

Just then, she heard a familiar voice call out to her softly but firmly. "Minnie, would you mind if I stroll along with you for a spell?"

"Hello Frank, good to see you. I reckon I don't mind if you do. You out enjoying the sunshine today or tak in' care business?"

"No ma'am, I was really hoping to see you come along."

"And for what reason you out here looking for me? I done already told you I'm knocked up for somebody else, Frank."

"And I done told you it don't matter who you knocked up for; what matter is who you gone end up with."

"I never wanted to end up with a young'un and no husband. I always dreamed of a happy family life. My pappa always said you only come around this way one time, so I'm going to enjoy my go round, no matter what."

"Me too, Minnie, I mean a happy family where the young'uns have a mother and a father in the house," he said, smiling.

"It don't take much for most folks, but I know it's gone take a good man for me."

"Minnie, I ain't never minded working just as hard as the next fella, and I been told that some folks think I'm a pretty decent young man. You get 'round to needing a husband, let me be the first to know. One thing I figure and you need to remember is every family needs a good man to take the lead and protect its members. "

"Mmm huh, they all say that; good day, Frank."

"I don't know what they say, but I mean what I say and don't you forget it."

"If you say so, Frank, but you betta live up to all your talk."

Frank reached into his suit jacket pocket and pulled out a ball point ink pen. Then he unscrewed the pen and took the small pen in the top out. "To me, Minnie, a young'un is like this little spring." Frank then held the spring clutched tight in a closed fist. "If I open my hand too fast, the spring will fly out wildly but if I open my hand up slowly, I can almost determine where the spring bounces off to. I would love to keep our young'uns safe, give them a sense of self- esteem, and teach them to think on their own. All I need is for you to give me a lifetime to do it in, all right."

"Now that you've established that you gone be round for a while, I'll need to talk to my uncle Johnny this time and get his opinion on things. Besides Uncle Johnny and my ma, the only other people I talk to in town is Tom and that gossiping Emma from time to time."

As soon as they arrived at the front walkway, Frank said good evening and started off. "Thank you again, Frank. I appreciate you walkin' and talkin' with me."

"Believe you me, it won't be the last time I talk to you. No Lord, big mama, this won't be our last conversation. I do believe you might have my nose wide open," Frank chided as he was stepping backward, then turned and departed for the evening.

The next few days seemed like the busiest and most exciting that Minnie had experienced in her life. Emma had put the word out that Bessie Smith had recorded a song for South Bend Records. Minnie couldn't be happier for her. Her own activities were overwhelmingly hectic. She had to see the mid wife to find out how soon the baby would be arriving. She continued to clean for her customers, help cook for the Sunday dinner sell, and continue her schooling. She mended clothing for her Uncle Johnny and helped Jane with her quilting. Yes, the weekly activities would be overwhelming for some people, but it was almost a normal week for Minnie.

One cold and clear Saturday morning in February held the biggest surprise. The midwife said the baby would almost certainly not be here for another three weeks, but Minnie woke up in the worst pain she had ever felt. It was even worse than being shot, she thought. Minnie thought it was odd that her bed was wet, because she knew she hadn't had a bed wetting accident. Johnny had stopped by that morning to pick up some pants Minnie had mended for him. He and Jane were sitting down in the living room chatting about how good the dinners were selling and the need to get a larger place to cook, because the kitchen was getting too small. Suddenly they heard Minnie screaming for Jane. Johnny was up the stairs in a flash.

"What's the matta, child?" Johnny asked, trying to catch his breath.

"Get the midwife, Uncle Johnny, my baby comin'," Minnie managed to get out before the next pain hit her. After begging the Lord to make the pain subside, she explained to Jane that she thought she was dreaming about the great pain she having, and woke up to find that her bed was wet. Meanwhile, Jane— herself a trained midwife —was gathering some clean towels and getting the hot water ready. Johnny knew if she had to, Jane could deliver the baby without a hitch. When Johnny returned with the midwife, Mrs. Simmons, Jane had everything ready, although she was a nervous wreck. Mrs. Simmons hadn't been there ten minutes before Minnie went to pushing. The baby's head started to emerge and then a whole little person.

"A boy," Jane said, her voice full of joy. No sooner than Mrs. Simmons had cleaned the baby off and handed him to Jane, Minnie began to push again. "Lawd have mercy, it's twins"" Jane shouted. Well I be dog gone, it's a girl." Downstairs, Johnny heard the first cries from the baby. He ran upstairs, there was Jane washing the baby off. "It's a big ole boy"" she exclaimed. "And a fine girl too, twins." Mrs. Simmons was cleaning off the girl.

"Yeah"" Johnny sang out. "Gone name him William, ain't you, Minnie?"

"Seem to me you done decided that for me, Uncle Johnny. Let me see him, ma."

"Soon as he clean, child. He's a fine ole boy."

"Well, let me see Maxie, is she clean?"

"Yeah, I like that name too, Minnie." Johnny repeated it: "Maxie... Maxie...Maxie."

After taking care of Minnie's post-natal needs, Mrs. Louise informed Minnie that she looked good and not to go outside for at least a month, no cooking, no hair washing, and all the other precautionary measures to take during that time. Jane had finished cleaning up the babies and Minnie finally got the chance to hold them in her arms. "William look like pappa too, don't he, y'all?"

"Sho' do," Johnny said with a big grin on his face, "gone be tuff like him too."

"We got us another William Heard," Jane whispered. "Maxie looks like a doll. This is a powerful blessing." Johnny brought up the new rocking chair he had been hiding away for Minnie's special day. The word spread down Twenty- third Street like wild fire and the gifts poured in.

CHAPTER V

Diapers, clothes, and all sorts of baby things came pouring in from everywhere. There were so many visitors that Minnie couldn't remember who brought what. Jane got everyone to sign a list, and those who couldn't write, Johnny wrote their names and addresses for them. They all received thank-you cards the next Sunday. The first six weeks was a major adjustment period for Minnie. It seemed that the babies had their days and nights mixed up. What a hard job, raisin young'uns, and I got two, she kept thinking. They were so soft and cuddly. Minnie loved to see them cooing as she sang her lullabies to them.

Johnny was on his way over to visit with Minnie, Jane, and the babies, when Rev. Foster pulled up. Rev. Foster appeared to be somewhat nervous as he got down off his buggy to greet Johnny. "Sorry how things turned out between me and Minnie, but I want you to know I'm as proud as a peacock to be the daddy of those children. And I plan on be being a good one if Minnie will let me." The two men walked inside. Johnny told the Reverend to wait while he'd go and tell Minnie that she has a visitor.

"You tell him he can come up here and see his babies if he wants."

Rev. Foster cautiously entered the bedroom. He spoke softly to Minnie, and she coolly to him. He walked as though he was walking on egg shells. Rev. Foster smiled broadly as he looked at his newborn son and daughter. "Can I hold one of them, Minnie?"

"Do you know how?"

"I guess I better if I'm gone want to keep'em sometime, if you don't mind."

"Maybe after awhile, I don't know 'bout right now. Listen, Thomas, I don't want to treat you bad about seeing your young'uns, but I don't want nothing else to do with you."

"I can understand that, Minnie. I'm just thankful you giving me the chance to be a part of William and Maxie's lives." Rev. Foster had not abandoned his responsibility to Minnie during her pregnancy. He sent money every week by Johnny, who kept and saved it for the babies. Little William and Maxie had a good savings started.

Lil' William woke up briefly to be fed before he slipped back off to sleep. Minnie wondered if she could produce enough milk for the two of them. Jane came upstairs to check on them and spoke to Rev. Foster coldly, adding that he should keep his visit brief. With the wash tub in hand, Jane was ready to give the babies a wash- off. "Ma, he just went back to sleep" Minnie said in a whisper, "but Maxie's up." Jane had made the babies some sugar tits.

"What are those, Minnie?" Thomas asked shyly.

"Sugar in lil' rags to pacify these two between feedings."

"Do they work?"

"We don't know yet, these are their first ones. You can come by on Sundays after service to spend time with the babies."

"I sure will, Minnie, thank you, that'll be just fine with me. I guess I better run along so you ladies can get back to tending them babies." Rev. Foster knew that he had fared well on his visit. He not only got to speak to Minnie again, even if it was cool and brief, but he got visitation privileges to see his son and daughter.

Jane gently undressed and submerged the little pair one at a time into the tub. First she bathed Maxie and brushed her hair. Lil' William loved the water. Soon as that little butt hit the warm water, he would start squirting pee everywhere, including his grandma's face. Jane would laugh as she tried to avoid the stream shooting up at her. "You wakin' up good for Grandma, now ain't ya, ole big- headed boy?"

After their baths, she showed Minnie how to keep the umbilical cords clean with a little alcohol. Jane sat in her rocking chair with William. After a sugar tit and a little rocking, he went right back to sleep. Jane kept Maxie playing with her. This allowed Minnie the time to write a letter to the school explaining the birth of her children, and that she desired to continue her schooling as soon as possible. Johnny delivered the letter to the school that Monday for her. The school's director, Mr. Bradshaw, made arrangements with Minnie's instructors to send all their present and upcoming assignments to her, but someone would have to pick them up and return them to the school. Minnie was delighted when Johnny came back with her lessons, as he called them. Six weeks seemed to have flown by. William and Maxie seemed to be eating more and more as the days went by. William was so greedy, Minnie thought she might need two more breasts to keep up with his demand. Rev. Foster kept his word and visited every Sunday like clockwork.

Minnie made it back to school in the spring. Frank immediately came over to her and told her how much he had missed her and thought about her. "I can tell, that's why your rump been by to see me so much."

"Well, I thought you would be busy with your babies and all, so I figured I'd wait for you to get back out and then ask you to marry me."

"Ask me what?" Minnie asked with her mouth hanging open.

"Will you marry me, Minnie?"

"Don't play with me like that, Frank Whatley. I mess 'round here and say yes and you don't really mean it."

"I mean it, Minnie. Can you take a ride with me after class?"

"I reckon I can spend a little time with you this evening without causing too much commotion at home. I've got to talk this over with my ma and Uncle Johnny at the family meeting tomorrow."

"I ain't marrying your mama and uncle, so why I need them to say o k?"

"Cause I do, mister, and if you serious, you'll wait and see what my folks say."

"All righty then, big mama, I'll wait."

"You better and you better be good to me and my babies."

"I'll be good to you, your babies, and all our babies too." Then Frank's tone and mood turned very serious. "I just want you to know something about my family that I've never spoken to another soul about. My father was murdered working in the same line of business that I do now."

"Oh Frank, I'm so sorry. What happened?"

"One night, he was making a pick up, and was robbed and shot. His half- brother was running the business back then. The two of them never had a close relationship until right before he was killed. My family blames him for the whole thing." He told her that even though the rest of the family had ostracized his uncle, he had remained neutral on the terrible matter.

Minnie was probably the one person in the world who knew exactly how he felt. She had always found Frank so easy to talk to. And before long, she had divulged her own family secret. She had confided in him what she could never tell Thomas. She painfully recalled the whole story for him, spilling it out like an over- boiling pot of rice. Frank gently held her in his arms. "If my pappa gave up his life so I could go on with mine... If he and his brothers made that kind of sacrifice for me, then I've got to do something positive with mine." The fact that they had entrusted one another with the ghosts from their past only served to forge an unbreakable bond between the two of them.

Finally the classes were dismissed for the day. Minnie thought her heart would burst from the excitement of the proposal she had just received. When Minnie and Frank came out of the side exit of the building, a shiny black horse- drawn carriage was waiting. Frank had prearranged for Bo Mealy to be his driver for the evening. Bo and Minnie had an open dislike for one another, but managed to exchange cordial greetings. Bo rode them to the north end of Lookout Mountain. After he stopped the buggy in what appeared to be a garden, Bo got down and helped Minnie, then he turned around and handed Frank two fresh red roses and a small box. Frank walked Minnie over to Sunset Rock. From this majestic vista, even though Frank always dressed dapper and professionally as a business executive. He dropped to his knees and made official supplication for her hand in marriage. Frank gave her the two roses and slipped the ring on her finger. Minnie fought hard to hold back the tears from falling to her cheeks. The ride back was out of this world. Minnie had grown to love the beautiful scenic attractions and salubrious climate of the Chattanooga area. The evening was gorgeous, not a cloud in the sky. The stars were shining bright, so bright that they all seemed to be winking at her. They laughed and talked a lot more on the way home about their future and more children. Minnie couldn't wait to ask Jane for permission to marry Frank, even though with or without it, she was going to marry him anyway. She wanted Jane to be just as happy as she was about it. The proposal turned out to be a great shock to her and she vehemently opposed the idea of a quick marriage, and then to someone she knew nothing about. "Child, what ya doin'? I ain't never met this man, gal. Why you rushin' to marry 'im?"

"Mama, I done took my time and I know what I want so just stand with me now. Please."

"I don't know nuthin' 'bout dis buck, but if'n you think ya love ' im and he ain't the fightin' kind, go on and marry ' im."

"You mean it ma?"

"I don't like it," Johnny said, "but I won't fight you on this, Minnie." He felt that Minnie had not gotten to know the man in such a short period of time.

Minnie was blissful ; she had what she wanted, almost. "Ma, one more thing, we gone stay here with you, o k?"

"Dat's up to you and your husband, Minnie, it's fine wit' me."

The next evening, after Minnie and Jane finished cleaning the kitchen and counting the profits from the dinners, the two of them talked about opening a restaurant. "Me and Uncle Johnny been talkin' and we think it's time to find a larger kitchen to cook these dinners."

"I been sayin' dat too," Jane replied.

"So, it'll be all right with you if I check into it, Ma?"

"I reckon, child, but don't go out bull headed and buy nuttin' without us first talkin' 'bout it."

"Thanks, Ma, now can I ask another favor of you? Will you keep Lil' William and Maxie for a little while? I need to go talk to Frank."

"Go on, child, but don't go stay long."

47

"Yes, ma'am, I won't go stay long. Thanks Ma, for everything, I love you."

After Minnie had whisked out, Jane softly replied, "I love you too, baby."

Frank was sitting on his front porch drinking a shot of whiskey when Minnie walked up smiling as she approached him. "Hey, big mama," he said smiling back.

"Hey Daddy," she said to him for the first time.

"That mean what I thank it mean, Minnie?"

"Yes, yes, yes, everything is settled. If you think we gone get married with blessings, then the answer is yes."

Frank drank his shot straight and yelled, "Thank you, Lord""

"Frank, there's one thing you must know; my ma go where I go, I ain't never leavin' her."

"I wouldn't ask you to do that, big mama. "

"Thank you, Daddy Frank."

"Wanna go dancing for a little while, Minnie?"

"Not tonight, Daddy, got to get back to my babies. One more thing, Frank; I want to open me a place, my kitchen's getting too small to keep sellin dinners out of it. Will you help me find a place sorta cheap?"

"I reckon I can have Mr. Moore find us something cheap."

"Why Mr. Moore, Frank?"

"Cause he's got a kindly face and only a kindly face can get something cheap in Chattanooga, o k?"

"All right, Daddy, just let me know somethin'. "

"So when, Minnie? "

"When what? "

"What day we be getting married on?"

"How about we wait till school is out?"

"That's just fine with me."

"Frank, I don't ever want to be worried 'bout my man slipping round on me, you understand? I'll cut your throat for that."

"No need worrying 'about that, mama. I don't do that now, so I know I won't when I got you at home. You a mean little ole woman, ain't you?"

"Ain't nothing little 'bout me, Daddy, and yes, I can be mean when I have to be."

"Well, all right, big mean mama."

"Good night, Frank Whatley."

"Come on, Mama, let me get you back to your babies."

The small talk on the way home produced an agreement to settle for a wedding to be performed by a justice of the peace instead of a local preacher. They decided this way would be less of a burden on everybody. The next morning, Frank went and spoke with Mr. Orland Moore about a building up town that would be fitting for a restaurant to operate out of. The Crabtree Café had closed about a month earlier and a lot of kitchen supplies had been left behind. Frank knew Mr. Moore would not be partial to helping him out because he was the syndicate boss in the Southeast. The man Frank called boss. They ran the numbers business, as Frank called it. Mrs. Cole ran a small portion of their gate for them, as did many others. Mr. Moore had been after Frank to expand into boot leggin'. Now Frank's request would give him the necessary leverage to convince him to do so. The building was huge, with two kitchens, and there was a second floor with a large conference room and three offices, the biggest of which had a back door and stairs that led down to the main kitchen and gave easy access to the back door. Mr. Moore also had plans to move the monthly gambling game he hosted into the offices of the facility. He had ordered dinners from Minnie consistently and was crazy about all the food. Now he could offer catered meals as a perk for the high rolling participants.

Frank agreed but stipulated that no whiskey was to come into the restaurant, and that these were two separate deals. The building was Frank's for the mere sum of $5,000. "Make the deed out to Minnie Lee Whatley."

"Who the hell is Minnie Lee Whatley, Frank?"

"That'll be my future wife. One more thing, J.D. Lang and Reverend Foster conspired to mark up food prices on Minnie behind her back. Is there some way for us to get back at them for doing the girl like that?"

"Let me talk to my lawyer. I know a thing or two about the law and your future wife is entitled to pursue civil action in court against these wanna be slick suckers. She can possibly sue the two of them ass holes for slander, conspiracy, liability, and anything else I can think of. Frank, I could use other means to get the money out of these scum bags but I won't. In this instance, though, I will use an attorney and make sure she gets a tidy sum. I hate that son of a bitch, J.D. Lang. We'll see if he and the preacher boy want the negative publicity that comes from extorting money from an innocent young woman. That arrogant cock sucker has always been a thorn in my side. Here's the deal. I'll get twenty- five percent of what we sue the bastard for. My attorney will get twenty- five percent and your wife will get fifty percent. This is going to take some arm twisting. Let me get back to you on this thing. Go ahead and ask your bride- to- be if she wants to proceed.

After Frank left, Mr. Moore called his attorney, James Copeland. He was a brilliant attorney with extensive knowledge in tort and criminal matters. He had an unblemished record when representing Mr. Moore in either area. Mr. Copeland, as he demands to be called by his peers, likes to keep a pocket full of candy so whenever he greets someone in the court room, whether it's the opposing attorney, judge, or average Joe off the street, he would hand them a piece of candy. He figured this gave him a psychological advantage over his opponent. He had reasoned that this put the other person in a better and more cooperative mood right at the onset of whatever deal he was trying to barter. Mr. Copeland knew all the dirty tricks the law allowed, every loophole, and used them to his advantage. His only vice, he was a known womanizer and loved to booze it up occasionally. This was a common thread he and Orland Moore shared. This shared iniquity made them two close friends as well as long time business associates. Mr. Moore often chided with James Copeland about the need to keep him on retainer for eternity so that he could one day find a tiny loophole in the Ten Commandments that just might allow them to get into heaven. The two also shared a common hatred for John Corynth and J.D. Lang. Corynth and Lang had kept Mr. Moore and Mr. Copeland in the dark on a secret agreement that had blocked Moore and Copeland from closing a deal on a hotel that had burned down in 1908 on Lookout Mountain.

When Mr. Copeland arrived, Mr. Moore excitedly told him that their opportunity to crush Lang had jumped up like a rabbit in the bush. Mr. Moore highlighted all the intricate details of the sordid extortion scheme cooked up by Rev. Foster and Lang. Copeland's eyes lit up with an evil gleam. "I always keep a load in the chamber when I'm out in the bush for stupid rabbits that jump. I'm going to roast that deceitful bastard." They got a good chuckle out of the fact that they had Lang by the balls. "I want all these damn people to realize that this family is under my protection, Mr. Copeland." Mr. Moore gave Copeland a full briefing on the deal that he had cut with Frank and Minnie, on how the settlement would be split in three parts. Mr. Copeland said he would demand them to pay $50,000 and he guaranteed that he would get it. In only two weeks, the mere threat of using the local press to expose the co-conspirators produced payment in full.

Thomas did have to get one well- administered but not so physically revealing beating at the hands of Bo and Reedy Mealy. The brothers whipped the Reverend with a two- by- four but they used a copy of the local directory and taped it to his backside to cushion the blows. The not- so- brutal mock whipping further motivated Rev. Foster and Lang to pay expeditiously. Frank and Minnie kept their part of the money in the safe at Mr. Moore's office. They planned to use this money as an educational fund for their children.

Having $50,000 of their money taken away in a lump sum hurt Thomas and Lang worse than any type of negative publicity exposing their conspiracy to the public may have caused. It gave Minnie the sweet taste of payback and revenge that she needed. It also put a deep gulf of hatred for Minnie and Frank in Lang's heart that rivaled his bitter feelings towards Copeland and Moore.

That afternoon, Frank went to get Minnie. He wanted to meet her mother and the twins, but most of all, he wanted to surprise Minnie by taking her to visit her new building that would soon be used to house her very own place of business. Jane spotted him walking up the walkway to the house. She jokingly called upstairs to Minnie that her husband was coming up the walk, even though she had no idea what Frank looked like. Jane just knew that this fellow had to be Minnie's Frank that she was always chattering about. He was as black as an ace of spades, and as handsome as a prince in shining review before his royal subjects. Frank had coal black, wavy hair, and stood about six- foot- one, slim, fine, and in top physical condition. He was a good- looking man even by Jane's standards. Before he had a chance to knock on the door, Minnie had raced down the stairs and jerked the door open. "Howdy big mama," he said, not noticing Jane standing in the background.

"Frank this is my mama, Jane Heard. Mama, this is Frank Whatley."

"Howdy, ma'am."

"Hello, young'un, done heard lots 'bout ya, now let me tell you sumptin'."

"Ma," Minnie protested, smiling. "You marry my child if'n ya wanna, but don't hurt her or I'll bring da hide off ya myself. Other den dat, I got nuttin' else to say 'cept I'm please ta meet ya. "

"Yes ma'am, don't worry, I'm not marrying her to hurt, her but that's not to say we won't never spat none, because she can be mean as the devil sometimes. "

"I gots nuttin' to do wit no spattins, but if'n ya gots to hit her, leaver her here wit me. "

"Won't be none of that, Mrs. Jane, ma'am."

Frank asked for and received permission to introduce Minnie and her mom to his family. They met Frank's brothers, Walsh, Joe, and Gussy, and his mother Frankie. Amazingly, they all seemed to genuinely like one another. Frankie was an American Indian and rarely spoke a word other than to talk about her people's history. Frank and everyone else adored his mother's sense of integrity and the sweet disposition that she had about her personality. Frank shared with Minnie some of the old stories his mother had taught him about her family history. She was Creek, a division of the Muskhogean tribe. She had told him that for her people, Lookout Mountain was the rock that comes to a point.

His mother had instilled a deep sense of pride in her children about how they had indeed descended from the indigenous peoples of this great continent. Frankie taught her children that their ancestors were mountain people. That at one point in time, their forefathers were the sole protectors of this vast yet little disturbed natural habitat that was part of the region in

North America known to the Indians as Chattata. Frank had learned that not so long ago, these mountains were only remotely accessible to other ethnic groups. His forefathers had gathered a storehouse of ecological knowledge about this mountain that had served them well when it came to protecting Lookout Mountain's eco system. Frank had a plan to increase awareness about the problems facing this region as far as preserving its natural resources. He felt that far too many people never thought about how fragile the ability to sustain a clean ecosystem on this and other mountains was going to be in the future. He also felt that not enough attention had been paid to the plight and well- being of the original inhabitants of this region. His concern was for both humans and animals. Frankie had taught Frank and his siblings that now everyone who came to this wonderful place had to become mountain people. Only unity would help solve these and other problems facing the area. She told them time and time again to preserve all forms of life, and that they must respect the dignity of man. All the Whatley children were taught that the name Chattanooga comes from the Indian phrase Chado-na-ugsa. Finally, Minnie learned that the only way that Frankie and her family had escaped the Trail of Tears was their tribe's dark skin complexion. This allowed them to mix in with the black people.

"Well, Minnie, if you can get your mama to take another ride with us, I want to show y'all something."

"Well, Ma, let's go."

"Y'all don't need me to go with ya nowheres, child."

"Please, ma'am, won't take but a short spell."

"I reckon, boy." Minnie noticed that Jane seemed to like Frank or she would have never agreed to go any further with them. They all loaded up into Frank's new Ford and headed uptown. Frank pulled up to a storefront at 204 Ninth Street. After helping Minnie, Jane, and the babies out of the car, he walked up to Minnie and handed her a deed and a key to a door. She looked at the deed and started smiling, her eyes twinkling like diamonds. Gently rocking Maxie on her shoulder, Minnie couldn't stop herself from smiling.

"Frank, I told you to look into it, not jump up and go out and buy a place for me." They went inside as soon as Minnie could calm herself down and stop fumbling with the key. The previous owners had left a new stove and a fairly new refrigeration system that was state of the art. There were tables and chairs to sea t 150 people, and plenty of spare room. Minnie asked when the previous owners would be removing their things. "This building and all that's in it belongs to the lady named on the deed you holding, big mama, lock, stock, and barrel."

"This lady don't exist yet, Daddy Frank."

"She will tonight," Frank replied. Neither of them was paying attention to Jane, who was herself pleased to see Minnie so happy.

William's cry broke into their ears like a bullet, jolting them back to reality. Minnie got a bottle out of the rag she kept them in. "Ma, do you like the place?"

"I love it," Jane answered. "Now what we owes you young'un?" Frank looked puzzled. The question seemed blunt and harsh to him.

Before he could answer, Minnie interrupted, "I plan on making the big office mine, so when I'm tired, I can slip up the back stairs and lock the door."

Just then, there was a loud knock at the front door. They turned to see Sheriff Leroy Ponterford with his gun drawn. "What the hell are you folks doing in Mr. Moore's place?" he demanded.

Minnie snapped, "This here place belongs to me, Sheriff, and don't be pointing no gun at my family."

"You better have some paper work saying you own this property or you gone find your smart mouth ass in jail, nigger gal."

"Here's the deed right here and don't ever call me no nigger gal no more neither."

The sheriff checked the paper as though he couldn't read. "Hmmm..... this is you, huh gal?"

"Yes it is," Frank said, "we got the deed from Mr. Moore this morning, sir."

"Who you, boy? I done seen you 'round here before, hadn't I?"

"Frank Whatley, Sheriff. I'm sure you remember me from Mr. Moore's office. This here's my wife Minnie and her mama Jane."

"Is that your automobile outside, boy?"

"Yes sir, that's my car."

"Let me see your papers for it. O k. I'll be checking with Mr. Moore to make sure ain't nothing funny about that deed. By the way, what y'all planning on doing in here anyway? Ain't no niggers never operated no place uptown before."

Minnie spoke before she knew it. "Ain't no niggers gone run this place either, and don't never call my man no boy, peckawood."

The sheriff's face reddened, then he smirked and said, "You one upitty lil' gal, ain't you? We gone see 'bout bringing you down to your place with the rest of the niggers."

"Suh, don't threat my child or you peckawoods all a die," Jane said. Just the look in her eyes let the sheriff know she meant every word.

"You folks have a good day," the sheriff said as he backed toward the door.

Frank was looking more like a hero every day in Minnie's eye. She was starting to hope he would live up to that same status in the bed room as well. The fact that he had never mentioned or approached her disrespectfully only intensified her desire for him. Moreover, she thought he was fine as hell and wanted to see what he had in his britches. Meanwhile, Ponterford made a beeline to Mr. Moore's office. He burst in, yelling, "What the hell do you mean selling prime real estate to them niggers? What the white folks gone think? They gone burn 'em out. That's what they gone do and you know it."

"Damn it, calm down, Leroy," Mr. Moore said coolly. He had been expecting him all day and knew exactly how he would handle the situation. "Shut your mouth sometimes and use your ears, man. Now, there's about fifteen or so colored eateries in Chattanooga and hadn't no damn body burned them out. These people can cook the best damn food in the world, bar none I tell you. The deal I made with them good folks is gonna up all our pay around here, especially yours. Ain't nobody gone burn these people out cause you ain't gone let 'em, you hear me?"

"I ain't standing in the way of good white folks for no niggers, Mr. Moore."

"The hell you ain't. I pay you more in a day than any of these other good white folk can pay you in a week to protect what I say protect. Now you will treat them folks with dignity and respect, and make sure no harm comes to them or their place. You understand me, Sheriff Leroy Ponterford?"

"Yes sir, Mr. Moore, I do, I just don't know how the other whites gone take this."

"They gone take it the way you make 'em, just like everything else around here. As a matter of fact, when they open that restaurant, you and me is gonna be the first and most frequent customers they have. Bring all your deputies the first night too; dinner is on me that night." You know Frank Whatley is my right hand in this town, and I take damn good care of my hands, Ponterford. That's who I count my money with, son. Now get out there and protect my money. That's what you get paid for, not to cut my damn money off. I believe you have a job to do, Sheriff."

Ponterford was about to leave when he asked, "What about John Corynth? He and his wife have owned the Southern Eatery for almost fifteen years. Hell, that place is the reason the Crabtree had to close down in the first place. The Corynths' place stayed busy on Sunday until that gal and her mother started selling dinners, causing them to lose the colored business. Them folk make a decent living over there, Mr. Moore, and they gonna want to fight for it."

"Hold on, Sheriff. Do you really think they want to go down that road? Go get Corynth and bring him over here right now."

The round trip took only ten minutes. Mr. Moore barely had time to formulate his offer to Corynth. When they arrived, he excused the sheriff and made his offer to John Corynth short and sweet. "We are prepared to offer you the equivalent of the last ten years' income for your restaurant. This is a one- time, no- compromise offer."

"No insult to you, Orland, but that place is me and my wife's dream, and no amount of money is enough to sell that."

"I repeat, this is a no- compromise offer. I do regret that the place was a dream come true, but no dream can last forever, Mr. Corynth. Bring the paper work over proving the income, and you will get that amount in cash. Have the building cleaned and empty in thirty days. Have a good night, Mr. Corynth."

John Corynth rose very unsteadily from his chair. "I can't believe some niggers had you run me out of business. This ain't over, Orland. Not for them niggers it ain't."

"Those folk work for me, Mr. Corynth. It wouldn't be wise to start trouble with them. Now take this money and be happy. Never let it be heard that you attacked or had someone attack those folk or their new place."

"You want to know what I think of you, Orland?" Corynth asked with malice and contempt.

"No sir, Mr. Corynth, I don't want to know what you think of me. I figure if the Good Lord wanted me to know what you or any other man thought of me, he would have given me the ability to read minds. Since he didn't see fit to give me that ability, it ain't none of my damn business, nor do I care what you think of me, mister, now have good day." Corynth left enraged and filled with hatred.

Meanwhile, Frank and Minnie had dropped Jane and the babies at home. Frank picked up Bo and Reedy Mealy and headed for the justice of the peace. All the way there, Reedy was trying to talk Frank out of getting married. This steamed Minnie to no end. "Shut your damn mouth before I put my foot in it, Reedy."

The ceremony lasted all of ten minutes and most of that was spent with Minnie and Reedy rolling their eyes at each other. After the short but beautiful ceremony, Minnie and Frank drove Bo and Reedy back home. Frank had a joyous smile plastered across his face. He had by chance alone met, befriended, and f allen in love with his dream girl. Now by choice, he would have the golden opportunity to stay with her for the remainder of his life, united in holy matrimony.

At Minnie's Café, from the planning stages to opening night, Minnie and her staff Emma Mae Johnson, Rhae Hollings, Brenda Coles, Louise Roberts, and Tom Worthy, along with Jane, worked like a well- oiled machine. Emma Mae was messy and loved to keep things stirred up, but she was a dedicated, hard worker. In fact, she would spend more time at Minnie's Café than anywhere else. Opening day came and Orland Moore was right there along with Sheriff Ponterford and all the other white officers. Once the town's white citizens saw this, they joined right in with no trouble. They raved about the large portions, the lovely Caribbean decor, the romantic ambiance, the lighting set, but most of the talk — what little went on at the tables — centered on how delicious the food tasted. Some of the best they had ever eaten. From time to time, acts of racism and vandalism were carried out against the café. These things happened in spite of the best security possible.

CHAPTER VI

Neither of the love- struck newlyweds could have predicted the long odyssey that they were about to begin. It would be a romance that would border on scandal, myth, and to some, a bit of legend. The marriage was the talk about town. Emma Mae and Rhae Hollings were the head gossip mongers, as usual. The two of them were out front leading the throngs who wondered why Frank Whatley would marry a woman with another man's babies. After all, he was one of the most eligible young bucks in town.

That first night of marriage for the newlyweds was the beginning of what they hoped would be a lifetime of bliss. The happy young couple knew that if they lived up to the vows that they had exchanged, the two of them just might come as close as two imperfect humans could get to being in a state of grace. The blessings began to pour in like manna from heaven for this marital union. William and Maxie were three when Salema was born.

Salema was named after the city of Jerusalem. The name means "safe haven" and was perfect for her. It was almost a prognostication on her parents' part for giving her such an odd name, because that is exactly what this daughter would eventually become to this growing family.

From day one, William was over protective of his baby sis, as he affectionately called the new center of the Whatley universe. Johnny adored all of Minnie's children and kept William with him almost twenty-four hours a day when ever possible.

William watched over Salema even closer after witnessing an incident where Maxie had snuck and drank some bleach by accident, thinking it was soda water that she was sneaking into while no one was looking. Ma noticed that the toddler was slow in her responses and quite nauseated. Jane questioned William, who was always very smart and brutally honest. She quickly got to the bottom of the cause of Maxie's ailment. Jane hurried and retrieved a small jar that she kept some mayapple root in. She gave Maxie a small chunk of the raw root, and the herb induced vomiting immediately. Jane was always using the home remedies and root medicine she had learned from the old African slaves she knew as a young girl. She passed this lay medical knowledge on to Minnie.

One afternoon, while Maxie was out with Rev. Foster on a father-daughter lunch date, William was supposed to be watching Salema play in the big backyard with the high porch that had steep stairs, stairs that William and Maxie still had to help the baby up and down. William let Salema get out of his sight while he was trying to trap grasshoppers in an old glass jelly jar. He had climbed the back fence into a small field behind the house. At that very moment, Frank was cutting through the alley coming home. Frank could see from his vantage point that Salema was almost two- thirds of the way out of the back yard. The baby had at this point gotten herself wedged between the gate and the house. She was desperately trying to squeeze her way past the gate to the front of the house. So as to not alarm either child, Frank slowly crept up behind Salema and eased the little explorer from her self- induced trap. Then he took her inside the house, where Minnie was in the kitchen cooking and talking to Johnny, who had stopped by to discuss business about the crops, and of course, to see the children. Never saying a word as to what had transpired outside in the yard, Frank turned the baby over to her mother and proceeded to return to the back yard, where William the great bug collector was hard at play. Frank jumped the fence into the slightly overgrown field. He took an interest in the type of bugs that William was after. He even gave him advice as to how to catch the grasshoppers, telling William to add a small amount of fresh green grass to the bottom of the jar.

After they had caught several bugs, Frank popped the question : "Where is baby sis, William?" A blank stare born of panic and concern replaced the wide, buck toothed grin that had once covered William's face less than a fraction of a second earlier. At once, William began to frantically call out for his baby sis. Together, he and Frank jumped the fence. William started running toward the stairs, but Frank cut him off. "William, do you think she could get up these stairs on her own?"

William became flustered and threw both hands up. His hazel eyes filled with tears. He ran around the house, screaming at the top of his lungs at a pitch so high, Minnie and Johnny came running out of the house. Minnie was holding the baby in her arms but William was so upset as he ran toward Minnie and Johnny that he never saw Salema in her arms. "I lost my baby, I lost my baby"" William was screaming so loud that neither Minnie nor Johnny could understand a word he was trying to say. Johnny snatched the boy up off his feet and hugged him to calm him down. Johnny and Minnie then turned to Frank to see what in the world was so funny. By now Frank was doubled over on the porch laughing so hard he couldn't catch his breath.

"What's wrong with you, Frank?" Minnie asked in a cold and harsh tone. She was mad as hell at Frank. How could he sit there laughing while her son was so upset? After Frank caught his breath and explained to them what had happened, Minnie and Johnny then saw how serious little William was about the whole thing and they roared into laughter themselves. William wasn't joining in; he was mad now. He was holding onto his baby sister's hand and looking at the three of them as if they were demented. Over half a minute went by before he could calm himself down to catch his breath. After he stopped crying, he loosened his grip on Salema's hand.

With a serious stern look on his face, he threw the jelly jar down and walked in the house with his little sister. This may have been humorous to the adults present, but this little man saw no levity in losing his baby sister. This incident only reinforced his already strong protective instincts. From that day onward, William took on this overprotective attitude with all of his younger siblings. As Johnny was leaving, he mentioned to Minnie that he had received a wire from Uncle Ricky Lee and Aunt Lillie. He was going down to north Georgia in a few day to meet up with Babe, Tara, and what ever male cousin Aunt Lillie sent to drive them. The wire merely stated that they had a small surprise for him to pick up.

When Emma arrived to open the café Sunday morning, she noticed a lot of glass around the front door. Someone had thrown a brick through the second floor windows into the office that Mr. Moore sometimes used on Friday nights. When Tom arrived at work, she asked him to clean it up. Tom replaced the broken window panes and they went about their daily tasks as if nothing had happened. That was the way they dealt with random acts of ignorance. Sunday was extremely busy at Minnie's Café after church. It seemed like every family in town, black and white, came there to eat. Emma, as usual, kept everyone close to the window that went into the kitchen entertained, talking about the latest events from the previous night.

James Timmons, the oldest of the Dirt Dobbers, had brought further shame, scorn, and scandal on their already sullied family name by allowing Tom Worthy to perform oral copulation on him in the outhouse of the Chicken Shack, a local juke joint.

The story she stuck to is this: Tom supposedly promised James four dollars if he would let him perform the dirty deed. But after James prematurely ejaculated leaving Tom soiled and unsatisfied, James received no payment, leaving him both satisfied and angry at the same time. James threatened to beat Tom up, but backed off after realizing that he was completely over matched. Tom looked like a gigantic blue-black-colored gorilla. The man stood six- foot- four and was built like a Greek god with 240 pounds of muscle underneath all that femininity. Further more, how would James explain to everyone why he wanted to fight him to start with? The very last advice Tom gave young James, "Learn to hold a small load before you try handlin' a heavy load like me." Chidingly, Minnie told Tom to keep his business at the Chicken Shack there and please don't let it flow over to work. Tom just laughed at them and shook his head back and forth saying, "I ain't ashamed if y'all ain't ashamed to be talkin 'bout this shit while the saints out there eating after church." That really broke the staff up with laughter. Even the customers were starting to wonder what was so funny. Jane had to step in and insist that they get back to work.

Tom Worthy was the best dish washer / janitor / cook in the state of Tennessee, as far as he was concerned. Further more, he was probably the best closer in the restaurant business, and he didn't mind flaunting his physical prowess and stamina when it came to getting the job done. Minnie loved Tom and the rest of her staff for their work ethics and she paid them very well for it. Every employee at Minnie's Café had a love for playing the game Po- keno, and they would spend countless hours playing at the restaurant after closing or at the home of who ever wanted to host a weekly game. Before everyone had pick out the boards of their choice to start the game that night, Tom pulled Minnie aside. He confided in her that the gossip did hurt his feelings. After consoling him, she tried to make the moment a little easier by joking with him, "In the future, Tom, don't put your business in the juke joint outhouse, 'cause these folks will kick it in the streets before a cat can lick his tail."

Tom busted out laughing, snapped his fingers so loud it sounded like a twenty -two pistol fired off, smacked his lips together and said, "Please, miss lady, you would've taken advantage of the opportunity to tackle that monster yo'self if you didn't already have Daddy Frank." That was the way many days of hard work ended at Minnie's Café.

That same spring, Frank and Minnie both graduated with honors. He had his degree in engineering and she had hers in accounting. Minnie took advantage of what her degree offered, especially at tax time. Having two successful businesses allowed her to put her degree to practical use. She was very proud of the career choice she had chosen. But Minnie was a mother, and the children demanded her undivided attention whenever she was with them.

As Jane began her regimented morning of cooking breakfast and house cleaning, simultaneous noises distracted her. At what might have been precisely at the exact same moment, she heard a buggy pull along the side of the house and Minnie running to the bathroom to throw up her guts. William was up with his grandmother, waiting on the first biscuit out of the pan. He heard the noise on the side of the house and jumped on a chair so he could see who was out there, but he saw nothing. Jane and William walked to the back door and there in full view, a wagon full of memories. Jane eyes immediately welled up with tears as she caught sight of her husband's favorite quilt, covering this wagon's rear end. She wondered if this was a cruel joke being played out by someone who might have found out about her family's past.

A slight muffled giggle from behind the house revealed the culprit; it was Johnny. He stepped from behind the house wearing what Jane recognized as William Heard's favorite hat. He ran up the stairs, hugged Jane, and began to tell her the incredible story about the wagon. Minnie, who had just stepped out of the back bathroom into the kitchen, heard the entire unbelievable story. When Johnny met up with Babe, Tara, and Buster, they had with them a surprise of mammoth proportions. Two- thirds of William and Jane's precious possessions had been salvaged the night they left for Tennessee, by Uncle Ricky Lee and his brothers. They loaded the items on William's old wagon and stored it at Uncle Ricky Lee and Aunt Lillie's. "I've got another surprise for you; come on out, gal," Johnny said with a big smile on his face. Minnie thought she was seeing a ghost. It couldn't be, but it was Babe. Minnie and Jane were overjoyed. They both rushed and gave Babe a big hug.

Minnie could not believe that Babe was back with her once again. "I just declare, Babe"" Minnie yelped, "It's only been five…six, oh my Lord, six years, can you believe it? I'm so happy you're here, Babe."

After the hugs between Minnie, Jane, and Babe were over, she introduced Babe to William, Maxie, Salema, and Frank, who had heard all the commotion and came out of their bedroom to see what was going on.

Everyone's undivided attention turned to the wagon. Remarkably, all the hand crafted cabinets and bedroom furniture that Uncle Buddy Lee had built was by some miracle back in their possession.

"If this don't beat a hog a- flyin'"" Minnie exclaimed as she ran her hand over her father's favorite quilt. Her excitement grew when she pulled the cover back that revealed all of their other belongings. Jane wanted to unload every piece by herself but opted for a seat near the back door with supervisory duty as to where things should be temporarily placed. As each item came in the door, she felt that she had more and more of her William back. By the time Johnny and Frank had finished unloading everything Jane remembered the weapon drawer her husband had built under the wagon. Somehow, five of their rifles and a shotgun were still there, along with thirty dollars. William had designed this hideaway drawer for his hunting trips and delivering corn whiskey. Minnie was torn between the joy she felt from being reunited with Babe and the emotions that welled up deep inside of her from seeing the things that were once in the home where she grew up. Chatter filled the living room as Minnie and Babe tried to catch up on the things that had happened in their lives over the years. William was playing outside on the wagon, acting like he had a team of horses attached and he was driving through town with a load of fresh fruit and vegetables for sale, imitating his Uncle Johnny. The sun was shining, but rain came pouring down. "Come up here, boy, outta dat rain." When William was up on the porch Jane gave him some folk knowledge. "You know when the sun shining and it rains, dat means the devil is beatin' his wife."

William stood on the porch gazing out at the rain, wondering where the beating was taking place, and what the devil's wife had done wrong. He ran in the living room and interrupted his mother and Babe's conversation. "Why the devil always beat his wife when the sun shines and it rains, Mama?" Babe answered him, "It's just something old folks say, baby, it's not happening for real." Everybody including William started laughing, but he still had his doubts about the whole thing.

Minnie got around to asking Babe if she would be interested in some cleaning work that she had available. Of course, Babe jumped at the opportunity to start making some money. Assimilating Babe into the household was not awkward at all. She was a very private and slightly introverted young lady who spent most of her time working or in her room. From their childhood days, it seemed she would only open up around Minnie. Frank wondered if Babe spent her time alone because she was uncomfortable or home sick. Frank had Minnie ask her cousin if she wanted to go out to the Chicken Shack with them one night. Babe's first response was a resounding "No way" but after some arm twisting from Minnie, she finally agreed. Jane agreed to baby- sit as long as they did not come home drunk and not be able to take care of the children the next day.

Plenty of fellas were making passes at Babe. They couldn't help but notice her thick, shapely figure and strikingly beautiful looks. Only one idiot caused any hint of trouble because he erroneously thought she was acting stuck up because she wasn't very talkative while he was desperately trying to converse with her. He was smiled at and dismissed politely, along with all other prospective would- be suitors. Babe was not looking for a man; she had one at home. Babe told Minnie she wanted to get away from Rome because every report she had heard from Uncle Johnny was that things were going good for them in Chattanooga. And having work right away would allow her to save to be able to afford a place of her own, so that her fiancé Willie Clayton could move up. That night, they all had a ball, and everybody did get a little tipsy, but nobody over did it. They got home after 2:00 the next morning.

No sooner had Frank laid his head on the pillow it seemed, when he heard someone beating on the back door like the world was coming to an end. Frank was both angry and apprehensive as he opened the door. It was Reedy Mealy. The news he brought both startled and shocked Frank. "Four thugs attempted to rob Ms. Cole, Frank. She said they knocked at her door about three this morning and pretended to have bad news about her son Michael. Though she was half asleep, she was able to shoot two of 'em. Both them in the hospital in bad shape I hears, the other two ran. The young would- be robbers didn't know she never came to the door at night without her pistol."

The two who ran were later identified by Ms. Cole and were now in the basement of Mr. Moore's office, hog tied. Mr. Moore had sent Reedy to bring Frank to deal with the situation. Frank grabbed a fresh T-shirt and the britches he had on just a couple hours earlier, and they headed uptown to Mr. Moore's office.

On the way over, Reedy told Frank they had also found out that two of the boys were from Boone Heights and the other two were from the Willa Homes area. When they arrived, Mr. Moore, while outwardly remaining calm, was fuming and Frank could see he wanted harsh punishment delved out to these young thugs. Mr. Moore had not been down to the basement, but told Frank to handle them two as a local problem; he did not think the situation called for what some others would want to do to these boys. Furthermore, he did not want the embarrassment of them knowing that these young boys had tried to rob one of his places to begin with. They were told to send them home with a strong message so that any other person who intended to use violence or intimidation against his people could see what the end result would be.

Frank stopped on the way to the stairs and retrieved some thick tape and a couple of two- by- fours from the hall closet where the supplies were kept. He threw one to Reedy and they both began to swing the lumber to warm up.

Once in the basement, Frank told Reedy to go into the room where the two were and blind fold them and tape their mouths shut tight. Reedy stood only five feet six inches but had massive forearms and weighed in at 215 pounds. He was as strong as an ox. Reedy opened the door, snatched the youngest of the pair by the back of his hair, picked him up, and threw him in the hall where he landed at Frank's feet. Though not able to scream out, they both moaned real hard for about fifteen minutes before they passed out from the terrible beating — a beating that left them both with all four limbs broken in multiple places. They would also need several hundred stitches to close gashes that were seemingly everywhere. For nearly five minutes, it was a competition to see who could expose the most white meat the fastest. Reedy wanted to kill them. "You can't beat men like this, Frank, and let them live. They'll have too much hate in them after a beating like this."

Frank disagreed and over ruled him. "We were told to send a message, and this is the one we're going to send." Any way he was sure these two wouldn't want any more trouble if they survived this beating. Both were unconscious but breathing when they were dumped in an alley in Boone Heights that morning.

Frank stopped at Mr. Moore's office to fill him in on the events that took place in the basement after he left, but before he could say a word, he was offered a bottle of top shelf whiskey and asked to bring Reedy in for a couple shots if he wanted to join them. Reedy jumped at the offer. He came in and sat down on the couch and listened as Mr. Moore told him and Frank what it sounded like from his vantage point in his office. Mr. Moore smiled with approval. He then instructed Frank to set security patrols for all the work locations. Frank suggested that Reedy be placed in charge of night security, whereupon the three of them agreed on a schedule. Reedy received more responsibility and a boost in pay after administering one good ass whipping within the boss's hearing range. Frank had left his pocket watch in the basement and went to retrieve it. He noticed that the room had been cleaned with bleach. The smell of the bleach filled his nostrils. It was so strong that he had to rush back upstairs as soon as he grabbed the watch. Gasping for air as he came back upstairs, he asked Mr. Moore, " Who... in the hell... used all that bleach down there?"

"I had three of the boys clean up all that blood they left behind. Nothing gets up blood better than bleach, not even saw dust. You should know that as much as you fish and hunt, Frank." Mr. Moore then stood up. "I want you to start thinking about going on a safari to Africa with me and some of my staff that share our love for hunting. I want me a giant black rhino head on my wall. Boy, a white rhino would be great, but that would probably mean going to South Africa, and I don't wanna go there. Animals, not bad folks is what we'll be hunting over there, all right, Frank." Mr. Moore laughed as he turned up another shot of whiskey ; he was already there. Frank never got the chance to respond to Mr. Moore's offer because Sheriff Ponterford was knocking at the front door. So Frank and Reedy left out the back before he could see them in the blood -soaked clothing they still had on. Ponterford had stopped by to ask Mr. Moore how he wanted the situation handled with the two boys still in the hospital. "Well now, Sheriff, we don't wanna prosecute those boys for trying to take money from people who make money outside the law themselves, do we?"

"These niggers need to be taught a lesson, if you don't mind me saying so."

"From what I've been told, they damn near dead now. How much more of a lesson do they need, niggers or not?"

"If I could at least catch those two that run off, we could run them down to the station and bust their heads open," Ponterford said as he started towards the door.

"Yeah, you do that, Sheriff, and have a damn good day."

Frank told Reedy he didn't want to take a trip to Africa, even though he wouldn't mind having the opportunity to hunt wild game. It was about 2:00 P.M. when Reedy dropped Frank off at home. Rest was the only thing on his mind as he ran up the back stairs. Minnie was scrubbing clothes in the big tin wash tubs they kept on the back porch. She stopped him before he entered the back door. "I got one question for you, Mister. Where you had to run off to this morning after we barely got in the house? And I see you running with that no good Reedy Mealy too." All the time she kept scrubbing clothes.

Frank thought that either this woman is crazy or she's just kidding, so he turned to walk in the house to get cleaned up. He figured she had to see all the blood on his clothes. She couldn't believe he was just going to walk off and ignore her. In a fit of anger, as Frank opened the door, Minnie swung the wash board as hard as she could, striking him with brutal force across his lower back. "I told you I ain't putting up with no carousin', Mister."

Excruciating pain shot up and down his spine as Frank buckled to one knee. As he regained his footing, he could see William standing in the kitchen staring at the whole scene. "Mama" Why you hit my daddy Frank? Daddy Frank, Daddy Frank"' William called out. He was confused and hurt by what he had just seen. She had started carrying a straight razor in a handkerchief and was reaching in her bosom to get it when she caught sight of her son, and stopped searching for it. Shocked and stunned from the blow, Frank turned and walked toward the stairs. He never uttered a word. Only then did Minnie notice all the blood on his clothes. She called out to him but he kept walking. She started down the stairs after him, now desperately concerned that someone else had hurt him.

He never turned around. "Mama, you know I don't believe in fighting no woman, so just leave me be." The pain was so severe, he wondered if the blow had broken his back. Frank managed to cover the ten- block walk up the alley to his brother Walsh's house. When Walsh opened his door for Frank, he fell in his arms. Seeing all the blood, Walsh panicked thinking someone had stabbed or shot him. He only calmed down after Frank filled him in on the whole story. Minnie had watched him as far as she could see and then went to calm William down and finish the wash.

There was a knock at the front door. At this time of day on Sunday only meant one thing: the café was busy and there would be no day off for Minnie. Minnie opened the door for Emma, who was about to explode from her eagerness to spill the latest dirt. After telling Minnie that it was getting way too busy at the café and that her help was needed, she mentioned the sordid events of last night's attempted robbery. By the time she got to the part about Reedy and Frank looking for the two boys who had gotten away, Minnie cut her off. She told Emma to hurry back to work and assured her that either she or Babe would be there to help out. She almost pushed Emma out the door, then rushed to Babe's room and burst in without knocking. "Child, I feel as foolish as Willie Joe Neckbone, and you know anybody with a name like that, head has got to screw on and off. Babe, I done made a plum fool out of myself. "

"Hold on now, calm yourself; what in tarnation is you going on about, Minnie?" Babe was still a little cloudy from last night. After she heard the details, she lit into Minnie. "What the hell you hit that man for? Oh Minnie, shame on you, I ain't getting in your business, but you was wrong and you know it. You better find your husband and apologize. You need to get that temper under control, cousin. "

"Well sir, I done figured that much out on my own, Babe. But you right, I ain't had no right hitting Frank like I did. Babe, I need you to take William to the café and help Ma and Emma out for me. Lord have mercy, I hope this man can forgive me for act in' a fool. "

"Give me a little time to wash my face and we'll head on over. Where do you think Frank went to up that alley? "

"He's probably at Walsh's house, I hope that's where he went. Babe, please don't say nothin' 'bout this to anyone. "

"When have I ever talked to anybody 'bout what we talk about, Minnie? I never have before, and I ain't 'bout to start now."

Minnie and Babe decided that Babe would drive Frank's car and drop Minnie off at Walsh's. On the way out the door, Minnie told William to grab a pile of towels she had washed for the café. As she was about to get out of the car, Minnie noticed William trying to stuff a towel in his pants pocket. "What in the world are you do in' with that towel, boy? "

"Mama, you know I gotta get Mr. Tom before he pop my legs with his towel." Tom loved to play this game with Minnie's children that he had taught them. He called it pop the legs with the towel. Minnie told William that the café was full and to leave Tom alone and let him do his work. She knew her feeble warning wouldn't stop him from playing with Tom. When they pulled up in front of Walsh's house, she gave William a hug and told him to behave. She thanked Babe and walked up to Walsh's door.

Minnie was greeted by Walsh at the door very dryly. "I don't fight at my home and I don't allow no such carryings on here either," he told Minnie before inviting her inside.

"I didn't come here to fight nobody and I know I was wrong for hittin' Frank in the first place, Walsh, and I'm sorry. That's all I come down here for is to let him know that I didn't mean him no harm. I just lost my temper. "

"You most nearly broke that man's back 'cause you lost your temper over him working. "

"I don't mean no disrespect, but I ain't discussin' my business no further. Can I see Frank, please? "

"I reckon so, he laid across the bed in there sleep."

Minnie entered the room as if she was afraid of how he would react if he heard the sound of her voice. "Frank," she whispered real sweet and low, "I'm so sorry I acted a fool and I'm so ashamed. I don't know what I'll do if you don't find it in your heart to forgive me. I promise you..."

Just then, Frank reached out and grabbed her hand. "That lick hurt, woman, make that your last one, you hear me? I can't re-raise you and I don't need a new mama. I came to Walsh house 'cause he can keep his mouth shut about things and this won't get spread all over town, but I ain't for no fighting, Minnie. I respect you too much to carouse on you, didn't we talk about that before we got married?"

"I know we talked about it, we talked about a lot of things. Can't we put this behind us and go home? I'm so sorry, Frank."

"Well I'm through with it, Minnie."

For the next three nights, Frank was pampered with long back rubs until all the soreness subsided. Then the real making up began. Jane and her quilt club were meeting at Mrs. Rosa Duvall's house after their family meeting that Friday night. Mrs. Rosa had the rare ability to cure babies of the thrash infection. Johnny had shared great news at the family meeting. The fall crops were doing so well that he would need extra help and could now hire on three permanent workers. Johnny had implemented a form of selective harvesting that allowed him to preserve the fertile topsoil on his small farm. He also started growing strawberries, grapes, small fruits, and other leguminous plants that he had extensively cultivated. Babe suggested to Minnie that she take the children out to the farm for the week to help work. Minnie quickly agreed. She couldn't believe they were about to have the house to themselves. Frank had been busy washing vegetables for the cafe that he, Johnny, and William had unloaded before the meeting started. He had done a very thorough job washing the tomatoes, cucumbers, and okra. For a fraction of a second, he thought about starting on some mustard greens, but changed his mind. He knew that touching them meant a blessing out from Minnie was sure to start up. She did not allow anyone but Jane to wash greens in their home.

The weather was seasonably cool that evening, so everybody grabbed a sweater. Johnny volunteered to drop Jane off at Mrs. Rosa's. The children were so excited to be going to their uncle Johnny's farm, they almost forgot to say bye to their parents. After giving them a hug, they ran out to the truck. Minnie assured Jane that she would be there to pick her up in a few hours, then she thanked Babe for keeping the children as she saw everyone to the door. She also hugged Johnny and thanked him for everything he was doing for her.

As soon as she heard Johnny's car pull away from the house, she swung into action. Minnie started a fire in the fireplace, grabbed a pile of quilts, and made a pallet next to it. After freshening up and slipping into her night clothes and grabbed the ointment she had been using on Frank's back for his nightly back rubs, she walked over to the table where Frank had neatly placed four bushels of freshly washed vegetables and gently grabbed his hands and led him into the living room. "Are you ready for a very special back rub?"

"Where's the young'uns and everybody else?"

She motioned for him to lay on his stomach and she straddled his legs. In a low, sexy tone she replied, "Ma is at Mrs. Rosa's house quiltin'." She leaned over and started lightly kissing him on the back of his neck. He could feel she had on no panties. "Babe and the children went to the farm with Uncle Johnny." She rolled him over on his back. Three hours of sweat filled love making ensued as she slipped his long hard penis out of his pants and into her pulsating, wanton vagina. Frank cradled her full firm buttocks in his strong hands and began to rock her as if she were in a rocking chair. After about their third or fourth ride, an earth- moving orgasm weakened them both as they lay collapsed onto the sweat- soaked pallet. Trying to catch her breath and speak at the same time, Minnie managed to get the words out. "That....huh has got to be... a baby. The lovewe just made...huh was too good for it not to be. It was perfect, Frank. I promise you, if I'm pregnant and it's a boy, I'm naming him Frank Jr."

The love making session had completely drained both of them, and after some hugging and petting, they both nearly drifted off to sleep. Suddenly, Minnie sat straight up. "Ma" Frank, get up, we got to pick Ma up from Mrs. Rosa's. Hurry up and get dressed. Lord have mercy, Ma gone kill me."

Four hours had passed in what seemed like no time at all. They both threw their clothes on grabbed a sweater and hurried to the car for the short ride to Mrs. Rosa's. Minnie cuddled up to Frank and laid her head on his shoulder. She nearly drifted off to sleep before they pulled up to the house.

When they arrived at her home, Mrs. Rosa greeted them at the door. They were surprised to see Jane and the others still laughing, talking, and stitching away. Jane was not nearly ready to go home. So Minnie and Frank took a seat in the living room and waited for about thirty minutes as Jane and her friends finished their quilt. Frank reminded Minnie that they had left the living room a mess. So they decided to pull the car to the back when they got home. That way Jane would go straight to her room and they could clean up their mess.

After a week of hard work on the farm, Babe and the children were back at home. School would be starting soon for the twins, and Babe had a long- awaited guest coming to town. The letter she received stated that Willie Clayton would be arriving on Friday at 2:00 at Terminal Station. Johnny watched her face light up with joy as she read her letter. "Where the two of you plan on staying, Babe?"

"I guess we gone have to rent a place."

"No, you don't have to do that." Johnny suggested they move down the street into his house. He saw it was just going to waste away because he was always at the farm. "I want to help you any way I can, Babe. This way you can keep savin' your money."

"Johnny, I'm so happy to be a part of this family. You, Minnie, Cousin Jane, Frank..." Babe became emotional and couldn't finish the thank you she wanted to share with him.

Johnny gave her a hug. "All we got is each other," Johnny reminded her as he headed for the door to make the short hump back to his farm. The twins and Salema had a great time at the farm, and for the most part were well- behaved, though they had trouble concentrating on the small tasks assigned to them. The adults were happy to have the noise of the children back home. To their surprise, they had missed them terribly.

First Baptist was full to capacity that Sunday, and Reverend Black, the pastor, preached a stirring sermon, "Why You Should Be Baptized." After the service, Frank dropped Minnie and Jane off at the café and headed to the farm to help Johnny install a new irrigation system they had devised. Rhae Hollings met Jane and Minnie at the back door of the café, urging them to hasten their steps. Tom had cut the tip of his right pointer finger nearly off while cutting up some chickens. The accident had just taken place as they were preparing more food for the day. Tom had soaked a piece of a clean towel in lamp oil and wrapped the finger up tightly to stop the bleeding. Minnie ran outside to try and catch Frank before he left but he had already pulled away and did not hear her calling him. When she came back inside, Jane and Emma were looking at Tom's hand while he sat as if nothing had happened.

Minnie took one look at the finger and asked Emma to take him to the hospital and bring her the bill. Tom was refusing to go until everybody insisted. He only agreed to go after Jane asked him to do it for her. Tom was afraid of two things: snakes and needles, and that was his real reason for not wanting to go to the hospital. Minnie was aware of this, so she asked Emma if it would be all right if she drove him in her car instead. The cut had bled through the bandage that Tom had made, so Jane wrapped it in a new towel and he and Minnie took off for the hospital. On the drive to the hospital, Tom let Minnie know, "This ain't even hurting, but if they got to stick me with a needle, I'm gone scream like a you- know- what Ms. Minnie."

She tried not to laugh but neither one of them could hold it in so they both burst into loud laughter. "Tom, how in creation can you be laughin while you bleeding like a hog?"

"I told you it don't hurt." They arrived at the hospital and received swift service. The cut only required six stitches and took only a few minutes to close.

Tom made the stay much longer than required when he lost his composure as soon as the doctor approached him with the needle. Tom screamed and fell off the small hospital bed landing on the floor with a loud thud. He slowly raised his head from the floor and fainted. Three male staff members had to be called in to help lift him back onto the bed. The doctor made use of the time he was unconscious and sewed the finger back together. One of the nurses was sent to the waiting area to find a relative or friend. When Minnie entered the room, Tom was just awakening. He pretended not to remember his cowardly act and sprang off the bed as though he had conducted himself as valiantly as a gladiator.

On his good hand, Tom snapped his fingers and said to Minnie, "You ready to go, girl?" Minnie paid the bill and offered to take Tom home. She suggested he stay off a couple of days until his finger healed properly. He looked at her as if she had lost her mind. "If you don't get me back to work, I bet we gone go round and round in this here buggy. This little scratch ain't stopping me from working. I sho' ain't going home to sit with my daddy and hear him complain all damn day."

"You sure you can work with your hand like that? What the doctor say?"

"He sho' didn't say go home and sit with Daddy. Now you better get this buggy headed to the café." Minnie agreed but made him promise that if the finger started bleeding, he would have to go home until it healed.

Minnie's Cafe was packed. Some people had been waiting for up to fifteen minutes to be seated. All the staff were shocked to see that Tom had returned to work, and relieved he was all right.

CHAPTER VII

The first day of school was approaching. William had new Buster Brown shoes and fresh short sets to wear. He hated wearing short pants because he was self- conscious about his knocked knees. William had an annoying habit of dragging around in the mornings when getting ready for school. Maxie had always done everything before him. She walked, talked, and could feed herself before he could. She suggested he tie his books up with a belt and carry them in front of him to block any view of his knees. Minnie always made them walk to school together.

On the morning of the first day of school, and mostly because the books kept hitting his legs, William kept lagging behind all the other children walking to school. Maxie had warned him several times to keep up with her. She continuously implored him to keep up with her. But he was his usual stubborn self and wouldn't even make an effort. So she waited for him to catch up, and when he did, she unloaded a furious round of hard slaps to his head. He took off running to school and was the first student to arrive.

Maxie was always so reserved and quiet. She was the teacher's pick from day one. School seemed to come so easy to her, as did most other things. She was always an honor student and very well- mannered. William, on the other hand, was stubborn and just short of being a hellion.

After the twins had left for school, and before Salema woke up, Babe told Minnie and the rest of the family that Willie was coming on Friday, and of her plans to move into Johnny's house. "Oh Babe, I'm so happy for you," Minnie said, giving her a hug. "Is there anything we can do to help out?"

"Minnie, after everything you already done, I can't ask you for nothing else. Anyway, I done saved almost every dime I made since I been working for you."

"Babe, you gone have another mouth to feed. I'll increase your split on the cleaning ten percent and I don't want to hear another word about it. I want to do this for you; remember, we here for you." Babe tried to put up a slight protest, but finally offered her gratitude and accepted Minnie's term.

The after- school chatter among the twins was about what everyone had done over the summer. They changed their school clothes and after a light snack, completed their homework. Afterward, they asked their mother if they could go on the back porch and play rock teacher. A few other children came over and joined in the game. Dwight Timmons, the youngest of the "Dirt Dobbers" came over as well and was dominating the game. He was being a bully as usual. To the other children, it seemed Dwight fought with someone different every day. William told him if he couldn't play any nicer than he was playing, then he could go home. Dwight promptly proceeded to beat him up. The fight stopped when Maxie punched Dwight in the nose and made it bleed. Dwight ran home and told his mother Helen, who — after she had stopped the bleeding — came down the street to the Whatley home to find out what had happened.

After a few loud knocks at the door, Babe opened it to find Helen standing there fighting mad, yelling and cursing. Babe opened the door for her after a few loud knocks. "One of these little bad ass young'uns down here busted my boy's damn nose."

Frank, who had been in his room stretched out across the bed resting, came out after he heard her cursing. He stepped in front of Babe before shecould say a word. "Ma'am, I don't curse in my house and nobody else will either. You and everybody else 'round here better respect my house, my wife, and my children. Ain't no bad young'uns living here at this address, so go on away from here."

Helen knew exactly who Frank Whatley was, so she never opened her mouth to give any rebuttal to him. She turned and meekly walked off the porch. As she reached the bottom of the stairs, in a very low humble tone, she muttered, "Please, Mr. Frank, if I could just ask that my boy not be hit in the nose again because it bleeds so easy and I can't hardly get it stopped once it starts." Helen then walked silently back down the street to her home. Lucky for Helen, Frank came to the door and not Minnie.

Friday morning was cloudy and overcast. Frank and Minnie gave Babe a ride down to Terminal Station. She tried to hide her excitement, but they saw that she was both nervous and happy. The ride down East Twenty-third Street to Market Street was a blur to Babe. She never noticed any of the passengers in the arrival area. They were all human silhouettes in her mind. Everything and everyone seemed to breeze by right before her eyes. The train had arrived ten minutes early and the passengers had begun to gather their belongings.

Babe spotted Willie. He had his back turned to her and was picking up his trunk. She eased up behind him and grabbed and hugged him around his waist. "Darn it, I've missed you."

He turned around with a big grin on his face. "My Babe," he said as he picked her up and swung her around in circles. Willie Clayton was a nice- looking, big strong corn- fed country boy with broad shoulders. He just needed to take better care of his teeth. Frank and Minnie were waiting outside. When they saw the happy pair come out of the station, Frank pulled down to pick them up, and Babe introduced Willie to them. Minnie welcomed him to Chattanooga and told him how much Babe and everyone else had been looking forward to his arrival.

Frank helped Willie load his trunk up and asked, "You hungry, man?"

"I could eat a horse," Willie replied. So they headed down East Main to the café. All Willie could do was look around at the new sights. This was his first trip to the city. He told Minnie he was glad to get away from the boring country life, and that he had missed Babe terribly. The most Willie did at home was shoot pool all day long. He said he had gotten so good that no one back home could beat him. Frank just listened. Babe made it known that Chattanooga had many other things to offer besides pool halls and hustling at pool. Willie just laughed, "I can see that already." They arrived at the café and introduced him to Ma and the crew. After he had three plates of food and two glasses of iced tea, he wolfed down a slice of pecan pie and some peach cobbler.

After he had finished eating, Babe let him know that she had to get back to work and he should rest until she got home. "You'll need it this evening."

"Well now, if I'm gone need that much energy this evening, I might need a little something to help me get some sleep. You got anything stronger than iced tea in the house?"

Babe responded tersely, "You know I ain't allowin' no drinking in my cousin's house 'less 'n he says so."

Frank offered to take him for something stronger to drink and a short tour of town. They first stopped by the boot leg house Frank operated, and picked up a bottle of whiskey. Then he showed him all the hot spots in the area. Willie could tell right off that Frank was a very intimidating force on the streets of this town. A blind man could see that Frank had the entire city of Chattanooga on fire from the energy he created when he was present or made an appearance anywhere. The many noticeable stares of admiration from the opposite sex made Willie immediately love being seen about town with him. The Chicken Shack, the Blue Flame club, the prostitute stroll, and finally the poolroom — that was all Willie needed to see; the tour stopped right there. All hopes of him resting until Babe got off work were out.

When they walked in Smick's Pool Room, only six other guys were there. They were shooting nine ball for a dollar a game. Frank recognized a few of them. John Henry Timmons, the father of the "Dirt Dobbers," had the best stick in the area and was currently winning all the money. He had long ago abandoned his wife and children for what the streets and fast women had to offer. Willie asked, "Anybody mind if an old country boy get in the game?"

Tim Roberts spoke up. "Course you can, but I'm up next." It was Tim's day off work and he had been waiting for half an hour to play. Willie called the game after him and watched John Henry leave him without a shot and scoop up Tim's dollar. As luck would have it, John Henry missed his first shot after he broke the balls. Willie was about to run the table but thought better of winning the first game and missed intentionally. After he lost, he sat down next to Frank and told him that he had thrown that game and wouldn't lose again. They had a couple drinks while John Henry ran the table for four straight wins. It was Willie's turn again. Frank asked John

Henry if he wanted to bet a buck on the side and he agreed. Then he started joking with Willie telling him not to be scared. Show 'em how its done in Georgia That was the beginning of the end for John Henry that day. He never won another game. Altogether, when Frank and Willie left that night, they had won nine dollars. Frank was still happy with the three he had won. They walked out feeling pretty tipsy and elated with the results of the pool game. John Henry, Tim, and the others were a little upset and felt like Frank had set them up. They told him the next time they shoot pool with Willie, the end results would be a hell of a lot different. They really couldn't be too mad, though ; Frank did share his half gallon of whiskey with them. So they didn't have to spend any money on beer and booze that day. On the way home, they stopped by the dime store so that Willie could buy Babe a gift. Frank dropped Willie off, shook his hand, and told him it was good meeting him. Before going home for the evening, he went to check on some business. When he got home, Minnie was sick at the stomach. "What's wrong, mama?"

"I'm probably pregnant as a fish. I guess you plan on keepin' me barefoot and pregnant."

Frank just laughed, "It ain't my fault you feel so good."

CHAPTER VIII

Not by design, but over the next decade, Minnie gave birth to six more offspring. Frank Jr. was born August 10, 1918 ; Arselee, October 25,1920; Doyle, December 28, 1921; Celeste, March 28, 1923; and finally Cecelia,

January 16, 1926. Minnie's brood of children reflected true physical evidence of how one person's gene pool could dominate another. Her genes dominated over Thomas's, with William and Maxie, but with Frank, it seemed as though Minnie had served only as an incubator. All the children she had borne for Frank looked as though they had been produced in a chocolate factory. They had produced a variety of Frank Whatley look-alikes. All the babies were delivered by the midwife combination of Jane and Mrs. Rosa Duvall.

Frank and Minnie instilled a code of all for one and one for all in their children from the start. Minnie insisted that the highest level of personal hygiene be maintained, especially for the girls. Clothes worn were always ironed and neat; no wrinkles were allowed. The home was kept spotless; everyone had chores. The children had a very regimented daily routine, especially during the calendar school year. They had to change out of their school clothes immediately upon arriving home from school. Then their home work from school had to be done, and after a snack, they had those chores to get done. Only the boys were to mop floors. This was the only work rule that Frank imposed. He said girls should not have to do that kind of labor. The boys hunted with Frank, and everyone except Doyle loved to swim in the huge creek on their uncle Johnny's farm. Doyle was afraid of the water. All of the girls could clean whatever kind of fresh game was bagged, including deer, rabbits, chickens, or fish, with the best of hunters. All of

Minnie's children had very poor visual acuity and had to wear prescribed glasses at early ages. However, she did not allow them to use this as a crutch to lean on in any facet of their life. Though there were not many, if there was a fight between any one of them and another child, they were all to give the opposing child a good whipping. This would serve as a deterrent to any other would- be enemies of the Whatley-Foster clan.

Minnie's favorite saying to them was, "Love ye one another as ye have been loved." She opened every family meeting on Friday evenings with that phrase.

During that same decade, Babe had not conceived once. From the first day he hit town, the pool hall was Willie Clayton's favorite place of employment. He worked mostly out on the farm with Johnny. William was entering puberty at the time of Cecelia's birth. One day, Minnie observed a fight between William and Dwight Timmons through her back window. The fight was a complete cake walk for Dwight, as he left her son with a black eye. "Boy, you pick in' up the wrong kind of battle scars. You should be ashamed of this black eye," she said teasingly. "If you gone fight, I guess you better learn how. That little mannish tail scamp Dwight is gone keep beat in' your rump if you don't know what to do in a fight." William wanted to know right away where he could go to learn how to fight. Minnie explained to him, "Fighting is stupid, but if you want to know how to defend yourself, I'm with you. Street fighting and boxing are different. The ring has rules; there are none on the streets. You use whatever is nearest you and end the fight as quickly as possible on the streets." So she gave him twenty- five cents and sent him to the Y M C A to get lessons. The twins were twelve at the time.

Maxie wanted to take lessons too, but William told her girls couldn't come in the gym. Before she knew it, she had replied, "I can whip your ass and Dwight's too." Minnie told her to watch her fast mouth or she would wash it out with lye soap. Her punishment would be to walk her brother to the gym.

Minnie always had to admonish Maxie about not wearing winter coats or sweaters in cool or cold weather and again on this day she gave Maxie a stern reminder to put on a sweater before going out to walk William to the Y M C A. From the moment Maxie walked him to the gym and he began hitting the heavy bag, he loved boxing. He later would say, "She started off walking me to the gym, but I wound up walking her every place else after that."

Over the next ten years, he would become a gold glove boxing champion. The fights with Dwight stopped after a one- punch knockout about a year after he started boxing. Frank Jr., a.k.a. Rico, was a very intelligent boy from the start. Almost everyone except William called Frank Jr. "Rico." William preferred "East" for some reason. Rico also had a very cunning side to his personality.

Arselee was sweet and rather introverted. She always seemed to be in the shadow of her brothers and sisters. She was a loner and seemed to not need many friends or associates to be happy. Celeste was a busy body from the opening bell, and was the spitting image of her grandmother Frankie. She was extremely intelligent and a pretty girl, though it seemed she was always physically ill. CeeCee was the nickname everyone gave Cecelia. And she was spoiled rotten by the entire family from day one. She was so pretty and looked like a chocolate- covered baby doll.

All the children were adjusting fine except for Doyle. He had been born with a speech impediment, so some of his teachers thought he was retarded. Minnie insisted nothing was wrong, just that his speech was impaired, and won them over with her firm demands that he be educated and treated normally. She realized that education is the great arbiter of who wins and who loses in American society. Minnie met with her son's educators and a plan was devised to keep Doyle in the least restrictive educational environment possible. Doyle was placed in a regular class room setting, and given extra attention from his teachers in the areas of most concern. It was determined that Doyle would get direct instructional services and some special accommodations from his teachers in areas such as phonetic awareness, language structure, and linguistics. Minnie and the rest of the children helped out at home with extra help in study habits, reading, writing and spelling after school. Doyle was given the optimum opportunity to be a successful student. He performed as an average student with this pillar like support from his teachers, mother, and family.

Everything was going great for the family and the community in general. Then came Black Tuesday and the Great Depression. After October 29, 1929, the headlong plunge of the nation's economy into the trough of depression seriously affected the entire Chattanooga community. Long- established business concerns were forced to close their doors. The Great Depression took its toll on Minnie's Café also. Yet during this time, the business never failed to clear a small profit. That was due in large part to the activities of Frank and Orland Moore. Add to their clandestine ventures the fact that Minnie's operating cost to run the café was cut to purchasing mostly dried goods and the cost of utilities because the bulk of her food supply came from her uncle's farm and her building was paid off. Further, she still had the gold coins her father left her. Frank saved gold coins also, and this proved to be a valuable reserve during these lean years. The shock of the collapse of the economy did not leave Minnie's family feeling the despair that some felt. Less than a year earlier, the family had attended the gala opening of Lookout Mountain Hotel at which Paul Whiteman's Orchestra was a major attraction. Frank had suggested they expose the children to nice affairs such as this, so they would be used to more than one kind of culture. Now less than a year later, Lookout Mountain Hotel, like many an optimistic enterprise of its kind, was doomed to failure. Many households could not keep their budgets afloat, and for the first time, persons who had maintained financial integrity failed to meet personal obligations to creditors.

Chattanooga's situation in general was helped to a large degree by the diversification of its industry. The Tennessee River and the area tributary to Chattanooga is perhaps the richest mineral region in America, as respects both quantity and diversity of resources. Coal and iron, limitless in quantity and of a uniformly high grade, are found in every hill and mountain. Gold, silver, copper, zinc, lead, mica, asbestos, and gem stones are profitably mined within eighty miles of Chattanooga. These resources are augmented by the successful quarry on a daily basis of white, black, and mottled marble, all excellent building stones. Cement, slate, calcareous lime, kaolin, sand, and potter's clay are also found in inexhaustible quantities. Poplar, pine, gum, cherry, cedar, ash, oak, hickory, and other hard woods are accessible from the Chattanooga area.

These natural resources created some work for the men in the area and new government social programs came into being. These things served to stem the general feelings of despondency that gripped the community and most of the nation. For the people who resided on Twenty-third Street, this turmoil served as a unifying agent for them all. Housing, in fact, became most difficult for many. As circumstances afforded them, Minnie and Frank used their rental properties to house dozens of families who had not a dime to live on and all were fed three meals a day on a daily basis. Minnie's Café served as a place where anyone hungry could get a decent meal, money or not. Skin color didn't matter. Johnny helped anyone who wanted to plant start a garden. He also gave away fruit and vegetables by the basket to who ever needed food. Minnie and her family' s benefactions to the community during the Depression years were of inestimable value to the community.

One of the programs created to relieve, manage, and sustain the resources of the region would play a central part in the rest of the family's progression : The Tennessee Valley Authority.

CHAPTER IX

Frank hired on with the TVA as an engineer in 1934 and never worked any where else. He loved his new job ; it was his life long dream come true. He had always loved fishing in the Tennessee River, and now protecting it and the mountains that he adored were part of his secular work. Frank now had first hand access to, and could pass information about the TVA projects and study programs to Johnny. This gave Johnny a heads- up on programs that the agency could provide before any other farmers had knowledge of their coming into existence. Frank had become a junior member of a team of men who were commissioned to design ways to stop the ruining of topsoil in the Tennessee Valley, along with the gross depletion of forestation in the area. Protecting the local natural resources for the future was a giant step for a black Native American. Minnie was proud as a peacock of her man ; she planned a party at the café to celebrate.

Minnie received a letter that week from Maxie telling her that she had something important to talk to her about. She would be home from school for two weeks on Friday. Salema was quietly becoming a very stacked and enticing young lady. She had the interest of more than just the young boys in the area. William was coming home on break too. He brought a stunning surprise home with him : a beautiful young bride with a figure like a Coca-Cola bottle. She was from a family of Gypsies, and her name was Ethel Garrison, now Ethel Foster. He was madly in love and so was she. At first, public reaction to the news was negative. William was shocked to be greeted and gestured to with a cold shoulder, especially from all the young ladies in the area. He was becoming quite the player, the field bachelor type, before he left town for agricultural school.

Only one of the local young ladies seemed to be genuinely friendly, and her name was Jeanette Strong. Jeanette and Ethel hit it off right away. In fact, Jeanette was the only person to show kindness of any sort toward Ethel besides William's family members. In reality, this is the way things started out for the young bride in Chattanooga with those of the female gender anyway. Some of the girls were even scheming on how to break this marital union apart from the moment they heard about it. The ringleader of the home wreckers was ex-girlfriend Suzi-Mae Williams. She lived in one of Frank's rental houses with her mother, Mary. Minnie privately called her mother "Blue Mary" due to her dark skin complexion. She never let Suzi or her mother hear the nickname; it was only said after they were no longer in Minnie's presence. Even Thomas took a while to warm up to Ethel because to him, she seemed to be such a quiet, mysterious young lady. Thomas could clearly see that Ethel was not sneaky or deceitful; he just had apprehensions because he never did trust quiet people. But Minnie liked her from the start because nearly every word out of Ethel's mouth was about William.

William and Salema remained close over the years while he was away at college. Some friends had written to him, informing him of rumors on the street about Salema and an older boy. He had planned to see if there was any credence to the gossip while he was home. The party was planned for Saturday after the closing of the café. What William found out after a little investigating Friday shocked and amazed him. He had talked with Salema's best friend and confidant, Lloyd Spencer, and Lloyd broke his oath of secrecy under the threat of dire physical harm to his person. He finally broke down and told William that Salema feared she was pregnant with the child of a married man who had presented himself as a college student. It was her first sexual experience. He was afraid to tell the identity of the man, for fear of how William might react, but he was too afraid for himself not to tell. The young man's name was Steve Barry. He was not married, William later found out. He did have another female interest by the name of Ruth. In fact, he really was a college student. Lloyd told him that Salema was afraid to tell Mrs. Minnie about the pregnancy, and that she had contemplated abortion. Only the horror stories about hangers being used on young girls had stopped her from using that option. Lloyd said he felt a sense of relief now that someone else knew the whole dirty little story.

William's first reaction was to go find this low life and crack his head open. He thought about discussing the issue with Minnie to try and cushion the blow for her and Salema. "Hell no, she gone beat the daylights out of my sister," he reasoned to himself. First he wanted to talk to Salema and find out from her what had happened. He was the one person in the family, he thought, who could understand how she felt. It was widely rumored that he was the father of a three- year- old girl named Betty Lou, mothered by Louise Deshazer. Louise was his first intimate experience, but they broke up after the baby was born. He accepted his paternal responsibility and provided financial assistance for the child.

The day William and Maxie left for college, Uncle Johnny gave them both bank books. The books went to separate savings accounts he had set up with funds that Thomas had paid to him for support of his children. He had been paying from the time they were born. Although Minnie refused to accept the money, he had saved every penny for the twins. William had no doubt Betty Lou was his little baby girl. Minnie knew about and accepted the baby as she did most of her son's transgressions, the greater number of which she helped him cover up. When he walked in the house, Frank was talking to Minnie and Johnny about a plan to bring new conservation methods to the Moccasin Bend area of the Tennessee River. The TVA did not want any other minerals depleted from the river basin. William sat and listened as Frank explained how years of over planting crops like corn and tobacco without rotation of fields had eroded and depleted topsoil in the eastern region of the Tennessee Valley and that in the western wing of the valley, the soil was sick as a consequence of erosion and leaching which followed in the wake of King Cotton. The topic was of great interest to William because he was studying agriculture in school.

Frank further explained how these conditions were making rain the enemy of man, causing the thin topsoil to be exposed to the elements and wash away during the smallest rain storm. One of the last factors that was affecting the soil in the area negatively was the rapid deforestation of the mountains that surrounded the Tennessee Valley. Removing the forest was causing the rain water to run too rapidly down the mountain sides, thus eroding all underlying topsoil. The mountains usually soaked up this water like giant sponges, but now greedy men were taking all the trees. Frank and his group of scientists and engineers were going to devise a plan that would help to nearly eliminate this ruin to the region's soil and resources. These men were determined to bring an end to the annual phenomenon of the April- through- December flash floods of the Tennessee River, and stop the river from turning into a flash stream that was washing away the productive soil of the hills and lowlands. Frank and his team were planning to make the river slow down and walk through the valley, and help the people by silting and devising a system of dam s to control the flow of the mighty waters of the Tennessee River.

One of Frank's first tasks was to help map the region. He was also entering Johnny into a study being scientifically monitored by the TVA for local farmers. Johnny had implemented a plan years earlier that had included building mole hills with all plowed- away soil. He strategically placed these mounds around all of his fields that he used for planting, and annually rotated these fields. This had saved the majority of the precious topsoil on his land. Long before other farmers around him, Johnny had grasped the concept of the complicated dynamics of soil conservation. Frank now had

Johnny and Minnie's undivided attention. This most interesting agriculturally based conversation going on between the three older heads of the family gave William the opportunity he needed to talk to Salema discreetly. William politely excused himself and went to the kitchen, where he could hear Salema and Arselee talking as he walked down the hall. They were washing vegetables for the café that Uncle Johnny had just delivered, and listening to the blues on the radio. He walked in and hugged Arselee and told her that she could go out and play, that he would help finish washing vegetables for her. She darted out the back door before he could say another word or change his mind.

William started his conversation with Salema. "I realize that you're becoming a young woman, so if you choose not to discuss your personal affairs with me, I'll understand. But if you need someone to talk to or help in any way, I'm here for you. Always know that whatever I have, you have and it'll always be that way." She knew he wasn't a judgmental person and that she could trust him with her deepest, darkest secret. He had never betrayed her trust.

Salema was always strong and straight to the point when she spoke. She turned toward him and said, "William, let me put it like this. I've only talked to one person about this and that's my friend Lloyd. But I do think I'm pregnant. I know folks saying that Steve is married and making a fool out of me, but that boy ain't no more married than the man on the moon. My problem is that I'm in dire straits with Ma, Mama, and Daddy."

William thought for a minute before he opened his mouth to speak. "Salema, one thing in life I'm learning is that there are so many ways to be made a fool of, you can't duck them all. Not to say that you have been made a fool of, because what you are going through is just part of life. As far as being in dire straits with the family, they ain't about to throw you in the streets because you got pregnant. The worst thing that can happen is Mama killing your ass, and she can only do that once."

They both started laughing, she walked over to him, hugged and thanked him. "I needed to hear that."

William told her jokingly, "Daddy Frank won't let Mama do to much to you any way. You know you've always been his favorite girl. Hell, he won't half way allow Mama or nobody else to whip any child around here if he's at home, ever since his little incident with 'Stanky Chank' talking to him in Grandma Frankie's mama's voice."

Stanky Chank was William's nick name for Celeste. He was referring to an incident that happened when she was three. Frank was a staunch disciplinarian who believed in the use of corporal punishment. Celeste had broken a glass in the sink while throwing a temper tantrum because she wanted more sun tea. She had already drunk two full glasses and Frank told her she'd had enough. Celeste pitched a fit and started whining and jerking her shoulders. Frank had grabbed a switch to spank her. When he drew back to swing at her, she cocked her head to the side and spoke very calmly in a different voice, saying, "Frank you don't hit your mother." His eyes bucked and he froze as she repeated the phrase. He dropped the switch and turned and walked out of the house. He never spanked her again. Being part Indian, he thought his daughter could possibly be possessed by some ancestor. At the very least, he thought this child was odd.

Salema knew she had a great rapport with her dad and that he was a very understanding man. The thought of disappointing him or her mother was tearing her apart inside, especially since she was his first born and the twins were doing so well. She knew her parents' top priority for their children was getting a higher education and becoming productive adults, able to function on their own. Now here she was, not out of high school and pregnant. This would break her parents' heart and she knew it. William told her he would try and find Steve and introduce himself, and let him know he was there to help. Neither one of them had any idea that the word on the streets was that William was home looking for Steve to beat him up. Steve had heard all the talk and had rounded up his cousin Leon, who had a reputation for being a bad ass.

Ethel had been taking a nap, and had slept for about two and a half hours. When she woke up, she went looking for William. Everyone had started getting ready for the party by then. Even after giving birth to all her children, Minnie was still built like a brick shit house, Frank would always say. Tonight she wore a chocolate brown two- piece dress suit. The dress fit tight to her body and had eight rows of tassels wrapped around it from top to bottom. She pinned her hair up in a beautiful ball with curls falling around her neck ; she looked absolutely gorgeous. Frank wore a medium brown wool three- piece suit, a beige and medium brown tie, medium brown and beige two- toned Stetson shoes, and a medium brown Stetson hat. He always had his pocket watch chain hanging from the inside of his vest in front of him. Frank looked super dapper this evening. His white shirt was perfectly starched and ironed. He wore his beige cashmere top coat to complete his ensemble for this party. This was the first adult party that Salema had her parents' permission to attend. All the children would be able to be present for about forty- five minutes to an hour to honor their father, then they would be carted off to the house, so that the whiskey, dirty down home blues, and grinding could get started.

Tonight, because she was old enough, Salema could stay until midnight. When the family arrived at the café, it was packed to the gills. Emma and the staff were working the party for Minnie. They were getting paid and partying at the same time. It seemed like all the people they ever knew were there, and some they had never seen before. Even upstairs was full. All of Frank's family was there. Some of his distant relatives he had not seen for a long time, including his second cousin, Annison showed up. The turnout for this party was overwhelming. Mr. Moore, Mr. Copeland, and some of their cronies were there. The whiskey was flowing as if it were legal, and there was enough food to feed Pharaoh's army. William found Salema and asked her where Steve hung out on the weekends. She told him he usually drank wine with some of his friends up on the railroad tracks behind the freight station on Alabama Street. They had an old empty box car that they had made into a sort of club house used for their drinking and sexual exploits. As he was leaving out the back door of the café, Salema and Ethel walked out with him. He kissed Ethel and told his new wife that he would be right back.

William wanted to explain to Steve that everything would be all right, and that he would help him and Salema get the rest of the family prepared to deal with the arrival of a new family member. As he drove up Market Street, he could see the old box car as he approached the intersection with

Alabama Street. He pulled his Ford truck along side the railroad tracks and walked over to the third rail, where the car had sat for nearly seven years, decaying. Loud talking and laughter filled the air as he got close to the tattered side door, which was pulled closed. As he slid the door open, he could see three guys passing a bottle of wine around, drinking directly from the bottle. A train was passing on the main track on the other side of the car, so he could barely hear anything as he grabbed the floor and pulled himself quietly inside without being noticed. William jumped up into the car and attempted to introduce himself and ask if they knew Steve Barry.

Steve yelled, "This is the son of a bitch that's after me"" Before William could get another word out of his mouth Leon and Douglas rushed him. Douglas grabbed him from behind and held his arms over his head. Leon pulled a knife out of his pocket and stabbed him twice in the upper torso. William was completely surprised and had no time to defend himself from the attack. Douglas outweighed him by at least a hundred pounds. William weighed about 165 pounds at the time. When Douglas let William go. He slumped to the floor of the box car and grabbed hold of the bottom of Steve's pants leg. Steve lost his balance as William took hold of his pants and tripped and fell face- to- face with William. The train on the next track had cleared, and the silence in the box car was deafening.

With every breath, William could hear a hideous whistling, a wheezing of air, coming from the hole in his chest. Not knowing whose leg he was gripping, William whispered to the nameless face in front of him, "Will you please let…Steve know that I didn't come… for no trouble…wanted to help."

As Leon and Douglas jumped down out of the car, Leon hit his hand on the side of the box car and dropped the knife. He bent over to look for it, but it was too dark to see anything around or under the car. Douglas heard the knife hit the ground to and joined his now partner in crime crawling around on the ground looking for the weapon. Douglas stammered out in a nervous whisper, "Man, you killed that nigga. We better get the hell outta here." The two of them then scrambled to their feet and took off running across Alabama toward Market Street. Steve heard what William had managed to whisper and stopped trying to pull his leg free and stayed behind to help him.

William pleaded with him, "Please… don't leave me out here to die by myself."

Steve could see that William was gravely injured. He was scared as hell but he knew he couldn't panic. He picked William up and asked: "Where your keys?"

"My keys in my britches," were the last words he uttered before losing consciousness.

Louise Deshazer's younger sister Sally was in her boyfriend Sherman's car, parked not far from where William had left his truck. They had pulled up shortly after he did, thinking this was a good spot to make out for a few minutes. They saw Leon and Douglas jump out of the box car and run. She thought she recognized William's truck, since she had seen it many times before at her home. Then they saw Steve coming in their direction in a very fast trot carrying William in his arms. Sally and Sherman got out of the car to see what was going on. When she saw how William's tongue was hanging from his mouth, and blood was running out of it, she started screaming. She nearly pulled William from Steve's arms, getting blood all over the front of her dress. Steve was barely able to keep hold of William after the run from the box car. He laid William in the bed of the truck and searched frantically through his pockets for his keys. He was muttering something incoherent after retrieving the set of keys from William's pants pocket as he ran toward the driver's side door.

Sally was horrified and distraught at what she was seeing. "Where are you taking him?"

"To the damn hospital'" he yelled. Steve sped off in the truck, tires screeching, slinging rocks behind.

Sally and Sherman had heard about the party being held at the café that night, so they jumped in the car and raced over there as fast as Sherman's car would get them there. Maxie had just managed to drag Minnie into her office no more than five minutes before the door burst open. The only thing that Minnie could clearly see as Salema and Sally came flying in the office was the blood on Sally's dress. Maxie had just told her mother that she was pregnant. The only words Minnie could get out before the office door came flying open were, " If this don't beat a hog a- fly in'. Great day in the mornin', I'm gone be a grandma." Salema led Sally in by the hand, they were both crying and screaming that somebody had hurt William.

The music had stopped, and it seemed like everyone was trying to get to the office to see what had happened. There was a crush of people outside the door. Maxie shut and locked the door as Sally proceeded to tell them what she had seen. Minnie was horrified by the words she was hearing. She immediately jumped out of her chair. "Where they take my child?" She snatched open her desk drawer and grabbed the extra set of keys she always kept there. Minnie fumbled with the keys in her hands nervously but managed to find the right key and open the back door to the office. She and the girls ran down the back stairs to the main kitchen's rear exit. Minnie had used the smaller kitchen for the party and figured no one was in the big kitchen as Jane called it.

When they reached the back door, Jane turned on the main overhead light. "What's gwoin' on?" Jane hated crowds and had come back in the kitchen for some peace and quiet. "Come on ma, we gotta go" is all Minnie said as she ran back and grabbed Jane by the hand.

"What done happen ta dis young'un?" Jane asked as she noticed all the blood on the front of Sally's dress. As Minnie opened the car door for her, she began to explain to Jane what was going on. Jane leaned forward and closed her eyes as she listened to Minnie break the terrible news to her that someone had hurt William. She never opened her eyes ; she just clasped her hands together and started saying a prayerful, quiet chant, slowly rocking from side to side.

There were several police cars parked in back of the hospital when they arrived. When Minnie parked, Maxie told her mother to hurry inside, that she would help Jane get out of the car. Salema had bolted from the car and was already in the lobby looking for someone to question when Minnie came running inside. Sheriff Ponterford was standing off to the right of the front desk talking to Steve and a hospital official when he noticed Minnie run in the back door. He walked down the corridor and called out to her. "Mrs. Minnie, may I please have a word with you?" he asked politely. He led her off to a small waiting area and began to discreetly talk in a low tone. He gave her all the information that he obtained at the time, starting with William's condition. "Your son's condition is extremely critical. The doctor said he done lost a lot of blood."

"So where is he now?" Minnie asked, her voice trembling with pain.

"They got him in the operating room undergoing emergency surgery now. He was stabbed twice, Mrs. Minnie. One wound had punctured a lung, and the other may have lacerated his liver. That fella Steve over there brought your son to the hospital, and was present when he was attacked. He said he didn't stab him, but he knew who did and was willing to identify the person or persons." He told her that the doctor had left instructions for the family to wait to receive word from him after he finished surgery as to William's condition. Sheriff Ponterford lowered his head and humbly said to Minnie,

"All we can do is pray for your son to make it at this point. I'm sorry this has happened." He went on to assure Minnie that the culprits would be apprehended and that justice would be served.

Just as he was about to turn to walk off, Frank, Mr. Moore, Mr. Copeland, and Ethel came in the hospital through the front entrance. Numerous relatives and friends had followed them over from the café. Before they walked inside, Frank had instructed those assembled out front to wait outside for him to come out and give them word on William's condition. The group of them walked over to Minnie and the sheriff. Mr. Moore quietly asked the sheriff if he could speak to him privately by the back door. The two of them walked off speaking in very hushed tones. Frank grabbed

Minnie and hugged her, asking how William was. She filled him in on his condition and started crying. Frank was trembling but he kept his outward composure and held Minnie tighter. Salema and Maxie had been talking to Steve after Sheriff Ponterford and Mr. Moore walked off down the corridor. Steve was brutally honest about the incident. He gave the complete blow- by-blow story to them. He even told them that he had heard that William was out looking for him and how he had recruited Leon and Douglas to watch his back. After he had finished, he turned to Salema and asked her to marry him.

She frowned up her face and answered, "Nigga, I know you are not serious. Do you think I'd marry you after you done had my brother stabbed?"

Maxie was very angry as she was nearing the end of the horrid incident. She started speaking a little louder than even she realized. She shouted at Steve, "So you really set my brother up, you dirty mother fucker." She was normally so reserved. Frank loosened his grip on Minnie and they both turned to see what was going on down the hall. Maxie then slapped Steve so hard that it must have knocked all the taste buds out of his mouth. Salema grabbed him and Maxie punched him in the face, real hard two times. He was struggling to get away from the grip Salema had on him, but couldn't.

Frank rushed over, as did Sheriff Ponterford, and broke up the scuffle. The sheriff threatened to arrest everyone involved in the fight if they didn't all calm down. Frank sternly but calmly reminded both girls that William was in critical condition, fighting for his life and that they should both remember that and maintain a sense of dignity. Both Salema and Maxie immediately deferred to him and began to calm down. Sheriff Ponterford heard Minnie ask Maxie what she meant by "Steve set William up."

While Maxie was explaining, the sheriff hurriedly started walking for the back door with Steve. He wanted to defuse any further drama in the hospital lobby. After she heard the short version of what happened, Minnie called out for the sheriff. He stopped and turned around just short of the door. She walked toward him and looked directly at Steve as she approached. When she got within earshot, she told Steve that she appreciated him waiting and making sure her son got to the hospital. Then she told him that she would pray for him; she thanked the sheriff for how he had handled things, and turned and walked back over to the rest of the family. Sheriff Ponterford then pushed Steve out the door and put him in the back seat of his patrol car and took him to the station.

Frank had finished talking to and consoling both Maxie and Salema. He asked Maxie if she would drive his car and go pick up her father. He wanted her to let Thomas know what had happened to his son and get him down to the hospital as soon as possible. Even though the two of them had never spoken a word to each other in all these years, Frank never interfered with or stood in the way of the twins' relationship with their biological father. Both Maxie and William called him Daddy Frank and both had a special paternal bond with him as well as with Thomas. The natural bond they had with Thomas didn't stop either of them from loving Frank dearly. Salema volunteered to ride with Maxie, and the two of them took off after Maxie walked over to check on Jane. Jane was sitting in the waiting area still chanting and praying. "Please leave my baby with me a lil while longer if ya see fit ta do dat. But take him on home to glory if he has ta suffer ta be here with us."

Maxie hugged her and she and Salema took off to get Thomas. All the time Ethel had been talking to the hospital administrator and making inquiries as to which doctor was performing the surgery and what kind of credentials he had. He told her the physician's name was W.C. Martin and that he was the best in the city, bar none, white or colored, even though he happened to be colored. His colleagues always referred to W. C. Martin as "The Natural." It was reputed that he had the most delicate, yet firmest and steadiest hands in the operating room, of all his local peers. Ethel was assured that all that could be done medically for her husband was being done, and that the family would get a briefing as soon as he got one.

For a nineteen- year- old newlywed bride, Ethel was holding up extremely well emotionally. She knew she was facing the possibility of becoming a young widow. Most young women her age would have crumbled under these dire circumstances, but she felt a certain sense of strength and spirit of optimism surrounding William and his family. And it was quickly rubbing off on and sustaining her through this ordeal. Frank had been talking to and thanking Mr. Moore and Mr. Copeland, who were about to leave, for coming and showing their concern for his family when Ethel walked over from her conversation.

After the men left, Frank and Ethel started looking for Minnie, who was nowhere in sight. Frank suggested that Ethel check the ladies' room. He strolled calmly down the corridor to the back door. As he walked past a custodial closet, he heard his wife's voice coming from inside; she was crying and praying. He stopped and stood quietly and respectfully outside the door. He could hear her saying in a sobbing low tone, "Lord, I realize that I ain't never done nothing for myself. Everything good that ever happened to me you made it happen. You made all this possible for me, you gave me my Ma, Frank, and William, Maxie, Salema, Rico, Arselee, Celeste, Doyle, CeCelia, the café, everything I got you gave me, and it's all been so good to me. But I need you now more than ever before, Jesus. I'm not ready for my baby to leave me, not yet, ummm ummm." She started moaning, and finished her prayer, "Lord, if he leaves me now, I don't know what will become of me, I'll be a mess. Please don't take him home to glory yet, he been one of the joys of my life, Jesus, I ask this prayer in the name of our Lord Christ Jesus amen."

Frank couldn't stand to hear her crying anymore, so he tapped lightly on the door. When she opened the door, he gently wiped her eyes and nose with his handkerchief and took her in his arms and hugged her as she broke down sobbing again. The raw emotion of her prayer had tears running down Frank's face too. He felt that William was his son as much as anyone else's, and he was torn apart by this as much as she was. "We can't lose him now, Frank," she said as she trembled in his arms from crying so hard.

"The Lord got the last say in all that, Mama, so stop crying. He gone take care of William and the rest of us like always, you'll see. Come on now, show that faith like you always do. William needs us to be strong for him now. Hold your head up, the Lord gone make a way for us. He always does, doesn't he, Big Mama."

She couldn't help but try to smile through all the tears. "Yeah, Frank, he does make a way for us. We've been blessed."

Her eyes were swollen and red, but she was still pretty, Frank thought. He bent over and wiped the dust off from the knee area of her dress, then he took her hand and led her back down the corridor. Minnie thought about the fact that she had not seen Babe or Willie all night at the hospital. She asked Frank where she was, "I asked them to stay behind at the café and help clear out the people left behind and kind of clean up a bit before closing the building. She had wanted to come but agreed that would be the best way to help you out."

Minnie looked down at Frank. With a very loving gleam in her eyes, she softly asked, "Daddy Frank, you try to think of everything you can to take care of me don't you?"

He looked up at her and laughed just a wee bit. "That's all a man can do is try and do his best for his wife and children, big mama."

He stood up and they held hands as they walked toward the waiting area where Ma was sitting. They could see Maxie, Salema, Thomas, and his wife Olivia enter the lobby. The girls also had one of Thomas's young under studies with them. The young and handsome protege's name was J.D. Mayes. He had grown up a member of Thomas's church and was an awesome personality in the pulpit. Thomas was visibly upset and nervous. Maxie formally introduced her father and step father for the first time. Frank extended his hand and the two men shook firmly. Thomas thanked Frank for sending Maxie to tell him about William, and asked if the doctor had come out of the operating room yet. Minnie spoke up, "no, we're still waiting. She shook Olivia's hand and spoke very warmly to Thomas.

Olivia told Minnie that she had been praying for William and the family on the way over, and she would keep them in her thoughts and prayers.

Minnie replied, "Thank you, honey, we need prayer right now. I appreciate you sending up another one for that child laying up there on that table."

Thomas then asked Frank if the two of them could have a word in private. The two of them then walked down to the rear lobby. Thomas spoke openly, asking if he could call him Frank instead of Mr. Whatley, and speak candidly without causing any hard feelings. Frank told him sure, he could call him by his first name. And as long as Thomas didn't plan to disrespect him, he had no problem with and fully expected him to be forthcoming in his conversation. He told Frank that for the first couple years after he lost Minnie, he felt not only foolish for his own actions, but that he couldn't help but feel a sense of jealous y and resentment toward him. Thomas said that the passing of time, the maturation process, and meeting and falling in love with

Olivia helped him see he was wrong for those feelings. Finally he expressed his gratitude for the way Frank had handled the situation with the twins. The only problem either one of them ever complained to their father about involving Frank was when the children were about twelve years old. William tried to use the fact that Frank was not his biological father as an excuse for him not have to accept any discipline from him. If Frank were to offer him any advice on any subject at the time, William would reply in a smart tone, "That's not what my father said I have to do"'"

Frank handled the situation with the wisdom of Solomon. He sat William down and told him that he was happy that he loved his father so much, and that he wanted him to continue to value and respect Thomas's opinions. But he was the only daddy in his house and as long as William decided he wanted to live under his roof, he was not to ever mention his father's opinions and rules in his home again. William grew to realize how disrespectful he had been to Frank, and to his credit, he later apologized. And it was Frank and his great uncle Johnny who had taught William to hunt and fish. Thomas didn't fish or hunt. Of course he was a fisherman of men of sorts as a preacher.

As Frank was about to reply to Thomas, Dr. Martin walked out the door to the lobby. He looked bushed, but he was all smiles. Thomas and Frank hurried down the corridor to join the rest of the family. Doctor Martin asked who were the parents. Frank, Thomas, and Minnie all spoke up at the same time. "We are," they all three said in unison.

Doctor Martin chuckled and said, "That's a new one on me, one man, three parents. Any way, it's nice to meet you folks and I've got great news. Remarkably, and I do mean remarkably, your son pulled through the surgery." You could hear the entire family breathe a collective sigh of relief. He said that William was still in extremely critical condition. That he had lost a lot of blood upon arrival to the hospital. "So thank God and whomever got him here when they did. A few minutes later and we could not have helped him at all. He would have drowned in his own blood due to the puncture in his lung. We were able to fix the lung and stop the bleeding in that area very quickly. Our real blessing came when we discovered that only a small laceration to the liver had occurred and we able to save that organ. Those factors and a large dose of God's grace probably saved your son's life tonight. I was just the tool he used to get the job done. Now I want you all to know that I've decided to spend the night here at the hospital. I'll be in the doctors' quarters on the floor William's on, so if any complications arise, and I don't expect any, I will be here on the premises."

The entire family started thanking him and asking if they could see William. Before he could answer, Jane stood up and walked over to where he was standing. She grabbed his hands, "I specially wants ta thank ya fa being the tool the Lawd was able ta use ta get my grandson through dis." Doctor Martin just smiled and told her he was honored to be able to do it. He told the family that the three- and- a- half- hour surgery had drained him and he needed to take a nap. The nurse would let only the parents see William tonight. Ethel quickly, and some what loudly disagreed. The doctor told her that as a young bride being put to this test of faith and stress level, she would be first. He had no idea William was married at such a young age.

Again Doctor Martin reiterated that he was fatigued and needed some rest. They all thanked him again and he disappeared through the same door that he had entered. Minnie had noticed that by the end of the doctor's briefing, Maxie was holding hands with young Reverend Mayes. Thomas asked the young preacher to please offer a prayer before the people assembled outside left. The entire group of them on the inside then walked out to the rear of the hospital.

Reverend Mayes waited until after Frank had given everyone who had waited very anxiously but orderly outside all this time a briefing on William's condition. After they all stopped celebrating, the young minister gathered everyone around him in a circle. He asked Thomas, Frank, Minnie,

Olivia, Jane, Maxie, Salema, and Ethel to hold hands with him in the middle of everyone. After closing his eyes and bowing his head, he said a short but stirring prayer that bordered on being a mini-sermon. "Father God, we come to you tonight on bended, humble, prayerful, and yes Father, thankful knees. Thankful Jesus for all the blessings that you bestow on us and provide in abundance daily. With your eternal wisdom, Lord, you set up the family arrangement for mankind, Father. And we are most thankful for this provision, Jesus. Lord, we thank you for this family, and for watching over their son William in his hour of need, Father. We realize tonight that while we are in this race of life down here on this earth you prepared for us. Lord, that we are either headed into the storm, in the middle of the storm, or on the way out of the storm. But no matter where we are in the storm, you are there with us, sweet Jesus. We give thanks and praise to you tonight for carrying William through this portion of the storm. Father, we know you can do all things and through your son, all things are possible. We know you see all things, Father, and that we don't need to mention all the acts of generosity and kindness that Mr. Frank and Ms. Minnie have extended over the years to the people of this community. Because you've already written those good deeds down, only to be recalled on the day of your judgment of all mankind.

"But Father tonight, we just want to thank you for keeping William down here with his family and all those who love him a little while longer, Jesus. We want to close by saying thank you for all your many wonderful blessings, Father. We offer this prayer in the name of the Father, the Son, and the Holy Spirit. Amen. And Amen again."

As the throng of people began to exchange good nights, Maxie walked over to the young preacher and grabbed both his hands. She was looking at him with the warm glow of love when she noticed her mother staring at them. But she was so proud of the prayer that he had just delivered that she paid no attention to her mother's stare. Maxie said good night to everyone, and walked off with Reverend Mayes. Thomas wanted to see William before he and Olivia left for the evening. He and J.D. had driven their own vehicles to the hospital, trailing Maxie in a three- car caravan, and were in no rush to leave for home. So Frank, Thomas, Olivia, Minnie, Jane, and Ethel proceeded to go up to room 345 as instructed by the night shift nursing supervisor.

William was awake and drinking a little water with the assistance of a nurse when they entered his room. He looked drugged and weak, unable to speak. Frank, Minnie, and Jane all lined up on the side of the bed the nurse was on. On the other side, Thomas, Olivia, and Ethel lined up. Ethel slid up on and sat down on the end of the bed. William nodded off for a few seconds, then opened his eyes and smiled at everyone. He tried to mouth out the words "thank y'all." Or at least that's what it looked like to most everyone. A couple of tears ran down the side of each cheek and William drifted off to sleep. Thomas held his right hand and Minnie and Frank both held his left hand. Ethel was unconsciously rubbing and gently stroking his right thigh. "It looks like William need some rest. My heart has been filled with joy just seeing him smile again," Thomas related. He told Olivia that it was time for them to go home and that they would return in the morning. He would assign another minister to deliver the Sunday message this week.

Minnie asked Jane if she was all right now that she had seen William open his eyes and smile at them. Jane just rolled her eyes at Minnie and smiled. "Yes, by the good grace of God. Yes Minnie, I'm 'bout ready fa bed now."

Frank motioned to the door and everyone except Ethel started out of the room. She walked about one step toward the others and announced, "I'll be staying here with my husband." She asked Minnie to bring her a change of clothes, a bath towel, and her tooth brush. Minnie looked puzzled for a second, then she agreed to fill the list for her new daughter- in-law. The two couples shook hands in the hall and bid each other farewell.

Jane never said one word to Thomas or his wife all night. Thomas attempted to say good night, but she never acknowledged his gesture.

CHAPTER X

That Sunday morning, before she left the house, Minnie sat the rest of the children down and explained to them what had happened to William. Rico was very upset and she had to calm and comfort him and the rest of the children before she left the house that morning. Minnie first wanted to make a quick pit stop by the café on her way to the hospital to see William. She wanted to get Ethel some breakfast. She had also packed the things to deliver Ethel for her change of clothes and ablution needs.

As soon as she walked in the back door of the café, Emma and Tom started asking her about William and the rest of the family. Minnie thanked them for their concern, and told them that it looked good for William, and that the rest of the children were fine and that she was so proud of all of them. She thanked God and said, "The Lord has really blessed Frank and I with a great bunch of children."

Emma just laughed, "I'll say he has, Ms. Minnie. You know we all love them children of yours and we been praying for William all night long."

Emma was looking at Tom out of the corner of her eyes as Minnie turned to walk away from the two of them. Minnie asked them if the staff could make out without her today because she would more than likely stay at the hospital all day. Tom assured her things would be taken care of as if she were there running things her very self. Emma quickly reinforced his support by telling Minnie that they were surprised to even see her in the café at all today under the circumstances. Minnie packed a big to-go breakfast for her daughter-in-law. She even managed to get a laugh out of both Emma and Tom when she left, by telling Emma to keep the gossiping down to a minimum today. Even though she knew for herself that Emma just could not resist the temptation to stir up slanderous, scandalous conversation.

Minnie stopped At the Ninth Street Drug store and bought a dozen red roses and a big get well soon card. Then she drove the short distance to the hospital and made the trek up to the third floor like a lady on a new baby delivery mission. She could hear William's voice as she got near the door to his room. He was groaning and saying that he was sore all over. When she turned the corner, entering the room, she saw him sitting up on the bed facing her. Ethel and a nurse were helping him to his feet. William wanted to walk to the rest room on his own. When he looked up and saw his mother, he just started grinning from ear to ear. Minnie just stood in the door shaking her head from side to side, smiling. She had tears of joy streaming quietly down her cheeks. When she wiped her eyes, she could see that there was a stack of get well cards on the foot of the bed. The room was full of flowers ; they were everywhere. Mr. Moore had sent some, Ms. Cole, Mr. Copeland, Frank, Johnny — and half of Chattanooga it seemed. The hospital staff had started taking some of the flowers in to other patients. There were just too many of them coming in for William, even his old boxing coach from the Y M C A had sent him flowers. Dr. Martin walked in before anyone could say a word. He looked much fresher than he had the night before. He told the nurse and Ethel to hold on for one moment; he wanted to check something out before he let William get up on his feet. He spoke to everyone in the room and asked them to give him a moment alone with William. Dr. Martin had the nurse help him lay William back down.

After he checked the wounds and made sure that no stitches had torn and that nothing had re opened, he admonished both the nurse and William for rushing things along much too fast. The doctor told him that he had never had a patient so eager to get out of bed after such a catastrophic injury. He asked William to hold out his arm, so that he could give him a shot of pain medicine. "Slow down, champ, we're still in the middle rounds of this fight. Save some gas. You might need some for the late rounds. We still have to watch for blood clots forming in your legs. So stay in the bed, young man, until such time as I say you can get out of it. Until then, you are gonna have to get used to a bed pan. Now that might do a little damage to your ego, but it will save your rump from tearing open those wounds and have me tear a hole in your rear end."

"Take it easy on me Doc. I ain't go much rump left to tear." They all started laughing but William had to make himself stop because of the pain.

The rest of the family had assembled in a small waiting area a few feet from the room. Johnny and Frank chatted about how they both wanted William to finish school and expand the farm even more than its present seventy acres. Johnny expressed to Frank how devastated he knew the family would have been if they had lost William. William had such a special bond with everyone and served as an essential glue that held things together for a bright future for his generation of the family. Dr. Martin came out and asked that everyone help keep the patient in his bed until further notice. He let them know that everything was progressing very well and that the best thing for William was to rest. "I'm sorry family, but I've just given him a pain shot and he'll probably sleep for about two or three hours. If you're quiet though you can go in and spend a few minutes with him before the medication takes full effect." He then said that he had to continue his rounds and check on his other patients, and would be back in a couple hours for a follow- up.

As everyone entered the room, William started to apologize to his mother for putting her through all this. Then he said something that made everyone laugh. "I had some street doctors try to perform surgery on me last night. But a real doctor came along just in time to really get the cuttin' part straightened out, now it looks like I might be all right." And with that said he drifted off to sleep.

Ethel had just returned from eating her breakfast, and taking care of her needs. Ethel let her mother-in-law know she felt fat... fat, full, and refreshed. She had missed the doctor's briefing, so Minnie brought her up to date as to the latest instructions.

Maxie and the Reverend J.D. Mayes walked around the corner holding hands. As they entered the room, everyone else had just turned to leave. Suddenly they became the center of the entire group's attention. The couple spoke to everyone and turned to leave the room with them after they saw that William was asleep. As they walked down the hall, Babe and

Willie came walking up the corridor toward them. Minnie told them that the doctor had given William a shot to make him sleep, "It'll be a couple hours before we can see him."

Maxie came over and asked Minnie if she could speak to her in private. "Excuse me ya'll." The two of them walked away from the rest of the family to a vacant waiting room. Maxie filled Minnie in on her history with J.D. "I noticed you noticing the hand holding. Mama I've known him since I was a little girl and liked him since day one. And he being the father of this child I'm carrying, mama, he wants to get married."

Minnie was all smiles and very pleased the young preacher wanted to do right by her child.. She told Maxie to just tell her what she wanted and it was hers. "It's your day, baby. I been waiting for this day to come and now its here." Minnie opened the door and called Babe into the room. After they made sure that the door was shut, she whispered to Babe, "Child, Maxie getting married to that handsome young preacher out in the hall. Lord have mercy, we got us a wedding to plan."

"Does Thomas know Maxie,"Babe asked. "J. D. has already asked daddy for my hand in marriage, and since he thinks of him as a second son, he jumped for joy." Frank always wanted whatever Maxie wanted for herself to be happy. Minnie asked Maxie if she wanted their engagement announced to everyone. Maxie's answer was that the engagement would be short. She told Babe and Minnie that she wanted to get married before she started getting too big from the pregnancy. Therefore, she wanted to have the wedding within the next month. "That's all right by me"" Minnie almost screamed.

There was a tap on the door. Babe opened it, and Frank and Johnny came into the small room that was now getting a little crowded. They wanted to know what all the loud talking was about. They had heard Minnie yell out and were anxious to hear what was so exciting. "Maxie has broken the news of her engagement to J. D," Minnie boasted proudly. Frank looked at

Minnie and shook his head. "You just now figuring out the two of them were a hot ticket in town, big mama?" Then he gingerly stepped over to Maxie and hugged her, telling her that he was so happy for her that he could turn a flip.

Johnny gave her a big hug and congratulated her as well. Then he informed them that he had to get back out to the farm, and would get back to the hospital before visiting hours ended this evening. He had a huge harvest to bring in this year again. Frank also had to depart, so he told Minnie that he had some business to attend to that would take him a few hours at Mr. Moore's office. So Frank and Johnny left together.

Minnie suggested that she, Maxie, and Babe go eat at the café. She was anxious to start planning a wedding. Maxie said she wanted to wait at least a week before she made a formal announcement. She also told her mother that she wanted J.D. to join them for lunch. When they joined Willie, J. D., and

Ethel, who had been inadvertently left in the corridor by everyone, Maxie asked the three of them to join in on a group luncheon at the café. Then she pulled J.D. aside and whispered to him that they had everyone's blessings on their marriage. Maxie was as giddy as a teenager on her first date.

When they got outside to the vehicles, she jumped in the car with J.D. and slid over right next to him like Minnie always rode next to Frank. Babe had just purchased a brand spanking new Ford, so Minnie asked to ride with her and Willie. Babe had always driven like a green- eyed granny, so it took them about three minutes longer than Maxie and J.D. to arrive at the café. Maxie spotted Brandy, J.D.' s older sister and her husband Curtis sitting inside at a window table. J. D. waved at them through the window and his sister beckoned him inside with a "come here" wave. Brandy was his only sibling, and the two of them had always shared a very........ very close- knit relationship. J.D. had shared with Maxie the fact that he did not like to fight as a small boy, so his sister had to fight for him. At any rate, she never allowed the neighborhood bullies to pick on her younger brother simply because he was a pacifist. Brandy always knew J.D. wasn't scared of the other boys, he told her he thought fighting was barbaric. This was an early train of thought that J. D. and William had in common. It was also one of the first things that attracted Maxie to J.D.

Maxie walked inside the café with her new fiancé. J.D. introduced Maxie, whom both Brandy and Curtis already knew, for the first time as his fiancé. Louise Roberts came over to ask Maxie if she would be eating in the family area of the restaurant. She informed her that she would and that her mother would be arriving in a few minutes with more people. Louise spoke to J.D. with the usual "Good morning, Reverend Mayes," which Maxie loved to hear him addressed this way by other people. As a girl, she felt the title Reverend gave her father great dignity. Now she had her very own reverend to cherish and love.

Because of his dynamic, intellectual style of preaching J.D. was rapidly becoming the most popular young preacher in town. When Minnie, Willie, and Babe came in, they walked over and Maxie introduced them to Brandy and Curtis. Curtis works as a supervisor at a warehouse that supplies most of the local grocery stores' dry goods. Though well- spoken, if he chose to speak, was very quiet, and a rather nice looking young buck himself.

Minnie told Brandy that she looked forward to meeting her mother, and that it was so nice meeting her and Curtis. Then she invited them to join in on the luncheon that was slowly turning into an unofficial engagement celebration.

Brandy and Curtis followed everyone else into the private family area and were treated to all they could eat on the house. Brandy said to J.D. "I am so proud of all that you've accomplished. Most, if not all the men who had been bullies when we were children were either in the chain gang or dead. Those men lost most of the important battles in life because they only depended on themselves to fight their battles." J.D. was very flattered by what his sister had said and of course, Maxie was overjoyed. To her, her little brother had become a man of great dignity ; who always depended on God. And was about to be married to one the prettiest, most popular young ladies in town. Before everyone sat down, Minnie excused herself so that she could go back in the kitchen. Maxie and Babe started talking about William as everyone got seated. When Minnie got in the kitchen, no one saw her approaching except Tom. Emma was shooting her mouth off as usual, and never heard Minnie creeping up behind her. She was grandstanding and loud talking for Tom, telling him that Ms. Minnie thought her children could do no wrong. Tom tried to cut her off, saying, "Now just stop it, Emma, you know how much we all love those spoiled ass children of Minnie's."

Emma was not to be stopped ; she cut Tom right off in mid- thought. She said, "Looka here, two of Minnie's daughters is pregnant, without as much as a constant beau, let alone a fiancé or husband. And top that off, with William darn near bout gettin hisself killed over Salema. Minnie can kiss my ass if she thanks them some angels she got. Honey, them some little demons, if you ask me. I still love 'em, though."

Tom was standing with his eyes bucked, batting his eye lids, scratching the side of his head, trying to signal Emma as to Minnie's presence in the kitchen. When Emma finally got the hint that something was awry, she turned around and Minnie was standing right behind her. Minnie had her hand in her bosom on her straight razor. She thought better of pulling her razor and cutting Emma. So Minnie just lit into Emma verbally. "Look- ah here, you snuff bucket; kissin' ass ain't no crime so you can kiss mine.

Hang it on a lamp pole and lick it like a sweet jelly roll bitch. I ought to take this razor and cut them damn lips off of that big mouth of yours. Emma, you must jump out the damn bed first thing in the morning with stirring up shit on your warped mind. You keep me and my young'uns out your damn mouth. 'Cause the next time I hear you scandalizing my family, it's gone be you and me."

Tom came around the prep table, and carefully led Minnie toward the stairs up to her office. Tom put his arm around her shoulder and hugged her.

"Minnie, come on here, girl, you know Emma got a problem with that mouth, child," he said as they walked up the stairs.

Emma was standing at the large prep table that she and Tom had been working at, with her mouth hanging open in shock. She was literally in a ball of tears. She called after Minnie, telling her she was sorry, that she was just clowning with Tom. But Tom turned toward her on his way up the stairs with Minnie and told her, "Honey, just hush for a little while and go wash your face." Minnie never paused or looked in Emma's direction as she walked away. She continued up into her office as Tom addressed Emma.

When Tom entered the office, Minnie started laughing and he couldn't stop himself from joining in. Tom almost fell on the floor, he was doubled over so far. He made it over to one of the three chairs around Minnie's huge oak desk, and laid his head on the crook of his arm on the corner of her desk. "Oh child, I'm so glad the Good Lord let me be in here today to see that loud mouth cow finally get hers. And no, you did not trust to tell her to lick your tail feather, like a sweet jelly roll.... whew....I thought I was gone fall out in that kitchen when you said that, girl, for real. Minnie I'm, just glad you didn't cut her ass. They will take you to jail, girl, and you got too much going on right now for that kind of foolishness."

Minnie finally got her self under control and told Tom that she did not want any hard feelings between herself and Emma. "But Tom, honey, I knew someone had to stop her from thinking any subject is open to gossip at work. And today was a good day to put a halt on that mouth from running in the kitchen all the time. You know Emma can be a real earth- disturbing bitch sometimes with all that gossiping. And we all know she don't care nothing about hurting other people's feelings. Hopefully this will teach her big- mouth rump to calm it down and respect folks more, at least for a little while anyway."

Tom just poked out his mouth and said, "Yeah, right Minnie. We'll be lucky to get two good weeks of peace around here."

Minnie reminded Tom and herself that she had a room full of family and guests downstairs eating in the family area. Minnie hurried Tom out of the office and rushed back to the dining area. She acted as if the whole scene with Emma had never taken place. The only other person she mentioned the ugly verbal spat to was Babe, and she waited until later that evening to even do that.

Back in the kitchen, Tom had gotten Emma calmed down and assured that she had done no permanent damage to her relationship with Minnie. He did take advantage of the opportunity to rub in about her always gossiping, and not being able to handle the repercussions, After he had pried a smile out of her, "Hmmm..... I see we can dish it out but we don't take the punishment so well, do we, Ms. Emma?"

Emma just ignored him and called out for Louise to come pick up the rest of the order for Ms. Minnie's family. She had placed an apology note on the serving platter with Minnie's name on it. When Louise picked up the order, Emma gave her instructions to make sure no one except Minnie saw the note. She told her that she would be watching her to make sure she didn't read it herself. Louise delivered the note with Minnie's food very discreetly. Minnie read the note and just smiled to herself.

As Louise was setting Willie's plate in front of him, he clicked his mouth and sniffed in deeply. "This here food always smell and taste so good, it don't make no earthly sense"" Willie exclaimed. Willie couldn't seem to stop cutting his eyes toward Louise, and Babe noticed it every time she walked in eyesight.

She leaned over to whisper in Willie's ear, "Did you lose something in that gal's behind, fool? I see you can't take your eyes off her rump." Willie tried to look shocked and innocent. But he couldn't fool Babe; she had seen the act too many times before.

He just gave his usual lame statement. "Come on now, Babe, a good man don't leave steak for hamburger......ha....ha...ha."

Only thing, Babe wasn't laughing. She was growing tired of Willie's song and dance act that included hustling all night and womanizing. The Willie Clayton Show had been playing the last ten years, with Babe footing the bill for nearly all the expenses. Babe poked him in the ribs with her elbow and told him to at least act like he had some respect for her in public, even if he wasn't able to appreciate the quality woman he had at home.

Maxie and Curtis were joking with Brandy about wanting a house fu l of children. Brandy said she wanted as many as Curtis could produce. She was already expecting their first child. Brandy was entering her third month of pregnancy. Now J.D. And Maxie's baby would be born almost at the same time, plus Salema would be having her baby around that time too.

Just as the conversation was getting juicy with potential names for the coming boys or girls, Frank, and Ma walked in with all of Minnie's other children. Frank had wrapped up his meeting with Mr. Moore and went by the house and picked up the rest of the family. Doyle jumped in his favorite chair at the table and asked Minnie, "When we get to see William?"

She answered him as only a mother would. Minnie laughed and told him, "As soon as you eat all the vegetables Ma gone put on your plate." Celeste chimed in, "We all ate food at home before we left. Daddy cooked for us and now we're ready to go to the hospital to see our brother. Salema and Arselee agreed, they were ready to get to the hospital as well. Rico never even sat down at the table; he stood by the door that led into the kitchen that they had entered. Before everyone departed, Minnie introduced Brandy and Curtis to everyone as J. D.'s sister and brother -in-law. Then she asked Jane to ride in the car with her and Babe so she could be the person to break the news to her about the upcoming marriage of Maxie and J. D.

Maxie had been at Ma's right hand from the time she was able to understand that Jane was her staunchest supporter on earth. Minnie thought it would be next to impossible for Ma to let Maxie go. Now to lose her to marriage since she never wanted her to leave home or Tennessee for college. Cecelia wanted to ride with her mother to the hospital, so she ran and grabbed Minnie by the hand as they were leaving the café. After all the seating arrangements in the cars were settled, the small caravan took off back to the hospital. When Minnie told her mother of the pending nuptials, she got a pleasant rather shocking surprise. Jane reached toward the sky and said, "Praise Jesus. I sho' couldn'ta picked a finer boy fa her myself." Ma was all smiles. She took a deep breath, looked at Minnie and said, "God sho' is good all the time. Now let's git my boy on to da house away from dem ole doctors...... mmm...hmm."

Jane put her arm around CeeCee, who sat between she and Minnie, and gave her a snug hug. Cecelia tried to pull out of her grandmother's strong grip but to no avail. As Jane released some of the pressure, CeeCee just closed her eyes and rested her head on her grandmother's side. The other children rode over to the hospital with their father. Frank had to pull the car over for a moment to give Celeste and Doyle a stern, mean stare for elbowing one another. Celeste demanded more room on the car seat, and told Doyle to scoot over a little bit. He said he had no more room to scoot, so she elbowed him and he elbowed her back. Arselee told her daddy what was going on in the back seat. Just from the glare in Frank's eyes the children knew to behave, he didn't have to use corporal punishment; they knew when he meant business.

He admonished them that they had better not get down to the hospital showing out, or he would have to show out with them. They all knew what that terminology meant, so they all put on their good children's faces.

Salema and Rico were riding in the front seat looking straight ahead. It seemed they were both strictly focused on seeing William. It almost seemed the two of them were completely oblivious to the discipline that their father was meting out to their siblings seated in the back seat of the car.

Rico was every bit of Frank's true junior, as he was so aptly named. He was very mature for a boy his age. He even emulated his father's style of dress as much as he could. Everyone who knew the family knew that Rico loved William's dirty bath water, and would take a drink of it if the dirty water made him more like his big brother. He shared the same protective instincts for his sisters as William. Just as William was close to Maxie and

Salema. Rico and Arselee had an unbreakable bond. The two of them called each other partners in crime. Rico had learned to box, play the girls, street game, and hunt, all mostly from William.

Although Rico was far more advanced than his peers academically in school, he preferred the knowledge that the streets gave him over book knowledge. William could see this trait in his younger brother and always steered Rico toward doing the right thing and to keep his priorities straight as to what was expected of them by their parents. He was a good positive role model for him to follow in many ways, except for the girls and the streets. William figured his little brother had to learn about what was going on from somebody, so why not teach him the right way himself.

When the family arrived back at the hospital, Frank devised a system for two family members at a time to go up to the room and visit William. Each pair would have a ten- minute time limit on visitation. Everyone else had to wait downstairs in the lobby area. Ethel and Minnie attempted to go first, but Cecelia wouldn't let her mother's hand go, so Frank allowed her to go with Minnie. Rico and Jane would go next. When Ethel and Minnie walked into the room, Dr. Martin and another doctor had William standing on his feet next to the bed. Dr. Martin introduced Minnie and Ethel to Dr. Price, and then both the doctors held William by his hands and allowed him to take a few steps around the room. William was all smiles as he made a small circle around the room before the two doctors helped him get back into the bed. Dr. Martin asked William if he had felt any sharp pains during his short stroll, as he checked his vital signs. William answered that there was only soreness around the area of his incisions, but no sharp pains. Dr. Martin was happy to get this positive reply from his young patient, and told Dr. Price that they could leave him to his visitors. His vital signs were all normal, and starting in the morning, he would supervise a walk down the hall by the nurses for William.

After the doctors left, Ethel started asking what else the doctors had said before they walked in the room. She and Minnie both wanted to know what led the doctors to get William out of bed for a walk. "Dr. Martin had some concerns about blood clots forming. So he thought it would be a good idea for me to start taking short walks to keep the blood circulation flow normal.

CeeCee was standing at the head of the bed next to William. She rubbed her hand on his forehead gently and asked him? "Do you feel better now that I'm here?" William did his best to control the laughter that was built up behind that announcement. Minnie tried to look as serious as possible when she told CeeCee that she had made her brother all better just by visiting him. As Ethel and Minnie began to get comfortable, Rico poked his head in the door, "Daddy said it's our turn to visit." Jane then entered the room and sat on the foot of the bed across from Ethel. CeeCee went straight over to her grandmother and stood next to her and started rubbing William's feet. He told her to stop, that it was tickling him and the laughing made him hurt.

So at that point, Minnie told Ethel that they had to take CeeCee and let Ma and Rico have their visit to themselves. Rico let Jane and William talk for a minute. William could tell he was antsy about something. "Come closer to my bed." Rico had sat down in one of the two chairs in the room. "I prefer staying in the chair." Unable to refrain any further he asked, "How did those guys get the jump on you, and what kind of repercussions are we going to take? You always told me that if someone hurt me bad enough, that the rest of my brothers and sisters would make them pay for it. Now shouldn't we make these fools pay for this?"

William looked at Jane and smiled; she just turned her head as if she couldn't hear their conversation. Ma never interfered in any of her grandchildren's relationships. William spoke slowly in his response to his younger brother, because he did not want him to think that any thing he had taught him before was to now be contradicted. "Well, East, you right, something should be done to those idiots for squirreling me like they did, and I been told that it's being handled by Daddy."

William knew that Rico wouldn't dare question his father about the situation and would now be assured that the re would be repercussions for those cowards. At that point, Rico got out of his seat and walked over to the side of the bed. He looked at William and said, "I sure am glad you're going to be all right, guy." Then Rico told Jane that their time was up and that they had to go back down to the waiting room so that two more could come up and visit. He leaned over and hugged William and walked out of the room.

Jane started laughing and told William, "Now dat is a mannish boy if I ever did see one. All his big words and all....he a real sport, I tell you the truth."

William just shook his head, "Yes ma'am, Ma, I think there was a little old man locked inside of him when he was born."

Then Jane leaned over and hugged William's neck, " Thank the sweet Lawd my boy is gone be just fine." Then she rose up off the side of the bed and slowly started making her way to the door. As she passed Salema and Arselee in the hall, she was singing and praising the Lord. Jane noticed Minnie and Frank standing off to the side talking; the look on their faces suggested the subject must be very serious. Frank had been telling her the details of his meeting with Mr. Moore from earlier that afternoon. He had wanted to wait until this evening when they were alone and things were quiet. Then he thought better of that idea, because deep down inside, he felt Minnie and the rest of the family deserved to hear this news right away. He had just finished telling Minnie as Jane approached.

Minnie couldn't believe what she was hearing. "Well I just declare, its strange how things work out sometime, ain't it, Frank?" She then told Jane that they needed to talk. The two of them sat down and she began to unfold the mystery to Jane. The two young men who had stabbed William were dead. They had been involved in a high- speed chase with the sheriff's department on a road that was narrow, and lost control of their vehicle and hit a tree. They were both killed instantly. It seemed terrible to the two of them that the two families now had to bury their sons.

After everyone had finished their visits to William's room, Minnie and Frank went in and told him what had happened to Leon and Douglas. William looked off to one side, "I'm sorry, but I can't say that I'm sorry for them at all. To me they got just what they had coming."

Frank just told him that he understood how he could feel that way and maybe one day he wouldn't. He told William, "With the help of the Good Lord, you probably gone be coming home soon. Them boys ain't never coming back to their families again." "Daddy, I do feel bad for their families, but they didn't care if I made it or not. In fact, they tried to make sure I didn't make it, as far as I'm concerned. So they just got what they was trying to dish out to me."

Minnie said she felt the same as William, except she hated to see anybody die, but in this case, Douglas and Leon had tried to murder her son. So their untimely demise which was brought on by running from the law and justice, meant that justice was served as far as she was concerned. She told Frank and William that she was only concerned with her son coming home healthy and well.

Ethel was standing in the door of the room and had overheard the entire conversation. Frank and Minnie had their backs to the door and they were blocking William's view so no one ever heard or saw her come in. What had happened to Douglas and Leon was not to be kept from her or anyone else. Minnie and Frank just wanted to talk to William first. Ethel's voice startled everyone. "I agree with everyone. It's because of this tragic act that was committed against my husband that my heart has no mercy, or forgiveness for their families lost." So to her, Douglas and Leon had gotten what they both had coming to them. Ethel said she was staying at the hospital until they let her husband come home.

So as Minnie and Frank were leaving, Minnie agreed to continue bringing her fresh clothes and her hygienic she needed for her daily ablutions every morning for the next couple of days. When Minnie explained to the rest of the family what had happened to Leon and Douglas. Rico just smiled. "All right.... yes. You mean Daddy got the police to kill them fools. Now that's playing it smart, Mama."

Minnie looked at him as if he had gone crazy. "Boy, what in the world are you talking about? Where did you get a fool notion like that from?"

"William told me during my visit that Daddy was going to handle taking care of these cowards, and by the way things turned out, it looks like he did a great job."

Minnie could not believe her ears. How could her teenage son be so cold and callous about the death of any human being? She grabbed Rico by his collar and pulled him close to her face. Minnie was getting angry and she could feel herself wanting to choke some sense into his head. She told him in a low mean tone, "Your daddy didn't set nobody up to be killed by the sheriff or nobody else, you thick mule- headed boy. Have you lost your mind?"

"Mama, I'm sorry, I was just going by what William said," Rico managed to squeeze out humbly.

"Rico, them boys had a mamas and daddies and families that loved and is going to miss them too. Now they probably got what they had coming tothem, but we ain't gone celebrate nobody's death in this family. You understand me, mister?"

Rico hurried a "Yes ma'am, Mama." Minnie and Frank were almost the last two people able to intimidate and get this type of response from their son. The rest of the family had sat waiting, all with bated breath until Minnie let Rico's collar go. "Sit your mannish tail down and hush your mouth." Any of the other children would have at least been a little bit embarrassed or had tears in the corner of their eyes. Not Rico; he didn't care what anyone including his parents thought of him. He was a strong character to say the least for a fifteen- year- old. After the short meeting was over, Jane let Minnie know that Rico was telling her the truth. That William had told him the story about his father to keep Rico from trying to go out and get revenge on the boys himself. Minnie listened and did not give any reply to her mother or feel any remorse about chastising Rico.

Minnie did take him with her to visit William the next day, and the three of them talked about the revenge to be taken when they are attacked by outsiders. As she and Rico were leaving, Dr. Martin was standing near the nurses' station. He asked Minnie if he could to talk to her about releasing William to go home in the morning. She said, "W hy sure, I haven't had no better news in a good little spell, Doctor."

Dr. Martin said if things continued to go well today that there was no reason for William not to be able to go home tomorrow. Then the doctor turned and asked Minnie, "Who is this handsome, well- dressed young man?

Does your husband know about him, Ms. Minnie?" Minnie could see in Rico's eyes that Dr. Martin was making a powerful impression upon him. "This is my son Rico, Frank Jr., he's going to become a future leader in Chattanooga one day." Rico loved the way his mother introduced him to the doctor. He liked the power and self- confidence that seemed to simply exude from Dr. Martin. This was a very important moment, and Minnie was not about to waste it. She let Rico know that he could be in a position of leadership one day, and she fully expected him to get there.

After a firm hand shake and cordial greetings between the two, Dr. Martin asked, "What fields of interest do you plan to endeavor?" Rico replied, "to become the owner of as much property and real estate as I can. Then start a new insurance company for colored folks to buy life insurance policies that pay larger death benefits than those presently available." Dr. Martin turned and asked Minnie, " How old is this young man and how does he do in school?" Minnie smiled and told the doctor that her son had just turned fifteen in August and that he was a great student. Dr. Martin went on to say, "Well, I hope you've got ten more like him at home, honey bunch, 'cause he's got some very bright ideas already. Keep up the good work in school, young man, and one day you'll more than likely have all the things you want. There is nothing that can stop you from reaching your goals except yourself from a lack of effort. So tomorrow is the big day for Mister William to go home and you can have your older brother back." Dr. Martin told Rico that it was very nice to meet a young man with his aspirations, and agreed to meet Minnie in the morning to sign William's release papers.

Why Minnie to sign the papers when William has a wife?

CHAPTER XI

On the ride home, Minnie noticed that Rico had his chest poked out a little farther than he usually kept it. So she knew his self- esteem was at an all-time high and she planned to keep it that way as long as he could begin to show just a little more humility. She began a conversation about selling insurance by asking if she could become an investor in his company when he started it. "I am still trying to figure out the profit margin and if enough people would be interested in buying better benefits." Minnie couldn't help but smile; she barely kept herself from laughing aloud. Her entire attitude changed about the subject as she stopped in front of the house.

Minnie turned to look at her son, she saw the intense focus and fire in his eyes. "Was he really serious about this matter or just being Rico?" she thought to herself. She decided to change the subject. "So how do you feel about being a part of your sister's wedding?"

"You know, I guess I'm kind of excited about it. If this J.D. makes my sister happy then I'll be happy for her. You know mama this is a first isn't it?"

"What?" "This, us spending time alone. I'll always remember today, the visit to the hospital was pleasant, and I really liked Dr. Martin. But now mama can I go visit a friend for awhile?"

After a nice hug she told him yes, but not to stay gone too long, because supper was already on the table. As he walked away, she stood there looking after him in amazement; he was so mature for a boy his age. She stood there thinking to herself as he disappeared around the corner and out of sight.

Minnie started up the small walk way to the front porch stoop, when Maxie and J. D. pulled up to the front of the house. Minnie spoke to J.D. before he even got out of the car. "I'm fine, Ms. Minnie, how about yourself and the rest of the family?"

"Well, J.D., I'm fine and it look like everybody else is fine too. Dr. Martin said it look like he might let William come home in the morning if things go all right tonight."

"God is good all the time, ain't he, Ms. Minnie?" J.D. said to her, smiling.

"Yes sir, he is. I know he done brought us a long way. We sure couldn't have made it this far without the Lord. Where in creation the two of you coming from anyway?"

Maxie was standing next to her fiancé smiling as he spoke to her mother; now she answered swiftly. "We were at Uncle Johnny's farm helping him a little bit and telling him all about our wedding. Mama, did you know Uncle Johnny been at that hospital before day every mornin to see William?"

"Child, that don't surprise me none, you know how crazy Johnny is bout that boy." Minnie continued her analysis, "I hate to admit it, but besides his brothers, William might be the one person Johnny loves most on this earth. And sometime I wonder how lonely he must get being out there on that farm all this time all alone without a woman or a wife and children of his own. I always ask him and he always says his work for us is his woman, and that all of you is his children. We take for granted all he does for us year in and year out; he been there making it so much easier for us to get along. After the wedding we gone give him a big party and say thank you, knuckle head. He won't take money from me or Frank. Even if I bring the subject up, he has a temper tantrum like a little child. Johnny don't even know he gets a check from the café every year in the bank. Maxie, why are we standing out here in the streets discussing our business? Let's go in the house and eat supper. Some of these old nosy folk might be gettin an ear full of our family business. You know what I say bout these folks round here. You don't have to put your business in the street, just put it on the curb, and these nosy Negroes will kick it in the streets for you."

J.D. had never heard that analogy and thought it was both hilariously funny and brutally honest. He was still laughing as they entered the living room of the house, and fell down on a chair. Maxie promptly grabbed him by the arm, and gave him a lift out of the chair. She knew her mother didn't like anyone flopping down on her furniture. J.D. was on her mother's good side and she intended to keep him there.

The three of them had supper together and made lots of wedding plans. J. D. said he wanted his mother to help plan some of the wedding and Minnie agreed. Maxie said she would ask Jeanna if she wanted to be involved in the planning process for the wedding. Tentatively, they had agreed to hold the wedding at Thomas's church and use family members exclusively as part of the small, traditional ceremony. J.D. wanted to know about a couple of his best friends being ushers. So everybody agreed to ask Jeanna to have lunch with them tomorrow after William was settled in at home to discuss the wedding. They had two weeks to make the wedding come off the way Maxie had dreamed. J.D. and Minnie were determined to make it happen.

Arselee and Celeste had (finish) cleaning the kitchen and asked if they could go sit out on the front porch stoop until the street lights came on. This is where they always entertained their friends in the evening after supper. Minnie was agreeable with that as long as all their chores were finished.

The girls wanted to tell their friends all about the upcoming wedding plans that they had just listened in on. Salema was already sitting on the stoop with a couple of her girl friends and Lloyd. Bernice and her sister Beaula had stopped over to visit Salema as well; they were two of her closest girlfriends. As a matter of fact, Beaula may have been the very first child who ever introduced herself to Salema the very first day she went to a public school.

Arselee wanted to know who Maxie had chosen as her maid of honor; she figured Salema had that assignment nailed down. As the discussion heated up among the girls, Rico stepped around the corner with three of his friends. Parnell, who is one of William's and Rico's oldest friend had just returned home from a tour in the United States Navy. And Parnell had brought a friend home from the navy named Commo Berryhill who had been discharged at the same time as he had..

Salema noticed that Parnell and Rico called him by his nick name, Berry, as they conversed. The other boy who was with them was Rico's partner and closest friend, Billy Russell.

The young ex-sailor in town couldn't keep his eyes off Salema all night long. It seems Berry was enthralled from the moment he laid eyes on her.

Salema too, for the first time in her life was feeling the very same way about him as he was feeling about her from the very start.

Usually young men had to pursue Salema for some time before she showed any interest at all, but something was very different this time around with Berry. It took Steve six months to get a date, but this was not the case with Berry. After an introduction and some small talk about his adventures in the military, he let her know he was attracted to her. "I mean no disrespect, I just couldn't help myself. For the first time in my life I don't feel shy talking to a young lady. So it's got to be you cause something just compelled me to let you know how I felt." As soon as he asked if it was possible to see her again, she agreed without hesitation.

All the other people seemed to have vanished from sight as they were talking or it might have seemed that way to Salema. During their time together in the navy, Parnell and the other sailors used to tease Berry about being shy with girls. The little personal conversation Salema and Berry had seemed to last for only a short while before Celeste rudely interjected herself into their conversation. "Where you from?" Berry answered, "New Orleans Louisiana" Celeste then bombarded Berry with a whole line of questions about the lifestyle in the Crescent City. She wanted to know how much partying went on down there. Was the water dirty? What kind of food did they like to eat? How many French people lived there? Berry was very patient, answering each question that she posed to him to the best of his ability. He really didn't know how many French people lived in New Orleans. But he told her that the French people had a great influence on the culture of the city and the state of Louisiana. Her final question was what kind of sports they liked to play and if Berry could play any kind of sport. "Because ahh, you know everybody in the Whatley and Foster family can play almost every sport good," she boasted. "We run track, box, play baseball, football, and I know we are the best roller skaters around here. Every Saturday night is roller skating night for the colored kids in Chattanooga and we skate faster and better every week. Man, we play everything," she went on to say rather cocky and confidently.

Berry told her they liked to play baseball mostly, and that he loved the game himself. "I never liked to brag on myself but most people say I'm pretty fair when it comes to pitching a baseball. Some people even told me to tryout for one the Negro Leagues."

Salema then took the opportunity to reclaim control of the conversation by inviting Berry to play a game of softball and go skating with them sometime.

Then she offered him an invitation to the wedding and reception. Berry gladly accepted both offers. Berry's acceptance raised Salema's anxiety level to the point where she couldn't wait until Maxie's wedding day had arrived.. She really liked Berry's humility and confidence in himself, plus he was really a good looking fella, she kept thinking to herself. Before the conversation could continue, Minnie was at the door, beckoning all the children inside for the night. Salema said a very discreet good night to Berry and everyone else, and the Whatley clan was forcibly retired for the evening.

Parnell teased Berry all the way home, telling him he was whipped before he had even smelled the draws. All Berry could do was laugh because he knew his nose was so far open that a freight train could have ran through it. He kept saying, "P," (his nickname he called Parnell), "this is the one, boy... I'm telling you. I can feel it in these bones, man."

The two of them then agreed to conspire to make Salema and Berry a couple. Initially, Berry would pretend he couldn't roller skate and would need some lessons from Salema. Then he would monopolize all of her free time with movies and skating. They went so far as to devising a six-month-to- the- altar plan, but first Berry wanted to find a job. He also wanted to go home and tell his family that he was moving to Chattanooga, permanently. Berry had saved a nice little nest egg for himself from his military salary.

He had enough capital to get himself a place of his own and sustain it for at least a year.

The days that led up to the wedding seemed to fly by. Salema had not seen Parnell or Berry since the night she met him. She had heard through gossip that they had traveled to New Orleans to visit Berry's family together, and would be back in town in time for the wedding. Salema was a little worried at first that Berry might not come back, but she was reassured that he had left word that he was coming back to town. Berry also left word with Parnell's sister that the only reason he was coming back is for Salema. But she had another problem to deal with first.

Frank wanted to talk to her about her pregnancy. The two of them had not had time to discuss the matter, since events with William had transpired so fast. Frank told her that after William was settled in, he wanted to have a word with her about her future. Salema trembled with fear at the thought of having to talk to her father about this life-altering subject. But she knew the time had come to face the repercussions of whatever course of action her father was going to take.

Salema had predetermined that she would tell her father that she was prepared to take care of her baby by herself. That she was prepared to quit school and get a job to support the two of them, if need be. The only problem with Salema's plan is she never would need it. Frank had already made up his mind that the family would do everything that they could to be supportive of her.

When the two of them finally sat down after William's arrival home, Frank without hesitation let Salema know he was disappointed that things had turned out this way. "I learned a long time ago that babies come when they want to, not always when we want them. And you're not ready to raise a young'un on your own, not yet. I'll never turn my back on one of my children. Was I angry? Yes, of course, I think any father would have been, but this situation with William has shown me how precious life is. Don't get me wrong I think you are much too young to be having a baby. On the bright side of it all; she'll be our little family blessing." Frank went on to say with a big smile on his face, "My first grandchild, and I'm going to spoil her rotten." Salema was so relieved the way their conversation turned out.

Before her father left the room after hugging her, he told her that he loved her very much and to keep her head up and not listen to the nasty things that some neighbors might have to say about her being pregnant without being married.

She really didn't know how to respond to his acceptance of the situation because she had only prepared for the worst. Frank lifted her head from his shoulder and looked her in the eyes and said, "Let this be the last time something like this happens to you. You understand me, little woman? And you gone finish school on time, and you better not let this pregnancy make you miss a day of school. Those are my rules and don't break 'em. If the baby is a girl, I want you to name her Gwendolyn for me, you hear. I don't know a name for a boy yet, except I don't want no more Franks or Williams, and that's for sure."

Salema smiled at him and answered simply, "All right, Daddy, anything you say. Thank you so much for not being so mad at me. And for not talking to me nasty and mean about this, Daddy. I didn't mean for this to happen to me right now and I'm sorry."

"Don't be sorry, Salema, it's a blessing. Just don't let us be blessed again until you be married, understand me, young lady?"

"Yes sir, Daddy." Ethel called for Daddy Frank from the living room; she didn't know he was talking with Salema at the time. She wanted his help getting William to the restroom. Dr. Martin told them that using the toilet would be the only area of concern that William might need some help with when he gave the home care instructions. This was his standard procedure for his patients, before he released them after trauma surgery. He was one of the few physicians around who showed this form of bedside manner and care. Frank hurried into the living room, mistakenly thinking something had happened to William. Ethel laughed to herself, because she could see the tightening around Frank's eyes as he entered the room. He always looked so mean to her as if he was fiercely concentrating to discern every detail of everything he ever looked at, even after Ethel reassured him that she only needed help getting her husband to the restroom.

Frank never smiled; he just did his usual teeth grinding that showed the bones extending on both sides of his slim face at the jaw bone, and a nostril sniffle. William had very little trouble using the restroom, and joked that he would be able to go like a grown man with no assistance by tomorrow. Ethel had cooked enough breakfast for the entire family, when she had intended on fixing just enough for William but thought about everyone smelling food and not seeing any when they woke up. So she cooked a big breakfast just like Ma and Minnie normally did. Jane just sat and watched from her rocker, taking advantage of an opportunity to have a meal cooked for her for a change.

Minnie had stopped at the café early for a change, since they released William before eight that morning, much earlier than she had expected. This happened because his family showed up at six- thirty A.M. again much earlier than usual. So Dr. Martin took advantage of the opportunity to get the release out of the way for the staff and himself. This afforded the staff the ability to get the tedious paper work done as soon as the first shift day started. The hospital bill had mysteriously been pre paid, so the family did not have to come up with one red cent to cover costs for William's stay. The conversation Mr. Moore had with the hospitals administrator the night of the stabbing had taken care of medical costs.

When Minnie walked in the café, Tom lit up like it was the Fourth of July. "Girl, it looks like you got your bounce back in your little step this morning …huh, Ms. Minnie?" Tom chided as he spoke.

"I guess if you say so, Mr. Tom, but I do have to say God is good all the time."

Emma followed closely by remarking, "Ain't that the truth. Oh...by the way have you heard the rumor going around town about Willie trying to go with Louise behind her husband and Babe's back?" Minnie gave the gossip a closer- than- usual listen this morning because she had her own apprehensions about Willie and his loyalty to Babe. She still offered no comment and went on with business as usual. The information was stored for future reference in case she felt Babe might need the family's assistance in any way.

Minnie jumped right in with Emma, Tom, and the rest of the crew and immersed herself in her work. The afternoon flew by and the work never seemed easier for Minnie ; she needed to be here away from all the stresses of home today more so than she had in a long time. The café stayed busy and her mind stayed off of everything going on at home.

The rest of the week went by just like that, rather uneventful, leading up to the wedding. All the plans were now in place and all they were waiting on was arrival time at the church. All the children asked for and received permission to go skating Saturday night, the traditional night that all the colored children in town went to the rink. Salema had asked to go Friday night with Lloyd and some of her girlfriends; for the first time ever, they wanted to go on Friday because one of their friends was a white girl named

Susan who had invited them to go with her. The only problem was, they did not know that an unspoken never- enforced policy existed at the skating rink.

Star Light Skate Rink was owned by Mr. John Corynth, and did not allow interracial skating. Corynth's son, John Jr., managed and ran the rink when he was home from college on weekends. He was known as a real blue blood, high society red neck. What John Corynth didn't know was that John Jr. wasn't as squeaky clean as Daddy thought him to be. He had manyskeletons in his closet that some of his peers had let slip out to a chosen few females, among whom Salema's friend Susan happened to be one.

Susan had confided in Salema a long time ago that she knew for a fact that John Jr. and his friends sold large amounts of hemp at home and at school. Salema called it "devil in the bush," the name she had heard Minnieuse for the herb some young people liked to smoke. No one had ever tried to mix races at the rink before; the colored children automatically knew to come to the rink on Saturday nights.

So when the group of friends showed up all giddy and pumped up from all the conversation they had on the walk to the rink, they received the shock of their young lives. Salema and Lloyd were in front of the group when they arrived at the door of the rink. Salema made sure that Parnell heard about the planned skating event; she invited him and Berry, who had just got back in town. They were right behind Salema and Lloyd with Susan standing with them. They were told by John Jr., who had about ten of his friends standing at the door with him. "You know blacks is only allowed to skate on Saturday nights and don't bring a white girl with you even then."

"We got the money to pay tonight and it don't matter if my friend is colored or white, we can skate together if we want to," Salema replied.

"Oh...I see, you one of them little uppity Whatley niggers ain't you, girl?" John Jr. shot back at Salema in a haughty tone with his bird chest poked out displaying a false sense of bravado for the eyes and a steel cold racist tone for the listening pleasure of his assembled crew. "Now, before you answer me, you listen here: Your nigger money ain't no good here until Saturday, you hear now? Come back on nigger night, rich little nigger girl."

Berry spoke up, "You need to watch your mouth and don't let another nigger come out of it or I'm gone shut it for you." John Jr. laughed, Just like a colored boy, get mad and resort to violence."

Lloyd said, "Come on, y'all, let's get away from here and tell Ms. Minnie how we being treated up here by this white boy."

"That's right," John Jr. yelled as they turned and walked away, "go tell your rich nigger mammy." He and his friends were all laughing loud and yelling

"Nigger money is for nigger night"" A few of them started yelling that Susan was a nigger lover, but she just shook her head and ignored them.

Luckily for Susan, this event didn't carry over to her high school the next week. Salema knew it would not only carry over to school, but that Minnie and Frank were going to be incensed when they heard how they were treated. She was absolutely right. Lloyd broke the whole story to the two of them on the front porch. After Frank calmed Minnie down from her initial hot-tempered reaction to the event and was able to stop her from going to the skating rink at that very moment. He told her, "Maybe we should go inside and discuss the matter in private. Between the two of us we should be able to devise a plan."

After they got inside, Frank hugged Minnie and said, "Hey, mama, you been through a lot in the last month, and tomorrow we have a child getting married. We don't need to see the Sheriff tonight or have no drama with Mr. Corynth. We'll deal with him and his son another day another way. Let me see how Mr. Moore feels about this situation Monday, and then we can come up with our plan for what happened tonight. But we ain't gone let nothing interfere with Maxie's wedding day."

Minnie smiled, "Well sir, you right, Daddy. Let's just enjoy this day and thank the Good Lord above we still all together." As she was slipping out of his arms, she said in a low tone, "I still want that smart mouth ass boy and his daddy taught a lesson about nigger night."

Frank just laughed and changed the subject. "I brought the last of the wedding dresses from Mrs. Rosa's house on my way home this evening, did you see them yet, mama?"

"Frank, I ain't had no time to see nothing this evening and you know it. I was just getting in the door good when them young'uns come runnin up on the porch talkin about that foolishness at that skating rink. Where did you put them?"

Frank went into the closet and pulled the beautiful lavender colored dresses out so Minnie could get her first look at the design she and Maxie had created. They were stunning, to say the least, she thought to herself as Frank watched from across the room as she admired the finished product. Mrs. Rosa Duvall and the ladies in the quilt club had volunteered to make all the dresses on short notice for this wedding because all the girls in the wedding party, including and especially Maxie, were all either family members or like family to them. They did a spectacular job on the wedding gown; it rivaled any thing sold in the fanciest stores uptown. The children were all getting in the house for the night and Minnie didn't want the girls sneaking to get a look at their dresses, so she called them in to see them. She knew if any one got dirt on one of them, she would half kill them, so it was better to let them look at them in a controlled environment. CeeCee was very impressed with her little gown; so was Arselee. Celeste wanted to try hers on right then. But that idea was quickly dismissed by Minnie. Salema just stood back, watching everyone and smiling to herself. She was daydreaming of her own wedding day, envisioning the day when it would be her turn to walk down the aisle as a bride. Little did she know that outside powers were at work to bring about that day sooner than she ever dreamed possible.

That night before Maxie's big day was spent preparing the church by Frank, Thomas, Minnie, and Olivia. The two couples worked feverishly and deep into the night transforming the church into a floral paradise of white lilies. Lilies had always been Maxie's favorite flower. The funny thing about the two couples working together to prepare the church was they seemed to get the work done in near total silence. But it wasn't an uncomfortable silence; they were just all too busy working too engage in much conversation with each other. They finished with the beautiful floral decor in time to get about six hours of sleep before they would have to be right back for the wedding ceremony.

The next morning after breakfast, the house was a mad house, with everyone trying to get ready for the wedding at one time. Frank had to stop the circus and organize the house by gender in different sections of the house. Minnie, Jane, Ethel and the girls had the rear and he, William and the boys had the front. After that, it took only about thirty minutes and everyone was ready for the trip to the church. The family looked awesome.

Pastor Black had accepted with honor the invitation to perform the ceremony at Rev. Thomas Foster's church, an unprecedented act, since they had never stepped foot in each other's church before today. Not that they'd ever had a personal problem with each other; they just had the two biggest congregations in the city that stood on opposite sides of town, competing for parishioners.

Minnie and the girls helped Maxie get dressed last. She looked gorgeous when she stepped out to take the short ride to the church. Her hair, already naturally wavy, was styled to perfection for her day of wedding bliss. The church was packed to capacity with family and friends when they arrived at ten fifty that morning for the short ceremony. J.D. and Maxie wanted the nuptials over early so the families could have all day to party.

Freddie and Sophie Lucas, J.D.'s grandparents had made the special trip up from Selma, Alabama. J.D. could do no wrong in their eyes, especially his grandfather's. When Maxie and Thomas started down the aisle of the church J.D. stood there proudly with a big grin on his face. He was as proud as a game rooster, waiting for his bride to be standing at his side. Pastor Black asked, "Who gives this woman to be married?"

Thomas answered loud and clear, "I do." With that he released her arm into J.D.s for the rest of the couple's earthly lives together. After they exchanged traditional vows, J.D. was ordered by Rev. Black to kiss his new bride. His hands trembled ever so slightly as he pulled back her veil and kissed Mrs. J.D. Mayes for the very first time. Minnie and Jeanna and Thomas and Frank all had tears in their eyes as the couple ran down the aisle out the church to the car waiting outside to take them over to the café for the reception.

It had been a lovely wedding, and as everyone filed out of the church, the sun was shining bright from behind a big white pillow like cumulus cloud. The weather was optimal for an outdoor picnic or a wedding reception. Frank told Minnie that he would ride from the church to the café with Mr. Moore. So he gave her his car keys so she could drive some of the children over with her. Uncle Johnny had already taken Rico and Doyle with him. Minnie knew that Frank probably wanted to discuss the issue about John Corynth with Mr. Moore. Frank did just that, and once again Mr. Moore had just the right recipe for how to deal with the situation.

Mr. Moore told Frank that he owned another huge building that was empty; it was of a double size that encompassed both the 218 and 219 Ninth Street addresses. Now together, Mr. Moore and Frank would devise a plan to turn that building into a skating rink for all the children of Chattanooga, and take the entire market completely away from Corynth. They would punish him by taking all the money out of his pocket. Frank loved the idea. He and his engineering friends could install a floor ten times better than the one Corynth had in his rink. Mr. Moore agreed that if Frank did the renovations the building needed, they would be fifty-fifty partners in the proposed venture. "I want the name of our new rink to be called the Aurora because the light that shines from it on grand opening will be blinding to the existence of the Star Light. And just maybe a lightning bolt of wisdom might strike that ole fool Corynth that after this business defeat he'll come to see that it's the dawn of a new day for the way business is going to be conducted in Chattanooga, Tennessee. One thing for sure, he's gone get the meaning of Orland Moore's word; my people are under my umbrella of protection and Frank it seems he just refuses to recognize that." They stared at each other shaking their heads, grinning. After a farewell and a handshake Frank departed.

CHAPTER XII

Frank already knew he could get all the hard wood timber he would need from Johnny's farm. All he needed to do was convince some friends to invest some precious spare time to design a floor for the kids to skate on that was better and more modern than what Corynth had at the Star Light.

When Minnie and Jane entered the back door of the café, Louise Roberts told Minnie that Emma needed to see her as soon as possible. Minnie asked Louise if everything was all right with the café and the reception. Louise assured her that things were fine as far as those things were concerned.

Minnie headed straight to the big kitchen to see what was going on. When she walked in, she saw Emma sitting and talking with a young white girl. The young lady had a boy with her whom Minnie assumed to be her son. The child appeared to be about ten or eleven years old. Both of them were dressed rather modest, but neat.

Emma handed Minnie a letter that the young lady had shown her. It was old and the writing on it had faded a little, but Minnie could still make out the words, which were very touching. The letter had been written to the young lady by her sister during the Depression years. It spoke of a kind young colored lady who had fed and helped her with work during the worst days in the early part of the Depression.

The young lady's name was Lori; her son's name was Robert. She had escaped from an abusive spouse. Alone and with her son she had no immediate trustworthy or extended family to turn to and no place else to go. The grip of fear that she escaped made her not trust her dearest confidant with even a slight hint of her impending flight from her doomed marriage. Lori had not heard from her sister since the Depression; they had run away from an abusive father back then and were separated by early forced marriages that took them out of their father's home. She had only the thin hope that her sister had held on and stayed put in Chattanooga.

The name of the café was the only name Lori had besides Ms. Minnie's to look for her sister. "I'm so sorry ma'am to be interrupting your reception... but as you see that's how life's been for me, the wrong time. On top of everything else its my son's birthday and I don't have a pluck nickle and don't even speak of a gift...to give...him." She began to sob uncontrollably.

Lori hated showing up there like that, but she had been at her wits' end with her husband Jim. He was a drunken bar brawler who beat her incessantly after his weekly Friday night binges. His paydays only meant that he would bring home the bruises, not the bacon for his family. When the abuse spread to Robert; she had to draw the line at that point and get out by any means available.

Minnie was deeply touched by what had happened to this pretty young girl and her son. Lori was a stunningly beautiful young lady with long blonde hair and deep blue eyes that looked like the Caribbean waters south of Florida. Minnie gave Emma instructions to feed Lori and her son as much as they could eat. Then she said, "Honey, you ain't got to worry about finding no place to get away from that low down old man of yours. I'm gone help you and your boy. Are you sleepy, sweet heart?"

Lori couldn't help but tell the truth. She was dead tired and it showed on her face. "Yes ma'am, I'm bushed," she answered.

Minnie told her that she would go upstairs and prepare a private little room that she only used for special occasions. Minnie stored a cot that only she and Frank knew about back there in a closet. Minnie and Frank used the cot for their monthly private romantic dinner at the café alone after closing hours that usually ended with hot sex. Now the cot's existence was exposed to the crew. Minnie just said she had fallen asleep at her desk too many nights and had put it in the back room if she needed a nap ever now and then. Then she walked off to rejoin the wedding party.

She had Lori all set up and left instructions for Emma to bake Robert a birthday cake quietly so that Lori didn't know. Then she told Tom to go buy him some new roller skates in the size it looked like the boy might wear. Tom loved the idea and went right up town to the store to buy Robert's gift.

Doyle and Robert hit it off immediately; the two became inseparable as soon as they met. Doyle had walked back to the kitchen with his mother. He and Robert started talking as soon as he walked into the room. Doyle's speech impediment seemed none existent to Robert; he understood every word Doyle enunciated clearly. The two boys rode with Tom to the store.

When Minnie got back to the reception, Maxie and J.D. were just arriving. They had not even begun to dance the traditional first dance together. J.D. was lit up around the eyes; he looked so happy today, and so did Maxie,

Minnie thought to herself as she watched them enter the huge room together. They made a handsome couple. And all of her daughters were breath taking in their gowns, so she knew that she and Frank had their hands full trying to get them to the altar before the boys got to them first.

The room was filled with family and friends having nothing but fun. Frank sneaked in behind Minnie and peered over her shoulder to see what she was looking at. He could tell from her focus and smile she was looking at their children, so he whispered in her ear, "Them some fine young'uns, ain't they, big mama?" Minnie nearly jumped out of her skin but Frank's strong hands held her steady.

Mr. Moore eased his way over and asked if he could dance with Minnie, and Frank said, "I don't see why not, unless the lady don't want to." "It will be a delight Mr. Moore. I hope you can keep up. I've been known to cut a rug or two in my day." "Well it looks like I'm gone have to put them words to the test. Let's go madam."

J.D. and Maxie were finishing the first dance when Minnie and Mr. Moore started dancing all around the room. The children were staring in amazement at their mother. They had never seen her dance with anyone besides their father and never this close with another man, let alone a white man. But they danced so good together that after a couple of minutes, none of that silly stuff seemed to matter. Soon the entire floor was full of couples dancing. Before the children knew anything, they were all dancing with their friends. Minnie took the opportunity to thank Mr. Moore for taking care of William's hospital expenses. "I truly want to let you know how much I appreciate everything you've done for my family, Mr. Moore."

"Ah, we do what we can. Today we party and forget yesterday, better days are ahead for us, Ms. Minnie," Mr. Moore said in a vain attempt at modesty.

Salema and Berry spent the entire day exclusively together. Maxie and J.D. stopped the music to cut their wedding cake. Uncle Johnny gave a toast to the newlyweds and J.D. smashed cake all over his and his new bride's face and clothes. Now the bride and groom had to go change clothes. Just what J.D. wanted , to get Maxie out of her clothes and alone for the first time as his wife.

Jeanna really liked the toast that Johnny presented to the happy new couple. It entailed his vision for a very safe, productive future filled with lots of children and happiness. After Johnny finished, he asked the groom's mother for a dance. She hesitantly accepted but seemed to genuinely enjoy his attention during the rest of the reception.

William and Ethel were trying to do a little dancing, but he couldn't stand around long enough to finish a song after the cake cutting was done. So she put him back in the big chair that they had brought from home and had set up especially for him to sit in. "King William," Ethel kept teasing him. Of course, the same group of females who tried to stir up trouble from the beginning of their marriage were all there still lurking in the wings for one slip from Ethel. They had to show love and support for the king too.

In the mean time, Tom had returned from the store. It hadn't seemed like it, but he and the boys had been gone for over an hour and a half. Tom had gone mad buying things for Robert. Tom bought him two pairs of shoes, pants, shirts, and new socks and underwear. Tom used Robert to fit the clothes even though he had no idea all these things were for him. Tom had played a game on him by fitting Doyle out as well. Doyle asked Robert to come upstairs to the reception, but Tom told him that Robert couldn't come with him. So Doyle went and asked his mother to let him go home and change clothes so that he could play with Robert.

Minnie had never seen Doyle so excited to play with another child before. So she took a break from the festivities and took Doyle home and got him into a change of clothes. She also brought the other children a change of clothes.

It took her and Doyle about half an hour all together to assemble everyone's apparel. She listened as Doyle told her about the trip to the store with Tom, whom he loved dearly. He told her how many clothes and shoes Tom bought Robert. Minnie thought how happy it must have made Tom to be able to spend some money on a child. Minnie knew that Tom wanted children of his own, he just didn't want to do what it took to get them. So this was right up his alley; after all, he didn't have anything else to spend his money on besides his dad and himself.

Doyle said he really liked Robert; "Robert special like me," he told Minnie. Minnie couldn't see where Robert had any visual handicap, so she wondered if he could see something she couldn't. Her concerns were not all misplaced and were mostly borne from a mother's protective instincts, especially when it came to Doyle. This was his very first external relationship of any significant meaning, and because of his speech impediment, she wanted things to go well for him. Doyle kept smiling to himself on the ride back to the café. Minnie could only wonder if Robert was all he could think about. She didn't dare to interrupt his thoughts at this time, so she just let him have his space.

She did give him a temporary diversion when they pulled back up to the café. He was to tell all his brothers and sisters that they each had a change of clothes waiting for them in the car. So he burst into the reception room looking for his sibling wide- eyed and in a huff. He looked for Celeste first; he knew if he told her, he had in effect told everyone. He spotted her immediately and gave her the news. Celeste was happy because she couldn't wait to get out of her gown. Doyle spread the news to his siblings of the fresh change of clothes so fast that one could say, 'before a room could turn dark after the flick of a light switch,' Doyle was on his way back down to the kitchen for more fun and play with Robert.

Doyle showed Robert all the places where they played near the café, and Robert liked the railroad tracks the best. It was where he and all his old friends played a game called 'chicken' back home in Texas. Robert and his friends would let the train get real close to them, as close as possible, then run across the track just ahead of the passing train. It was a very foolish and dangerous game for little boys to be playing, but Doyle loved it immediately.

The sense of danger he felt gave him a never-experienced rush of adrenaline that excited him like nothing ever had before. Babe and Willie were waiting at the crossing in their car on their way to the reception after changing clothes from the wedding ceremony. They were both looking on in shock and horror as they watched Doyle play this insipid new game. Doyle looked up in stark fear as he ran directly toward Babe's horrified face behind her car's windshield. He was trying to hit the brakes and change directions at the same time, but he knew it was too late to turn and make it back across the tracks. More importantly, Babe had already seen his dumb and potentially life- costing mistake.

Babe leaped out of the car, she was trembling, she was so angry with Doyle. He had damn near scared the life out of her. She ran over to a tree that was next to the tracks and tore off three long thin young limbs to use as switches. She then grabbed Doyle and put him on both knees. Babe put his head between her legs and whipped his behind until the entire hundred- and- fifty- car train had passed by.

As the train cleared, all Robert could see as he ran across the tracks, laughing at first, was Doyle's rear end turned up, getting a blistering from Babe. He immediately stopped laughing. After Babe had finished tanning his backside, she asked, "Who is this boy Doyle?" He was currently unable to speak. "What's your name boy? Did you have something to do with what Doyle just did?" Robert stood there wide eyed and frozen with fear. It took

Doyle a few minutes, but he finally got Babe to understand what had just transpired at the rail crossing and who Robert was. Babe literally threw both the boys in the back seat of her car and headed to the café. She was livid with them for being so reckless with their young lives. Babe was also astounded at the influence that Robert seemed to have over Doyle. He had always been such an introverted recluse, she had thought; now this new boy had him running in front of trains. Doyle looked completely petrified as they all got out of the car at the café; he tried in vain to beg Babe not to tell Minnie and Frank about what he had done. But he knew his begging was to no avail; he was doomed to one maybe two more whippings, and that was all there was to it. Babe did agree to wait until after the reception was over to tell Minnie about what had happened, and this only served to prolong the boys' agony.

Now they had to anticipate the punishment all day, and that was a source of great mental anguish for both of them — especially for Robert, because he didn't want to be the cause of him and his mom getting kicked out in the streets because he played some silly game. He knew they had no money and no place else to turn if Ms. Minnie got mad at him and told them she no longer wanted to help them with their present life- altering quagmire.

So young Robert spent the majority of his eleventh birthday in mental anguish. When Babe and Willie walked in, J.D. and his sister Brandy and her husband Curtis were all dancing around Maxie in a circle, laughing and having a blast. The reception was going too beautifully to give anybody any disparaging news about anything anyway, Babe kept telling herself as she approached Minnie standing with Frank.

They all greeted each other and because of the enormity of the event, today's greeting was accompanied with hugs from everyone. Only Babe could see that the hug Willie received from Minnie was a little cool. She wondered what was bothering Minnie about him. Maybe Minnie finally had the confirmation she needed and could see how unhappy Babe had been shortly after Willie's arrival ten years ago.

Babe was planning to tell her that Willie was becoming increasingly more abusive both verbally and physically to her and that she wanted help getting him out of her life. But too many other negative things had been happening to Minnie, and Babe didn't want to add her burdens on Minnie and Frank. She had tried to handle things on her own, but now, they were getting too bad. She'd had enough of Willie hitting her and taking her money for his gambling habit. Babe had tried fighting back, but the attacks became increasingly more violent and Willie was much stronger than she was physically. So Willie always won and bullied whatever he wanted away from her and she wasn't going to take it any more.

Frank asked Babe to dance and the two of them headed for the dance floor. Minnie loved watching her man dance; he was so smooth, and as usual, he was very well dressed, even after changing out of his tuxedo. Willie headed downstairs for more flirting with Louise. Louise was about to get off of work early so she could go see her mother and spend some time with her. Her mother had been ill and she wanted to look in on her today. Willie caught her leaving the café and suggested he give her a ride to her mom's house. Knowing she would other wise have to wait for a ride from Tom or walk, Louise gladly accepted.

CHAPTER XIII

Louise and Tim were having some very serious marital problems that stemmed mostly from him losing money gambling all the time. She was unhappy because Tim never spent any time with her until late at night when he was drunk and broke. Furthermore, Louise knew that Tim openly caroused with other women. He had become extremely brazen with his extra marital affairs, and flaunted his ability to woo other women.

The two of them had married straight out of high school. Tim had only been with Louise sexually up until that time and wasn't very popular with the ladies in school, mostly due to the fact that everyone knew that Tim and Louise were already a couple since intermediary school. Louise had never had sex with anyone else but Tim in her entire life. But in the months and years that had passed, Tim had become quite an item with the young ladies. He was known for staying out all night, mostly on the weekends carousing the pool halls and juke joints. And he gladly took advantage of his new found popularity with the strumpets about town. He had learned all kinds of nasty little oral tricks that he tried on his young bride.

Willie bragged about all the money he was winning from Tim and his friends on a weekly basis on the ride to Louise's mother's house. This only served to add fuel to the already flaming inferno of contempt that burned in Louise's heart for Tim.

When they pulled in front of her mother's house, Willie asked, "How long you plan on visiting?" She replied, "Maybe an hour or so, then I'll get a ride home from my brother so I can cook and wash clothes. I don't even know why I bother cooking. That fool I'm married to won't eat dinner at home anyway." She opened the door to get out of the car.

Willie asked her to hold on for a minute. "You don't have to jump out so fast do you?"

"What you want, Willie Clayton? I appreciate the ride and kind conversation but what you really want with me anyway?"

"I want to pick you up from here in an hour after I've gone and taken some more of your husband's money. I want to pick you up and take some honey off his hands. I want to pick you up and give you a dose of this Georgia mule stick I'm carrying around Tennessee with me, girl. Hell, I want to pick you up and give you something that little boy you married to can't give you, a good sweet slow country screw. You know that thing of yours is popping like a thirty-eight pistol and foaming up like a bottle of beer."

No one had ever been bold enough to talk dirty to Louise before, and she was loving every nasty word of it, and she couldn't hide the fact that she did. After he had gotten her interest in having a libidinous affair with him, Willie pulled out a wad of money that he had partially bullied from Babe. "I'm going to take this little bit of money and damn near double it off your stupid old man and his friends while you visit your mother. Then I'll bring you back some of your money I take off your lame ass old man; after that, I'll take a little of his honey pot if you want me to."

Louise felt moist and excited by all the dirty talk plus the idea of sneaking and having sex with someone new. "We'll see about that when you pick me up in one hour, Mister, not one hour and one minute either, or I won't go with your ass no where." When she got out of the car and up to her mother's door way, Willie waved a good guy, good-bye as he pulled away from the house.

Oh shit"" he shouted to himself as he pulled around the corner, "I'm about to tear this nigger's old lady's pussy up this evening."

The comment that Tim made as Willie walked into the pool room was hauntingly true that day. Tim shouted from his crouching position over the eight ball he was about to shoot off the table, "Hey, country boy, I've got something to give your ass this evening."

Willie laughed uncontrollably as he replied, "U mm....hmm...you sho' do, son, but first I'll take that little lunch money your old lady gave your lame ass for work next week."

The gambling took its usual course as Willie cleaned Tim and his crew out as per weekly. Babe never even missed Willie; she was having such a great time with her family at the reception. Moreover, it was a source of stress relief for her that he had disappeared in the first place. It had begun to disgust her to see his face, after she had been so in love with him at one time in her life. Now she just wanted to hog tie him and whip his butt like he had done to her once.

Babe had allowed herself to be used, abused, and exploited for all these years, and she suffered silently because her pride wouldn't let her tell Minnie or any other family member. She didn't want everyone to know what a fool Willie had been making of her. Babe also had to deal with a part of her psyche that had a tinge of jealousy of Minnie for having so many healthy children, while she was apparently barren. To top it off, Minnie had Frank, who Babe thought was perfect for Minnie and a great guy, while she was stuck with Willie's dead beat ass.

There were so many diversions at the reception that no one missed her worse side not being attached to her at the hip. As Willie normally did when they were together; hawking her every move because he was afraid that at any time Babe might tell Minnie and Frank about his patterns of robbery and abuse. Willie knew how much Frank hated men who fought women. He also knew that he didn't want any trouble with Frank Whatley or his associates. So it was almost as if Willie was both sadistic and suicidal in his thought patterns where Babe and he were concerned. William had even struggled up from his big chair and danced with Babe and Ethel and Maxie and Minnie all at one time. William truly looked like a big pimp as he called himself, while all the women in his family danced around him. Salema, Celeste, Cecelia, and Arselee, and much to everyone's surprise, even Jane joined in on the juking.

J.D. and Brandy stood back and observed the dance together at the edge of the long table that had been reserved for the families. After the dance, Salema and Berry slipped off all alone for about ten minutes, and Berry got his first little peck of a kiss. It was a very modest kiss, not of the French variety, but rather respectable. This only encouraged Berry more to pursue his ultimate goal of marriage with more zeal than he had already shown..

Babe only missed Willie much later that night, nearly as the reception was about to end, and that wasn't for hours, after she was nearly drunk from all the champagne she drank. At that point, Babe was pretty groggy and ready to go home and go to sleep.

Minnie had a surprise at the end of the night; she wanted everyone to gather for a small birthday celebration. She had gone down to the kitchen and gotten Lori, who had awakened from her much-needed nap. Minnie introduced Lori and Robert to everyone at the reception. Lori was visibly uncomfortable being in front of all these strangers, ninety percent of whom were colored folks, ma king this even more awkward. Minnie helped soothe her by hugging her and having Emma bring out a big cake with thick white icing and " Happy Birthday, Robert" written on top of it in pretty ocean blue letters that almost matched Lori's eyes. Then Tom brought in all the things Robert had tried on at the store, and the entire room of people sang happy birthday to Robert. This was a far cry from how Robert had spent the day thinking this birthday would turn out after what had happened earlier at the railroad tracks. Lori stood at the front of the room with tears running down her face, and Minnie gently wiped them away for her.

Mr. Moore soon brought all the sappy behavior to an abrupt end when he contemptuously started singing a slightly drunken version of "Oh Danny Boy." Mr. Moore then handed Robert a hundred-dollar bill, complimented him on having such a beautiful mother, and wished the boy a hundred more happy birthdays to come. Orland Moore told Lori that if he could do anything for her or her son, to let him know and it was done. Lori was simply astonished at the mosaic of people she saw as she looked out over the people assembled for this reception. There were Indian, black, white, Spanish, all kinds of ethnic backgrounds all having fun in one room. This probably was her first time running in to people of color partying openly with white folk. More than that, the outpouring of love and concern for her and Robert they had never experienced before, not even from their own kin, let alone a group of complete strangers. Lori stood amazed and nervous at the front of the room and managed to ease a timid thank you out of her mouth to everyone before she resumed her position observing the party.

Robert told his mother that these were the nicest gifts that he had ever gotten on his birthday, as he was trying on his new skates for their first roll on the streets of Chattanooga. Lori made him take the skates off; she told him not to go out skating until tomorrow morning. First she wanted to know where Ms. Minnie was going to put them up for the night. And Lori did not want her son skating through the reception, disturbing the guests like a little wild heathen who had never received a gift before in his life. Lori could see how excited Robert was, and she could tell there was no way he was going to be composed rolling through the room.

Minnie had made Johnny aware of the plight of Lori and Robert and set arrangements up with him to have them stay in the empty bunkhouse at the farm. The bunkhouse was very nice and would be comfortable and private for Lori and Robert. Minnie also knew that a little boy from Texas probably would be happy out on the farm, more so than he would in the city in one of Frank's rental houses anyway. Robert's paternal grandfather owned a big farm in the big state, as Lori called Texas, and Robert loved spending time out there every summer.

Minnie walked over and told Lori of the plans that had been made for their accommodations out on the farm. She also told Lori that she should rest up tomorrow and Monday so she could begin to wait tables at the café on Tuesday, so she could make some money. "I think that the peace and quiet of being out on the farm for the next couple of days will do you and your son some good."

Minnie pointed over to a corner table where Jane, Mrs. Rosa, and some other ladies from the quilt club were standing and juking next to their chairs, and smiled to herself. "Child, if this don't beat all"" she exclaimed to Lori. "It's so nice to see Ma having a big time for the first time in years."

"Well honey, it looks like you and Robert is set, so come on, let's go juke with Ma." Minnie grabbed Lori's hand and literally dragged her out to the dance area where the older ladies were cutting the rug. It wasn't long before Mr. Moore, Mr. Copeland, and two of their friends had joined the dance. Frank saw what was going on and he came over and joined in on the fun.

Back at the pool hall, Willie had made short work of Tim's bank roll. Before he left to pick up Louise from her mother's house, Willie bought Tim a fresh bottle of whiskey and loaned him five dollars to keep gambling with. This would give him sufficient time to knock Louise off in the sack, and guarantee Tim's whereabouts for the next couple hours. After Willie picked Louise up, he handed her seventy dollars of Babe's money. Willie pretended like he had won most of it off of Tim and his friends. Then he headed straight for his and Babe's house. As soon as they were inside the front door, he started kissing her and seductively removed all of Louise clothes, licking her all over her body as he took them off.

Louise was on fire as she melted in his grip from a near orgasm. The sensation was oh so delicious as the head of his penis penetrated her for the first time. Willie was much more well- endowed than Tim was, and Louise was loving the difference in diameter and length. Louise was having back- to- back- to- back orgasms for the first time in her life. She had never sweated like this with her husband and never had sex in so many positions that Willie was maneuvering her into with ease. One time she hollered out so loud that the neighbors could hear her. Willie never noticed that Louise was scratching his back raw from the heat of their passion. He was too drunk from all the whiskey he had consumed at the pool room.

After Willie exploded in orgasmic rhythm with Louise, he fell into a coma like sleep. Louise had just had her mind blown apart from the intensity of the pleasure she had just experienced. She lay stroking his head and staring at him for a long time before she finally slipped out of the bed and walked the short distance to her home. Louise felt a strange sense of revenge and fulfillment with the libidinous, adulterous act she had just taken part in.

As the reception was about to come to an wonder ful end, J.D. and Maxie stood up in the front of the room and thanked all the guests for coming. J.D. was a little tipsy for the first time in his life. But he had enjoyed this reception with his family and his new family like no other. Babe, after all evening, started looking for Willie. Minnie told Babe that she had seen Willie break for the door as soon as he saw her go dance with Frank when they had first arrived, and had not laid eyes on him since then.

Babe asked if she could ride home with Frank and Minnie. Frank had taken Ma and the other children home earlier, and had planned on staying late at the café to be alone with Minnie and their cot. But he relented to the pressure from Minnie to take her cousin on home and come back to the café, but only after Babe announced that she needed to talk to the two of them together about some problems she was having with Willie.

On the ride home, Babe proceeded to tell Minnie and Frank all the ugly details of the years of abuse she had endured right under their very noses, how it had escalated to out- and- out robbery and beatings; and now she could no longer tolerate it.

Frank was incensed; how could any fool hurt a gentle soul like Babe? Especially Willie, of whom she had provided every material need in his life for. Willie had to be crazy to hurt someone in his family, and as fine of a woman as Babe, Frank was thinking to himself nostrils flaring and teeth grinding.

Plus Frank hated men who beat on women. Minnie was about ready to jump out of the car she was so mad. "Let's find this nigger and skin his ass right now, Frank. I mean it and don't you try to talk me out of it either. I don't want to hear none of that 'Let's wait and make a plan' rationality foolishness right now either. We getting ready to pay this nigger back for the old and the new. I been knew Babe that Willie had you taking money from cleaning these houses but I didn't know he was beating you up and taking the damn money for his pleasures. I didn't say anything because you was doing all the work anyway. Honestly Babe, I never liked your country fool no how, now I find out he been beating you on top of everything else. I can't stand the way he smirks and cuttin' his eyes like he's a big sport, then smiling like an ole Chess Cat when he know he done pulled some shit over on Babe again and again right up in our faces like he just making fools out of the whole bunch of us around here. Let's hog tie him to a stake and set his ass afire, Frank."

"Oh no doubt, if Willie at this house or out in the streets, he's getting an ass whipping tonight," Frank replied, "and he's getting out of that house this evening with nothing but the things he came to town with and no more." Frank usually refrains from the use of profanity but he will use the word ass because its in the Bible. No doubt, Frank is ready to give Willie what he really need.

When they pulled up to the house, Minnie jumped out of the car and ran inside with Babe and Frank hot on her tail. They found Willie knocked out butt naked and uncovered, lying in a still- wet sweat sex puddle. The vast amounts of moistness that Louise had produced had long since dried up and left Willie's penis looking like a glazed doughnut. Minnie started to shake Willie to arouse him from his sleep, but Babe stopped her immediately.

Babe ran over to the dresser and retrieved several pairs of silk stockings. Then she instructed Frank and Minnie to help her turn Willie over on his stomach without waking him up. " Shhhhhh.... let's get this bastard tied up, y'all. I'm going to show his ass what it's like to get a ass whipping."

"Beat the dog shit out of him, girl," Minnie whispered. After they carefully flipped him over with only two light moans and no resistance, Babe tied him to all four big bed posts on her huge oak bed with the silk stockings. After Babe went into the bath room and got Willie's leather razor belt, she commenced to giving Willie a brutal ass whipping. He awoke struggling as mightily as he could against the silk stockings, but the more he pulled, the tighter the knots in the stockings became.

Soon Willie was suspended in mid air with nothing but natural ass exposed to the wrath of Babe and the razor strap. Willie was yelling like a bitch as Babe whaled on his back and backside until she nearly passed out. Then Minnie took over until Frank said that this was enough of the preliminary ass whipping and asked Minnie to halt the brutality for a moment.

The momentary reprieve that Willie had been given was only so that the level of punishment could be upgraded. Frank looked at Minnie and Babe and told them to take a minute to catch their breath. Then he wanted them to pack up only the things that Willie had brought to town with him and no more or no less. After they had packed his few belongings, Frank cut Willie loose from his stocking bonds and picked him straight up off the bed by the back of his hair. Willie cried out in sheer agony as he was led to the front door of the house butt naked and thrown out onto the front porch and down the stairs.

He kept yelling, "Please don't do this, Frank, please don't"" But Willie's desperate cries fell on totally deaf ears except for the neighbors he managed to awaken with his high- pitched yells. As they walked along every few steps, Frank would unleash a vicious kick into Willie's posterior, lifting him off the ground with the furious force of every blow, causing Willie to scream out in an even higher pitch than the razor strap had caused earlier.

Frank lectured Willie as they went along, "Man, didn't you know what would happen to you if you messed with one of mine?" By now, every neighbor on the street was on their front porches, watching as this embarrassing inevitable moment of self- induced fate came to Willie Clayton. The pointed-toed Stetson shoe that Frank wore hurt to the bone with every kick in the butt. When Frank turned Willie loose, he told him that if he ever heard tell of him setting foot around any member of his family ever again, that he would rue the day that his mama had his no- good dog ass.

Then Babe and Minnie, who had been following right behind them as they walked up the street, opened up Willie's suitcases. They casually strolled into the middle of the street and began to distribute all of Willie's clothing all over the street and stomp on it. The razor strap had opened several nice-sized gashes on Willie's legs and back, so bending over was a giant task at this point. The hard kicks in the rump only made matters twice as bad for Willie as he hurried to pull a pair of pants on to cover his nakedness. Willie had no money or any place to go as Babe, Frank, and Minnie turned to finally let him limp away like a wounded dog. Babe ran back and spit directly in his face. As Willie reached up to wipe the spit off his face, Babe told him to let it drip off slow and not to touch it, or she would have Frank kick him in his ass one more time for good measure. So as Willie stood there with the wad of saliva dripping from his face, Babe couldn't help but slightly titter as she railed Willie for the final time. "You ain't nothin but a damn fool and I was a even bigger one for staying with you all this damn time. But I'm free now, nigger, I'm finally free, and we stomped that ass tonight, you got to see what its like to be grown and have somebody beat on you like you they damn child …"

Babe broke down and started crying, then she slapped Willie again right in his mouth. Frank had then asked Babe to let them go home, but Minnie told him to let her finish. Babe said, "I'm finished with this piece of shit, baby. Let's go on home, Minnie, like Frank said."

As they turned and walked back down the street toward the house, Babe asked Minnie, "Can you believe I wasted all these years trying to fix my weaknesses so I could be stronger for a weakling of a man like that? Child, I ain't gone waste another minute worrying about the areas of my life where I'm weak. I'm gone concentrate on my own strengths from here on out. If I'm strong enough to take all the shit I've taken and still manage to provide for a household on my own, I can make it on my own without a no- good man dragging me down."

Willie was truly a battered and broken man as he limped away in the direction of Tim and Louise's house. He was disoriented and didn't know what time it was or how things had transpired like they had. In his mind's eye, he had fallen asleep after pulling off a Don Juan move of historical proportions. What a shame for his last conscious moments to be spent spanking some wet ass, only to be awakened getting the ass whipping from hell. Willie needed to retrieve the money that he had given Louise earlier in the evening, so he could get somewhere to lay his head down for the night. He thought better of the idea of knocking on Tim and Louise's door at this hour of the morning or night. So he found a nice warm box car along the railroad tracks and slept in it for the night.

Babe talked to Frank and Minnie for half the night before they finally left and she was all alone in the house for the first time in years. She was lonely, hurt, relieved, and yet a bit scared at the same time. More than anything, Babe kept thinking of how she had felt the days and months that led up to Willie's initial arrival in Chattanooga. She was waiting for her knight in shining armor to come and light up her life and make all her days and nights happy. Instead, Babe now felt that she had laid waste to the majority of her youth, wasting it on Willie. Willie Clayton became her worst nightmare and was no more than a complete loser and a lout. Willie had turned out indeed not to be Babe's knight in shining armor, but rather a simple and plain bumpkin who was loud, abrasive, and a total vexation to Babe's very peaceable spirit.

Babe knew that tonight was the beginning of the rest of her life, and that she was about to be reborn as an adult woman for the very first time in her life. The very thought of finally being able to make any arbitrary decision without any one person to consult or get approval from excited Babe to no end. She no longer had to live in stark fear of coming home from work with her hard- earned money, money that she worked long, arduous hours for only to have someone take it away from her before she could even pay her bills. Babe slept like a newborn baby who had finally gotten he r days and nights straightened out. The next few months seemed to Babe to be the best of her life.

The next morning for Babe was truly a joyous one. One of life's simple pleasures seemed so much more serene this morning; just to take a hot bath all alone seemed to be a brand new experience.

Minnie left the house early that morning so that she could stop by for a very brief check up on Babe, though she had little doubt that Willie would ever bother or try to retaliate against her cousin again. Then she went to rudely intrude on and make a short visit to the bride and groom. J.D. and Maxie were still asleep, so Minnie decided to ride out to the farm and check on Lori and Robert while she had some rare free time on her hands. Ma had made a fresh batch of tea cakes and Minnie wanted to see if Robert would enjoy them as much as all of her children did. So Minnie had a bag full for him to eat if he liked them. If not, they surely wouldn't be wasted with Johnny there ready to gobble up all the tea cakes in his sight.

In all the excitement the night before, Babe had never mentioned the incident that happened on the railroad tracks the previous day. So Robert never brought it up either; he figured, why bring more trouble on himself if no one else brought up the subject. Minnie had deduced perfectly that the farm would be the best environment for Robert to be in to get adjusted to being uprooted from his previous life so abruptly. Lori told her that she had to go out and look for Robert when she woke up at six this morning after they had gotten settled in the bunkhouse after two in the morning.

The nap Minnie allowed Lori to take at the café had been the only reason that Lori was able to get up so early that morning. Just being on the farm had given Robert a burst of energy that could carry a boy his age for hours on end. As soon as Robert had eaten his breakfast, he was skating down to the barn to feed animals or help out in any way he could, and Johnny didn't seem to mind Robert at all. As a matter of fact, Johnny seemed for the most part to genuinely enjoy having the boy around. Lori thanked Minnie again for helping her, and asked her why she was doing so much for them. Minnie told Lori, "It seems to add a vital source of energy to my soul when I'm able to help others who are in need. Maybe the Good Lord blessed me just enough so I could be in a position to help other people." Minnie didn't know all the reasons; all she really knew was, it made her feel good to help others and she loved doing it. Minnie figured she had worried Lori enough and finally said, "Lori, child, I gotta go and pick up Rico up and take him shopping for some new shoes."

It seemed that Rico's feet were growing so fast that he was in need of a new pair of shoes every other month nowadays. After dancing at the reception just about the entire night, last night, he complained that his present pair of shoes, which Rico had just been wearing for a mere three to five weeks now, were getting just a bit uncomfortable and much too tight. Minnie hated to see children ruin their feet wearing the wrong size shoe. Rico had long used this t id bit of info about his mother against her and thus was able to stay draped in the latest foot wear and attire. The fact that Rico loved the reputation of being a very natty dresser who wore new shoes all the time only served to boost his ego.

This more than the comfort of his shoe probably fueled Rico's seemingly desperate need for having a new pair of shoes bought for him all the time. Rico was always very manipulative and cunning when it came to getting the ladies — even his own mother — to cater to his every whim.

The night before at the reception, Rico had tried his normal mellifluent approach with Lori that he took when he hit on women. Offering to provide all of life's luxuries at only a very nominal toll to her person, Rico tried the nonsensical line that prostitution was very stress- free.

"I can show you how to make ten times the money you been getting paid slaving at the café. Listen, if you willing to start out by partaking in the life at a young age, whore work won't be detrimental to your physical outward beauty over a long period of time. But now working in the café on your feet all day, that's gone wear and hull you out." Rico whispered all this in Lori's

146

ear, finishing up by telling her that he was a part- time pimp around town in his secret life.

Lori just laughed him off and sent the youngster on his way by simply telling Rico, "Hey, son, I'm country, not stupid. Give yourself the opportunity to grow up to be a man first."

Rico just gave Lori a dirty, glaring look as he slowly walked back over to his small group of friends that he spent the entire evening with at the reception.

Lori's first impression of Rico was that of a little wannabe city slick street wise thug before he was ready to assume the responsibilities of the role. But Lori kept the incident and observations to herself and didn't dare communicate them to Minnie. Lori knew better than to offer biting opinions to people about their children, especially when you first meet them, and they are the hand that presently feeds you.

Minnie was about to leave when Uncle Johnny hollered at her to come and talk to him before she left. Johnny told Minnie that he was pleased to have the little boy out there with him this morning, that time seemed to fly by much faster than usual this morning. Robert was skating around the pig pen area at a fast pace, distributing corn and feed mostly on the ground but at least where the live stock could eat it.

Minnie asked Lori to bring Robert with her to the café in the morning and made arrangements with Uncle Johnny for them to ride into town with him; then she took off. Minnie drove away feeling good about the prospects that life now held out for Lori and her son, as opposed to what she had to live through with her father, then husband.
with her

Afterward, she picked up Rico and they went to the store and purchased him a new pair of brown Stetson shoes and a suit for church on Sunday.

"Thank you again, Mama, for continuously upgrading both my foot apparel and my top- shelf suit attire," Rico spewed as they walked out of the store. The conversation was sparse and concise for the ride home. Rico now already had what he wanted from his mother, so his topics for conversation were now very limited.

Minnie dropped Rico off at home and headed to the café for a busy day at work. Rico did indeed have a secret life in reality that neither Frank nor

Minnie knew anything about. Rico had been drafted, and had accepted the position of leader of a notorious street gang of young thugs his age, with several members even older than he was. None of the gang members had the cool demeanor, heart, or fearless attitude that Rico seemed to have naturally. Further, not a one of them was as clever and manipulative as he was, and they all looked to him for guidance and initiative, in their petty criminal endeavor that they undertook.

Rico would later come to think that gangs were for cowards and that he had been a foolish, immature young boy to ever get involved with one. But that would be years and several life- altering mistakes later. For now, he was the crowned king of the k. p.s. The activity and association that the gang presented would prove to be a powerful and negative influence on the rest of Rico's life.

CHAPTER XIV

Emma had already spread the word to the staff on the events that had taken place at Babe's house when Minnie arrived that morning. Louise was in total shock and wondered if she would face any reprisals for having laid up in Babe's bed the night before with Willie. Louise didn't dare act as if she was too interested in where Willie had spent the night, having heard that he was left totally destitute and penniless.

Louise walked out in back of the café and began to tear up at the thought of what had happened to Willie. Then Louise heard a light whistle from the hedges that surrounded the back edge of the cafe's property. Willie had snuck back there in hopes of seeing Louise this morning.

Louise first became very wary, then she hesitantly approached as she thought she recognized Willie's voice whispering. "Psssst...psssst, come here, gal, I need to talk to you for a minute." Willie was crouched like a cowardly dog, sweating like a run away slave, behind the corner of the hedge. He was ready to take off running if he was spotted by a family member or a friend of Frank's. "I can't let these crazy folks see me round here. I don't want no more trouble from Frank or those folks he run with."

Willie looked and smelled like hell. He went on to ask if he could get some of the money that he had given Louise back so that he could get some place to stay temporarily. Louise reached into her bra and retrieved all of her money that was tied tightly in a handkerchief. Louise had learned to keep her money like this from watching Minnie and Jane; she noticed that they stored it there for safe keeping. Louise had about 80 dollars all totaled and just handed it all to Willie. Willie tried to feign as though he would give the money back, but Louise insisted that he take all of it.

"When and how am I going to see you again, Willie?"

"We'll figure out a way; first let me get a place to lay my head down. Until then, we'll meet in the evenings after you get off work, at Lang's Grocery Store. But I need to get the hell away from here right now before one of them see me and tell Frank." Louise could see that Willie was clearly shaken and wanted no part of Frank Whatley in a violent or confrontational situation ever again. This meant that remarkably, Willie was now free and available for the taking. Louise practically floated back into the café on cloud nine; she had never felt so light on her feet in her life.

Frank had discussed his plans for designing a floor for a skating rink with his two most trusted co-workers that morning. Jimmy Covington and Henry Bosworth, two brilliant engineers, who were happy to provide Frank with whatever assistance he needed. Frank had helped them with a project for irrigating the men's father's farms in the past. Frank had basically used the same plan that he and Johnny had used out on the farm to help Jim and Henry out. So the two of them had no problem with this sort of quid pro quo situation that had worked itself out on its own.

Frank had impressed the two men with the simplicity and efficiency of his irrigation system, and now it was their turn to help Frank out with the skating rink floor. Henry suggested they plan a dual floor system, one with a ramp for advanced skater s and a flat floor for beginners and intermediate-level skaters. Frank loved the idea from the start.

Jim expressed some reservations on how to keep the children from trying the ramp too fast who weren't ready for advanced skating. Frank assured Jim that he would work out a system to avoid such instances. This rink was going to give the children more options and the ability to increase their expertise in skating. After hearing Frank's very convincing argument in support of Henry's ramp idea, Jim conceded and gave his support. Jim said, "Let's add some pool tables to the place. I think it would also help by consolidating both recreational activities in one building."

Frank agreed with Jim and kind of figured that by adding the pool tables, that this would also give their rink a distinct and definitively different feel than Corynth's Star Light. Frank adapted both men's ideas and asked when they would be available to get started. Both men were so eager that they agreed to draw up some plans that evening. All three agreed to meet at the café at six that evening to eat, then go to the building where they would install the floor to get its accurate dimensions and start drawing up plans for a new skating rink.

That evening at the café, Frank arrived at five forty- five so that he could have special service set up for his two guests when they arrived. Minnie was shocked to see Frank in the café to eat; he very seldom came in for a meal. Frank said it was because he loved the food so much, he didn't want the menu to become to familiar to his taste buds. Plus, Frank appreciated the fact that he was blessed and privy to have the same cooks at home. Never mind the fact that either Frank, or one of his daughters almost always cooked dinner at the house and they all had great culinary skills in their own rights.

Henry and Jim were punctual, as usual, and sat at the table where the Whatley family usually ate in private, for the first time, Jim and Henry had unlimited access to the food in the café on Frank, and they both took full advantage and gorged themselves to an uncomfortable level of fullness.

They were both in total bliss and had gaseous stomach pain, if that is at all possible to accomplish. Still, the three men managed to pull themselves away from the table and down the street to the new Aurora Skate Rink to be. After carefully measuring the building's inner walls, they drew up the preliminary plans for the dual- floor rink to come into existence. Frank was now pregnant with a new business baby, and he was bursting at the sea ms to see how the baby was going to look upon a hopefully healthy birth.

The plans called for nine regulation- sized tables to sit in the entrance or outer room. Then the customers could enter the beginner and intermediate floor area. Then the grand paradise for the advanced skater, an indoor ramp built to maximize speed and control. There would be two locker rooms equipped with restrooms for the different genders, to make it comfortable for storing and changing shoes and skates. They designed a counter to the left of the entrance and a hidden click counter at the door. It was a similar type of clicker to what county fairs and traveling carnivals used. It was a very innovative way for the rink to keep an almost accurate count of paying customers and gate receipts. Frank would only let Salema and Minnie know of the counter's existence.

The three men stayed at the rink much later than they had anticipated because after they had drawn up the final plans, Frank went out to his car and retrieved a bottle of whiskey. It was his way of saying thanks and celebrating the beginning construction of the Aurora skating rink. Each man swallowed the three straight shots of whiskey in rapid succession before Frank said a sincerely heart felt thank you to them both. Henry admonished Jim and Frank not to be late for work in the morning as he drove off.

Frank felt blessed to have white male friends who were not bigoted, living in this geographic location of the world. He knew that it was almost unheard of, and a total dream to have the type of co-workers who would confidently hold this plan of the proposed rink to themselves and help him plan it.

One saying about most of the men in this area of the country held firm and stood true: They believed in a man's action, not his skin color. Those men who had survived the years of the Depression with one another held it to be true that if they could count on you in hard times, you could always count on them to be there for you, no matter the color of his skin. All the family men in these parts, colored or white, knew that they could count on Frank to be in their corner if things ever got tough.

Ethel had just begun to put the supper away when Frank came dancing into the house. He was unusually happy and in a great mood for it to be a work night. Ethel wondered, when Frank asked her where Minnie was at. Frank was bursting at the seams and anxious to tell her the news about the plans being complete on the rink. Minnie had been washing Ma's hair in the bathroom and wasted no time coming into the living when she heard Frank's voice.

Frank produced the drawings from behind his back and showed them to Ethel and Minnie. The sketches were at first a little hard to make out for their untrained eyes. But Frank showed them a simple way to figure out what they were looking at. Soon both Minnie and Ethel could clearly make out the schematic configuration of the plans for the inside of the rink. The building was going to be transformed into a beautiful fun palace for the children in the community.

Maxie and J.D. came in the front door about that time and were the first to hear that the family was going into the skating rink business. J.D. loved this idea for the young people of color in Chattanooga. He was a staunch advocate for children in the colored community in every facet of their lives, especially when it came to them having ample recreational facilities. J.D. and a group of young ministers were instrumental in bartering a deal with and getting the local Y M C A to start a colored baseball team for the youth in the community. The team was always one of the strongest in the region.

Maxie was in her last semester at school and would be graduating in six weeks. She asked if Frank and Minnie wanted her to come home and run the skating rink. J.D. stepped right in and said he didn't like that idea at all.

"Oh no, we can't have Mama at the skating rink all night on the weekends. That would not be becoming of a minister's wife, now would it?"

Maxie smiled and told J.D. "I couldn't stand to be away from you at night long enough to run a business anyway, even if it was just running the business into the ground.

Minnie could hardly believe that in six weeks, her twins would both be the proud owners of college degree s. Now if she could only get the rest of her children to get on the path to higher education, she would have accomplished one of her major goals. She had promised herself to make her life count. Improving the lot of her posterity, and getting her children a better education than what she had was a priority.

The next week was so hectic for Frank, he thought he needed to be two men in one. Every day needed ten extra hour in it to get all the things done Frank had on his to do list.

Johnny had begun to clear all the biggest oak trees in a systematic way so as to weed out and not totally clear all his oak trees. Johnny was still able to provide Frank with a more than ample supply of hard wood for the floor of the rink. By week's end, the major bulk of the building supplies had been ordered and paid for; some had even been delivered already. Mr. Moore hastily assembled a professional construction crew, and the work on the Aurora was to begin the following week.

The construction crew began to demolish the interior of the building bright and early on Monday morning, so that soon its floor would begin to reshape itself into the form of a skating rink. One of the demo experts found a huge crack in the building's foundation that lay directly in the door way between the building's two biggest rooms. These rooms were to be used for the flat skate floor and the ramped floor. The crack in the foundation could have created an unsolvable quagmire, but Frank figured out that the crack had not weakened the entire foundation of the building.

In fact, it looked like the previous owners had dug this hole purposely for some odd reason. Frank had a wild idea, but he needed more help from his engineering friends to pull it off. So Tuesday, just before lunch, he asked

Jim and Henry to meet him again at the café for more planning. Henry and Jim both wanted to eat more of the delicious food at the café. Since both of them hardly ever got out of the house on work nights and they had enjoyed the first night of planning at the rink so much, Jim and Henry jumped at the second opportunity.

After they had once again gormandized themselves at the café, the three men took off for the skating rink. Jim took one look at the crack and jokingly suggested an in- ground fish tank. Frank was amazed and never saw any levity in the suggestion, because that is exactly what he had in mind.

"Do you think we could make it work?" Frank asked. Henry looked at them, "You're both crazy for coming up with such an idea, but it just might work. The only problem might be getting a pump set up large enough to blow in enough fresh air for the fish.

Frank suggested they design an old- fashioned covered bridge to traverse the new tank and stock it with oversized cod. Jim said that only a group of men who had to work at the T. V. A. could have come up with this bold and innovative plan for a skating rink. Frank offered to pay the two men money for the extra services that they had provided him, but they both politely refused his offer.

"Come on now, Frank," Jim said in a very serious tone, "just go get the damn bottle of whiskey. And let's have us a couple drinks, hell that's enough pay between three old friends helping each other out."

Henry added to Jim's train of thought by chiming in, "Jim and I ate enough of Ms. Minnie's food to cost you a week's wages anyway, Frank."

Frank again told the men that he couldn't thank them enough for their assistance. After they had finished their now- customary rapid- fire shots of whiskey, Frank surprised both men with their personal half gallon of high- grade moon shine to take home with them. This kind offer of deep appreciation did not offend either man's sense of pride, so Jim and Henry both gladly accepted the shine.

When Jim and Henry left, Frank stayed and began to get the hole prepared for the planned project. Before Frank knew it, he had been working nearly all night long. The time had flown by, he had become so engrossed in the work he was doing that Minnie had gotten worried and came looking for him. Her foot steps in the empty building caused Frank to first draw, then cock his pistol and aim it in the direction of the foot steps that he heard approaching.

When Minnie turned into the main flat skating rink floor, all she saw was a big barrel pointing in her face.

"Frank, don't shoot, it's me, baby, it's Minnie," she shouted. "I was worried about you, man," she said as Frank lowered the weapon and she slipped ever so gracefully into his arms. "Man, what you gone do, kill your fool self trying to fix up this darn place?"

At that very moment, Minnie noticed the huge hole in the floor. "Well, sir, if this don't beat a hog a- flying, is this what the hell you been up here doing all night, Frank Whatley?"

Frank just looked at her and tried to explain as simply as he could about what had happened with the hole in the building's foundation. When Frank had finished, Minnie teased him, "You and your co-workers think y'all can fix or make anything." Still, Minnie loved the idea, and thought that if Frank could pull it off, the rink would have a serenity to it that no other building in the area would.

Being the disciplinarian that she naturally was, Minnie wanted to know how Frank planned on keeping a sense of order among the youngsters at the rink. Frank told her that he planned on posting a list of ten rink rules at the front door. The punishment for breaking any of the ten rules would be a life time ban from entering the rink. Frank further explained that he planned on making the inside of the rink so much fun that no child or young adult would want to risk being barred.

"How much longer will I have to wait for my husband to want to come home to his bed. Frank just looked into Minnie's still- lovely hazel eyes, "I'll be home before you can put your car in gear." They both drove on home and Frank slept a little past ten the next morning and went in to work late, something he had never done before.

Frank was a strong believer that punctuality and responsibility go hand-in- hand. The good thing for him was he never had to report his time for getting paid at work to anyone but Henry, who was their lead engineer.

Henry was also responsible for turning in everyone's pay sheet at the end of each week. Since Henry knew where Frank had been the night before and since he had never been late or missed time at work, he figured Frank had gotten caught up in the project at the rink and needed some rest. After all, Henry knew that things had been extremely busy for Frank lately. Plus

Frank's work supply orders at the job site and his strategic mapping plans were all well ahead of schedule.

The subject of his late arrival was never even mentioned when he arrived at work, and it was a long time before he was ever late again for the T. V. A. due to personal business.

Frank knew that today he had to take the boys to the barber shop after he got off work and he wanted to talk to Rico about an incident at school. One of his female teachers had caught him in the hall between classes, kissing one of his young, alluring female classmates. Minnie wanted to beat his behind, but Frank wanted to talk to him instead. As usual, Frank won out in the debate as to how they should best handle the situation with their son. Minnie kept saying, "If you spare the rod, you spoil the child." She was specifically referring to her own son being spoiled rotten and in need of a good hard trip to the wood shed. There was no room for tact or compromise as far as Minnie was concerned, when it came to meting out discipline to her children. Frank took a more diplomatic approach to child rearing. He did too much talking to the children in her perception of his inter actions with them.

When Frank picked Rico and Doyle up to go to the barber shop, he made Rico aware that he had a problem to discuss with him as soon as they returned home. Mr. May, the barber who had given both the boys their very first hair cuts, loved to play a game called the dozens with Rico. They played in a clean, respectful manner, as Rico still had to be mindful that he was a child, keep his manners, and defer to Mr. May as an adult. That was the only way that Frank allowed this type of relationship to develop between Mr. May and his son. Plus, the two of them were very entertaining to him and all the rest of the customers present whenever Rico came into the shop with his dad for a hair cut.

As soon as Frank and the boys walked in, Mr. May started in on Rico. "Hey, old water- headed boy, how you been doing? Frank, that boy must have gotten his head from his mama, 'cause you got a small pea head and he got ten- gallon- hat head."

Rico cut back at Mr. May before his dad could say a word. "Oh ye of few, or should I dare say, diminished tonsorial skills, you show your jealousy of the youth of today so obviously. Too bad your hey day has passed you by and now you have to see a young stud like me take all the pretty girls from you." The men in the shop all laughed at the language and smooth style that the youngster used to deliver his rebuttal to Mr. May's verbal onslaught.

Rico sat back in his chair to get a cut and Mr. May stood behind him with a big grin on his face and picked up his cup and took a nice swig of whiskey.

"Ahhhhhhh.........." Mr. May had to let out a sigh of relief from the harshness of the straight whiskey's taste.

Rico turned his head away from Mr. May and said, " Come on now, Mr. May, you about to burn the hairs out of my nose blowing in my face like that, sir. That's why you can't cut nobody's hair right no more, Mr. May, all that whiskey you sipping on got your hands shaking a little bit too much."

Rico and Mr. May were really pushing the limits of Frank's tolerance for their game. Frank cleared his throat to signal that he had heard just about enough of it for the day. Frank's nose was sweating profusely on the tip by now and he had an evil gleam in his eyes as he glared at Rico.

Frank addressed his son in a manner so as to not to completely publicly embarrass Rico but to reign him in a bit. "Hey there now, young man, don't get too big for your britches and get brought down a button loop or two. Remember you're talking to a grown man. Don't insult his habits in front of customers." Then Frank gave a chuckle and sat back down. He had brought the game to an end and Rico didn't know if he should be smiling or scared to death. Rico did know he had to deal with what must be a hot issue as soon as he left here, and he was apprehensive as to what that issue was. Not knowing made it all the more stressful and agonizing. The wait was a form of mental punishment that Frank used on his children.

Doyle, who had sat looking and laughing at the verbal sparring and exchange between his brother and Mr. May, was happy when his cut was over. Doyle hated to get a hair cut; he didn't like the way the little pieces of cut hair felt on his neck. After each and every hair cut, he would race to the restroom and wash his hair and body.

Frank took Rico out on the back porch and had a heart- to- heart talk about safe sex. Frank had heard that his son was already sexually active; rumor on the street had it that the sexual activity was even with several adult women around town. Frank warned Rico about sexually transmitted diseases like syphilis.

"Are you fooling with a lot of these loose women, son?" he asked Rico.

Rico knew one thing about his father: If you told Frank the truth, he would not hit or whack you. But if Rico had lied merely one time, Frank might knock him off the porch. Frank still imposed sometimes severe corporal punishment on both his sons with maximum force. So Rico told the truth right off the top. "Yes, Daddy," he spoke up boldly, "I've been with some women around here. I'm not about to tell you any fabrications about it. But I'm not trying to get any disease or father any children out of wedlock."

Frank then told Rico, "Slow down, you have plenty of time for that foolishness, concentrate on getting your education Junior, you're a very smart young man. Don't waste yourself out in the streets. The same thing going on out there in them streets today will be out there in fifty years. So stay from out there so much Rico, the streets will hold you back in life, they don't let you grow. The streets keep colored people running up and down them until they lose their youth, and eventually they die out there in them streets. Is that all you want from your one life, son? I'm not raising you up for the streets to take you away from me and your mama, you understand Junior?"

Frank only called him Junior at either his few moments of endearment or discipline time. Frank used a stern, almost nasty tone, nearly barking at Rico. "I'm placing you under close scrutiny for a long time until such time as I see a change in the direction that you're presently taking." Frank also told Rico that the re were other disturbing reports that he was beginning to hear about the company he was keeping for pals these days.

Before he let him leave, he reminded his son that he lived in a community that acted as a village; all the adults could either discipline or reward its children. Frank had an ear on the pulse of the activity in the streets of the community. So it would be next to impossible or at least very hard for Rico to continue any clandestine activity. Frank wanted him to know that he was at least going to be privy to the word on the street, especially about him or any other member of his family. He was trying to convey the message to his son that rarely does a man come along that the street life does not totally consume and eventually annihilate if he chooses to take that path in life. Few live to tell of their adventurous memories of street conquests to their extended offspring in their golden years.

When their discussion was over, Salema was waiting to pull Frank's chain. What his daughter asked him nearly caused him to have a heart attack. "Berry has ask me to marry him in two months and I accepted, if you approve daddy," Salema blurted out. " Do what" marry you?"

Before Frank addressed Salema any further, he turned away from her, threw both hands in the air, and exhaled. "Lord have mercy, what's next with these young'uns of mine?" Frank turned around and fired a barrage of questions at Salema. "Have you lost your mind, girl? You'll just be graduating from high school in two months, won't you? How long you been knowing Berry? It couldn't have been too long, Berry just came to Chattanooga from the Navy not too long ago, didn't he? I mean does he know you're carrying a baby?"

Salema answered all of Frank's questions with a simple reply. "Mama already said it's all right to get married, if it's all right with you. She already gave me and Berry her blessings."

"Your mama did what?" Frank was livid now. "I guess my entire family is suffering from some type of lunacy. We need to have an emergency family meeting, tonight." Frank stormed off the porch into the house and left

Salema standing on the back porch. Minnie was waiting for him. Frank held his composure extremely well, and calmly asked Minnie, "Have you gone completely mad? How long Salema been knowing Berry for you to give them your blessing to get married?"

Minnie's rebuttal brought back both Frank's ability to think rationally and his blood pressure level. "Frank, how long did you know me before we fell in love? And how do you know these children are not in love with each other as much as we still are today?" Minnie stepped up to him and pulled him close to her by his waist, with a cunning little smile on her face she said, "Let's back our daughter up on this marriage and let her and Berry run the skating rink for us, Frank. Yeah, I know they young and impulsive, but they got us to help them along the way, don't they, Daddy?"

Frank took a moment and truly listened to Minnie's voice on this matter. She always had her way of making Frank see both sides of any issue if needed when they arose in the family. Frank agreed to compromise on the issue, but held back giving his blessing to the proposed marital union.

There were still many questions that Frank wanted answers to before he would consent to any arrangements of matrimony for Salema. Frank was still angry and needed some time to sort things out in his head. He told Minnie that he was going over to his brother Walsh's house for a little while to clear his thoughts.. He kissed Minnie and headed out the door. When Frank arrived at his brother's house, he never even got the opportunity to open his mouth about all the drama going on at his home.

Walsh greeted him in his usual warm way, but Frank could sense that something was bothering him terribly and he wasted no time filling Frank in on the problem. "What's wrong Walsh? I see it on your face. Where's ma ma?" Mama's in the bed, weak and sick. None of the doctors can find anything wrong with her. She says that her head hurts all the time and no energy to get out of bed." Frank told Walsh, "Help me get mama cleaned up right now, I'm taking her to see Dr. Martin." But Walsh told him that Frankie had already seen Dr. Martin that afternoon. "Dr. Martin couldn't find anything medically wrong with her, either. Her suggested that the family keep a close eye on her, and if her condition changed, to bring her back to the hospital."

Walsh had a problem because during the day, both he and his wife Lizzy worked, so there was no one home with Frankie most of the day. Frank suggested that he take Frankie home to stay with him and his family. "That way," he told Walsh, "someone will always be at home with her, you know the crew I've created over there." They had a laugh at that. "Minnie and I will work out a schedule conducive to having someone there with mama at all times." Walsh agreed that for now, this would be the best arrangement for their mother's care.

Walsh and Frank packed up Frankie's clothes and belongings and loaded them and her in Frank's car. When Frank drove up, everybody was shocked to see him with his mother and all her belongings. Everyone was happy to see Frankie, especially the children. They all enjoyed a special bond and relationship with their paternal grandmother that was vastly different than the relationship that they had with Ma who lived right in the house with them, so they had access to her almost anytime they wanted her, except of course when they were in school or if she stayed long hours at the café working, or visiting. For her grand children, going over to Uncle Walsh's house to visit Grandma Frankie was a major event, even though the distance between their house and Uncle Walsh's house was less than two miles.

Frankie had a soothing effect on her grandchildren; she was the sweet grandmother, Ma was the disciplinarian of the two. Jane never felt or displayed any form of petty jealousy toward the relationship the children had with Frankie.

From the day Frank introduced Jane to his mother, Jane had fallen in love with her warm, quiet personality too. As fate would have it, the joy that the entire family felt upon Frankie's arrival to live with them would be literally very short- lived.

Frankie stayed in the bed all day long until that one evening when she asked Frank to be sat in the living room so that she could watch the sunset. Frank called Rico and Doyle from their room, and they helped him set Frankie up in a big rocker in front of the window. Frankie said to him with her soft spoken voice, at this point is just above a whisper. "The pain in my head don't hurt so bad no more, and that she was very sleepy. Frankie asked for her favorite cup so that she could drink some coffee, thinking the cup of strong black mud coffee might wake her up a little bit.

Frankie reclined in front of the window that evening in the same manner that she normally did at home with Walsh and Lizzy. Frank finally convinced her to lie down for the night. The next morning, Minnie had already gotten out of bed, helped Frankie get cleaned up and dressed by the time Frank woke up. Frank was a little behind his normal morning routine, so he hurried to get dressed so that he could leave for work. Frank went in to look in on Frankie before he left the house for work.

"How you feeling this morning, Mama?" Frank asked her as he helped her into the living room and into the rocker.

"I be all right, I reckon Lord willin'," Frankie answered in her soft, high-pitched voice. "And Frank," Frankie whispered, "I love you too, you turned out be a fine son with a fine family."

Frank was stunned by this verbal outburst from his mother; she had never said this much in one given conversation before today. But he had to leave for work, so he just kissed her head again and left for work. Frank and his co-workers had a big legal decision that was going to be handed down today. A group consisting of about nineteen privately owned utilities in the state of Tennessee had challenged the legitimacy and legality of congressional authority to create the T. V. A. The legal challenge being contested in the nation's court system could put an end to the progress in the region and to job security for many men in the area, and could bring an end to the entire existence of the T. V. A. Frank left the house optimistic of a legal victory for him and his co-workers.

Frankie sat in the rocker looking out at the gorgeous day that was developing outside. Minnie came in the living room and checked on Frankie after she had been cleaning her room and the bathroom. Frankie was sitting with her head slumped down, leaning toward her right shoulder. Minnie couldn't see her face and presupposed that Frankie had slipped off to sleep for a short nap. Minnie walked into the living room to check on her. As Minnie got closer to Frankie, she softly called out to her, "Ms. Frankie.......Ms. Frankie?"

When she got around in front of Frankie, Minnie could see a small stream of blood running from Frankie's nose. Minnie went into the bathroom and got a clean towel and soaked one end of it in cold water. She went into the living room and gently leaned Frankie's head back and held the cold wet end of the towel on Frankie's nose. Frankie looked at Minnie and smiled, then she breathed in deeply. When she exhaled, a big gush of blood rushed from her nose and she never took another breath. Frankie had suffered a slow bleed then a major blow out of a blood vessel in her brain.

The bleeding into an empty cavity of Frankie's upper skull was the cause of the headaches and sleepiness she experienced in the day s leading up to her demise. Frankie had died suddenly and almost painlessly with a warm smile on her face, and in Minnie's arms. Frank's mother had died as peacefully and quietly as she had lived.

Minnie immediately went and knocked on William and Ethel's bed room door. They had slept late for a change this morning; so had Ma. Ethel opened the door to the bed room, after they exchanged good mornings to one another, Minnie told Ethel that Frankie had just died in her arms, and that she needed Ethel to go get Frank from work, but not to tell him that his mother was dead.

William got up and got dressed ; he was getting along very well and was regaining his strength back. William stood in the bathroom and wept like a child for about fifteen minutes. Frankie had always been his grandmother too in his eyes. After he regained his composure somewhat, he went to Jane's room. Ma was all ready to cook breakfast. Jane had slept late for the first time in months. Minnie had not disturbed Jane because she was so happy to see her mother get some much- needed rest. Plus, Minnie didn't want to wake Ma up first thing in the morning with the news of Frankie's death. William

asked Jane if she had been in the living room yet. Jane answered, "Um....
umm... Not dis monin I ain't, baby, why you ask?"

William got straight to the point, the way Ma liked things. "Ma,
Grandma Frankie's in the living room dead, it looks like she had a massive
brain hemorrhage."

Jane pushed her way past William out past the parlor into the living
room, where she checked on Frankie. She looked up from holding Frankie's
hand and flopped down in the chair next to her and started crying. William
stood and waited while she grieved before he helped her to her feet. Minnie
sent William to get the sheriff.

Ethel and Frank had pulled up to the house before William could pull
off to go get Sheriff Ponterford. William tried to act as normal as he could
when he said, "Good morning, Daddy Frank," as he pulled off to go get
the sheriff. Frank spoke and went inside; he and his co-workers had gotten
the news that the law suits had ended in a judgment in favor of the T. V. A.
The people in the Tennessee Valley who depended on the protection of the
resources of the region had won a very important court battle, and Frank was
eager to share the good news with Minnie. Ethel had merely told Frank that
she was told to tell him to come home and no more.

Frank wondered why Minnie had sent Ethel to get him from work so
early. He figured his mother had gotten worse and Minnie wanted to take
her to the hospital. When Ethel pulled in the yard, she pulled around to the
back door, and Frank walked in the house. Minnie called Frank into their
bedroom. The next thing Ethel heard was Frank's voice saying loudly, "Oh
Lord, don't tell me that, Minnie........oh no." Then she heard Frank begin to
sob loudly, he bawled like a baby for what seemed like forever.

Ethel went into the living room where Jane was and had returned to her
seat next to Frankie's remains. In no time at all, it seemed William was back
with Sheriff Ponterford. The sheriff came in and walked over to Frankie,
then checked her vital signs. He then walked outside and instructed two men
from McCall's Funeral Home dressed in suits to come inside and prepare the
body for removal from the premises.

Frank had not fully regained his composure but he could hear that
people were in the house, so he came into the living room. Frank walked
over and stood over his mother's lifeless body. All he could see was her saying,
"You turned out to be a fine son and you have a fine family." Then he smiled

because Frankie looked so at peace to him, as though she was merely taking a nap.

When the men began to prepare Frankie's body for removal from the house, Frank left the room. He did not want to witness his mother being carried out of his house for the final time, so he walked out on the back porch by himself. Minnie had been standing back in the shadows, watching Frank in case he might need her assistance in any way. She followed Frank out on the porch and put her arms around him from behind. "I know it hurts, baby, but she really is in a better place than if she stayed down here and suffered just so we could have her around. And none of us is that selfish, are we Frank She went so peacefully, with a smile on her face. Your mother didn't suffer and linger in pain. She got tired and went on home to be with the Lord, baby."

"I know........I know you right, Minnie, but it's probably the worst pain I've ever felt in my life. I mean my stomach is cramping on the inside as if somebody kicked me in it. My mama is gone, all her knowledge that my children barely had the opportunity to learn is gone with her. But I know she would want me to be strong, so I'm gone be strong for her and for my family." Then Frank began to weep again and Minnie just held him in her arms and rubbed his back and head.

After the body had been removed, William came to get Frank to sign for the funeral home to prepare the body for a wake, funeral, and internment. This good cry allowed Frank to get a lot of the initial pain and shock out of his system. And though Frank's mood remained extremely morose for a long period of time, he was able to display a great deal of emotional continence at his mother's wake and funeral.

Frank asked Minnie to go with him to Walsh's job. "I need to let him and the others know that mama has passed on." Walsh thought something was wrong when he saw Frank and Minnie pull up in front of his job. Neither Frank nor Minnie ever bothered him at his job, especially Frank, unless it was a dire emergency. Walsh rushed out to see what was wrong. Frank pulled him to the side a little bit and told him the terrible news. Walsh was devastated by the news of his mother's death. He was not prepared to hear that his mother was gone.

Frank and Walsh stood hugging and rocking from side to side. They were both sobbing like little babies, in broad daylight, on a public street, mourning their mother together. "I'm so sorry, Walsh......I'm so sorry........I'm gone miss her so much." Finally, they let each other go and Frank reached in his pocket and got a fresh handkerchief to wipe his eyes then blow his nose.

"This is the Lord's will, and we have to accept it, Frank, and try to keep on doing our best," Walsh said between sniffles. Minnie had gone inside and informed the supervisor that Walsh's mother had died, and that he would be leaving for the day.

After they had informed and tried to console Joe and Gussy of Frankie's death, the brothers sat down and started to make the final arrangements.

The Whatley brothers agreed to have the wake in Frank and Minnie's parlor at their home, then have the funeral at Rev. Black's church, First Baptist. First Baptist was large enough to hold the large number of people likely to attend Frankie's funeral. After all, Frankie had four of the most popular sons in town, although only a very few people actually knew Frankie very well personally.

The wake was sad and the children took their grandmother's death extremely hard. Celeste and Cecelia were nervous about having the casket in the house with them all night long with the dead body of their grandmother in it. The girls had conjured up images in their vivid and fertile imaginations of Frankie getting up out of her casket during the night.

The funeral was a bit more subdued, mostly due to the out standing job that Pastor Black did officiating the service and in delivering a very comforting eulogy. He stressed to the family to use the peaceful spirit and mild manner with which Frankie had lived her life, to permeate the church for her home going. The choir sang, "I'm Going Home to Be With the Lord" and Pastor Black comforted the family and throngs of friends with a eulogy fit for a saint.

Rev. Black said, By her conduct, Frankie had exemplified proper Christian behavior, this we could see by her living habits. She had been a chaste woman in many ways. Frankie Whatley had clean speech and conduct, not just on Sunday at meeting time, she practiced these things as daily habits. In every facet of her life, Mrs. Whatley reflected clean moral behavior and that's something to be proud of. Neither time nor space nor the pain s that death cause, can ever separate a family from their beloved. We can only hope that time will ease the pain. Loving families can transcend and defeat death's temporary sting by remembering that we all have the hope of seeing our loved ones who precede us in death again in the resurrection that God has said is yet to come." *(Where is the beginning of this quote?)*

Rev. Black told each person attending, "Hold on to and cherish the warm and wonderful memories of family and holiday gatherings. Keep on as Frankie had, teaching and watching children grow and impacting each other's lives from our first cries as a baby in powerful ways. Finally, Pastor Black called Frankie a woman of substance who had taught her children the history of her people, and one of the great, strong, yet quiet characters of her time. "I know we are all going to miss Frankie. I know I am, but we got to let her go and rest in peace just like she lived, in peace and silence."

Frank was very happy with the content of the words spoken about his mother, and after the service was over, he approached and thanked the pastor for his kind discourse. Pastor Black hugged Frank and the entire immediate family as they began to file out of the church behind the casket to go to the grave site for internment.

After the short grave side service was dismissed, all the family and friends gathered at Frank and Minnie's house for the customary food and drink, and the continuation of the celebration of Frankie Whatley's life.

(wording) That was the norm in the colored community and Whatley family, after a funeral service was held, good eating and lots of drinking and partying. Frank told Salema that he wanted to talk to her, Berry, and Minnie as soon as possible when they got home after the service. He told Salema to round up

Berry and meet him in the parlor before all the guests began to arrive at the house.

When Salem and Berry entered the parlor Frank said, "This is how it's going to be. Berry, you want to marry my daughter, I suppose?"

"Yes sir, Mr. Whatley," Berry nervously answered.

Frank went on, "W ell, I reckon I can't stop y'all if you really want to get married and you love each other. But I can say this. That baby Salema is carrying is a Whatley and that's final. She not gone be a Berryhill. And yes I'm positive it's a girl. Now Salema, you are going to name that baby what I told you to name her, you understand?" "Yes sir daddy." Salema replied jubilantly. "Plus I have a surprise for you, the two of you. This project I've been working on for the past few weeks is a skating rink I'm building and me

166

and your mama have decided that we want you two to manage it." "Daddy are you serious?" Salema was so happy, she just couldn't believe it. She had her hands covering her face, and eyes bucked giggling like a little six year old. "Now Salema, you have to finish college as scheduled."

"All right, Daddy, thank you," Salema answered. She felt that she had been dictated to but maybe approved of. It didn't matter, she was happy, she was getting married to Berry. Frank shook Berry's hand and told them to plan the wedding for two weeks after the graduation.

Minnie was in total shock as Salema and Berry left the parlor. She had never seen Frank take such a 360-degree turn on an issue of this magnitude in all the time she had known him. She approached him to congratulate him on being open- minded about the matter, Frank turned to look outside the door to the parlor. "I feel like someone is watching us," he said. Sure enough, Celeste was standing to the right side of the door, eavesdropping.

She had heard the entire conversation transpire between Salema, Berry, and he daddy. Celeste looked intently as she addressed her father. "You think your decision was just and fair? I think it was domineering and tyrannical. I'm never going to allow you to pick when or where or who I get married to."

Frank was astonished at the level of disrespect that Celeste blatantly displayed towards him. "You fast tail little girl, you know better than to be standing out here looking in grown folks mouths when they're talking."

Before he could get another word out of his mouth, Minnie took over the conversation and disciplining. "Don't you stand your fast tail rump up the re talking to your father like you a grown ass woman. I'll get some switches and whip your ass until it ropes like okra. Now get your fast tail rump in there and get you something to eat and don't you ever let me hear you talk to your father like that again, not in your entire earth disturbing life, you lil heifer."

Celeste turned and scrambled out of the living room toward the kitchen as the first guests arrived at the front door from Frankie's grave site. Minnie laughed as she asked Frank on her way to answer the door, "Can you believe Celeste had the nerve to stand there talking to you like that? Standing there rolling her eyes at you like she just as grown as you are these days."

Frank was still very leery about disciplining Celeste. Today was a very sensitive day for him in that regard, because Celeste had said to him in the past that she was possessed with the spirit of his grandmother.. Now that Frankie was deceased, Celeste probably had planned on taking full advantage of her father's superstitions on death as soon as possible, that day, only to have Minnie spoil her plans of daughter-daddy mind control and domination, before she could hatch her devious little scheme on Frank. Celeste never tried that antic with her father ever again after that day.

The house was over run with people after about ten minutes of continuous arrivals at the front door. The entire extended family and a host of friends gathered together at the house. Together they exhibited the type of courage that Rev. Black spoke of in his eulogy, that allows the human family to survive the devastation that the sudden death of a loved one causes.

That night, after all the family and friends had left for the night, Frank saw that Doyle was taking the death of his grandmother a little harder than the rest of his siblings. He called Doyle into his bedroom and gave him a sterling silver and jade pinkie ring that belonged to Frankie. "Doyle, I know you miss your grand mama, and she would have wanted you to have this ring. Now you make sure you take good care of it, you hear me?"

"Otay Daddy, I done dake dood dare of dat wing, dank doo." Doyle smiled a wide grin as he slipped the ring on his right pinkie finger.

"You more than welcome, now get on in there and act like the big man your grand mama knows you are.."

Doyle couldn't walk out of the room for staring at the ring in disbelief, that he was now its proud owner. Frank stood at his dresser smiling with a light mist threatening to drip from his eyes, as he watched Doyle bend the corner into the hall. Minnie appeared in the door way as Doyle disappeared. She asked Frank what had made Doyle so happy. Frank told her about seeing Doyle a bit sad, standing in the kitchen, so he had given their youngest son a ring that he figured Frankie would have wanted him to have.

Frank's words were almost as mellifluous to Minnie's ears at that moment as the words that Rico used to woo his women. Minnie marveled at the fact that in his moment of most severe personal pain, Frank still had the where with al and mental clarity to put his child's concern ahead of his own grief for his mother. Why should this surprise me? Minnie slowly began easing her hands up the back of Frank's shoulder blades as Frank stood at the dresser with some of his mother's jewelry spread out in front of him on the top of the dresser. Having a man who felt the compulsion to serve and protect his family in a balanced way was indeed a blessing that Minnie wasn't about to take for granted. She rubbed Frank's shoulders and started to try and relieve some of the pent-up tension that had gripped him since he walked in the house a couple of days ago happy to have just learned about a court decision that secured his and his co-workers' financial lives, only to find out about the sad, life-altering news of his mother's untimely demise.

"All right now, Minnie, that feels too good. Now stop it, woman, you gone start something we can't finish in here this evening." Frank was trying to wiggle away from her strong yet velvety touch, but he was trapped between Minnie and the dresser, with no place to run or hide. A knock on the bedroom door saved them from things going any further. Arselee swung the door open after only hearing him ask who is it.

She wanted to tell her father that she loved him and that she understood how he must be feeling, because she was hurt too. "I really loved going over to Uncle Walsh's house to spending the night with grandma. All the girls would sleep with her and she always let me snuggle right up under her. That made me feel safe and secure; she could sense that I think. And she made me proud of my Native American Indian heritage and history, just like the preacher said today at the funeral. Y'all know what I was thinking in my room just now, Mama and Daddy? I was thinking to myself that I'm going to miss my grandma, Frankie, but I can let her go and rest in peace. Because I know she loved all of us. All I came in here to say is I'm glad she was my grandma and she made me proud to be able to say that I'm a Whatley. Both of my grandmothers understood and understand that I am a very sensitive young lady. I can be myself when I'm alone with either of them, not like everybody else around here."

Arselee turned and walked out without waiting on either one of her parents to reply to her spontaneous and rare verbal display of emotions. She was probably the one child of theirs who had inherited most of Frankie's genes that made her so introverted and sweet. But Arselee had a duality in her personality that did not exist in Frankie's; she had a bit of both Frank and Minnie's mean streak, locked inside of her, as well. If a person managed to push the right buttons in the correct order, then that unfortunate individual would soon find out that there was a broom-riding witch lurking beneath the depths of her sweet, shy public persona. Even having such a rage inside of her didn't take away from how loving Arselee was as a person. A whole lot of pushing had to occur before the witch would ride her broom.

CHAPTER XV

That night was made easier for Frank by the comfort that his children provided in words, as well as the promise Doyle had made to preserve his heirloom he had inherited from his grandma. The next week also helped, as Frank and his co-workers had to immerse themselves in their projects. The size and scope of the remodeling and refurbishing of the building for the skating rink kept Frank more than twice as busy as the average Joe. Then he still had other clandestine business concerns in operation and those entities were still growing. Frank still experienced times when he was very morose, but the passing of time and the full schedule he kept made it a little easier for him to bear the burden of losing his mother and the resulting devastating grieving process.

The time that had elapsed since Lori and Robert had arrived in town had helped them out immensely as well. Lori had gotten her routine at the café down to a science, and Robert had forgotten all the original feelings of home sickness and of missing his dad. They were adjusting to a tranquil rural life of full independence very well now.

The next five weeks flew by and remarkable improvement was being made on the skating rink. Frank figured, as did Mr. Moore, that they could open in about two more weeks; Frank was pushing for three more weeks at the most. Both floors were near completion and the tank for the cod with lighted floors and walls was fully operational at this point. The covered bridge had been installed over it and half the construction workers spent their lunch hours sitting around the bridge, staring at the fish.

Ever since he went back to work after the funeral, Frank had the overwhelming feeling that he could not get enough work done fast enough. It seemed to him that he always had the most irritating, nagging feeling in the back of his mind and in his gut that he had something more to do. Johnny had provided him with the finest trees that he had available and had been a very good listener to Frank on the rare occasions that he opened up to anyone.

Today, Johnny had asked Frank to bring Mr. Moore with him so he could talk to them about something that was important to the family. On the way up the main road to the house and bunkhouse area, Mr. Moore spotted Johnny's prize bull, Timbuck. "Now that big ole pretty stud bull sure would be a nice mount for my wall of fame, Frank."

Frank hated sport hunting and called the wall in Mr. Moore's office "the wall of shame," mostly because Mr. Moore didn't even kill most of the animals that he had mounted on it in the first place. He had either paid someone to kill them or bought them at a sporting goods store. Or he had cut a deal for some of the animals in the back rooms of lodges on the African savannah. Time and time again, Mr. Moore would banter on and on about his safaris in places in Africa like Swaziland. Mr. Moore had a vast well of knowledge about the small African kingdom, which he more than gladly shared with Frank. Mr. Moore spoke of his visit there in the mid twenties to hunt large game in the territory and land under the control of King Sobhuza the Second's monarchy. Mr. Moore had told Frank that colored people everywhere could be proud of the fact that the British had only administrative control and not full authority over the tiny nation nestled between South Africa and Namibia. Even though Swaziland is the second smallest country in Africa. King Sobhuza and his people in Swaziland had never been totally subjugated by any European nation, unlike most other nations on the African continent. Mr. Moore spoke of the near- temperate climate in the higher altitudes of Swaziland and how the plateau teamed with such a wide variety of wild life species. He spoke of the prolific and diversified bird life in Swaziland, where over 400 different species of birds can be seen, such as rarities like the bald ibis and blue crane. Frank was fascinated by tales of up- close encounters with live game like aardwolf, black- backed jackal, red duiker, honey badger, klipspringer, oribi, vaal rhebok, wildebeest, white rhino, serval, and zebra.

Although Frank had the ultimate level of respect for Mr. Moore, he had no respect for men who hunted any species of animal to near depletion just for the sport of it. Frank knew that deep down inside, Mr. Moore had respect for all of these majestic beasts. He just wanted to be able to look at the animals all the time by mounting some of them and placing them on his wall of shame.

These mounted animal trophies allowed Mr. Moore at any given moment while he was sitting in his office to take mental flight back to the jungles and plateaus of Africa. Frank never let Mr. Moore know how he really felt on the matter. As far as Frank was concerned, it was none of his business what hobby Mr. Moore chose as long as it didn't affect him, the ecology, or his family. But now, this twisted love affair that Mr. Moore had for stuffed animals was about to affect one of his family members.

Johnny loved him some Tim buck, and Frank knew it would be next to impossible to pry or negotiate the bull away from him. Tim buck was the model of consistency when it came to producing a fold; to Johnny, Tim buck was one of the main pillars of this farm.

Johnny had gotten word from north Georgia that Beau Jennings, Will Jennings's only son, was running the farm into the ground after his mother's death, and was selling the top land on the farm where the main house and the house that he and his brothers had built once stood. Beau was keeping all the top- grade low land for the Jenning's family to move to and build a new home there and live. Johnny wanted to solicit some help in getting a white face that could be trusted down there to purchase that top land for him, Jane, and Minnie.

Mr. Moore got out of the car and gazed longingly down in the direction where Tim buck stood grazing on some hay. "Now I sure would love to see that old bull preserved for all eternity. It would be a shame to see a beautiful beast like that grow old and die when I could give him eternal life on my wall of fame, Johnny."

Johnny looked down the field, and before he knew it, a flash of anger over came him. He looked at Mr. Moore and said, "Now you might have Frank and everybody else around here convinced that you can piss up wind in a thunderstorm and not get wet, but I'm not so sure you got me convinced it can be done yet, Mister. My bull ain't for sale, now or ever." Mr. Moore started laughing and walked a couple of steps toward the bull but stayed in ear shot of the conversation between Frank and Johnny so he could hear.

"Frank, I need some help with getting a trustworthy white man to go down and purchase some land for me in Georgia. You know ole Will

Jennings's wife Heather died and their son Beau done almost lost everything they owned. Now in order for him to save any of the land his daddy owned, Beau needs to sell some top land pretty cheap and we need to get in on it and tie that land up right now." Johnny winked at Frank so that he would know to play along with what ever he said. "Now, we don't need no money, Frank, just for the man to deal with them good ole boys for us and bring back the deed in your name for me. Will you help me out with this thing?"

Mr. Moore slowly stepped back over and boldly interjected himself into the conversation. "Now I might know an ole boy down there in Georgia that I can trust with my life that can get this land deal wrapped up by the end of the week if I can get that bull mounted by then."

Johnny almost jumped up in the air but managed to keep his composure as he shot his hand out to shake on the deal. Johnny's hand came rocketing out so fast that he hit Frank's arm on the way to shake Orland Moore's hand on the deal to purchase the land that held the remains of all his brothers.

Frank merely wanted to discuss the fact that Minnie had a very bad dream a few nights back and wanted Johnny's opinion of her dream. "Minnie's uncle Buddy Lee had appeared in her dream and told her that William Heard wanted to ask Minnie if her ma could come on home to take care of him and his brothers. She said Buddy Lee appeared in ragged clothe and had a gaunt physical appearance as though he had not been eating good. The dream scared her so bad; the next morning I found her curled up in a fetal position in her mother's bed, with Jane holding her in her arms. Johnny tried not to seem as if the dream bothered him at all, but it scared the daylights out of him in reality. Johnny's only reply to his niece's nightmare was to say, "Come on now, Frank, we all know that dreams ain't real. She's probably bothered by the fact that Frankie just died, so she just scared she might lose Jane, that's all it could be, Frank."

At this point Frank was ready to accept anything that sounded half way rational. So he quickly agreed with Johnny's concise analogy of Minnie's bad dream and dropped the subject altogether.

After Frank had left that day with a load of trees, Johnny decided he would talk to Minnie about the dream when he'd take her, her weekly supply of meat that he processed fresh for the cafe's usage.

When Johnny breached the subject with Minnie, he never told her that Frank had discussed the matter with him; he simply made a comment about a night mare that he had about his brothers. William had come to him in a similar way about a month before Frankie died, saying that he needed Jane to come and take care of him, and it wasn't the first time that Johnny had the dream. That's why it scared him so bad when Frank told him of the dream that Minnie had.

Minnie told Johnny, "I do declare, that dabb blasted dream got away with me so bad I didn't know what to do with myself, I was so scared I near bout peed on myself when I got up. So I just ran in Ma's room and jumped in the dag blasted bed with her. Johnny, I tell you the truth. I wouldn't know what I'd do without Ma. I know its gone near bout drive me mad when she takes her journey on home to glory, but I can't let her know that's how I feel. Ma expects me to be so strong all the time but I'm not as strong as she is and I know it."

Johnny said to Minnie, "Listen, you have just as much as Jane if not more, shoot for as that matter most men I know, so stop the pity party, it don't become you very well." Before Minnie knew it, she was ready to start slinging Johnny around the café as if they were still teenagers back in north Georgia. But the inclination to wrestle was now replaced with a smile and a thank you at this point in their mid life juncture.

Jane had been listening to the entire conversation between Minnie and Johnny from her station around the corner from the two of them. So Jane tried to ease both their minds as best she could by coming around the corner and telling them both off. "Next time them dead folks bothering y'all in your sleep, tell them I ain't ready to die and take care of nobody yet, and y'all stop tryin' ta push me over in a grave or rush me away from here too. I got too many babies ta take care of down here. I ain't ready to go nowhere right yet, if the Good Lawd willin'." Then Jane turned and went back to her work station with a sly grin on the corner of her mouth, to finish cutting up vegetables.

Knowing how much they both still needed her is what had kept her going all these years and it meant the world to Jane mentally. Neither Minnie nor Johnny ever gave Jane any rebuttal, or back talk, as she preferred to call it. They gave each other a raised eye brow and wide- eyed look of acknowledgment that Ma was still the queen, and deferred to her seniority.

Salema had asked and got Jane, Mrs. Rosa Duvall, and several other ladies of the quilt club to once again enlist themselves to do the sewing for her wedding gowns. This time, the ladies had plenty of time to get the dresses ready for the grand matrimonial ceremony. And this wedding was going to indeed be a grand affair. After all, it was Minnie and Frank's first born daughter, not that Frank thought any less of Maxie. But he was going to give Salema away in a first- class all- the- way gala.

CHAPTER XVI

The graduations were awesome for the entire family. Rico was so impressed with the college scene that it was a task to get him to leave campus after the twins' commencement ceremony. Salema had walked with her class the weekend before and she was not enjoying seeing all the possibilities marriage and pregnancy would deny her. She as happy to see her siblings accomplish their goals of getting a college degree, yet depressed at the thought that she may not get hers.

Maxie could see what she was going through, and she managed to get away from J.D. long enough to try to comfort her little sister. "Come here, Salema, let me tell you something about college. Now you been up here to see me and William, so you know it ain't easy and these knuckle heads want more bedroom knowledge than they do book knowledge anyway. Plus you gone go to school, Frank Whatley gone see to that, Ms. Salema. And on top of everything else, you got all of us and Berry's fine ass, and you got a baby coming. Girl, hold your head up high. What's wrong with you? Let's enjoy our lives, honey, college ain't the end of the damn world and you know it. You're about to get married next week, girl, then start managing a beautiful skating rink. Not one of these people out here graduating can say they got a ready- made business to go start operating, not even me," she said grinning a bit. "Come on now, do you realize how blessed you are, woman?"

"Thanks Maxie for coming over here and talking some sense into me. You right, what am I thinking about, I am blessed, Yes I am blessed," she said laughing. While she and Maxie hugged Salema thanked her again for helping her to see the opportunity she had before her and for caring.

"After awhile you gone be too big to be a maid of honor for me, if you keep swelling up like you been doing the past couple weeks."

"Salema, you know Ma gone make our dresses where somebody got to really be staring up your tail to make out that we showing a little bit."

Frank and Minnie decided to have a joint graduation celebration that would be small in number because the wedding was going to be the following Saturday. Frank had taken Berry inside the skating rink to work on the refurbishing every day since the engagement was made official. Salema and Berry would get their very own set of keys to the building after the wedding reception. He had helped Frank design the kitchen for the rink, which turned out to be a small version of the cafe's large kitchen.

Frank was becoming very fond of Berry; he could see that they had a lot of things in common and shared many similar personal qualities. The major difference in the two men was their family background. Both of Berry's parents were raging alcoholics, and his worst nightmare was following that path in life. Other than that, the two men had more in common than differences in personal character, their likes, and dislikes. Frank loved baseball, hunting, fishing, playing solitaire, owning as much of Chattataas he could and po-ke-no; so did Berry for the most part, except for the latter two. By the time the wedding day came around, Berry had completely won his father -in-law over with his hard work ethic and the fact that Frank could see him light up when Salema came around him.

Salema asked Maxie if J.D. would perform the ceremony for her and Berry, and Maxie called J.D. over and asked him if he would perform the rites. J.D. was overwhelmed by the honor and immediately accepted. All he wanted to know was if the couple wanted to use traditional or their own vows. Salema was stuck on traditional, but only as far as the vows were concerned; the rest of the wedding ceremony was going to be personalized and purely contemporary.

Salema had chosen a Caribbean sky blue material that almost matched the decor in the café for her gown. Maxie's gown was a tad darker than hers, and the rest of the girls in the wedding ceremony dresses were rainbow. Berry's tuxedo matched Salema's dress and M. L., who was of course the best man, and the groomsmen's tuxedos all matched Maxie's dress. Frank had the back yard transformed into a garden paradise for the ceremony.

The night before the wedding, he called Salema into his bedroom and gave her a large sum of money and a set of keys to a house. This was his wedding gift to her and Berry. The home had two bedrooms and a restroom with inside water, a toilet, and electricity. Salema was over come by her emotions and started to cry. She had not fully considered the fact that this was her last night at home with her brothers and sisters; she was leaving home for good tomorrow. She felt like a vulnerable little girl instead of a grown woman who was about to be married the very next day. The reality and magnitude of the union she was about to enter into hit her like a ton of bricks. And to say that she developed a case of cold feet would be an understatement. "Daddy, what am I doing, am I ready for this?"

"We all ask our self that question right about now, Salema, but you got to ask yourself that question, not me. Pray on it tonight and ask the Lord to guide your heart. Do you love him enough to sleep out doors with him if you had to?"

"Yes, Daddy, I do, and I'm not just saying that either. I mean it from the bottom of my heart."

Rico was a groomsman in the wedding, and he needed some shoe polish for his dark blue Stetsons, so he knocked on the door to his parents' room. Frank handed Salema a handkerchief and gave her time to get her face cleaned up before he let Rico in the room. Rico asked for and received permission to take a fresh can of his dad's polish for his shoes. He was excited about how dapper he would look to all the women at the wedding. As he bolted from the room, he told Salema to make sure she had the photographer make an extra picture of him by himself at the reception. Frank and Salema looked at each other and laughed at the enormous size of the ego that had just taken over their conversation. The funny thing to both of them was how no one was even going to be thinking about a picture of Rico at the reception except maybe Rico himself. Frank called him back from down the hall and told Rico that he needed him and Doyle to help hang some streamers in the back yard early in the morning. Frank and Berry had made some rainbow- colored streamers that matched the dresses in the wedding to hang along the walk way to the altar. The yard was all ready for the big day and so was the family. This wedding would begin the real healing process, for most if not all the Whatley clan after the death of its quiet matriarch.

When Frank woke up the next morning, he couldn't believe his eyes and ears; it couldn't be thundering and lightening outside. There were none of the usual signs that an impending storm was on the way the night before. But here it was at six in the morning, raining cats and dogs outside. Frank had gotten up early so that he could set up all the chairs in the garden area, where the wedding was going to be held. He looked out of the kitchen window and could see that the entire sky wasn't dark, just one big area was looking rather ominous and pitch black. Frank could see the cloud pattern moving out of the area fast, so he surmised that the thunder head was just passing over quickly. He was right; the passing shower only served to clean up the entire back garden area, and by the time the wedding began, you could not even tell a shower had passed through. The yard was perfect and so was the bride.

J.D. was a little nervous and stammered over a couple of his words, but over all, he did a splendid job officiating the wedding ceremony. As he asked Commo Berryhill, "Do you take this woman, Salema Whatley, to be your lawfully married wife?" Frank cleared his throat, something that he had told

Berry he was going to do earlier that morning. It was an inside shotgun wedding joke between the two of them. Berry laughed when he heard the signal from Frank, and Salema wondered what was so funny. She gave Berry a kind of inquisitive look as she too started laughing a little bit.

But Berry quickly regained his composure and said, "I do." Minnie had figured out what her husband had done, and she elbowed him in the side with a light jab. Minnie smiled coyly to herself, knowing that she had really orchestrated this whole event in the hopes of her daughter being happy. It didn't take very much manipulation, because Frank would have known that Berry was the one for Salema any way if he had just looked for himself, Minnie was thinking as Salema repeated her vows back to Berry.

After the ceremony was over, Salema and Berry walked back inside the house, she asked him if he wanted to go see their new home. Berry was shocked; he had a room that he had tried to get prepared for a new bride to move into. "Where did we get a house, Salema?"

"Don't worry about it. We got the deed in our name, and it's all legal and ours. All we need to do is go down to the furniture store and pick us out the kind of furniture we want in it, Mr. Berryhill, sir."

"Shit, this is better than I even dreamed it was gone be," Berry shouted as Minnie opened the back door to the kitchen.

"Everything all right in here?" she asked as she entered the kitchen. "Y'all didn't get hit in the eye with none of that rice them fools threw right in your faces, did y'all?"

"No ma'am," Berry answered, "me and Mrs. Berryhill just fine, Ms. Minnie."

"Well, the café is ready for the reception that y'all asked me for, so I'm gone head on over yonder now," Minnie announced.

Jane came in the door and called Minnie. She wanted to ride in the car with only her or Frank, no one else, she said. Minnie took Celeste, Cecelia, and Arselee with her. Jane and Rico rode with Frank. Doyle was almost left at the house because he had to take the time to change clothes. Then he insisted on finding his best pair of skates to take with him so that he could sneak away and skate with Robert. Luckily for him, William and Ethel were changing clothes too, so they waited on him to get ready.

Berry had heard a local blues band that he said reminded him of New Orleans in the juke joint one night after he and Frank had wrapped up working at the skating rink. Frank had offered to buy him a few drinks, but Berry only had one. Berry always drank alcohol in moderation, but Frank saw that Berry was enthralled by the band, so Frank hired the musical group to play at the reception, and all the guests kept saying that they were exceptionally good.

Salema and Berry stopped at their new home and Berry carried her across the threshold of the front door way. When he put her down, he kept thinking what had been going through his mind as she walked up the aisle with her mean ass looking daddy. "How did I get lucky enough to marry this drop dead fine, dark chocolate princess?" The two of them ran through the house like two little children, looking in closets, cabinets, drawers, bathroom, everywhere. Finally they met each other in the master bedroom. Salema then realized that she and Berry had never had sex. "You want to have sex now, Berry, or wait until after we come home tonight?" Salema eased up close to him.

"Woman, if we start having sex now, we won't go to no reception. I done waited this long, damnit Salema, why did you have to go and say that? Ummm, let's go, let's just gone get out of here, now. We gone do some heavy duty celebrating tonight, baby."

M. L. had picked up Willie Hansley and a couple more of his old navy buddies from the train station the night before who had come to town for the wedding, so there was no limit on Berry's drinking tonight. M.L., the navy fellows, and M.L.'s mother Ernestine had made it over to the reception before most of the family members arrived at the café. They had already started in on a tub full of ice cold beer and had polished off about three each, that's including Ernestine, before any other guests arrived. Ernestine was known for being able to hold her own at the bar, no matter the potency of the chosen alcoholic beverage. She would also cuff anything that was not nailed down, and everyone knew she had a thief's mentality and a cold heart.

As soon as Doyle got inside the café, he sought out Robert. Tom Worthy, who had spent every day getting to know and love Robert at the café since Lori started working there, told Doyle that his friend was in the rest room and that Robert had been waiting for and talking about Doyle all morning long. It wasn't long before the two of them were off on another skating adventure.

Once again, Robert headed straight for the railroad tracks. As fate would have it, a train was about a quarter mile from crossing as they approached the main crossing on Alabama Street. Robert couldn't resist the urge to race the train, even though Doyle told him, "I not done do dat wit do no mo, do done dit in dwouble, Wabert." But Robert was already on his way up onto the crossing and paid Doyle no attention; he just flew across right as the train came whistling by. Doyle couldn't tell if Robert made it clear on the other side or not. He kept bending down, trying to see between the cars. It looked like he could see Robert lying on the ground on the other side of the train, but he wasn't sure. The cars were moving much too fast for Doyle to clearly discern if his friend had made it safely across in time.

As soon as the train cleared, he jetted for the other side. Robert was lying sprawled on his back, stiff as a board. As soon as Doyle leaned over to check and see if he was all right. Robert sprang up on his skates and started laughing because Doyle nearly jumped out of his skin from the fright. After Doyle regained himself, the two boys shared a good laugh and skated back down toward the café.

Mean while, back at the café, Babe had made it to the reception. She had sat next to Minnie and Frank at the wedding and Minnie wanted to introduce her to one of her male church members tonight. She had mentioned him to Babe after they came home from Frankie's funeral, but Babe said it was too soon after her break up with Willie to be meeting someone new.

Salema and Berry had gone back to the family home and to Berry's room, and both had changed out of their wedding clothes when they arrived at the café.

They came in the door both smiling and dancing with each other. This was their day and no one had to announce it to the world. The sparkle in each of their eyes said it loud and clear. If Salema and Berry had been shot off on a rocket into the cosmos at that very moment, the rulers of the universe would have had to add names for four new stars shining in the heavens, the glow in their eyes was so bright.

As the young couple danced around, Minnie stood staring at Frank, marveling at his maturation on how he was dealing with their children. Where as when Salema was a little girl, Frank had been stern and as rigid as a board, when it came to discipline or decisions he made, he was as stubborn as a jack bull.

But now on this adult matter and life-altering decision, he had become as malleable as potter's clay and had shown wisdom.

Johnny came and pulled Frank to the side; he had delivered Timbuck to Mr. Moore and picked up the deed to the property in north Georgia the night before. He wanted to present the deed to Minnie and Jane at the reception. "I'm so damn happy on the inside, I could bust open right here and die happy, Frank." Frank immediately stopped the band from playing and gathered the family around him in a circle. Then he let Johnny have the floor as he stood holding Jane's hand in the middle of the room. Johnny pulled the deed to the land from his pocket and handed it to Jane.

Ma looked at him confused and asked, "What dis foolishness you up ta, boy?" Jane handed the deed to Minnie and she could hardly keep control of her emotions as she looked at the piece of paper in her hands.

"Oh, Ma.........oh, Ma... Ma, I can't believe this...this is not real, Uncle Johnny, is this really true, it just can't be real. Johnny, how in creation did you pull this off, man?" Minnie hugged Jane and whispered to her that they now owned the land where her pappa was buried and they were free to go there now; it was theirs for real. Jane started rubbing her hair all over her head and crying so hard that Minnie had to carry her into the back kitchen. Minnie had closed the entire café for public business for this wedding reception so they were alone. Then Johnny came into the kitchen and the three of them stood together crying like little children.

Ma wiped her face and grabbed Johnny's hand and said, "I'm so glad dat the good Lawd let me live long 'nough ta see dis day. I can go on ta glory happy now, not dat I be in a hurry ta git dare yet. Oh, let's go have some fun'. My baby done got married up and we gets ta go on home ta our very own land. Ain't that a grand thang?"

All the while Jane was speaking, Minnie never stopped staring at her uncle Johnny. Was there no end to the gifts and miracles he had always brought into her life? And now this, her father could not have made a wiser choice of which of his brothers to send for this life long assignment of providing for and protecting his only daughter, and Minnie realized that at this moment more than ever before. It seemed this moment kept repeating itself in Minnie's life, and Johnny remained as selfless as ever, even in his finest, brightest moments he displayed genuine humility.

Rico and all the rest of the family came into the kitchen to find out what had upset Ma so much. Maxie and J.D. went directly behind Rico to Jane's side. Minnie explained in as brief terms as possible what had happened. After a loud round of applause, the family streamed out of the kitchen, led by Jane. She became the life of the party after receiving the great news about the ownership of what she believed was land that was Minnie's birthright, so to speak. In Jane's mind, she figured her family had made Will Jennings and his family most every dime they ever made. Just like the lazy, dependent upon other folk to do their work for them, people like the Jennings and others like them.

Berry got so drunk at his own reception that he had to be carried up the steps to his new home by his buddy, Willie Hansley. Babe met Mark Crutchfield, the church member that Minnie had wanted her to meet. Although he was a nice-looking guy, he didn't seem to be to Babe's liking right off the bat. But they had a great time dancing at the reception. Mark was a polite and perfect gentlemen. Babe even agreed to a small picnic the next weekend after church on Sunday.

As the last few guests straggled out of the café at the end of the night after the reception, Tom noticed M.L.'s mother, Ernestine, standing in the kitchen looking inside of the huge meat freezer. Tom could see that Ernestine had already stuffed what looked like a slab of salt pork in her big bag that she always carried, just in case the opportunity to cuff something arose. As Ernestine and M.L. staggered down the alley, Tom ran and got Emma so that she could witness the drunken pair. Tom and Emma almost died laughing at the sight of the mom and son buffoons stumbling up the alley.

CHAPTER XVII

One thing that neither J.D. nor Berry could ever get used to was the fact that both of their wives insisted on attending the weekly family meetings at their family's home on Friday nights. But neither of them ever complained about the meetings verbally or let the cat out of the bag that they disliked their wives attending, and soon they both began to love attending the meetings themselves. The raw honesty and sometimes heated debates were entertaining and informative to both men. Conversations were open and candid, and the overt legal family business status was closely watched over and strategically planned by the senior family members who were involved in the day-to-day maintenance and operations of the café, fifteen rental properties, and now the skating rink.

In just a week after the wedding, the skating rink was near completion; the only thing left to do was hang the sign outside and apply three to five coats of finish to the floors. Berry had learned a technique in the navy where he used a buffer in between coats of finish with some cold water that he sprinkled on the floor with a brand new paint brush. Berry could fully control and operate a high-speed buffer with a five-gallon bucket of cold water hanging from one handle. He would smoothly let the buffer glide over the rink's floor, dip the brush in the cold water, then he would start lightly flinging water in front of him. This gave the rink's floor a shine that made the entire floor look wet even after it had completely dried. Berry did the entire building like this in a twenty-four-hour continuous work stint that mirrored the long hours he used to put in on the ship in the navy.

Salema was proud of the stamina and stubborn attitude Berry had when it came to working. Plus she had never seen a floor shine as pretty as glass

184

and it was her man making it happen, and the whole family could see it. Frank was impressed, to say the least, when he first saw the floor; so were Minnie and Jane. Ma thought the place was amazing; she walked around like it couldn't be a real building when she first visited the skating rink. Berry had applied five coats of finish, and the rink looked great. Berry assured Frank that the hard finish would protect the hard wood floors and that he would maintain the rink and keep it looking just as it is at this moment. Berry would prove himself an integrity keeper over time on this, if no other promise he ever made were kept.

The sign arrived and was hung that afternoon, and the rink was ready for its grand opening that Friday night. That evening, the entire Moore and Whatley clans met at the Aurora Skating Rink for the very first time. Mr. Moore and his oldest son Lincoln were discussing the profit margin in such a business. Lincoln was impressed with the facility and wanted to know who was managing the day- to- day operations. Lincoln owned and operated three bowling alleys that were very successful. After he met Salema, they talked for the rest of the evening and Lincoln later told his father that he was very impressed with how sharp she was as far as business matters were concerned. Mr. Moore told him, "Well she's had two good example in Frank and Minnie on how to maintain a successful business, so we all expect Salema to do well managing the rink."

The next day, when he got home from school, Doyle couldn't wait to get to the café and tell Robert that the Aurora was opening Friday. Doyle asked Lori if Robert could attend the gala opening, and of course she said yes, as long as Robert was a good boy the remainder of the week. Lori knew this would put Robert on his best behavior and manners. Robert knew Friday night would be an excellent opportunity to release some rage and race a train. He couldn't wait to win the rage race. He was fuming on the inside; being pent up in the café all day.

Even though Tom made it as much fun as he could, it was still boring to Robert. Robert had grown very fond of Tom and the rest of the crew at the café, especially Ma. She was always feeding him something that tasted delicious, and he loved to eat. Minnie was always teasing Robert, telling him that he started off every morning eating because he was hungry, then spent the rest of the day filling his belly eating for taste.

On Thursday, Babe had gone to the department store to pick up some things that she needed for home and saw the latest roller skates for boys on sale, so she bought a pair for both Doyle and Robert since she saw how much they loved to skate together. Babe had planned on meeting the boys at the café before the rink opened up on Friday night, after she finished working. But when she got there, the two boys and every one except William had left for the Aurora's grand opening. Babe asked how Doyle and Robert had traveled down the street to the rink, and William told her that they had taken off from the café on their skates after everyone else had left in cars. It was only about a block and just across the railroad tracks to the skating rink, William had thought nothing of them skating over to the rink.

But Babe remembered the dangerous game that she had caught Robert teaching Doyle, and the fact that she had never mentioned it to a living soul. A frightening feeling of impending doom overcame her that something terrible was about to happen to Doyle. Babe hollered, "Come on here William, we got to get to them tracks right now""

Babe's premonition of doom had been right on point. As the boys reached the tracks, as usual, a train was coming. Robert readied himself for his mad dash across in front of the oncoming freight, as Doyle vehemently protested that he not make the dastardly effort tonight. "Do douldn't do dat no mo, Wabert, pease don do it. Let's dust doe do da date wink," Doyle pleaded to no avail with Robert. Robert made his usual last-second dash and seemed to clear the train.

As Babe and William screeched to a stop in Babe's car, Doyle was crouched down trying to see between the cars as they zipped by the three of them. William hollered to Doyle at the top of his lungs, "Where is Robert at, boy?"

"He dwied da wace da dwain I dee him on da gwound ower dare on da odder dide of da dwain."

As soon as the train cleared William could see that a tragic accident had occurred. Robert had slipped and lost his balance just as he cleared the other side of the train. Robert's left arm had gotten caught by the engine as the train went by him. The boy's left hand had been completely severed just above his wrist. William scooped Robert up and laid him in the back seat of the car. He told Babe and Doyle to get in and he took off for County General Hospital, less than a block away.

When they arrived at the hospital, Dr. Green was on duty. As soon as the doctor saw the severity of the little boy's injury, the team of medical personnel on duty swung into action. William shouted to the doctor, "Save the boy's life, please don't let him bleed to death," as they carted Robert off to the surgical wing of the hospital. William stood there rubbing the top of his head. Babe was trying to console Doyle, who was hysterical by this point. He kept asking Babe, "Is my fwiend gwone die?"

Babe assured Doyle that Robert would survive, and comforted him as best she could. She was so upset herself that she could barely keep her composure. Both hands were shaking as she hugged Doyle. Babe whispered to him, "It was the Lord that Robert and his mama here to us, don't worry, he'll bring him through this storm. O.K. Shhhh......now be strong and stop crying, boy after this is over ..."Babe felt a flash of anger but fought it back and kept consoling Doyle. "Just clean up your face now, be strong, and pray for your little buddy lying back there on that operating table." Babe called William's name and snapped him out of his state of shock that he had been suspended in mentally ever since he set foot in the door of the hospital.

William had immediately flashed back to his own recent attack, remembering he had just been here fighting for his own life. "William," Babe repeated for the third time, "go over to the skating rink and get Minnie and Frank and stop back at the café and pick up Lori as quietly as you can. Don't stir up no fuss and don't let everybody know what's going on over here at this hospital either. We don't want the same kind of mess and crowd over here like when you got hurt. Don't let Emma hear you tell Lori a word, you hear me, William?"

"Yes ma'am, Babe, I hear you loud and clear. I'm gone handle things discreetly all right. Doyle, calm down and stop crying and keep your head up like my little brother suppose to, you hear me, boy?"

Doyle straightened his face up almost before William's voice waves stopped reverberating across the air. That was the kind of raw power William had over both Rico and Doyle mentally. William did not even come close to following the logistical pattern that Babe had given him for rounding up Frank, Minnie, and Lori. He headed directly back to the café and called Lori out back. When she exited the back door, William said, "Don't ask me no questions, just get in the car."

Lori could tell by the expression on William's face that he meant business. She jumped in the passenger seat and as they took off, she panted out, "What's wrong? What's going on? Where are we going in such a hurry, William? Is something wrong with my baby?"

"Yes... yes, I'm sorry to be the bearer of bad news, but Robert has been hit by a train and he lost his left hand just above the wrist, it looks like to me, Ms. Lori. He was unconscious and headed into the operating room at the hospital when I left to come get you and my mama. I came directly to get you so I could get you up here as soon as possible."

Lori had a horrified look plastered on her face. How could this be happening? Things were going so well for them here in Chattanooga. Finally, she was going to be able to provide for Robert and herself a sense of safety and security, and now he lay possibly dying in a hospital because he chose to play chicken and race a train. William hurried into the rear entrance to the hospital. He escorted Lori into the waiting area where Babe and Doyle were sitting. Then he turned and left for the skating rink. Lori asked Babe what had they told her about Robert's condition. Babe had nothing to report except what William had already told her on the way over from the café. So Lori went to the nurses' station and they had no updated information for her either, but a ton of paperwork for her to fill out was stuck in her face immediately. Lori sat weeping as she tried to concentrate on filling in the spaces on the paper. Her every thought was with her son, praying for his survival.

William did not even speak to Salema or Berry as he went into the skating rink and located Frank and Minnie standing up front with Mr. Moore. He immediately whispered in Frank's ear what had transpired on the train tracks, and that they needed to quietly get over to the hospital. Frank quickly filled

Minnie and Mr. Moore in on what had taken place, and they all broke for the door with out causing a scene or calling any attention to themselves. Frank told Salema to make sure things ran smoothly at the rink, that a slight emergency had come up, but not to worry, things were under control. Salema and Berry both figured this was a staged move on their part to see how they would handle running the business with out them. After all, it was opening night and the place was packed to the rafters. They had no idea that such a catastrophic injury had happened to such a young child right under their noses.

When they arrived at the hospital, Lori was distraught. Her anguish had been intensified by a very rude and callous administrative assistant who demanded to know how the bill would be paid. Minnie stopped that immediately when she walked up and saw what was going on. "I'm paying every dime of whatever it costs to make sure that child gets the best care available." Minnie sat down at Lori's side and relieved her of the clip board that she had a death grip on and helped her fill out the remaining portions of her paperwork; then the doctor came rushing into the waiting area smiling.

Dr. Green informed everyone that the train's amputation had severed all the bones and arteries off cleanly and all he had to do was clean Robert's wound up and sew him up. "The biggest part of Robert's recovery is going to be mental, not physical," he told Lori. "There will be some psychological aspects to Robert's reaching maximum medical improvement after such a catastrophic injury at his young age. But all in all you have strong little young man in there." The psychoanalytical process could be life long for him. Because of the way he got hurt suggested to Dr. Green that there were some underlying issues that needed to be brought out. He asked if there were any questions and told Lori she could go in and see Robert in about fifteen minutes.

"Thank you Ms. Minnie, I don't know what I would have done without you being here with me tonight." Minnie told Frank and Mr. Moore to go back to the skating rink; that she was going to stay and comfort Lori and that there was no need for them to be held hostage, staying at the hospital all night long. Reluctantly they both agreed that it would be best to leave Babe and Minnie at the hospital and take Doyle with them. But for the first and only time in his life, Doyle refused to go with Frank when he called him. Doyle just sat clutching tightly to Minnie's arm.

Minnie looked at Frank and said, "Go on, let him stay here with me. He ain't gone have no fun anyway, as long as Robert is laid up in this hospital tonight."

Frank and Mr. Moore left and went on back over to the Aurora. The rink was full to capacity; it seemed all the kids in town were in the place. Salema handed Frank a wad of cash when he came up to the front door of the rink. Frank knew right then and there that he had to devise another system for collecting the gate at the Aurora. The present format of pay and walk past made Salema easy prey to any would- be robber at the front door clicker. So the next weekend, Frank made it so that Berry would handle the gate receipts from a small locked booth in front of the Aurora and each paying customer received a ticket.

Back at the hospital, William had left shortly after Frank and Mr. Moore departed, so Minnie, Doyle, Lori, and Babe all went in to see Robert. Robert had his head turned toward the wall, away from the door to his room. He heard the door open, but his arm was hurting a little more as the anesthesia that had been administered began to wear off. Robert lay quietly crying as Lori walked over to his bed. He looked so sad to her ;the first words he said were, "Mama, I'm so shame for being so stupid. Everybody must think we some ole country fools. Ms. Minnie you want send us away, will you? cause I really am sorry. I'm sorry mama for being bad, honest I am."

Lori reached out and grabbed Robert in her arms very carefully. She started to cry and just held him gently in her arms, silently staring at Minnie and Babe. Then she whispered softly to Robert, "I love you and I don't think you're stupid or country. I do think we need to find out why you wanted to risk your life and race trains. Don't you, Robert?"

"Yes Mama, I do. I don't know why I like to race in front of the trains, but I know I won't ever do it again. I was so scared, Mama, I just knew I was about to die right then and there. Once it caught a hold to me, I figured on being tossed around like a ole rag doll by that big ole freight."

Right about then, the nurse came into the room to give Robert a shot to make him sleep. Minnie told Robert that she was going to get him the best help that she could get and that they would be there when he woke up. Lori reminded Robert just how much she loved him and gave him a hug before he drifted off to sleep. A couple hours of strong female debate followed about how to best help Robert cope with all the immediate adjustments that he would be faced with upon his release from the hospital. The basic adaptations for meeting the necessities of facing everyday life would be his first big crisis. To fail at the onset of his rehabilitation would create an immeasurable distance psychologically for him to travel in order for him to get back a sense of normalcy in his life, and Lori already realized that.

Minnie's advice was to be patient, loving, yet firm, and to not show pity, and for Lori and everyone else to be sure to treat Robert as if he had never lost the limb in the first place. "Doyle was born with rickets that near bout took him right on away from here, and a speech impediment resulted from the rickets, but I refused to let him use those things as crutches to handicap himself. With the right kind of love and a whole lot of prayer, we can all work together to pull Robert through this terrible thing."

Babe inserted that some people who were whole-bodied at one time were sometimes very stern or down right mean at times. She also deduced that those embittered individuals with physical limitations were probably in reality very sweet people underneath their protective hard core exterior, but gave off impressions of having a hard, bitter edge about themselves because of their handicaps. "Lori be careful that Robert don't start to build complexes with the other children." Babe reminded Lori, "children can be cruel at times, playing practical jokes on one another, its inevitable that some knuckle head is going to tease Robert about losing his hand in a skating- slash- train accident, and the clubbed arm."

The three of them decided to inquire about being referred to a doctor who could help with the mental aspect of Robert's recovery when Dr. Green came back around to brief Lori. Lori thanked Minnie for her stepping up and guaranteeing payment to the hospital for the more than excellent medical treatment that Robert was receiving. "Lori, I ain't thought no more bout no bill after I told that lady I would pay for Robert to be taken care of. The most important thing for us to be concerned with right now is that your child is all right. I'm going to do what I said, not because I want you to feel like you're be holdin' to me, but 'cause the Lord blessed us so we are able to share our blessings and help others a little less fortunate than we are right now." The ladies concluded their conversation. Now they were staking a child's future on the approach they had chosen for his mental recovery after this most awful, traumatic event in his life. They hoped they had made the right choices for Robert. They all agreed that they had come up with as full and complete of an emergency contingency plan for a full recovery for Robert as they could muster with their limited knowledge.

Dr. Green came into the room. He informed Lori that if no infections or complications arose, he saw no reason to keep Robert for no more than overnight for observation purposes. So if he remained stable, she could take her son home in the morning. He wanted to see Robert again in ten days to check the wound, and then he gave Lori instructions for cleaning and changing the bandages. Dr. Green also referred Lori to a psychologist for Robert to begin seeing immediately.

After the doctor left, Lori asked Minnie and Babe to let her spend the rest of the night alone with Robert. She told them that she did not want to seem unappreciative of all their help, but that she needed the time to start helping Robert get the idea that she was always going to be the one person he could count on being there for him. Minnie understood what Lori was trying to say, and agreed to let her have the space she wanted to begin dealing with this harsh reality that her son was now going to need help overcoming.

That morning after the doctor checked Robert's arm over and everything checked out all right, Robert was released from the hospital. Of course, word had spread all over town by now that the accident had occurred and the results were being greatly exaggerated as the story passed along from one person to the next. From the moment they arrived back the farm, Johnny took charge of Robert's rehabilitation. Johnny tripled the amount of time that he spent with Robert previously. He monopolized the boy's entire day every day after he returned home from school. The most amazing thing about the tragic accident for Robert was, he had not been forced to miss one day of school although Dr. Green had given him two weeks out with a medical excuse, but he insisted on going that Monday after the accident occurred. Whenever Johnny could see that Robert was feeling sorry for himself, and would remind him that he still could write, eat, dress himself with out any help, and he could see himself do it.

There were still good days and bad days for Robert during the months after the accident. But all that changed one morning down in the barn. Robert loved one of the paint horses that Johnny owned, and he wanted to saddle him up for a ride. That day, Robert really learned to survive with one hand; he left the saddle loose and started to mount. After falling flat on his behind, he started to cry and feel sorry for himself. The horse proceeded to relieve his bladder as Robert sat having his personal pity party. The urine splattered him and he jumped to his feet. Angrily he adjusted the saddle and mounted the horse. Using his stump, he maneuvered the horse in the direction he wanted to travel. The stump worked to perfection because it was less sensitive to any pain due to the nerve damage in that part of his arm. His anger at the horse had proven to be the ultimate motivating tool for Robert to see himself as normal as everyone else, not some sort of mentally unbalanced, physically handicapped, maladroit adolescent, and that the arm offered certain advantages. He could hit objects, animals, or even people and not feel almost any pain what so ever by using the numb stump left behind in the aftermath of his personal tragedy.

After that morning, Robert began to use his arm for any- and everything, as if a hand was still attached to the end of it. Johnny had observed the entire incident with the horse that morning as he stood in a stall quietly, out of Robert's sight. His first inclination was to step out of the stall and help Robert up off the ground; then he decided to watch as the scene in front of him developed. Staying in the stall out of Robert's vision was the best help that Johnny could have ever given him when it came to coming to terms with the reality of his future.

In the days and months following the grand opening of the Aurora, the rink's gate receipts sky rocketed and so did Robert's confidence and self-esteem.

And the Star Light Skate Rink became a virtual tomb. The Star Light had been left in the dust, and truly blinded by the enormous response that all the children in the city had when they saw the regulation -size pool tables, the elegant entrance, the full-service candy counter with cold drinks, the bridge with the lit pond full of beautiful golden cod, the state-of-the-art floors, and the rest of the elaborate interior of the Aurora. Added to all this lavish material beauty was the warm, charming, personable Whatley children's daily presence, and Frank had a no- lose recipe cooking up at the Aurora. And that is indeed where the children spent every free moment they had from opening night onward. They were the free entertainment that motivated almost all the other children in the community, regardless of color, to want to hang out at the rink just to be around them.

Rico and his coterie were at the Aurora almost nightly and never missed a Friday through Sunday night. Minnie and Frank's children were the natural leaders of the community's younger generation. Maxie and Salema happened to go into labor on the same night. This coincidence was followed by an even stranger event. Ethel had broken water on a birth sac the same evening. Neither she nor William had any idea that she was even pregnant. In one eventful night, the Whatley, Foster, Mayes clan grew by three. Two girls and one boy. Maxie had a son and she and J.D. named him John Lewis Mayes. Salema had a girl and Frank had already predisposed with Salema's early pregnancy by naming her Gwendolyn Whatley before birth. He and everyone else would call his precious new princess Gwen. And Ethel and William named their surprise bundle of joy Wilma Foster.

As one would expect, J.D. started doting over and grooming John Lewis to behave and reflect the mannerisms of a preacher's son. William and Ethel spoiled Wilma rotten. But Gwen played a different role in the lives of the extended family. It seemed from the start that she held a far different, public, and slightly more prominent place in the lives of the family and community.

Lloyd who had cried more at Salema and Berry's wedding than anyone in her immediate family came over to their house every day. Rather, it seemed that way to Berry, and just pick Gwen up and take her with him wherever he went for the day. If Lloyd did not have Gwen, then Eleanor, one of Celeste's closest girlfriends, or some other person in the community would insist on baby sitting her. It seemed Salema's friends wanted to make Gwen the community's baby instead of Salema's. Then Salema had Frank to deal with; he monopolized as much of Gwen's time as he possibly could. Nothing was too good for her to have, as far as her grandfather was concerned.

Lloyd had a flair for fashion design and was attending cosmetic, hair, and clothes fashion school. Lloyd wanted to own a top- flight modeling agency and was determined that nothing or no one was going to stop him from doing just that. Minnie seemed to spend every free moment taking Jane with her to visit one grand baby after another. Frank, Minnie, and Ma seemed to be visiting or shopping for one baby or another every day.

In the months since Johnny and Frank had purchased the land in Georgia from Beau Jennings. Mr. Moore's representative in the area had also carried out his instructions to have someone clean up, refurbish, and furnish the main house and the big barn on the property. Minnie had promised Jane that as soon as Maxie and Salema had their babies, they would all take a trip back home to what was now their land, to see for the first time where William Heard and his brothers had been laid to rest. When Frank told Mr. Moore that he and his family were going to take a vacation to Georgia, Orland Moore surprised him. "Frank would you mind if I tagged along to get a closer look at the lay of the land you see. There was no way on earth that Frank was going to turn down such a generous offer as having Orland Moore travel on vacation with him and his family. Frank told Mr. Moore that he and his family would truly be honored to have him join them on the trip.

Johnny had asked Lori and Robert to make the trip with them also; he thought the trip would help Robert out immensely just by getting him away from town for a week. Lori agreed and so now this was going to be a multi racial group traveling in the Deep South together. Minnie was so happy that finally she was going home, and with a family who reflected her desire to keep her promise that she had made to her father so many years ago. Frank was a man who employed the same work ethic as her father had down at the barn, and out selling corn whiskey. Frank proudly said he put the "seven p's" philosophy to work for himself and his family daily, working from sunup to sundown. Frank said that "proper prior planning prevented piss- poor performance" and he practiced what he preached just as William Heard had done.

Inadvertently, Minnie had chosen a husband with near mirror qualities to the ones she saw every day working in the barn with her father as a young girl in north Georgia. The entire family coordinated plans so that everyone could be a part of what was becoming a great caravan trip back to Georgia. Jane could hardly wait for the day to arrive; there was only one problem left to hurdle before she and her daughter could make the short jaunt back to her William's remains. That was getting someone to cover at the Aurora for Salema and Berry for a whole week. That was solved by Mr. Moore's son, Lawrence, volunteering to handle the rink's operations for a week during the trip for his dad and Frank.

The week of the planned journey back home to Georgia was spent putting the final touches on the most exciting trip to date in Minnie, Jane and Johnny's lives. The night before they left, Minnie told Frank, "I never thought that the day would come that we'd be able to go back to the ground where I spent my childhood, and stand there a free woman." She told him h ow, from time to time over the years, she had nightmares of being taken back to Georgia in shackles like a run away slave to face murder charges.

Jane asked her dearest friend, Mrs. Rosa Duvall, if she would like to take the trip back to the land where she had spent the happiest moments of her life with William Heard. Mrs. Rosa had been a very patient friend with a discerning ear over the years of their close relationship. So she gladly accepted the invite and anxiously anticipated the trip to her friend's place of origin, and where Jane and William Heard spent their days of youthful marital bliss.

The morning of the trip, things went off like a military general had laid out a successful plan to invade an unsuspecting platoon of opposing troops. The days spent organizing this huge trip paid great dividends, because everyone was prepared and in his or her proper place at the proper time. The ride down was entertaining to Robert because he rode in the car with Mr. Moore, Uncle Johnny, and his mother. He found Mr. Moore's flirtations directed toward his mother humorous. How did this old man think he stood a chance with his mother, Robert kept thinking to himself. But nothing deterred Mr. Moore from his subtle suggestive comments he quipped out at every opportunity during the other wise polite casual conversation in the car. Mr. Moore complimented Lori on how her hair looked, her dress style, and her beautiful face, in a matter of a few short sentences. The lofty verbal praise made Robert a little more attentive along the ride than he otherwise may have been. The natural instinct that a son has to protect his mother came to the fore, so he had to stay on his p' s and q' s, so to speak, as far as Robert was concerned.

It was two in the morning when the large caravan of vehicles inconspicuously left the St. Elmo section of Chattanooga for Minnie's family sojourn back across the Georgia state line. For the first time since the tragic events on her pappa's birthday so many years ago, she was returning home with a rather large extended family of her own. And as fate would have it, she now owned the land that her family worked so hard to develop and enrich. The ladies had packed plenty of food for everyone, lots of sugar tits, and plenty clean diapers for the babies. They almost needed a truck for all the luggage they were bringing along for this trip. Luckily, William drove his Ford pick up, and all the luggage went into the back gate perfectly. The cab was so huge in his big truck that Doyle rode along with William and Ethel comfortably, even lying on Ethel's lap sleeping most of the trip.

As the long horde of vehicles pulled up, the big house that was once the throne of Will Jennings's kingdom, now belonged to the Whatleys. They all walked into the newly painted and furnished house, all done at the request of Mr. Moore and carried out to the letter by his representative, who had met them at the home with about seven other well- dressed white men that after noon. Johnny stood and watched Mr. Moore instruct his men as to where he wanted them to store everyone's luggage. Johnny laughed to himself as he thought back about his conversation with Mr. Moore about his bull Timbuck.

After Mr. Moore had pulled off the deal for the land to be finally in his family's hands, Johnny now not only thought that just maybe Old M an Moore might indeed have the ability to piss upwind and not get wet. At this point, Johnny thought he might have had the ability to peer up old Timbuck's rear end and give him the price of lard.

As the men were unloading the luggage, Minnie called Jane, Babe, Maxie, Salema, Arselee, Celeste, and Cecelia over to her. She led them down to the barn. As they were walking, she began to speak. "I been waiting all my life to show every one of y'all out here today what happened to me the day that changed my whole world for me. The day I'll never forget as long as I'm on thisearth. That day took my pappa and near about all my aunts and uncles from me. But now we are the proud owners of this here land that they buried them all on."

As the group of women reached the barn doors, Minnie grabbed the handles of both doors and flung them open. Daylight rushed into the dark, nearly empty, but very clean barn. Minnie walked over to where the tragedy went down and began to re-enact the whole scene for those present. It was riveting to all of Minnie's daughters to hear the story for the first time, right in the very spot that it had really happened.. None of them had ever heard their mother or grandmother mention a word of this incredible horror story. When Minnie finished, her daughters all gathered around her and hugged her as Jane watched and coyly smiled at Minnie. Jane was a truly happy woman at this moment for the first time in years.

Mrs. Rosa had followed the group of ladies down to the barn and had heard the entire story. She stood at the door with tears in her now fully enlightened and opened eyes. She now understood more fully the bond between Jane and Minnie more than she did before. Even though as a mother herself, Mrs. Rosa knew how close a mother and daughter could be, this was different. This mother and daughter had a secret that could cost them their very lives if it were to get out in the open and become public knowledge.

Frank was standing behind Mrs. Rosa, and he too had witnessed the cold, stark, graphic, and emotional re-enactment of the terrible altercation that had resulted in the death of a very rich, powerful, yet very disturbed and disillusioned man. Frank called out to let Minnie and everyone else that the luggage was all in the house, pretending he had not just seen the whole scene unfold before him. "Let's get some food on the stove, mama. We done drove all this way, brought all our family and friends." He kept talking as he approached the teary- eyed group of women. Opening his arms, Frank gave Minnie a glance out of the corner of his eyes that let her know he understood, and then he led them all toward the house with Jane on one side and Minnie on the other. Jane grabbed Mrs. Rosa's hand on their way by her, and they all headed to the big front porch together. Jane squeezed Mrs. Rosa's hand as they began walking away from the barn, and Mrs. Rosa reciprocated as they approached the stairs in a very discreet show of natural, mutual love and support.

J.D. and Maxie were lagging behind everyone on the front porch after the group returned from the barn. J.D. told Maxie that just from looking at this place, he could better understand why her mother had so much drive and determination when it came to her family and the café. Maxie said, "When we walked into that barn just now, I felt just how strong my mama really is for the first time in my life. Now I'm more determined than ever that we gotta do our part, J.D., to keep the family legacy going from here on out and let our babies know where they came from."

"Hold on now, Maxie, I know full well you ain't talking about moving me up in these mountains to preach to these people up here who probably won't set foot in a church a colored preacher spoke in."

Maxie had to laugh between words; she could barely get her reply out for the giggling. "Come on now, J.D. baby, there ain't no way I want to move away from my family and come up here in these hills. Man, that's not what I'm talking about."

Jane walked up behind the two of them and looked down the road a little piece toward the area where the house that she once resided in stood, and where the remains of her late husband were buried in the beautiful garden that she and Minnie had planted so many, many years ago. Jane asked J.D. and Maxie to drive her the short distance over to the site. As they were getting in the car, Rico walked on the porch and asked to ride along. The car's engine starting raised the curiosity of everyone who was standing in the front part of the house, which was literally everyone, since people had just started to recline and unwind after the ride down from Tennessee. Soon everyone was standing on the front porch, and Minnie headed for the car to go down to the old house's charred remains. Everyone else seemed to follow, and soon the entire caravan of cars and trucks was in front of the old house.

Minnie could see Jane standing with her head bowed at the rear of the old garden as she pulled up. Babe rode with Minnie and had stayed at her cousin's side during the day, giving the sort of silent support that she had always provided Minnie.

Babe stayed in the back ground most of the time, preferring to be alone while she was home for this return visit, and rarely seemed to want to talk to anyone. She spent her energy on improving her knowledge of her true potential and getting to know what Babe wanted out of the rest of her life. Her socializing was exclusively with her aunt Jane and Minnie, except when Minnie and Frank shared some quality time alone.

As Minnie got out of the car, she saw her mother ease herself slowly toward the ground so that she could kneel down on both knees. Jane leaned over and gently lay her face on the dirt. She was holding on to a small white cross with both hands that had the name William Heard hand written across the middle. Minnie was amazed to see that her mother was not crying at all; in fact, a warm, gentle, almost childlike smile was on her face. And Jane appeared not to even notice everyone gathering around her as she stared off into empty space. Rico stood over his grandmother and stroked her head, then Jane reached up and grabbed his hand. Seemingly in a trance like state, she said, "Dis here is yo root, hear my, boy? Dis is where you gone be at peace, boy. You listen ta me, Rico. Dis here land where you gone be at peace." Then Jane pulled herself up by her grandson's hand. Rico could not understand why his grand mother had said these things too him, and blew it off as just an old wives' tale from old people. He knew there was no way possible he would ever want to leave the city for this pathetic, slow country life.

Salema walked over to her mother. She asked her if this is the garden that she had told her about all her life. Minnie had told all her children that the garden at their house was never to be trampled in or desecrated by anyone. That the land it was on was to stay in the family always and never to be sold. Now they all understood why she felt so strongly about the garden at home. Salema and Berry stood holding hands and now their wedding in the garden took on new meaning to them. Salema turned and looked directly into Berry's eyes and made him promise her that together they would see to it that the garden that they were married in would always remain in the family at all costs.

Minnie walked over near the cross on her father's grave; slowly she scanned all the crosses down the neat row where William Heard and his brothers were laid to rest. The family members who had buried them here so many years ago knew that they would rest a bit easier in Jane and Minnie's garden. Now that Minnie was finally at the grave site, the whole scene seemed so unreal to her. She had to accept the fact that her father and uncles were all buried under there in the beautiful garden that she helped plant as a child all this time. Minnie felt almost as her mother did; she never shed a tear. "I've cried all my tears out over the years that I'm ever gone spill over that day in my life. My pappa wouldn't want me here sniveling like a baby, not now, not today. He would want to see me standing here with my children, strong and ready to face this cold world head on. And thanks to the Good Lord, I'm ready to do that today, because God been good to me, pappa, just like you knew he would be when you sent us up north. I'm glad that I was your child, pappa," Minnie said as she knelt down at the head of the grave. "I been trying to do what you asked me to do. Now we done been blessed to come on back home and now with the grace of God, this truly is our home now, pappa. Your family that came from your blood that was spilled on this ground ... guess what, pappa?

You'll never believe it, but we own this land that y'all worked so hard on all your lives. Yes sir. Its yours now."

As Minnie was herself seemingly entranced by the site of the graves, she continued her one- way conversation with her long- deceased father. As her daughters began to gather around her, Minnie finally noticed that she was not alone at the grave site. But at that moment, a billion people could have been standing around and Minnie would not have cared. Celeste, who was already susceptible to displays of over- the- top emotions of her own, was awed by seeing her mother and grandmother so openly displaying their deep love for a granddad she had never known. These two women always had it under control emotionally, she had thought up until this very moment. Then Minnie shifted gears and really gained momentum in her voice as she went on to say how her family had even been extended beyond her father's bloodline, by all the wonderful people who had become more than friends, like Mrs. Rosa, Tom, Emma, Rhae, Brenda, Mr. Moore, now Lori and her son Robert, and too many others to name them all. Now she had two sons-in- law that she thought the world of, and she knew that she was truly a blessed woman to have a husband like Frank. And she finally wanted the whole wide world to know that she thought her children were all wonderful jewels and God's most precious gift that he had bestowed upon her as she finished her long diatribe.

Celeste then grabbed the opportunity to jump in that she was looking for a little while earlier. She asked Minnie, "Mama, what are we going to eat for dinner way up here in these mountains?" Everybody couldn't help but start laughing, not only at the very bad timing of the question but at the genuinely innocent look on Celeste's face when she asked her mother. The reality of the situation to Celeste still boiled down to that while she and her siblings loved learning the family history and were visibly moved by seeing the grave site of their ancestors, by now the words seemed a bit archaic and only slightly entertaining on an empty stomach. Celeste acknowledged that all of this out pouring of raw emotion and sentiment is touching to the heart, and that's commendable and fine, but where is the food?

Robert was in complete agreement with Celeste, so were CeeCee and Doyle. All the children seemed to be famished and were tired of eating sandwiches and cold cuts from the Aurora's deli. After a few minutes, everyone was again gathered in the comforts of the gigantic living room of the Southern plantationowner- style home of Frank Whatley, formerly the home of the Jennings family for three generations. After everyone had gotten cleaned up from the wonderful meal that Jane and Maxie had prepared for the entire group all alone and without an ounce of help or interruption from any other human being in the house at Maxie's request, she wanted some time alone with her grandmother, and she wasn't going to be denied tonight. She ran her mother and sisters out of the kitchen in that order, and hogged all the private time with Jane preparing and cooking dinner.

Jane had a blast in the kitchen bantering on and on in her broken West African patois and fractured English about how life was as a slave girl on the plantation as a child. Jane had rarely breached the subject of slavery with anyone, but tonight she happily discussed her dreaded beginning as a chamber servant girl, as if it were the good old days. Maxie was fascinated by the detailed content of the conversation about human bondage. For the first time, she heard intricacies of her grand mother's youth she had never heard her utter before today. Jane explained that her grandfather on her mother's side of the family had been employed as the plantation's stud buck. He had, in fact, fathered — or in this case actually been used to sire — fifty- two children, all healthy laborers used to increase production and profit. Jane looked pained as she spoke of how she had only heard her master use the " N" word or the word "sucker" when referring to a colored baby. This had caused her to never use the word "sucker" or "nigger" in her limited, broken vocabulary at any time, not even when she referred to things like ignorant people, a piece of hard candy on a stick, or a gullible human being.

She told how during the course of her entire youth, she had to steal food for the field hands who worked long, arduous hours in searing heat in the field with her mother. How she had watched as slave children had to eat mush and fat back from a dirty trough that was kept under the house like animals, never being fed enough to get full. How men and women were staked to the ground and sometimes beaten to death in front of all the other slaves. Sometimes red pepper was poured onto wounds to compound the punished slave's agony. Babies on her plantation were frequently sold away from their parents at birth or very tender young ages. And how her father was a fully decorated Indian chief who had stopped having any relationship at all with her mother after her mom was forced to have a baby for a big, colored buck slave by their cruel master. Even after all his people had been sent on the Trail of Tears, Jane fondly recalled that her father had remained behind, hidden deep in a marshy, winding, and meandering swamp that most men were admittedly deathly afraid to enter. She said he lived in the swamp and woods to be able to keep a watchful eye on his slave children on the plantation. She said she lost touch with her father after being emancipated and meeting William Heard and traveling from near the ocean shores of eastern Georgia to the mountainous region of north Georgia on foot and near penniless. Homeless and illiterate, she had put her faith in the Good Lord and the husband he had provided, and headed northwest with only love as a support pillar and hope as a guiding light.

"Lawd have mercy, thank you, Jesus. I was free and I was in love." As she told Maxie about the exodus to the mountains. Jane was careful to be sure that the family history showed that there was a small sense of balance to the way colored s were treated by white people in the South. There were white folks along the way who showed good ole American Christian values, and many offered work for William and his brothers along the way so that they could make a few dollars to help with the journey. Some even gave them food and shelter to make things a little easier for the many colored s on the road together trying to find a better life for their families. Jane recalled how William taught her that as long as a man could offer another man either goods and services that the man needed or make a profit for such a man, the only color that mattered to men was the color of money.

When William and his brothers decided to stick together after the war, William implemented a rule for them all to abide by. It was that none of the Heard men would ever bed down with a married colored or white woman or give the white men in power the feeling that they ever wanted to or would if the opportunity arose. Every brother swore to adhere to uphold and never break the rule. William made sure that he raised the subject in his initial meetings about business after he had confirmed any arrangements to work on a man's property, especially if he and his brothers may possibly be left alone with the woman on that job at any time during the day, while they were completing any work. William made it a point of emphasis in his discussions with Will

Jennings before agreeing to live on his property with his family, working as blacksmiths and sharecroppers there.

Privately though, William and his brothers knew that some of the most beautiful and kindest women on earth were white. William and his brothers never wanted to make any powerful man, colored or white, feel threatened by their presence, about their women. This strategy proved vital to the survival of the Heard men. All these things taught Jane to not let color be a crutch in her life, and she passed that out look on life to Minnie. And now she could see the results of her optimism in the fact that her daughter and family had a mosaic of friends and loved ones from a diverse racial multi- ethnic make up and background. Jane's offspring never let race matter to them; they treated everyone the same.

After the conversation, Maxie hugged her grandmother and called everyone to eat; then she retired to recline with her precious John Lewis and of course J.D. Minnie and Frank had been engaged in a very interesting conversation with Mr. Moore about the future of business in Chattanooga. Frank liked the idea that Minnie told him that Rico had about higher benefit, less premium cost life insurance for colored people. He realized this could be a solid venture with huge profits. "Right now," Frank said to Mr. Moore, "would be a good time to spread out into the insurance field and start selling life insurance policies to colored folk that pay better death benefits for their surviving next of kin. Unlike the policies presently available for the colored that pay minimum benefits." Mr. Moore agreed that a small profit could be made, but he had reservations about whether enough people would put their trust into buying the policies. Mr. Moore figured they would do better by just selling caskets to people in the colored sector at a cost slightly over wholesale, by buying them in bulk then storing the caskets in a large warehouse.

The call to dinner ended the callous business discussion of profiting from the demise of others. J.D. blessed the food and everyone ate until they were about to burst open. Robert ate so much food, he thought he might split down the middle and spill all the small pieces of bacon Jane crunched up in the fresh pole beans that she and Maxie cooked with fried chicken legs and pork chops. Robert and Doyle both gormandized themselves; they were miserably full but blissfully satisfied. Celeste and the other children were all finished eating and washing dishes as Jane crept away from the table to put her plate in the dish water and then go to bed for the evening.

Rico wanted to talk to Ma privately before she retired for the evening. Jane had always given him the funding he needed for several correspondence college courses that Rico had taken and passed with flying colors. His grandmother had done this secretly for him since Rico was in seventh grade, and the courses had helped immensely, pushing him ahead of his peers academically. Prior to this trip, Rico had talked his grandmother out of three hundred dollars to pay for a Fathom course in what he had self -labeled as geo-neo- physics. Jane had paid for authentic courses in oceanography and seismology in the past for Rico. He had aced both subjects due to a desire that he had to know all the things he could about the physical make up of earth and our universe.

Rico made his thanks private and short as everyone else looked on. They all then got the chance to say "Good night, Ma," in a playful, harmonic unison as their grandmother was passing them by at the sink upon delivering her plate for them to wash. Jane turned and smiled at them without a word. She just gave a nod of approval for their veiled attempt at sarcastic levity, then hugged Minnie's neck real tight and headed off to bed.

Jane turned and said something that astounded even Mrs. Rosa as she headed into her assigned bedroom that night. " Lawd have mercy, I kin git sum real sleep at last, y'all. I'm home with my husband agin." Then she shut her door with a genuinely happy smile on her face for the first time in years and years. Minnie then excused herself from the room and said good night to everyone, including Frank. She announced to everyone at th at point that she was going to sleep with her mother tonight. Frank never exchanged a word other than good night, even though he and Minnie never slept away from one another, other than on the rare occasion that Minnie felt the urge, as she was feeling now, to sleep with her mother.

Jane had just gotten in bed as Minnie entered the room and got undressed and slipped into bed behind her mother. Jane laughed and said, "I knowed you be on yo way fo long."

It wasn't long at all before both women were asleep. Jane dreamed that she was in the kitchen of this home serving dinner to William and his brothers and her sisters- in- law. The dream seemed so vivid, as if it were really happening. Minnie was coincidentally having a strange repeat dream of uncle Buddy Lee coming to her. Only this time, he was fattened up like a pig on the way to the slaughter house, and dressed very nice with his clothes neatly ironed. Minnie could see her father in the distance with a big grin on his face, but he never said a word. Uncle Buddy Lee said, "Your pa wanted to say thank you for bringing Jane home to take care of us. William said, you done did 'bout everything he asked of you, and he so proud of you, he don't know what to do wit' hisself."

Buddy Lee began to fade away while he was talking, and Minnie saw something that amazed and scared her at the same time. All of a sudden, Minnie saw her mother enter the room smiling at her father and looking much younger in facial and physical appearance. Her dream too was extremely vivid and frightened Minnie so much that she woke up and sat straight up in bed.

The warm morning sun was shining in through the window, and the yellow glow of light beamed gently off her mother's face. Minnie did not even need to check her mother's pulse. Just the peaceful look on her face and the fact that Jane was laying on her back told her that her mother had gone on home to be with her precious Papa at last. Minnie screamed out at the top of her lungs, in an agony she had not even felt when she got the news that her father was dead. "Naw... naw.... naw, not my Ma, ohhhhhhhhh" Frank"" she shouted as she jumped off the bed and ran down the hall. Frank, along with everyone else, had been awakened by the yelling and was already on his way down the hall toward Minnie. "Ma dead, my ma is gone, she dead, Frank. Ahh......... Frank, I would never have come back here if I had known it would take her from me."

Frank immediately grabbed his wife to get her under control and begin to comfort her. Rico dashed past everyone with William, Maxie, and the other children on his tail. They all stood around their grand mother's bed, bawling uncontrollably in utter disbelief. How could she be dead? Rico stood at the head of her bed with an awed look on his face, rubbing her forehead gently, with tears streaming down his face.

Mr. Moore went into Jane's room along with Mrs. Rosa and confirmed that she had indeed passed away at some time during the night. As Frank stood in the hall holding Minnie in his arms, he himself began to weep silently like a little child, because the well of feelings in Frank's heart for Jane could probably outstrip the depths of the Challenger Deep's sockets in the Pacific Ocean. Frank had more than the utmost respect for Jane; he had actually revered the way she had such steadfast loyalty to Minnie and her family. Frank and his mother -in-law had a genuine love for one another. Jane knew that her daughter had indeed found her man from the day she met Frank. Jane never had any of the reservations she had with Thomas about Frank. Frank's purchasing the café only confirmed to Jane that he was indeed the real deal. Jane had seen enough to know that the love that Frank had for Minnie was woven out of the same type of cloth that she and William Heard had once spun so magically. Jane also loved the fact that Frank was a man's man who had treated the twins as his own from day one.

Mr. Moore went into the living room and waited until things settled between Minnie and Frank. One of his body guards then appeared in the hall and signaled to Frank. Mr. Moore told Frank that he would have his local rep send a mortician to the house and have the arrangements handled discreetly for the family. Frank just shook his hand and told Orland Moore how much he appreciated the kind gesture toward Minnie and his mother -in-law. Mr. Moore looked at Frank and said, "Frank, that was a grand lady in that room. She deserves nothing but the best now and I intend to give her just that."

"Mr. Moore, I agree with you on that whole heartedly, and once again I want to thank you for everything. Now if you all don't mind, I'm going to get Minnie a bit more comfortable with these arrangements and this terrible loss. As Frank passed by the room where Jane now lay in eternal rest, he noticed that Mrs. Rosa was still standing there with the children, crying. Frank just walked up beside Mrs. Rosa and held her hand.

Mrs. Rosa managed a little smile through her tears and said, "I'm only crying 'cause I know how much I'll miss my friend. 'Cause I know in my heart that she is at home with the Lord and she at peace. Don't she look happy and peaceful?" Frank noticed that Jane did look at total peace, like she was napping at noontime; her face showed no sign of pain or stress on it. Frank told Mrs. Rosa that he would truly miss Jane too. He reeled away from Mrs. Rosa, letting her hand fall gently back to her side as he left the room abruptly and headed back into the room that he and Minnie were sharing.

Minnie was on her knees, praying for God to give her the strength to weather the loss of her mother, when Frank entered the home's master bedroom. Babe was holding Minnie's hand and left the room as she saw Frank appear in the door. Babe had told her cousin to be strong, because they had the best relationship as a family ever, and to only miss Jane now because she has left them but she was home in glory. Frank brought the point on home for his beautiful, heart broken wife. When she finished her short, silent prayer, she looked over in Frank's direction. He smiled at her and said, "God allowed us to bring her home to be at peace with leaving you alone with me and these young'uns. She lived long enough to help you get financially secure and to see almost all of your young'uns grown up. The Good Lord brought your mother home to be with your father and her family that she loved, Minnie, and that's a blessing in it self. She was rewarded with living long enough to go from being a slave to owning the property that she worked on and helped to make rich. Now she came home to rest in peace, ain't that good of the God we serve to bring her all this way and let her not suffer any pain."

Frank gave Minnie time to digest that before finishing by asking his wife a stress- relieving question. "Now, Mr. Moore wants to help make the arrangements so that it will be easier for us to bear. Is that all right with you?"

Minnie weakly replied, "Ok, Frank, whatever you think is best is all right with me. Frank, my ma is gone, she gone for good, Frank. I never thought this day would happen to me. It happened to everybody but Ma; it seemed like to me she would live forever. All I can say is she gave me everything she had to give and I do mean every ounce of strength and love in her bones; she gave it all to me and I appreciate her for it too. Even when she shot me, I knew nobody on earth loved me more than her and my pappa. My ma only knew how to be who her folks made her out to be. And they taught her that no young'un was to disrespect a parent, no matter how old the child came to be."

Jane's mother would have came to the hospital and slit her throat if the bullet didn't kill her, under the circumstances which Jane had shot Minnie, if Jane had told her mother that she wasn't going to obey her orders, to cook, get the house clean, clothes washed, or any other task, whether it was domestic or otherwise. After explaining this out loud at this time to Frank and the rest of the air in the room, Minnie told Frank that she wanted to have a couple of days before having a funeral for Jane, so that she could give the friends that her mother had made in Chattanooga time to arrive for the service if they chose to make the trip. She asked Frank to call back to the café and let Emma know what had taken place overnight. That would be the only call they would have to place, and Minnie knew the word of her mother's death would then spread like wild fire in a dry forest.

CHAPTER XIX

The next person to hear the devastating news was Tom Worthy. Tom was completely overwhelmed with grief. He and Jane had a special relationship in the café. Jane's support and love for him was unwavering over the years that Tom had worked at the café. He spent every opportunity that he could listening to her mother wit about different subjects. Even his sexual preference had been openly discussed with Ma. Jane had given Tom the advice to never be ashamed of himself; she told him that the Good Lord did not make a mistake by making him. She always reminded Tom that God loves all his children, so he should love himself the way he was, not as others people would have him to be. When Emma gave Tom the news, he immediately excused himself to the restroom and wept like a child for about half an hour. After Tom had somewhat composed himself, he returned to the front of the café to announce that the entire staff was going to Georgia. "Emma, sweet heart, we gone shut this damn café down right now, honey, and head to Georgia, girl. Come on now."

Emma agreed and went out into the dining area and made a very tasteful announcement that the Whatley family had lost Mrs. Jane while on vacation. And due to this tragic news, the café would be closed for a few days in order for the staff to grieve and attend the funeral in Georgia. Several customers were visibly upset by the news; they had seen Jane working in the café for so many years and now she was gone. It wasn't very long before regular customers started bringing flowers to the entrance and lobby of the café. Before Emma and the others could get the place cleaned, secured, and empty, there were several rather large floral arrangements in the lobby. After the staff left, more small floral arrangements were placed at the cafe's front entrance. Condolences poured in as the word spread around town in Chattanooga of Jane's demise.

Tom organized a large group of local folks who wanted to drive down to the farm near Rome, Georgia. Jane would be buried right next to William in the garden that she had planted with her daughter so long ago. Emma and Tom rode in the lead car that led an even longer caravan of vehicles than Jane had left town with. As they slowly wound out of town toward the state line between Tennessee and Georgia that after noon, many towns people who knew the family stood and respectfully watched the vehicles leaving town. Some men even doffed their hats and some of the Whatley children's playmates and friends lined the road, watching and sending telepathic waves of sympathy heading south that day by many a person. All wished that they too could attend the funeral services and pay final respects to a grand lady like Jane Heard. When the long group of cars reached the farm, Minnie was overcome by the sheer number of cars. Where in the world would all these folks stay? Little did she know that the two twin bunk houses on the property had been fully restored, as the house had, by the very same construction crew. Paid for by Frank and Johnny, but in reality hired by Mr. Moore through his local temporary concierge.

So if the people traveling from Tennessee had enough love and humility to drive this far out in the woods, there was ample space to comfortably house all of them. Frank, Minnie, Johnny, and their entire family and a group of friends already assembled stood on the huge front porch and stared with blank faces as the large contingent from Chattanooga came streaming slowly onto the property. He looked at Minnie's face and could see the pride in her eyes as she observed this outpouring of love for her mother. As the front car stopped, Emma, Tom, and Emma's family got out of the vehicle. They were greeted warmly at the bottom of the stairs by J.D. and Berry. Brandy, Curtis, and Jeanna had made the trip down also. So had Walsh and Frank's entire extended family. There were still four bedrooms empty in the main house, so Frank's brothers shared one and Emma and her husband shared another. All the others were happy to spend their two nights at the bunk house.

Having all these friends around made the day a lot more comfortable for Minnie all of a sudden. With so many friends and so much talking going on, she had far less time to think about how much she already had began to miss Jane. Rico was taking this death especially hard, and so was William. Maxie called both of them in her bedroom. She shared all the things that Jane had spoken to her about the previous night in the kitchen. Then she told the two of them to miss her, "but let her go y'all. We always treated Ma with dignity and respect and she loved us back with all her heart. So miss her but let her go and rest. She was so happy to be at home with our grandpa. Now we got to go on and be strong like she was. We all got to die one day and I don't want nobody crying over me, and neither would Ma."

Rico merely said, "You're absolutely correct, Maxie."

William just walked over to his sister and hugged her, then he asked, "How you get so smart, woman? You must have been listening to some of the things I taught you over the years, huh?" The three siblings emerged from the room laughing and smiling, to the surprise of their mother who was watching as they came out in the hall. Minnie was standing talking to a man in a black suit from the funeral home.

After a short meeting with the funeral director, Minnie wanted to talk to the family alone. She let them know that Jane was going to be buried at sunrise, so that by sundown everyone could be on their way back to Tennessee and that by the time the sun set, her mother and father would spend their first night in eternal rest together. She suggested that for tomorrow's evening, everyone should try to get to bed early, if that was possible. "I'm ready to move on and I hope y'all are too." Minnie finished the meeting by telling the family the most important example her mother had set for them. "Ma taught me by the way she lived her life that I could over come any obstacle put in front of me. She always told me to put God and family first, then nothing on this earth could defeat me. It didn't matter if you was a man or a woman, if God and family is standing along side of you, nothing can defeat you. Put God first in your life and we will be all right, even after this great loss. So we gone keep doing as we've been taught. Love ye one another as ye have been loved."

As the family session was about to end, Rico asked to say something to the family. "Now, right here today, I make a vow to treat every one of you fair and just, and I must add, lovingly. So that in case we should come to an untimely demise due to time and unforeseen circumstance, I won't hurt so bad, I'll just miss you all terribly. Thank you Maxie for that lesson, I love you very much." They all had a laugh at the way Rico so uniformly phrased the bit of information for them, even at a time like this as they filed out of the room and head back out to the front of the house with all the others.

Emma and Mrs. Rosa had started cooking supper for what seemed to be an army of people. Mrs. Rosa took a small bit of comfort in the fact that all six of her children had made the trip down for the funeral to pay their final respects,

to Jane. Elijah, Beula, Mary Frances, Marion, Carolyn, and Perry Jr. had come to support their mother and keep her strong. Jane had been one of her closest friends and by setting aside the time as a united family and come to Georgia, her children showed the depth of respect and love that they had for Mrs. Rosa and her way of life.

Tom finally got the opportunity to be alone with Minnie and he took full advantage. He started sobbing and Minnie dried his eyes. She knew how close Tom and Jane were. Plus she knew how softhearted Tom really was as a human being. "Oh, I'm just gone miss how cold and calculating she could be, Minnie. And that sense of humor that only a few folks knew she even had, child ooh wee, she could keep me laughing back there in that kitchen all day long."

It wasn't long before the two of them were all laughs, reminiscing about all the wonderful parties and po-ke- no games they had shared together. And all the recipes Jane knew from scratch by memory were amazing to Tom; he would never be able to duplicate her sense of taste for seasoning food; it would always be just right. Only Minnie could season food the way Jane did. Maxie, Salema, and the rest of Minnie's daughters also had the gift for burning in the kitchen.. The conversation ended with Minnie telling Tom to be strong because his relationship with her mother had been based on mutual love and respect. So Tom would need only to miss his time spent with Jane; he could let her go to eternal rest with a totally clean conscious. Tom appreciated the comforting words that Minnie had spoken to him; the fact remained, he would have to face work without Jane ever being there again.

The next day was full of almost the same type of activity, except Minnie had to go to town the next morning and buy a new dress for her mother's burial. She picked out a snow white gown with a sheer pink lacy material covering it. The dress was gorgeous, and once they dressed Jane in it, Minnie went in to see her. Minnie then combed her mother's hair and styled it for the very last time. Then she applied a light bit of foundation and facial make up to Jane's still seemingly happy, sleeping face. Rico rode with his mother and waited until Minnie had finished before he entered the room. He smiled as he told his mother how peaceful and beautiful his grandmother looked to him. Minnie knew that she and her family were ready to move on and be strong as a happy, harmonious unit. Jane always tried to instill the good things she knew in her daughter and her grandchildren. Minnie could now see some of the fruits and benefits of Jane's labor.

Before dinner that evening, the mortician delivered Jane's body back to the house for the wake. The family and friends gathered all commented on how pretty, peaceful, and relaxed Jane appeared. After dinner that evening, William read a small tribute he wrote about his grand mother to the family and the friends gathered. "Slavery, adversity, tragedy, or any other obstacle could not stop her sense of resilience. She was blessed with longevity through all the stresses of life's trials and tribulations. She was the first person besides my mother and father and Daddy Frank that I knew loved me. If nobody else on earth loved me but her, then I know that her love was more than enough to carry and sustain me for a thousand lifetimes. I wanted to read this to everybody tonight because tomorrow it will be too hard for me to say these words. Now I know I'll be all right but still I thought it best to get it over with."

After William had finished and everyone had congratulated him on his beautiful tribute, he announced that Rico had been a major help with the tribute he had just read. Rico just shrunk away from all the compliments that people started to hand out in his direction. Everyone agreed to go to bed early so they could be fresh to attend the funeral at sunrise. Robert and Doyle had just come in from skating all over the farm and had to bathe before jumping in bed.

The funeral was conducted and the eulogy delivered with expertise by Rev. J.D. Mayes. After he delivered a tribute fit for a reigning queen struck down in her prime, J.D. asked if anyone would like to give a short personal testimony to the life of Mrs. Jane Heard. Mrs. Rosa spoke right up. She spoke loud and clear so that all assembled at the grave side service could hear her. "Jesus is the strength and joy of my life. Amen. And I know personally that Jane felt the same way about the Lord. Ain't no doubt in my mind that this friend of mine is at home with the Good Lord in glory this morning. Amen. Minnie, I want to thank you for bringing me with your family, so that I was able to be here with my friend. And I want to thank the Good Lord for blessing me to know your mother and this wonderful family y'all have. I want to say that you and these children can be comforted to know Jane gone be all right, she at home with Jesus, so you can rest assure that she sho nuff gone be all right. Father, thank you for seeing us through safely on this, my friend's final journey home to be at rest with her precious husband William. He is all she ever talked about when we were alone. William, Minnie, Frank and these young'uns was her whole world. When I think about what my friend stood for, all I can say to sum Jane up in a single sentence, I would say simply that she stood for family to me, and love for her family was the most outstanding characteristic about my friend's personality. And I loved her for that quality because my family is the most important thing on earth to me too. So I'm gone miss my dear friend till I go on away from here myself, I reckon."

J.D. then finished the service by singing a stirring rendition of "I'm Going Home One Day." After the service, Minnie, Johnny, Frank, and all the grandchildren covered the casket with dirt until the grave was finished. Then Minnie thanked everyone for attending what she labeled her mother's official home going a day of celebration of the life of Jane Heard. " Now let's go celebrate the life of one of the greatest women who ever lived, my mama'"" Minnie exclaimed as she threw down her shovel and headed back toward the main house.

Doyle cried the hardest that day, even though he managed to gain a good measure of control over his emotions by the time the service ended. The amount and variety of food cooked at the house for the family and guests was utterly ridiculous. Emma and Tom and all the women had been in the kitchen cooking all night long, preparing salads, and baking pies and cakes. Everyone spent the first few minutes after the service talking about the eulogy that J.D. had so masterfully delivered, and the rousing rendition of the great song he had put his heart and soul into singing. Rico was the last person to straggle away from the grave, but the first person in line for a plate of food. After he had completed his personal farewell to his grandmother, he made a bee line to the kitchen to begin feasting.

After a few minutes, the conversation started to pick up and laughter started to fill the air. Celeste and Arselee were talking about high school boys and the difference between them and college boys and army boys. Boys... boys... boys was the topic of the day. Frank stood back and observed, astounded by the fact that so soon after his own mother's and now Jane's death that the children had bounced back so soon. It made him proud to see that they had such strong love for one another. And the zest for life that his family seemed to share was strong enough to push past even the loss of its paternal and maternal foundation.

Mr. Moore had once again come through and provided the top of the line service for the family that his prowess aloud him. Frank knew that his boss's philosophy was to never put much money in the ground for a funeral dirge.

Mr. Moore had voluntarily committed himself to paying for the very best that money could buy for Jane. He explained his one-time thrifty expenditure by telling Frank and his other men that any woman who was a slave and behaved as regally as Jane deserved his best. Frank knew this meant he must have felt pretty strongly about Jane. That is just one of the affects that the demise of the grand lady of the family caused for those left behind.

CHAPTER XX

Frankie's and now Jane's death had left huge voids that were never going to be filled by another living soul. The Whatley household's standard of living never went south. But a case could be made by all the family members that services that Jane had rendered on a daily basis all alone were now taken up by and divided among all the beneficiaries of her work. What had taken one person a few hours to get done now would have to be split up between everyone to get done over the course of an entire day. Rico hated the extra duty of keeping the restrooms cleaned; it cut into his wayward social agenda and detailed itinerary for the young local females. Those facets of his life had been set in stone before his grand mother's death, neither of which was leading Rico to having a positive progression in his life.

Doyle and Robert continued their close friendship, and Doyle never seemed to care about having to keep the trash can empty in the house. Doyle had almost always emptied it for Ma anyway, so it was second nature for him to keep his newly assigned chore done. Ethel took over breakfast duty with the greatest of ease; she had been getting up early and helping Jane out since she had arrived, so it was no great effort for her to step it up a bit and prepare everything by herself now. Ethel never complained about any domestic duty she assumed for her new family; she loved having a family to perform them for.

One afternoon, soon after things seemed to be getting back to normal for the family, Ethel's new friend Jeanette stopped by to say hello. Jeannette had been beaten up by her husband Wayne, who worked as a pick up man for Mr. Moore in the numbers racket. Ethel noticed all the black and blue marks on her friend, but she wasn't going to pry or ask any questions as to their origin. William had come in from working out on Uncle Johnny's farm all night and most of the morning for a bite to eat and some sleep. Jeanette had not been in the house for five minutes before Wayne came knocking on the door. Minnie was pulling up to the house as Wayne entered, talking very nasty and disrespectfully to Jeanette, even deigning to use curse words in Frank's home. Minnie was shocked that Wayne — whom she knew only in passing — was treating the home of Frank Whatley in such a condescending way.

Minnie walked up and asked Wayne in a harsh, cold tone, "Did I just hear you disrespect my home, young man?"

Wayne had never seen Minnie approaching him from behind. He turned, startled by the voice coming from his rear, and answered, "No.... ma'am.... I didn't mean no disrespect, Mrs. Minnie." Wayne knew the entire Whatley family, and he all of a sudden snapped back to reality with the sound of Minnie's voice. He had lost focus on his whereabouts in his rage of anger, he explained to Minnie. "I'm sorry for behaving disrespectfully in your home, Mrs. Minnie ma'am, could you please forgive me?"

Minnie asked Wayne to step outside on the porch after telling him that she would be willing to forgive him, but to never use such foul language in her home ever again. Wayne was steaming as he stepped out on the front stoop and sat down. After Jeannette had been told to let them know if she needed help by Minnie and Ethel, she proceeded to go out on the porch to listen to the lame apology that Wayne now wanted to offer. Wayne threatened to punch her face in if she didn't get in the car and leave immediately. Minnie went in and woke William up so he could monitor the situation. "Don't you dare get involved in any altercation with that fool, William, just make sure he don't hurt the girl," Minnie told him.

As William got dressed, the argument on the porch escalated into a shoving match between Jeanette and Wayne. Jeanette was no match for her brute of a spouse. Wayne was a muscle monster at six feet tall, two hundred ten pounds. His only weakness was that he was all brawn, no brains. Ethel ran out on the porch to try and break the domestic skirmish up, but Wayne was having no part of being stopped, and shoved Ethel to the ground. William had turned into the living room and saw the big brute shove his wife as he approached the porch. William asked Wayne in a rather excited tone of voice, "Hey man, for some reason did you feel it was necessary to put your damn hands on my wife?" Before Wayne could respond, William was on the porch, saying, "I'm the only person allowed to put their hands on her, and Jesus don't allow me to hit or push on her. I'm gone have to knock you down, man, for what I just seen go down out here on this porch."

Wayne squared off to fight William, but was clearly afraid and William could see the stark fear in this hulk of a man's eyes. Wayne tried in vain to sound tough as he admonished William to get back away from him and stay out of his business. "I'm gone cut you if you don't get back, ole red ass nigga," Wayne said as he attempted to reach for his pants pocket.

William muttered, "If you come here cuttin', you end up at Carver from now on." Then he unleashed a furious ten- punch combination to Wayne's face. Wayne was caught with his right hand in his pocket and took the full brunt of each brutal, strategically placed blow. His nose was broken and blood streamed freely down his face. His vision was blurred so that he couldn't see a thing as tears flowed from both eyes. The very last punch was directed at Wayne's throat and had indeed met its mark and cut off his ability to breathe easily. As he gasped for air, he pleaded for mercy. But William was having none of it, and hit him with one last crushing right hand that sent Wayne tumbling off the porch. He now pitifully tried to crawl to his car and miraculously, Jeanette then turned on William. She started hollering for William to stop hitting her husband like that.

As William was about to start stomping Wayne into the pavement, she ran up behind and started to pelt William with rabbit punches to the back of his head. Ethel then started in behind Jeanette and attacked her from the rear. Wayne dragged himself along the ground and opened his car door. He pulled himself up and inside the driver's side of the car. It took him a couple of minutes, but he finally got his car started. Then, without any regard for his wife's safety, the cowardly dog pulled away from the curb, leaving his already battered spouse behind. Jeanette was screaming as Ethel whaled away at her, until William pulled Jeanette clear of the onslaught from his diminutive wife to safety.

Minnie stood in the door looking on in sheer disbelief at the level of ignorance she had just witnessed at her very own home. Minnie first called out to check to make sure that William and Ethel were both all right, then she went outside and helped Jeanette pull herself together. "Now how you gone be fool enough in love to fight for a man that's beating on you, child? Then the no- good dog run off and left you getting a beatin'. Is that the kind of man you want for yourself and your young'uns?"

Jeanette started crying, telling Minnie horror stories of a life of verbal and physical abuse with Wayne. The state had committed an almost as terrible mental cruelty, carried out and exacted against her and her children by over zealous welfare social workers guilty of violating her before Wayne. Invading her home with surprise inspections at odd hours of the night to insure that no man was present in her home. She had relented to Wayne's pressure and promises, and went against her personal beliefs about shacking up with a man. Jeanette never wanted any guy living over her children, but the stress created by the agents was too much, so she caved in and let Wayne move in with her to get rid of the welfare workers' constant harassment. Minnie listened and suggested that the young lady seek some help from the police to stop the beatings.

Minnie continued her strong words of advice and encouragement by saying to Jeannette, "I've always taught my children that charity starts at home and ends abroad. But I've also taught them that self- defense starts at home like wise. So, Jeannette, you've got the right to defend yourself against these ignorant men who think women are punching bag for them to go 'round here beating on." Then she promised to speak to Frank and see if Mr. Moore could talk to Wayne about his abusive behavior.

While Minnie was escorting Jeannette out, she thought about disciplining or chastising William, but then she heard Wilma start crying and remembered that her son was a grown man. She could offer advice, but he was married and Minnie was too considerate to humiliate William in front of his Ethel.

This was the second love drama that Minnie had either mediated or counseled today. Lori had confided in her that she had an ardent admirer of her own, a love story of epic proportions had been unfolding behind the scenes in her life. Mr. Moore's second oldest son, Jonathon, had been after Lori, asking about dating her from the day he met her. Jonathon was more like his father than any of his other brothers and was the apparent heir to the real family business. Jonathon had fallen head over heels in love with Lori, and was not going to be denied the lady that he wanted to spend the rest of his life with. Mr. Moore had shown that he was enamored with the young lady himself, so Minnie was afraid that the obvious conflict of interest would be too much for Mr. Moore to overcome. Therein lay the reason that Minnie felt Mr. Moore would never give his blessing to a marriage arrangement between Lori and Jonathon. Lori had only seen Jonathon three times on dinner or movie dates secretly planned and carried out in late- as- possible hours of the evening.

Jonathon even had the theater reserved three hours after closing for them to see a private screening of Gone with the Wind. Lori was smitten herself, but realized that she was still a married woman. And the hope of getting a peaceful resolution to her previous marital union would not be easy.

A third romantic front had shown its head after the trip from Georgia. Johnny and Jeanna seemed to be heating up as well, and this potential bomb shell had a strange twist to it. Jeanna hated the farm and had refused to even consider relocating from the inner city to rural farm America. So Johnny wanted to talk to William and Ethel about moving out to the farm and living out there and taking over the day- to- day operations of running the farm. Of course Johnny would still work out there and be the primary owner of the property; he would just move back into Chattanooga's city limits. And after the violent events of this afternoon, Minnie could not help but think it would be a good ideal for William to get away from the city.

Jeannette had just cleared the porch, but not before Minnie gave her the phone number to Babe's house. Babe had briefly made mention to Minnie the previous month before Jane's demise that she was going to start organizing and plan meeting on Saturday mornings for all the colored women who had been victims of domestic abuse in the city. Minnie planned to mention this at the family meeting on Friday that she was planning on attending the meetings herself and have each of her daughters attend. Minnie wanted the meetings to be more than bitch sessions that spent all their minutes bashing men. Instead she wanted to concentrate on how to stop this pattern of domestic violence, and this was also Babe's vision.

Babe wanted to stop the women from feeling guilty, as if they themselves had done something wrong and had deserved to be abused. When she had seen Jeannette off, Minnie scolded William and commended him at the same time, telling him, "I thought I told you not to take your knuckle headed, bull- headed, fool rump out there and start a ruckus out in the street. But, uh, ra, you had to go and do exactly the opposite of what I told your bull-headed rump to do. Son, you ain't learned by now, that anger is the poison that destroys whatever vessel is containing it. William, anger eats up your stomach lining and tears away your conscious. You gone have to learn how to settle problems and disputes differently. Some things are able to be fixed without busting somebody up side the head or kicking somebody's butt. Every time you get angry, you don't have to get fish- eyed, fighting mad.

Colored folks too quick to try to kill one another every time they get into it with somebody that's their own color. But look like to me nearly all of us will let white folks scare us to death and lynch us before we will raise a hand at one of them. We too quick to want to hurt each other around here, if you ask me. Ain't nobody gone change the way we behave towards one another but us. I'm the first one to fight if some fool hits me first, and I'll be the first to admit I got a terrible temper, but I ain't one to just haul off and start a fight. Colored folks try to kill each other over stupid little foolishness that if they just let go by, they more times than not likely to figure out that whatever they got so steamed up over will soon pass. But naw, Lord, that ain't good enough, we got to kill that negro or bust a head or get the police and put one another in the jail house. Somebody got to attack me or my husband or young'uns first. Even though I must say you did represent and defend this house and the family well out there on that porch today. I was proud of the way you stood up for your wife today; you gave that cowardly dog just what he needed. A good ass whipping. Now he knows how it feels to get beat down like the low down dirty dog he is. Going around here beating up on defenseless women. But William, you gone have to learn that you don't always have to whip a man with your hands. Sometimes you have to use your crafty mind to skin a cat too. We could have handled Wayne a lot easier by putting this matter in Frank's hands from the get- go."

"Yes ma'am, Mama, I know you right. I just lost my temper out there when I saw that fool put his hands on Ethel like he did."

"Boy, I done told you time and time again, a temper and a gun will get you in trouble but they won't come to get your fool rump out of it. Now I want you to go out there to the farm this afternoon and talk to your uncle Johnny about you, Ethel, and Wilma moving out there and taking over the farm. I think Johnny is sweet on somebody around here. He been thinking about moving back over here to the city and buying a new house. I think this will be the opportunity to put your degree to good use and to get you and your family away from all this commotion and confusion around here all the time. Lord, I don't know what in the world is coming over folks these days; they fight and want to kill each other over little or nothing. Anyway, please think on what I'm saying and get out there and see if y'all can come up with a solution to the thing. You know as well as I do that I need the farm to keep going so the overhead at the café stays down as low as possible. My uncle has been a blessing to this family, but if I have to go back to buying my produce from the market or another co-op, I might not be able to keep the profit margin at five to ten percent of gross dollars. So honey, I might be better off working for somebody else than to operate, so it would no longer make sense to be in business. Shoot, at that point, I believe I would rather close the café down."

This was one of Minnie's longest diatribes ever, and William was more than happy it was finally over. William was so hyped up at the thought of getting the opportunity to show the family all of his technical knowledge that he had worked so hard to retain. Now the time for application of his skills had come and William was more than ready to meet the challenge head on. After all, he already had on- the- job training out on the farm since he was a mere young strapping colored lad. William also had the benefit of having Frank and Johnny at his disposal to impart more knowledge to him than any of his classmates were privy to having access to. William was dressed in no time and on his way to the farm. Johnny had himself gotten dressed to come into the city and conduct some personal business. So William barely caught him before Johnny got out on the St. Elmo Street highway to town. The two of them stopped their respective trucks next to one another long enough for Johnny to tell William to meet him back at the farm house. After they got out and greeted one another, William just burst out with his willingness to immediately re locate to the farm. He told Johnny that he would agree to all terms and conditions set to help orchestrate the move as expeditiously as possible.

"Calm down now, young man, I'm just weighing out all of our options right along in now. I'm not looking to make any fast, foolish moves just yet. But now that don't stop you from coming on out here right now if you and Ethel want to do that. I've got three empty bedrooms in the main house that you can set up any way you want until I move out completely."

William agreed to talk it over with Ethel before he made any commitments to live on the farm. It would be a different discussion with Johnny still living in the house with them. Plus, William wanted to show his wife the proper consideration before committing them to the added pressure of taking over responsibility for the bulk of the day- to- day operations of the farm eventually. After seeing how well Salema and Berry were doing with the Aurora Skate Rink, William was in a sort of hurry to prove his worth to the family as earning potential goes, and he could feel it burning in his gut. There was no way he was going to let his little sis out do him. After all, she hadn't gone to college one day, and he had a solid degree in agriculture. Salema was fresh out of high school and due to her innovative father, she was already up and running as a business woman. William was just a teeny bit jealous that Salema and her husband were already making plenty of profit for the family coffers. But he never let it become a negative feeling that could grow into a rift that so often come between siblings over money. Salema had the type of personality built for giving great customer service to the retail or recreational consumer. She could keep all the children entertained while maintaining their respect. Salema had a good rapport with every hustler in town because they were all mostly employed by her father.

All the real gangsters in the colored community had respect for the young lady running the skating rink. The re were colorful characters who were known only by nick names. Most people never knew these men by the natural names given them at birth. They had monikers like Mr. Greasy, Mr. Florida Kid, Mr. Soldier Boy, Pee the Bed Slim, Shot Gun Slim, Burn The Highway Slim, who hustled as the coal man in the colored community. Burn the Highway Slim could bake the best pineapple cake around, and had shown Salema his secret recipe a long time ago when she was a young girl. Salema also learned how to stretch hamburger meat by adding torn strips of white bread to the meat as it cooked, from ole Burn t he Highway Slim. These men all treated Salema with dignity and respect. Each one of them looked out for her, because they revered her father as a man who had earned his standing in the street by his actions.

Frank Whatley walked it like he talked it, if you could get him to talk to you at all. And whatever code of ethics or standard of loyalty to the rackets they were in, he remained true to them. Whatever went on in the streets stayed out in them. Frank never gossiped or talked about other people's personal business, and street people respected him for that. Some even had begun to wonder if he had indeed retired from the rackets, since he was so very protective of his own personal and profitable business interests.

Since the family had returned from Georgia, he had spent every spare moment he had with his now pleasingly plump granddaughter, Gwen. If Frank was not at Salema and Berry's house visiting, then Minnie knew that he was carting John Lewis around with him, and making one of their younger daughters tag along as a baby sitter and diaper changer. Who ever drew the dreaded baby sitter job was eventually well rewarded for their effort. Frank made it a habit to never give gifts or reward a child of his for carrying out a chore or assignment that he chose to delegate to them. Later, after the fact, he would bring the tormented child who helped a new dress. Or give her or h im some money to go shopping for something new of their own choosing.

Gwen was spending more time with her grandparents than her parents; so was Wilma. Minnie doted over them as if she was trying to make up to God and gain his forgiveness for how stern she had been with her children, for having such a terrible temper herself, and for all the times she had whipped the grandchildren's mothers and father. Many times after the beatings were finished, Minnie knew that it was her anger that made her intensify the punishment that she had delved out., far past the amount of corporal punishment deserved for the offense that the guilty child had committed. Minnie was a totalitarian as a mother; her household was a model of how a democratic home should not be run. When it came to disciplining her children, she was a tyrant of the worst sort. Worst of all, Minnie was more than happy to live with her parental mistakes and ignore critiques of any kind, from any individual, about how she raised her brood of monsters, as she referred to her kids sometimes.

Time taught her to never shout at her grandchildren; hell, she could send them away with their parents when she grew weary of them. Minnie never wanted the luxury of sending one of her own children away when they were younger, after she had had enough of their antics and manure. The only escapee from most of the harsh whippings delved out by Minnie, for the most part, had been Rico. He was far too smooth for Minnie and could get himself out of just about any trouble with her. Rico was on the verge of becoming a young adult and he was a very egotistical young man who had decided he was going to get rich and live the easy life.

Rico had a terrible flaw in his perception of his parents' financial security; he had developed an innate sense of entitlement to the things they had worked hard to achieve. Frank Jr. wanted everything the easy way, handed to him on a silver platter. Life was a soft, cushy ride for Rico and he sometimes acted like a spoiled brat.. Unlike his siblings, he worked harder at getting out of work at the café and the Aurora than he did helping out running or maintaining them. Only when he was asked did he offer physical labor.

Doyle, on the other hand, was a server of the family and hard worker at heart. He was always looking for something else to help out with around the house. The good thing was that a sense of balance was kept by both sons and did not affect their brotherly relationship at all. Doyle looked up to and had the utmost respect for his brother his entire life. Of course Rico may have seemed to wear a super hero cape to Doyle, but his little brother grew to see his flaws as well. Doyle, at an early age, became aware that he did all the dirty little chores, jobs that Rico treated as if they were beneath his station as oldest son to Frank Whatley.

Rico recognized and deferred to the fact that his father thought of William as his oldest son. It was a complicated situation to Doyle that he never spent very much time analyzing; he looked at all his siblings equally. Not one of the children in the family ever referred to a sibling as a half-brother or -sister during their entire life course.

All of the Whatley children were spoiled. Maybe Frank insisting that they always be put first had not given Rico the hunger he needed to make his own mark in the world. Even at dinner or family functions that included food, Frank insisted that his children or any other children present at meal time be allowed to eat before any adult present. That was the rule at the Whatley home from day one. Maybe it was because as a boy, Frank had seen preachers be invited to his and others' homes for dinner. While the children waited hungry, the minister had first choice of the delicious food cooked, which was always the best the host family had to offer. The aroma alone was torture to those children, never mind the fact that most of the preachers ate nearly all the food that was prepared for an entire family. Some of the families that played host really could not afford such elaborate meals. And most of the guest ministers were aware of the pending dire financial strain that those poor folk faced. Some were just taking advantage of the opportunity to use their flocks at any cost to the children, who sometimes went hungry as a result of their unadulterated selfish gluttony. That never happened in Frank's home or at any event he hosted or attended.

Christmas was a carnival-like time in the Whatley home every year, just like it was when Minnie was a child. Fruit and nut baskets were everywhere around the house, as was cake, pie, candy, and cookies. And of course, gifts. So the children at 16 East Twenty- third Street were used to be being put first in life from the beginning.

Now a new custom was about to start. Rico had suggested to his father that the family should go and visit Georgia on a yearly basis. The entire clan could then take part in the maintenance and cleaning of the graves of their loved ones. Rico said that he always wanted to see fresh flowers at both of his grandmothers' grave sites on the anniversary of their deaths every year hence forth. Frank loved the idea and implemented the tradition as soon as he heard the words come out of his son's mouth. He never asked anyone else, including Minnie, for their opinion on the matter.

At the family meeting on Friday, Frank commended Rico for his considerate, loving idea and for the first time gave him a public compliment. What Frank had been made aware of earlier that day about Rico by one of his clandestine operator s in illegal gain did not surprise him at all. Rico was the ringleader and a co-conspirator in an unlawful but very profitable narcotics ring. Now Frank was about to divulge to Rico and the rest of the family that he was fully abreast of his son's activities outside the home.

Rico had been the master mind behind some of his peers starting to sell heroin in a small section of town where inside prostitution was rampant. The fact that the brothels were inside, away from open air, insulated the young punks from the almost ubiquitous police view of drug activity in Chattanooga. Rico and his little band of thugs were a somewhat sophisticated and very well organized unit. The margin of profit was incredible. Jane had slipped Rico money all his life, and he had saved a great portion of his allowances that Frank gave each child weekly.

When he counted his personal savings, Rico had enough cash to front the money needed to purchase a sixteenth of a kilo of heroin. The small package of pure China white opiate was so powerful that the group was able to cut it three times and still have the most potent narcotic on the streets of Chattanooga. This increased threefold the margin for profitability that the investor in the drug would receive after all the tapered-down dope sold. The only investor, who was none other than Frank Whatley, Jr., Rico had a specific group of trusted drug runners who served and catered to prostitutes and local junkies, most of whom were johns with secret habits and sometimes deviant sex lives.

Joe Flint, Russell Flint, and Billy Russell was Rico's muscle. These young men were making a ton of fast cash and keeping it all in a big pile. They had pledged to split only a small portion of the profits weekly so that they could split up a huge chunk after a year of selling. Then they would quit the drug business as rich young men who could then parl ay their ill- gained fortune into a legitimate business empire. This was the original plan the group came up with to get rich young. Joe, Billy, and Russell would not keep too much cash in their pockets, so things would continue to appear normal for the group. There was no need to explain the extra cash Rico suddenly had, because he always seemed to have more money than the boys his age. Rico only had one major problem: He had purchased his dope from an outside associate of Mr. Moore's. So it was inevitable that the word would get back to his father sooner or later about who the master mind behind all of the new heavy drug trafficking in town was.

The plan was working out just as planned at first; business was booming for the group and Rico. He actually had enough cash to go out and buy a new car or truck, or even a house if he had wanted. In the first two months of business, he had made enough money to buy three times as much of the narcotic as he had started off purchasing. The bulk of the money that Rico had used to go into the drug business came from his bogus geo-neo- physics correspondence course that he lied to Jane about. Prior to her death, he had deceived his grandmother to get the money for this detestable business and Rico felt terrible about how he had received those funds. On the other hand, he loved the fact that he now had some of the power that having lots of money gave a man, and he loved the feeling after only attaining a drop in the old bucket, as the saying goes. Women much older had always swooned over him, now, even more of them than ever were snapping at his heels.

In his young, immature mind, Rico knew he was taking a cold and calculated risk to improve his personal financial standing in the community. Now the time for reckoning had come sooner than expected for the young wayward entrepreneur who was willing to stoop to any level for a profit.

Frank, after complimenting his son, asked a question of him that bewildered the entire family assembled for the meeting, which, as usual, included Babe. "Rico, how can you feel so compassionately about your family and your people and sell poison to the young women from the colored community just to make money, son?"

Rico was stunned by the frontal stage he was on with the entire family looking on; his pride was hurt. By the cold look in his father's eyes, he also knew his goose was cooked, so to speak, so he instantly became defensive and offended his father with his smart- ass answer. "The same way you take in their money from your numbers racket, I figure."

Frank lurched toward Rico, but Minnie was between them and grabbed her husband's suit coat and held him still in front of her to keep her son safe. Minnie asked Frank, "What in the world is going on, Daddy?" Before Frank could get his answer out of his mouth, Minnie turned back toward Rico and back hand slapped him across his mouth" Rico was shocked by the force of the blow, and as he was recoiling his head from being turned by the blow's force, Minnie unleashed a verbal assault on her son. "Boy don't you ever lose your manners with your father like that again, you hear me, Rico? I will knock you in the middle of kingdom come if I find out you been selling that poison to these young gals around here, boy. I just declare I can't believe what I'm hearing. Frank, you mean to tell me one my own children selling dope in our community? Lord have mercy, Jesus" Well I'll be, if this don't beat all. Rico, lots of folks love pleasure more than they do the Lord. But I'll be doggone if I sit back and watch one of my own children throw away their lives and ruin other people's, and I just sit back and do nothing about it. You mean to tell me that you willing to throw your life away chasing in behind a dollar and loose woman? Half these skanks you around here laying up with old enough to be your mama. Now you think about it for a minute, what they doing with you besides using you? Rico, sometimes you so smart you don't think before jumping your rump right in the middle of something stupid. These old women and men out here messing around with these drugs and young folks lives is sick. You better stay your mannish rump away from 'em, if you know what's good for you."

Frank finally got the chance to speak, and speak he did. "For the young men like yourself who insist on selling drugs to the women and men in our community, they show others that they have no respect for the families that this stuff destroys and we should turn 'em over to the prisons. And I don't believe in putting our young men in penitentiary, but we got to start to save some of these young'uns from getting hooked on this stuff. At least we can start saving the ones that want to be saved, instead of getting more of 'em hooked on the stuff. Sadly enough, I see those out there in these streets that don't want to be saved. So I got sense enough to know we ain't gone be able to help all these folks, but we can start making a difference. At least my son don't have to be a part of the problem. Rico, you smart enough to know better, son, you possess the skills and knowledge to help stop people from victimizing the women in your community. But you choose to profit off the misery of others and for that I'm gone break your plate and take down your bed before I allow you to spend one more night in my home. Unless you speak up for yourself and convince me and the rest of this family that you done come to your senses. You can pack it up and get your grown tail rump on out here right now."

Minnie just gave Rico a very scared look ; she was not about to usurp Frank's authority or his ability to use this ultimate form of tough love to turn his son's behavior and actions around. Rico was insightful but still had deceit in his voice as he spoke up in his defense. "You're right, Daddy, this is a problem for colored folks to fix ourselves in our community. We can't wait on somebody else from outside to come stop folks from using or selling drugs in the colored neighborhoods. We got to stop it ourselves. I'm sorry, you all, I was wrong, and I will stop selling heroin."

Minnie felt patronized, as if Rico said only what he thought everyone had needed and wanted to hear. She wasn't satisfied with this appeasing apology and neither was Frank. Minnie insisted that Rico be allowed to remain at home and that he be required to attend the first six meetings of the battered women's group that Babe was still organizing. The first meeting was Saturday afternoon at Babe's house. So tomorrow was going to be the first part in a six-week series of proving ground tests that Rico would have to pass to continue living at home with the rest of the family. Minnie finished her remarks by telling Rico, "The space in this house and this neighborhood is going to stay in the hands of folks abiding by the law that says charity starts at home and ends abroad. You don't want nobody giving your sisters that poison and you ain't gone give it to nobody else's daughter either."

Frank agreed to give Rico the time he needed to turn his behavior around. "Six meetings is plenty enough time to show if a person means to change how they behaving. Okay, mama, I'll give you your six meetings. But if I don't see and hear tell of some things changing like I said, I'm gone take his bed down and break his plate." This was indeed the final word on this matter and Rico knew it. He had a six-week window of opportunity to prove that he had grasped the concept that he had to have the same type of respect and love for his community that he had for his immediate family. And that his views and mind had to be expanded to protect the women as sisters who lived in the extended community. Most importantly, Frank told Rico that he had to show his father by his future actions that he would not partake in the systematic destruction of his own ethnic group. This was impressed upon each of the children at this family meeting. Minnie told the family that if colored folks don't stop this dope and fighting now, one day we won't have to worry about the Klan. "Colored folks gone fool around here and destroy ourselves. I ain't gone sit back and watch my own people wipe each other out if I can help it."

Frank asked the children to be on the watch for their brother, and he did it right in front of Rico. Then he turned to Berry and Salema and told them to report to him on Rico's activity at the Aurora on the weekends. For the next two months, Rico could only socialize at the skating rink on weekends. No activity outside the home during the week after school. Rico gladly accepted his punishment, as he considered his other option of having his bed dismantled and not being able to live or eat at home any longer. He knew that he had sufficient cash to leave home, but capital alone was not enough to assume the responsibilities of adulthood and Rico had enough common sense to realize that.

Savannah had stopped by at the end of the family meeting and she had not heard any of the negative content of the meeting. Frank lit up like a candle when he saw her come in the front door of the house, and her arrival broke the tension in the air and gave Rico a much- needed positive distraction for his parents. True to form, Savannah did not disappoint Rico ; she even had a surprise visitor with her. Her mother Anna was in town. Frank was ecstatic to see his sister. Savannah charmed and made her uncle turn his undivided attention to her and her mother during their lengthy visit that lasted well into the night.

Frank had a couple of drinks and began to unwind and have a great time, telling jokes and laughing with his favorite niece and only sister. Frank had not seen Anna since his mother's funeral, and she was a sight for sore eyes. "Girl, you look good to me. I'm so glad you could come home for a visit when it's not for somebody's funeral."

Anna was almost as soft- spoken as her mother. She smiled and said, "Frank, it's good to see my family doing and looking so nice. I miss y'all so much up there in that cold city." Savannah had, in a round about way, almost followed in her mother's footsteps as far as choosing a spouse was concerned. Savannah too had sneaked off and married a biscuit- sopping Baptist preacher. Her husband's name was William Davie. William and Savannah were not like Anna and her husband, who had only one child, Savannah. They were already on baby number four of what would eventually number seventeen live birth children, with several miscarriages in between them. The names of the children were: Dorothy Louise, William Jr., Elizabeth Marie, Barbara, Donald Clifford, Carl, Margie, Annette, Bubby, Sylvester, Bennie, Ricky, Kenny, Sandra, Wanda, and Beanie. Gwen and Wilma had a host of cousins to grow up and play with because of Frank's one niece.

Babe also stayed after the family meeting, so the house was full of laughter as she and Minnie talked about their plans for the battered women in the neighborhood. Frank made it a top priority and carried out his attempt to spend as much time with his sister as humanly possible during her short visit to Chattanooga. Anna enjoyed all the attention her brothers heaped upon her, as well as having precious quality time to spend with her daughter and grandchildren. She spoke of missing the beautiful hot southern summers in Chattanooga. How they contrasted so vastly from the harsh winters with

Alberta clippers and the lake effect snow blowing in off the Great Lakes in Pittsburgh. And how life's course was so different in the North without a host of extended family members living within a close proximity of you on a day- to- day basis like it was when she lived at home.

The people in the North seemed less friendly and more inclined to stay to themselves. Unlike the more earthy, down- home Southerners, who spoke to one another openly as they passed on streets or sat on front porches waving at passing horses or cars, that Anna had grown up with. And it took Anna a while to adjust to their cold, callous attitudes displayed in public. But she soon learned that the tough exterior the people displayed was more a defense mechanism than anything. People were basically the same everywhere. Especially colored folks ; the northern person of color had the same diet as the southern person of color. Their children played the same games, the community operated on the same "it takes a village to raise a child" philosophy as Africans had always employed. There were no stark differences that Anna could detect.

When her days to visit had passed, Frank knew that he would once again miss her terribly. The meeting at Babe's house was set to start thirty minutes earlier when Minnie pulled up with all her daughters and Rico to Babe's house that Saturday afternoon. Ethel and William met the rest of the family members on the front porch. Minnie had to gather her children from the Aurora that afternoon; she had instructed them to meet her there for the sake of convenience. It was a central location where one stop picked up everyone, and a better alternative than being restricted to the house for the whole of Saturday morning for the children. Rico thought the meeting would be used to further crucify him, even though he had whole- heartedly made an effort to turn his behavior around. He had truly instructed his crew to stop the drug sales immediately.

Much to his surprise, he was not even mentioned or thought about at the meeting. Babe was too busy organizing and so was Minnie; from the moment she entered the door, she went to work. To everyone's surprise, Louise Roberts attended this very first meeting of the group of ladies, who would from this afternoon forward call themselves "Babe's formerly battered by bums" as an inside joke. Louise was six months pregnant for Willie, who she had kicked out of their home that the two of them had attempted to set up after he was kicked out by Babe; Louise then left Tim and moved in with Willie. Willie had continued the same pattern of abuse on Louise that he had set with Babe. Babe welcomed Louise even warmer than she did the rest of the ladies, and this made her relax and feel welcome. Louise had forced herself to come at Minnie's incessant request. Now she was more than happy that she did, as the meeting was opened with a prayer by one of the older ladies in attendance who happened to be an Eastern Star.

As the meeting got started, Minnie was the first speaker. "Let me start by congratulating Babe and each and everyone of you brave women for having the courage to step out on your on faith and face life where you are presently at. Each one of you could have become apathetic and just thrown in the towel, so to speak, but you didn't give up on yourselves. And I want all of you to know that God won't give up on you either, and neither will I. I'm gone do all in my power to help each woman here today with the Good Lord's help to guide me. I'm not gone take up too much time or stand up here bragging on how good my husband is to me in front of women who done had men beat on 'em or curse 'em in public or in front of their young'uns. Only one thing I'm gone mention about my husband is that his first interest in me was a human interest. He asked me how my child would have a daddy and how I would have somebody to take care of me and my young'uns if I did not let him be the person to be my young'uns' daddy and to take care of me. That man knew that I was knocked up for somebody else, but he was concerned about the welfare of the unborn baby. Not who had put the seed in me. All I'm trying to say is we need men who are not afraid to show how much they love us, all the time. Not insecure little boys willing to beat, abuse, and use you as a object of their passions. No woman should be beat by a man then expected to lay up with the person that just beat you half to death. We want the police to start treating these colored men who beat a colored woman the same way they treat a colored man that would have the nerve to go and beat up a white woman. And we gone get 'em to start doing it too. I bet that's gone put a stop to some of these ignorant fools thinking they can do any darn thing they want to, to colored women. I want each and every one of you ladies to know that my door is always open at the café or my house if you need any help at all, let me know. I'm not trying to take over this meeting. We all know that this is Babe's idea and her meeting, so I'm gone turn it over to my cousin at this time."

Lori walked in and sat in the back of the room as Minnie was finishing her short speech. She exchanged waves and nervous silent smiles of greeting toward almost everyone present, trying not to be more of a distraction than she already was, arriving so late. Babe spoke very eloquently about her years of abuse and how she had finally gotten the courage she needed to break free of her mental bondage. Now she had experienced the beauty of getting to know her true self, and this was a self- empowering growth period for her since she had left her tormentor. Babe admonished the women about being attracted to men for all the wrong reasons, mostly due to the material things men could and were willing to give or provide, always with a return of either physical or emotional attention from women. "These men who approach women to get them by buying them with money or things then feel as if they own a woman like a car or any other object they pay for. Just as they would beat a dog that they pay for, they will beat a woman that they pay for. So we got to learn to take care of ourselves. Most of us take care of ourselves, our young'uns, no- account men, and keep our mouths shut while we do it. And some of these so- called men still think they can beat us and we about to let them and everyone else know that those days are over. We are not tolerating men beating, cursing, or even looking at us mean no more."

Arselee had eased into the chair next to Rico and held his hand during the entire meeting, and as Babe went into the outlined mission for the new organization, she smiled at her brother. It was her sign to him that no matter what, she supported him, and especially if he was trying to do the right thing. Arselee had always been a pillar of support to Rico as he had also reciprocated the same type, backing up to her on many occasions. Salema let her younger brother know that she had his back also, but she told Rico that she was disappointed that he had chosen to lead his friends in the wrong direction. Celeste and Cee Cee just got up from their seats and both took a knee on their six- foot- four- inch tall, seventeen- year- old big brother's lap. Maxie watched from her seat behind her siblings and reached over and stroked Rico's hair from her seat. For once Rico had listened to his family and not tried to outsmart the entire clan and continue selling. His usual course would have been to put up a smoke screen long enough for the heat to abate, then return to business as usual. But this hard core love he had gotten from his loved ones had made him appreciate the fact that if the colored community did not stop drugs at their source, the drugs would eventually vaporize the entire ethnic group.

Babe clearly defined the mission of her ladies in attendance; it was to help raise the self- esteem of all women of color, starting with the newest female baby in the community. And especially the women present. "I want each and every one of you here today to know that a true woman like yourselves, all are to be treated as the precious gifts to men from our grand creator that we are, no matter what skin color you have." Babe told the ladies that women of color are more precious than any stone or substance found on this earth. Women of color are the mothers of all human life on this planet and should be held in the highest regard by all mankind, no matter where they are on this globe. "But men won't begin to recognize us for who we are until we force them to so. We have to carry ourselves with a lot of dignity and respect, then we make them

have to respect us in return. God did not put us on earth to merely serve and be used and abused. Without us, there is no them, so let's make these people start giving us the respect we deserve."

Rico stood up and started clapping as Babe wrapped up her speech, so did every person present. The proud group of ladies all agreed to start coming up with creative ideas to stop women from being battered and mistreated. The plan also included brainstorming together to help all the young girls in the community who were receiving assistance from welfare programs off the rolls, so that these young women's mental skills did not become permanently clouded. The ladies also wanted to help bring an end to the way these women were hounded by government officials who gave condescending lectures to these women about men and sexual activity. A plan would be implemented so that these women would no longer be subjected to the embarrassing late- night home inspection invasions, the constant harassing of women for having boyfriends, as the men were always referred to when a worker spoke of whomever the lady being violated happened to be seeing at the time — never were they called men — by these egomaniacal, over zealous government workers and agents.

The meeting adjourned with the ladies feeling better about themselves and the future. A new sense of empowerment had been fired up in these women, and no force was going to be strong enough to stop them. Each lady left more willing and vowed to make a greater sacrifice for the next woman being maltreated by another human being. Minnie and Babe began to educate as many women in the community as they could as to how the women in the community could ban together and make an impact on how they were being treated by the men in the community and the government. Celeste and the rest of the sisters were talking about how they were going to change the perception of how the younger men thought about the females their ages for the rest of the weekend. Each of the women at the first meeting did begin to come up with creative ideas for the group. Minnie even asked Mrs. Rosa to ask the still- functioning quilt club to make some night gowns for all the ladies in the group with "Babe's" stitched on the front with the letters "F. B. B. B." underneath. The ladies in the club made fifty- five gowns over the next six months. Slowly, the group did have a positive effect on many

Undeveloped

of the younger ladies in the neighborhood, who had somehow fallen prey to one stress of life or another and had gotten addicted to the placebo and short-lived pleasure that controlled substances offered.

Frank was pleased with his son's complete and whole hearted turn around that he witnessed over the six- week grace period he had allowed Rico. The effect that the meetings had on his son astounded him so much that he started silently contributing money to the group to buy anything needed for the women. Then Frank took things a step further b y secretly purchasing a small shot gun house and giving Babe the deed. Frank told Babe that the house was to be used as a safe house by the group for women who needed an emergency place to hole up. The group used the new house for ladies who were afraid for their lives because the abuse that they were suffering had escalated to that point, or young prostitutes trying to escape abusive pimps; even young female runaway teenagers sometimes slept there. The women of Babe's took turns cleaning the home on a daily basis, and the cabinets were always stocked with plenty of canned and dry goods.

Frank bought a new ice box for meat, and he got William to keep it stocked with fresh meat from the farm after he took over day- to- day operations from Johnny. Frank said he couldn't see much difference in who ran the farm, except that now Johnny had moved to the city in a big new house on Ninth Street, and no longer slept out on the farm. William had moved out as soon as he and his uncle came to terms on how they would operate as a team. No matter how long he ran day-to-day operations, William remained in total subjection to his uncle. This humility served William well, because while he had more technical knowledge than Johnny, he lacked experience in the year- round on- the- job skills that Johnny had nearly perfected. The entire family was still reaping the benefits the farm had to offer because of the timely transfer of knowledge and residence from uncle to nephew.

Johnny had asked Jeanna to marry him and she had accepted. Only two people knew of the engagement besides the wedding couple, and they were William and Maxie. Maxie had only learned because she had come out to the farm to confide in Uncle Johnny that she was as pregnant as a fish again with her second child. So they ended up exchanging good news that morning. Maxie and Johnny decided to make their announcements at the same time, at the family meeting Friday night. Minnie and Frank had another surprise announcement: Lori had accepted a proposal of marriage from Jonathon with the surprise blessing of Mr. Moore.

Mr. Moore had orchestrated a quickie divorce for Lori from her now ex-husband by sending six of his men to his home in Texas. Jonathon told Lori that the men made her ex-spouse a legitimate offer that he had enough sense not to refuse. Lori received an uncontested divorce settlement, along with substantial child support payments for Robert. Jonathon insisted that the child support payments be used to start a college fund for Robert, so Lori opened a bank account to deposit all checks mailed from her son's father. Mr. Moore only demanded that the wedding ceremony be traditional, Catholic, and private. Lori and Jonathon were going to be married this weekend in a private ceremony at the Moores' Catholic Church. Minnie and Frank had been invited to the wedding, and the entire family including Johnny had been invited to the reception. Robert was ecstatic about the wedding and idea of having a happy family at long last. He and Jonathon had a great rapport and he even agreed to act as an usher in the ceremony.

When Johnny announced his intentions to be married, all of his nieces except Salema and Maxie dropped their mouths open from shock. Celeste was so jealous, immediately not believing what she had just heard her uncle say. "Who you gone marry, Uncle Johnny?" she boldly asked.

"A wonderful lady that you already know very well, Celeste, J.D.'s mother Jeanna. We want every one of you who want to be in the wedding to be in it, especially you, little darling. But I'm going to have to insist on not having a wedding reception. Jane not being here for that would be too much for me. I hope y'all understand how I feel about not wanting to party right now without Ma at the party. I've already informed Lori and Jonathon that I'm going to make a short appearance out of respect at their reception, just to give them a small gift."

This invitation to be in the wedding made Celeste smile and calmed her at the same time. Celeste thought very highly of Jeanna, as did the rest of the family. Minnie told Maxie, "Hey, Mrs. Mayes, you already know that I want the baby to be named after Ma if it's a girl."

But Maxie immediately declined the request and told her mother, "If this baby is a girl she gone be named after my own mama, not my grandmama." An even bigger grin than Minnie already had on her face appeared after Maxie had finished what Minnie had originally thought was going to be a statement of total rejection of her baby girl name suggestion.

"Oh Lord, thank you, Jesus, this family meeting is a heap better than them last few we been havin'" Minnie exclaimed as she jumped around like a chicken with his head cut off in the middle of the living room floor. There wasn't a note of music playing in the whole house but she grabbed Frank and started dancing around the room.

Babe walked over to Uncle Johnny and hugged him. "Congratulations, Uncle Johnny, you got yourself a good woman and she got one of the best men I done ever knew besides a few like Frank and my own daddy. Maybe I might get lucky and find me a truly good man out there one day soon."

"Thank you, Babe, and I'm sure the Good Lord is still working on a man that's good enough for you, young lady."

Frank finished his impromptu mini waltz around the living room with Minnie, turned around, and insisted that Johnny have a congratulatory drink. "Well, I'm gone propose a toast to the last most eligible farming bachelor in town." Johnny agreed to have a drink with Frank. Frank called Rico, William and Johnny to the side. He allowed Rico to have his first mixed drink with him that day. Frank told Rico, "Hey, you'll soon be a man, so I don't want you out sneaking around town for a drink. I don't mind you drinking, so long as its done in moderation, after your graduation from high school this year, and you do it right here at home. And wherever you might decide to go to college, don't be down there drinking and acting a fool. Johnny, congratulations man, you and Jeanna deserve to be happy. I started to think you wasn't ever going to give up your exciting bachelor life."

Johnny just started laughing and turned up his drink. "Thank you, Frank. I just hope we can be half as happy as you done made my niece. Our family couldn't of went out and found Minnie a better man than the Good Lord brought her when He gave her you, and I'm not just saying that, I mean every single word of it from the bottom of my heart."

The two weddings were both very lovely ceremonies. Jonathon and Lori had the best reception that any couple had ever had in the whole Chattanooga area in the last ten years. The gifts were lavish and ranged from ski equipment to a new car for both Jonathon and Lori, from Mr. Moore and his wife. Jonathon already lived in one of the most modern dream houses on Sunset Rock Road. He had all the new appliances and amenities that a new home could offer, including an in- ground swimming pool in the backyard. Lori had caught a dream guy, and she wasn't about to let anything mess up her good thing for her and Robert. Minnie approached her to say congratulations after the couple acknowledged and thanked everyone for all the beautiful, expensive gifts. Tom Worthy had brought the new couple a very lovely lead crystal glass set that included a complete punch bowl set.

Lori had built a very special relationship with the whole crew at the café; she was considered part of the café family. Now she was quitting to become a homemaker and every day housewife. Tom stayed strong and held back his tears, but Emma wasn't able to keep hers from flowing as she gave the bride a toast. "This little frail gal came up to me early one morning as I was opening the doors to the café and asked me if I was Mrs. Minnie." Emma sniffled as she continued. "Little did I know she and her son would come to mean so much to me and all the rest of us. Congratulations, Lori, I speak for all of us at the café when I say you deserve to be happy, so does your son. We love y'all."

Minnie relieved Emma at the make shift speaker's podium in the middle of the converted floor of the Aurora, which tonight was a premier ball room. The rink was the only place in town big enough to facilitate all the guests. Before Minnie could start speaking, Lori walked up to her and held both her hands. Lori wiped her face as a couple of tears gently fell down her rosy red cheeks.

"Mrs. Minnie, God sent me to you," Lori started telling Minnie, "and I know that He did because I didn't know where to go or what to do. So I've already told you a million times but tonight I want the world to know how much you mean to me and my son. Thank you so much for every thing, although no words can say how I really feel, I can only say a simple thank you again." Minnie fought and kept her composure ; she looked out at the immense number of people gathered and laughed and said, "This child trying to make out like I don't do no wrong, but we all know way better than that. God did send Lori here, but not to me. Look like to me he sent her to be with Jonathon, and God don't make no mistakes as far as I can see. Robert is happier than he ever been in his life look like to me so we got a lot to celebrate tonight.

Jonathon, congratulations, you got yourself a fine wife and she got a fine young husband. Even for a young white boy, I always did say you was the finest one in town for your age, if I was a little.........y'all know I'm just kidding. Frank, sit down, baby. I'm just having some fun with these young'uns. Mr. Moore, you got a fine new daughter -in-law. Do you want to offer the traditional daddy- in- law toast?"

Mr. Moore came to the middle of the floor with Jonathon. Jonathon wiped his new bride's face, then he handed Lori his handkerchief as he hugged her. After a brief embrace, the happy newlyweds just held hands, standing next to his father. Jonathon could sense that Lori was still a bit nervous, so he asked for a chair so that she could be seated. Mr. Moore made his speech short and sweet. "Today, one more of my dreams came true. I was able to be blessed to see my son marry a fine, de cent, beautiful woman. I will do everything in my power to see that they are very happy. Congratulations, son, you too Lori, welcome to the Moore family. Let's have a good time, everyone"" Mr. Moore shouted as he helped Lori stand up from her chair; then he, Jonathon, and Lori started dancing in a circle of three. That kicked off a night to remember for Lori, Jonathon, and Robert.

The reception was awesome, so much food and whiskey that the people ate and drank late into the wee hours of the morning. Long after the wedding party had departed for home. Robert spent most of the night talking to Doyle, as usual.

The wedding the next weekend was a small family event done very tastefully in the back yard at Johnny's new home. J.D. offered the toast after the wedding. "This is a truly happy day for me, my mama, and our family. God has joined two wonderful people together. I could not be happier for my mother. Mr. Johnny, I think you a good, spiritual man and just what my mother needed. I watched her remain a chaste woman my entire life, and I'm not just saying this because she is my mother either. So I know you got a good wife, congratulations."

After a few hugs from family members and gifts were opened, everyone went back home, leaving the happy newlyweds blissfully alone. The next few months seemed to fly by to Minnie. Before she knew anything, Maxie had delivered a spanking new baby girl and named her Minnie Lee Mayes. Gwen and Wilma now had another first cousin to play with. Rico had his graduation from high school come and go and now he was a summer away from heading off to college. Arselee was next in line to finish her high school days the next year.

After Minnie Lee's birth, Rico went to Atlanta to attend Moore House College. Time appeared to speed up even more so than ever. The first eighteen months that went by were a blur. Before any family member knew anything, Arselee was engaged to be married before she could even leave for her freshman year at Spellman College in Atlanta.

Arselee and Rico had always planned to attend college in the same city. But she had met and fallen in love with a fellow by the name of Jimmy Mc Murray. Frank at first again refused to give his blessings to the union. This time he stuck to his guns. Frank never let his daughter know, but he didn't like Jimmy much for some reason. J.D. and Maxie were expecting their third child and Maxie had been a little sick during this pregnancy, unlike the other two. Due mostly to her own neglect, the problem that had plagued Maxie since she was a little girl had again reared its ugly head.

She had constantly run outside without a sweater or coat and caught a terrible head and chest cold that had grown into walking pneumonia. The bad thing for Maxie was that she was now in her final trimester of pregnancy. The baby was due any time now.

Arselee and Jimmy snuck off and and got married. Frank had long ago sensed that Arselee was by far the most sensuous of his daughters. And in Frank's eyes, she wasn't trying to do much about controlling the hormonal rage customary with being a very sensuous young lady. All that aside, he still showed Arselee with his actions that he loved her, but by eloping with Jimmy she had betrayed his trust. This was the most blatant act of rebellion that had been committed by one of his offspring, as far as Frank was concerned. He did not turn his back on Arselee, because she was the semi-guilty rebel. Frank had a certain amount of the burden to bear himself. So did Rico in an inadvertent way ; ever since he had been caught selling drugs some time back, Frank had slowly tightened the social screws on his younger daughters' lives, allowing less and less time for the girls to see members of the opposite sex.

Arselee, Celeste, and CeeCee were literally prisoners in their own home, other than being able to have free access to the skating rink on weekends. Frank had one obvious flaw as a father. He had a totally dysfunctional relationship with and was especially overprotective of CeeCee, who was becoming very much a stunningly beautiful young lady, even as an early teen. It was as if he had a sort of contempt toward his baby daughter. As if maybe he did not want any more children after Minnie had given birth to Celeste. Whatever his hang-up was, he never drew close to his youngest daughter, and he carried a deep sense of guilt because of his own actions. CeeCee was by far the prettiest of the Whatleys, even though her sisters were all gorgeous women; she was just like a baby doll that was growing larger and prettier. To top it off, she also was very intellectual to boot. CeeCee had already read many of the classics such as The Poems of Robert Browning, A Tale of Two

Cities by Charles Dickens, Twenty Thousand Leagues Under the Sea by Jules Verne, and Moby Dick by Herman Melville. Having had to deal with petty jealousy from other little girls at an early age had prepared CeeCee for the onslaught fro m boys better than most girls her age. She also had the benefit of being the baby in her family with four older sisters that she had watched go through the courting process. An over all dysfunction that the girls shared was that they had been reared in a household where the children were to be seen, not heard. If a guest arrived at the Whatley home to socialize with any of the adults in the home, the children were to disappear into another area of the home. Minnie had instilled in her children to never get caught peering into a grown person's mouth when he or she is talking to another adult.

So the Whatley children rarely went to their parents with personal problems or desires. The only adults to talk to were grandparents, and they were only available if no other adult was present. The family meetings offered only a small opportunity for the voice of the children to be heard, so for the most part they were casual observers of the adults. The greatest benefit that the children received was the mandatory sit- down family dinner every Friday night prior to the meetings. They let out all the details of their personal lives over great food every weekend around the dinner table. These dinner discussions kept their parents abreast of their children's daily activities, and were the most effective way the family communicated. Celeste was already dating her future spouse in her senior year of high school. His name was Willie Allen Niblet; he had come to Chattanooga from Darnelle, Louisiana to live with his father, Willie Sr. His parents had divorced when he was a boy. Now Willie had come to get a job where his dad was a supervisor at Diamond Heat Treating Corp.

Willie Niblet worked with his dad in the heat treating steel plant with a steadfast loyalty to the job, from which he was never laid off or terminated in his life. He was a very hard- working, extremely handsome young country boy who had all the young ladies in town buzzing about how fine he was and how hard he worked. Even though Celeste and Willie had gone through more traditional courting rituals, Frank began to question the pattern his first three daughters had set by getting married so young.

He asked Minnie, "Mama, do you think maybe I'm to blame for chasing our daughters away from home early?"

"Now Frank, I don't point fingers at a soul about what other folks choose to do with their own lives. These gals done got grown enough to make the bed they want to sleep in. They all hard- headed like they mama is. Let 'em learn on they own that a hard head makes a soft behind. We ain't went out here and chose no man for any of them gals, so if they like the men they choosing, I love 'em. Just as long as these Negroes don't beat on 'em or mistreat 'em, it ain't none of my business, once I done did my job and raised these fast- tail gals. You go on and let these young'uns worry you to death. They ain't gone make my hair no grayer than it's getting. I'm trying to worry about keeping you happy and around here for me. Maybe I been too hard on 'em I think sometime myself.

But I sure ain't gone spend too much time worrying over what I done already did with them young'uns. I sure can't take none of it back, so why worry my self over it?"

Frank was sitting on the side of the bed smiling as he listened to his wife's motherly wit on her maternal regrets or lack of them in this case. "Well, I reckon you right if they like it, I should love it, huh mama?"

"I reckon, Frank, we still figuring these folks we done produced out, and we're likely to never get that job done before we finished with whatever else the Good Lord got for us to do down here. Arselee grown and Celeste is near 'bout grown herself. Man, we ain't got but one more young'un in this house. So let them get on out of here so I can finally have a few minutes alone with you, will you? We blessed they getting married and moving on and not staying around here until they get to be old maids, at least they not leaving here shacking up."

Frank was still smiling, almost out- and- out laughing as the telephone started ringing. Both Minnie and Frank hated talking on the phone, so they agreed to just allow it to ring. But the phone kept on ringing, so Frank finally answered it. On the other end was Emma. She was extremely upset. She told Frank that J.D. had called the café looking for Minnie, and told her that Maxie had a little boy but that she had some complications, and they needed her to come down to Carver Hospital right away. Frank hung up the phone, grabbed his suit jacket, and told Minnie, "Come on, let's go to the hospital, Maxie's sick."

When they arrived at the hospital, J.D. was in the main lobby, distraught. He was totally out of control, hollering, "N o... no... no" Oh my GOD, please, please GOD no, not my Maxie, not my Maxie."A sheriff's deputy was trying to lead him into a small waiting room, but he was having a hard time, because J.D. was a strong, young, thin- framed buck, even if he was a preacher.

One of the hospital officials who knew Minnie by her face from the café approached her and Frank as they entered the lobby. "Mrs. Minnie, I'm so sorry to inform you that your daughter passed away this afternoon from acute respiratory failure, as far as we can tell so far."

Minnie was completely thrown for a loop by the devastating news and the way it had been delivered to her so bluntly as soon as she entered the doors of the hospital. She couldn't believe her ears and immediately yelled out, "Oh sweet Jesus, no, not my child" She ain't gone, they told me she was sick. How can she be dead already? Frank, do something"" Minnie yelled at her husband in desperation.

At that point, Dr. Martin appeared in the lobby and he took over the situation calmly and professionally. He got all the family there assembled in the small waiting room. After Frank got Minnie calmed down enough to talk, the doctor began to tell them how Maxie's demise had occurred. The pneumonia had engulfed her lungs and literally drowned her in the resulting aggressive infection. The hospital had nothing strong enough to fight the pneumonia strain that had affected Maxie. Dr. Martin then informed the family that the baby boy born to J.D. and Maxie was fine and healthy. Dr. Martin told Minnie how sorry he was that he could not do more to keep Maxie alive, but it was out of his hands when she arrived that morning. He and the staff did everything they could and had managed to save her baby for Maxie, which is what the doctor said she requested with her last breath.

As the doctor was finishing up his conversation, William and Ethel came in and William was out of control with grief. He had been told in the lobby that his twin sister was dead. Minnie did all she could to comfort her son, so did Frank. After a few hundred "why, why" questions, Minnie answered her son by saying, "God must have a better plan for her than we did, William. I can't believe she gone either. Now we got to figure out how we can make it pass this and help with these three young'uns that ain't got no more mama. Oh Lord, what am I gone do without my baby?" Minnie again broke down crying herself.

Johnny had driven Ethel and William over to the hospital from the farm after he had gotten a call at his home from J.D. about Maxie being sick. Johnny didn't think that death was imminent for his niece, or he would have reacted differently. Now he stood crying in the hall outside the waiting room. Johnny was a very spiritual man, so he soon gathered his composure and went into the waiting room and asked Minnie if she wanted him to help set arrangements or go talk to Thomas. Minnie thought about how this was going to break Thomas's heart. She asked Frank if it would be all right if they went over to tell Thomas and Olivia the terrible news.

Frank said, "Look, I don't know if I want to put you through seeing how hurt he gone be when you tell him he done lost his daughter. Big mama, you sure you can go over there or do you prefer me to take William with me and let him tell his father what's happened?"

"Frank, I can go over there. Maxie was my child, not William's. I don't mean to sound cold, but I can face up to the fact that she gone and it ain't nothin' that I or none of us can do to bring her back."

J.D. was almost catatonic, sitting in his chair in the waiting room with a totally blank stare in his eyes as if he was lost out at sea all alone. Johnny had called Jeanna and she had just arrived at the hospital as he was about to leave. Johnny had a good relationship with the head mortician over at the J. T. Trimble Funeral Parlor on Ninth Street. He wanted to start to make some initial contact with him but not any formal arrangements about handling Maxie's funeral. So many people had to be contacted. Johnny immediately after leaving the funeral home went and sent a Western Union telegram to Rico, telling him not to panic, but to call home as soon as possible. Rico called home that evening and received the tragic news from his dad about Maxie. Rico was on the very first train home that next morning.

Doyle was devastated by the news of his oldest sister's death that day. He had been staying out on the farm working with his uncle Johnny and William, since he had finished school himself last year. Doyle insisted on not having a party or revelry of any type after his graduation. He stood with William and cried into his hanky in near complete silence. Between sniffles, he kept saying softly to William, " It's done be alwight, otay."

William looked at Doyle after a few otays, and finally answered, "Yea pappa, its gone be all right after while. But right now it hurts like hell. I ain't lying, man, this is the worst I ever felt. And I know my father is gone be ripped apart by this news. Daddy Frank and Mama gone over there to tell him that his baby girl is dead. We better get out of this hospital before a whole lot of folks start coming over here after word get out that Maxie is dead. This is gone near 'bout kill me, Mama, Daddy Frank, and my father."

William and Minnie were right on point as far as Thomas was concerned. Olivia answered the door for Frank and Minnie and she could see by the sad look on their faces that the news had to be devastating. Frank broke the news to Olivia as soft and straight as he could. "We have terrible news for you all and every one of us. Maxie has passed away today and we need to make Thomas aware of the sad news."

Olivia herself slumped down into a chair by the front door. She was weakened by overwhelming grief at the news of her step daughter's death. Olivia had been in Maxie's life from a very early age and she loved her as dearly as if she had birthed her for Thomas. Thomas was in his study preparing a sermon when he heard Minnie's voice and came into the living room to inquire as to the nature of her surprise visit. Frank stood up to greet him and the two men shook hands firmly. Frank repeated what he told Olivia and he nearly had to catch Thomas, who immediately became sweaty and faint. "Not my baby, oh....my goodness. God in heaven, why not me, Lord?"

Thomas started crying like a baby, and Olivia got up and helped him out of the room toward the back of their house. Frank and Minnie were both crying again and felt very uncomfortable in the living room sitting on the couch until Olivia reappeared after what seemed an eternity. She said that she had called the doctor because she could not get Thomas calmed down. After a few minutes, an ambulance arrived at the house and the medics had Thomas whisked off in on his way to Carver in what seemed like only a few minutes. Dr. Martin was waiting with a trauma team on stand by and a strong sedative to get Thomas's blood pressure down before he gave himself a stroke from his raging state of grief. After the medicine's strong narcotic took hold, Olivia came out to report to Minnie and Frank that Thomas was all right and asleep. William went over to the hospital and spent the night with his father and his stepmother.

The next morning after his release, Thomas went by to visit Minnie and Frank. "I'm so sorry for the way I took the news, but I'm not ready to be saying good-bye to my little girl. I love the Lord and I know God don't make no mistakes, so I got to learn to live on. We all got to go that way and I know that, but it seem to me it ain't natural for a parent to out live their own child. Well, I just want to help in any way I can with the final arrangements."

Frank asked Minnie if she wanted him to step out of the room so that she and Thomas could make the arrangements. Thomas spoke up before Minnie could get a word out of her mouth. "I hope I'm not out of place for saying this, but Frank, I would prefer you stay right here for this."

Minnie looked at her husband and said, " Me too, Daddy Frank. I need you more than ever right now." Minnie had slept only about an hour all night herself. She was so depressed that she told Frank, " I wish I could get off this planet for a good month and just leave all this pain I feel behind."

The three made plans to have the funeral, with J.D.' s blessing, as soon as possible. Thomas also had a great relationship with the folks at J. T. Trimble Funeral Home, so he agreed to go talk to J.D. and set the date for the funeral. Babe had been torn apart by this death herself, but she had been at Minnie's side from the moment she heard the news. Arselee came home from her new ranch farm house on the land that Jimmy purchased for them to start farming just down the road from Uncle Johnny's farm. Frank asked to speak with Arselee after the funeral, one- on- one. The two of them had hugged for the first time since Frank had found out about her eloping with Jimmy. J.D. had the support of Jeanna, Brandy, Curtis, and his three children. He had felt abandoned at the hospital the day before, when all of a sudden he and his mother were the only two people left in the once cramped hospital waiting room. Frank had slipped away early that morning and went down to the neo-natal unit at the hospital and checked on yet un named baby boy Mayes. The baby was doing fat and fine. The doctors had come up with a formula for feeding him that was working to perfection so far.

Frank reported back to Minnie on the baby's status as he brought her breakfast in bed prepared by the staff at the café. Flowers were pouring into the café again, as well as at Frank and Minnie's house. J.D. and Maxie's house was being inundated with flowers and sympathy cards as well. Minnie insisted on going to be with J.D. and her grandchildren to help make the final arrangements with Thomas. Babe, Frank, Minnie, J.D., Thomas, Johnny, William, and Mr. Trimble sat down and set the funeral for that Saturday morning at eleven. The service was officiated by Rev. Black. Minnie asked him to keep the funeral short and sweet, and the pastor did just as he was asked. The entire funeral lasted a grand total of forty- five minutes. Most of the service was dedicated to the touching eulogy delivered in the usual fiery style that Rev. Black was gifted with being able to repeat time and time again. Rev. Black nearly whooped as he spoke of how Maxie had pulled her weight, on how she had to ed the line in a long line of chaste matriarchs, women of great dignity, servants of the Most High God. The service closed with the re nowned choir at First Baptist rocking the church singing "Rise Up and Walk."

After the inter ment, the family went over to J.D. and Maxie's house and ate and planned on how everyone would stick together and help raise the children. At the funeral, the baby was officially named Fred Mayes. The days following the funeral were extremely tough for the family, especially Minnie, William, and J.D..

One Saturday morning about three weeks after the funeral, a surprise source of comfort came to the door. A couple of Jehovah's Witnesses knocked.

Minnie answered the door. The man introduced himself and his wife as Gary and Susan McKee. He said, "Ma'am, this morning we are out sharing God's Word with our neighbors in the community. Speaking to folks about a subject that for some of us is very sensitive, and that is what hope does God's Word the Bible have to offer for our loved ones who have preceded us in death?"

Minnie asked the couple to come inside and have a seat. The subject had sparked her keen interest. She had been praying for a comforter, and it seemed to have appeared before her very eyes. Minnie told Gary that it was funny how they had come to the door this morning and for some strange reason she then opened up and shared with these two complete strangers the fact that she had recently lost her daughter. Minnie could sense that Gary McKee was a very kind- hearted man. And he was blessed with a soothing, calm speaking voice that immediately put her at ease with him. Her revelation led to a very candid Bible discussion on death. Many questions that had been in her mind were answered directly from scripture for Minnie. Minnie invited the young couple back and agreed to start studying the Bible with them on a weekly basis. Minnie really loved one scripture in particular that she learned that day, and that was Psalms 83:18. Minnie learned that God had a personal name that day and His name is Jehovah. This was fascinating to her, so she was lifted up in spirit by the short visit, and she was looking forward to more of them from Gary and Susan.

Mr. Moore had come by the house for a very rare visit after the couple had left. Minnie had just stepped into the restroom, so Babe answered the door. She was shocked to see Mr. Moore and four of his body guards standing at the door. Frank came into the living room to see who was at the door and was almost as shocked to see Orland Moore, even though they used to do this regularly when Frank was a young bachelor. Mr. Moore gave Babe his coat and sat down with his usual "I run the world" flair. "Frank, I've got great news if you are receptive to what I'm proposing. Recently I've been in touch with several agents for safaris to Kenya next July through the end of August. Frank, I realize that you probably think like most prospective travelers to Africa. Folks seem to think that they may have to stay in pup tents, mud or grass huts, and eat strange foods. But I've been on a few safaris, and nothing could be farther from the truth. We will be at a top reserve with excellent lodging that has private bathroom facilities, excellent food, cuisine specifically designed to cater to the discerning traveler's needs. I had some of the same reservations myself before my first visit to sub- Sahara Africa. I had a gargantuan phobia of being overwhelmed by mosquitoes and other bugs and insects. Add to that my fear of encountering these massive snakes on safari. Well, I must admit that not one day did I experience bugs that are nearly as bad as those at American parks I have visited in the South. And in all my travels in Africa, I've seen only two or three snakes and we had to go looking for them. Now just imagine during the evenings the dining tent will be filled with people from the four corners of the globe. Reveling in camaraderie, listening to soft jazz, enjoying the most sumptuous cuisine served to us by beautiful candlelight. After dinner and dessert, we sip whiskey, brandy, or warm cognac together, sitting around a roaring fireplace, listening to hyped- up bush lore from our very eloquent and entertaining host. Later, we can watch hippo graze only a few feet from our deluxe tent or the lodge. The night comes alive with the wild animal sounds and scents of the Africa that you've dreamed of. The untamed wilderness where a man like me senses that he is but a temporary guest, and not a complete controller of nature or the environment that surrounds him. Which, other than nature, that is exactly how I feel over here in America, as far as being in control of things is concerned. We will be escorted to dinner down a gorgeous fiery lit pathway guarded by spear- wielding Masai, because pizza- sized foot prints dot the path left there by hippo every few hours or so. So wouldn't you agree that carrying a spear is probably a great idea for our guides in the lodge area? I know you just lost a daughter, and that breaks my heart. Now Frank, I am not being insensitive I hope, by coming over here at this time. But I really feel, hell I know, that you and your entire family need to get away from here for a while. Do you hear me, man?"

Frank started to rebut Mr. Moore, but Babe cut into the conversation rudely but excitedly. "Excuse me, but did you say a safari to Kenya, Mr. Moore?" Babe wanted to make sure that she was not just imagining what she had just heard. It couldn't be that her and Minnie's dreams of animals making scary noises in the night and elephants standing nearby was close to coming to fruition. "Oh Lord, Frank, Minnie and I dreamed of going to Africa as young girls back in Georgia. This would blow Minnie away and it might help her heart to start healing a little bit if we could all go to the mother land together. I know for me, I might finally be able to sleep that gentle sleep that comes with self- contentment if I was to get to go to Kenya, Mr. Moore."

Frank did not need to hear any more; he was sold, hook, line, and sinker, but Mr. Moore sunk the hook in for good by promising a top- of- the- line 300-dollar- per- person- per- day A- rated facility with a full staff for every need a body might have. An excellent selection of wines and dessert would follow each catered meal. "Now I know we will be traveling with our families, but that doesn't mean we won't be able to still see all the beautiful women from around the world that will be traveling and staying with us at the lodge. Frank, the last thing I need to tell you I'll do discreetly." Mr. Moore then leaned in close to Frank's ear and whispered his real reason for this sudden long trip. "Frank, James Copeland has informed me that the federal government is going to be issuing secret indictments around the time we should already be out of the country. That's why I've already taken the liberty to get travel visas for all of us. Our tickets on the Booth Lines Passenger Liner are booked and paid for as well. Your entire family and my own are taken care of. It's up to you who you want to take with you. Frank, you have always been my closest confidant and most enterprising employee, so I refuse to leave you behind. But damn it, Frank, more importantly than that, you're my nephew and I love you as if you were my very own son. My wife and even my very own children know how dear you are to me. When I found out years ago that your father was my brother, my first reaction was one born of pure ignorance and selfishness. I never knew how much I had come to love your father until I had lost him to some senseless act of violence perpetrated by some young punks. I could have had security tight as a drum around him, but looking back on things, I guess I might have taken all of our safety for granted, even then. After your father's untimely demise, the rest of your family ostracized me; you're the only one who stuck by my side. I've done my best to keep an umbrella of protection around you and the rest of your family. Hell, I've done as much as I could without interrupting or just running your day-to-day lives. Do you understand me?"

Frank leaned back and thanked Mr. Moore. Then he informed Mr. Moore that the only members of his family who would be traveling to Africa would be Rico, CeeCee, Babe, Minnie, and himself. Doyle could not swim; he was afraid of the ocean and would never agree to get on a ship. Frank knew better than to try and force him. Celeste was in love and courting, so she would stay and work at the café with Arselee. Frank demanded that Celeste reside with her uncle Johnny during the trip. The group of thirty- five would cast off from New York and set sail for Africa June 5, heading for a final destination of the Masai Mara National Reserve, the finest reserve in Kenya. Mr. Moore had sixteen of his best-trained men traveling with his entourage, all avid hunters. Jonathon, Robert, Lori, and the rest of the Moore family also were along for the adventure of a lifetime.

Mr. Moore and his men left the house, and as they cleared the front of the house in his huge, black, shiny car driven as usual by his short, colored driver, Charlie Mack. Babe screamed in sheer excitement. Her high-pitched yelp caught Frank by surprise as she ran across the living room and jumped into Frank's arms. Minnie came out to see what was going on. Babe blurted out, " We going, we going, we finally going""

"What in all creation is you hollering about in here, Babe, like you done lost your rabbit ass mind?" Minnie asked her cousin as she looked directly at Frank. Babe jumped out of Frank's arms and ran over to Minnie. "Child, Mr. Moore just left here. He said he already paid for all of us a safari to Africa this summer, so you could get away from all this confusion and depression."

Minnie bucked her eyes in disbelief. "Babe, you got to be kiddin me"" Minnie shouted as the grown woman started skipping around in a circle, holding hands like to school girls in the middle of the living room.

The few months before the family's cruise ship embarkation were spent shopping by Babe and Minnie for the clothes that befit ladies on a safari. Minnie took CeeCee on countless excursions, after shopping for the trip should have long been finished. They both loved the time spent together in store after store, just being girls for the first time together. The quality time that Minnie was able to spend with CeeCee before the trip was special, and it served to strengthen an already strong bond the two of them shared.

The day the train was leaving Chattanooga for New York was a happy and sad one for the entire family. J.D. had brought the children to see their folks off, as had William and Ethel, Salema and Berry, Arselee and Jimmy, Celeste and Willie, Johnny and Jeanna, Curtis and Brandy, Gwen, Wilma, and Berry and Salema's baby girl Ethel, just born two months earlier, the newest addition to the ever-growing family.

Minnie shocked everyone attending by making the surprise announcement that none of the family members traveling to Africa would be returning to the United States ever again. The café was for Arselee and Celeste to run as they saw fit. Emma was to manage, and the staff was to be kept completely intact. Tom Worthy knew he had a job for life, Minnie told everyone, as he

WWII

stood openly weeping, dabbing his slightly swollen eyes with his hanky. Tom and the entire staff at the café had come to the train station to see the group off. Tom was astounded by the announcement. Then, as tears started to fill eyes, Minnie said, "Tom, stop that crying, child, you know I might come back home. It depends on how y'all start carrying on over here. All the mess in Europe, Northern Africa, and the Pacific, with the war. The American embargo on selling steel to the Japanese gone probably get us in this darn big ole mess, and I ain't wanting my son or nobody else's to die in no war. But as of right now, with the way these folks over here acting like they want to tear up creation, all the colored folks in this country done had to stand by and watch as President Roosevelt's New Deal expanded the role of the federal government into our everyday lives, causing the government to go into debt to provide jobs and colored folks can't say one word about how the tax dollars we send the government get spent. Well, one thing I can for sure, and that is as of today, the café is set with Arselee, Celeste, and a capable, courteous, professional staff. With Johnny, William, Ethel, and Doyle, the farm is in great hands; so is the Aurora with Salema, Lloyd, and Berry. The Aurora is a fun place where every child in Chattanooga can play together, no matter the color of his or her skin, and that should make the future bright for the city that I love so dearly. And for all the folks gathered out here today that know in your hearts that I love each and every one of you, remember one thing: Whatever has happened to me or any of us in the past or come what may in the future, y'all try to do like I've always tried to do, and what I pray I'm going to continue to do. Leave all your cares and concerns with Jehovah. God has always made a way out of no way for me. I have always believed and will always believe He can do that for all of us. I can say I hope it's peaceful and pretty over there in Kenya, and if it is, I'm staying. Good-bye, America, hello, Africa. Get ready, adventure, here I come."

MISS MINNIE (BIG MAMMA)

Dear Miss Minnie (Big Mamma):

Dear Miss Minnie, your name has been called. Come take a seat beside that wall. Blow you a kiss and let you go. You'll never sit in that chair no more. Dear Miss Minnie, your name and spirit lives on. The memories behind that chair remain; sadly enough you are gone. From that chair you loved and cared for all. You gave us strength and courage to carry life's ball.

Dear Miss Minnie, we remember you reaching out, opening your heart and home to whomever was in need. You gave and gave and we took and took. Indeed Miss Minnie your name has been called. Come take a seat beside that wall. You live Miss Minnie; you live. We miss you!

Kamar Ali Niblet
(kae)

About the Author

Kevin B. Niblet was born and raised in Northwest Detroit. He currently resides in Houston Texas. A husband and father of three who has worked at a myriad of occupations over his short life span. Some thirteen years ago Kevin was inspired by stories he used to listen to his grandmother tell him as a small child. These stories are the base used to pen this wonderful romantic fantasy. This story is a bit spicier than the tales that my grandmother told me as a boy. Just as I did, I am hoping my readers can take mental flight to the past glorious days of life in the southern parts of Tennessee and northern parts of Georgia that she loved so dearly. I promised my grandmother that I would take her back to the south one day. Now through the pages of this book I have kept that promise.

* INCOMPLETE SENTENCE; POOR ANTECEDENCY